For anyone who has questioned whether they were enough. (You were, BTW).

Ripple the Mesh

Puck & Pen, Volume 4

Sam LaRose

Published by Ink Stained Fingers Press, 2024.

RIPPLE THE MESH

First edition. November 5, 2024.

ISBN: 979-8224726691

Written by Sam LaRose.

Previously in Puck & Pen

Welcome to the fourth installment of the Puck & Pen Series! Just a reminder of what's happened in the story so far, as this series is best read in order.

In **Light the Lamp**, Pietr and Harper met and shared a first kiss in the bathroom of the Mounting Bison. Since then, they've fallen harder in love than either thought possible. Things got complicated after Pietr came out as pansexual on an Instagram post at Christmas, leading to an accident on the ice that put him out of commission for a month. During his recovery, Pietr introduced Harper to his best friend (and former Friend-with-benefits), Isaac Parker. The book ends with Pietr and Harper having a discussion about opening their relationship, specifically to include Isaac, after a fun threesome experience.

In **On the Power Play**, our main couple spent time in LA during summer break to solidify their relationship and expectations with their new shared boyfriend. Harper also gets propositioned by Misha Levin, a former Minnesota Northern Light and current Edmonton Roughneck player. Misha has some secrets and insecurities of his own –including his marriage to his best friend, Cecil Spitz. But their jobs and homophobia within Cecil's team has put stress on their relationship. At the end of the summer, Misha and Cecil visit Pietr & Harper at their new summer home in Wisconsin for a taste of what an open relationship could be like. Once the season starts, it's back to business and for Harper, that means making friends with the WAGs or "Wives and Girlfriends" of the other Osprey players. It's rough, but by the end she is finding it easier to deal with some of the wives over others. Pietr and Harper conclude the second book by going together to get inadvertently similar tattoos; lilac sprigs with appropriate queer flag accenting.

In **Top Shelf Biscuit**, Harper and Isaac spend some time together in Wisconsin. This culminates in telling Harper and Pietr's parents that the trio are in a relationship together. While Anya and Yuri are unfazed, Val in particular is not thrilled with the development. They are even more disappointed when the couple have a quickie marriage ceremony at the Mounting Bison. Meanwhile, Pietr's teammate, Gregor, has developed a crush on Isaac. During an evening out, after an afternoon of voyeurism, Isaac agrees to go home with the man —only to have the night come to an abrupt and early end. Misha also humors Pietr's interest in bondage play. A bonus short story further elaborated on what happened at Gregor's place.

Author's Note

A few reminders of what to be mindful of when reading Puck & Pen

- At this point, Harper's pronouns are she/her, BUT may still appear as They/Them by people outside her everyday life.
- None of these characters are representative any of queer identity as a whole.
- There is spice beyond this page! This includes but is not limited to detailed open door or "on the bed" sex scenes, multiple sexual partners, voyeurism, use of toys/sexual aids, light bondage, and dirty talk.
- Other potential triggers: gaslighting, childhood trauma, judgmental parents/family, cussing, "coming out" experience, discussions of past physical and sexual assault. (Specifically in Chapter 41).

Chapter One

"We have body language expert, Tasha McLeod, with us here today on Talk of Tampa. Tasha, who are we analyzing today?"

"I tell you, Gina, I love this whole dynamic that is happening with one of our favorite hockey players and his wife Harper Wyatt —and their boyfriends! Most of you know that Pietr Ivanov came out quietly as pansexual almost exactly a year ago today, after being traded from our beloved Gators. Last month we found out that they've been in a relationship with Isaac Parker, a former teammate of Ivanov's from LA. Now, just two weeks ago, we learned that Wyatt's secret boyfriend is none other than superstar Edmonton native, Misha Levin."

"Wow. That is a lot of love. ...Or is it?"

Harper sighed. She wasn't going to ask Anya to change the channel, but she wasn't sure she wanted to hear whatever this *body language expert* had to say about any of their relationships. For one thing, a single still photograph was not the way to read a person's body language. As an expert, she should know that. With every name drop, a photo had popped up.

"Let's start at the beginning. This is the photo that Ivanov shared last year on his Instagram, coming out. He and Wyatt are very close together. They're leaning into one another. Genuine smiles. Feet are turned. The hands together in the pockets. Very sweet. Very, very much in love. No doubt about it," Tasha continued.

"I sense a but?" Gina looked skeptical on the screen.

"*Let's fast forward. Here are some of the photos that were shared from the wedding. In the pictures with them together, they look comfortable. Happy. Again, genuine smiles. Very cute.*" Tasha had out a little pointer stick to wave around at the photos that were blown up and attached to cardboard on an easel between herself and the host. "*But in these with the full polycule, things may be slightly off with the other partners. Look at the way Parker holds himself, slightly away from the couple. Almost like he doesn't want to be there. Whereas Levin is very close to Wyatt, almost possessively.*"

"No shit," Harper spat out. "He was in a clingy mood."

"*These photos are from last week when the Roughnecks played the Osprey in Manhattan. It's obvious by the relaxed shoulders that the men are comfortable with one another. They've almost pushed Wyatt behind them. It definitely makes you wonder!*"

"Makes you wonder *what*?" Harper retorted. "Whether you made a poor career choice? Yes. You did."

"Harper!" Anya chided. "Is just for fun. No one takes this seriously."

"It's dumb." Harper sighed. "They pushed me behind them because of the cameras. After what happened at KongKon, none of them like me in front of an unknown camera."

"Understandable," Anya replied. "Here. Taste this." She handed Harper half of a small, filled cookie.

"Ooh, that's very cinnamon-y." Harper smelled it before tasting it. "It's good. What is it?"

"*Priyaniki*. We'll make *sbiten* later to enjoy with it."

"You say that like I know what it is, Anya."

"*Sbiten* is like a hot tea. This is a cookie." She waved the other half before shoving it into her mouth. "We'll have soup and dumplings too. Meat filled kind, not the fluffy bready kind."

"Do you need help with anything?" Harper offered.

Anya shook her head. "Go relax. Find Pietr and complain about the nonsense lady on TV."

"I complain about enough nonsense in general," Harper assured her.

"Then take these." Anya pulled out a plate to stick some chocolate chip cookies from a cookie jar on. She pushed it over to her. "Go sit out on the sofa and read or something."

"You want me out of your kitchen, Mama?" Harper teased.

"*Da*," Anya nodded, "you're very distracting while trying to cook and watch my talk show."

Harper picked up the plate. "Do I get milk or something with my cookies?"

"You know how to pour your own glass," Anya retorted.

Harper laughed. "Just teasing you, Anya. Let me know if you change your mind or need help with anything."

"I will, dear." Anya waved her off. "Go on."

Harper took the plate into the little living room, off the enclosed kitchen. Everything about Anya and Yuri's house was small. Pietr and Harper were staying a hotel nearby, as it was only a one-bedroom. In the three days that they'd spent in Florida, they'd visited three theme parks, seen the Winter Village at Curtis Hixon Park, gone to Busch Gardens, and let Anya feed them every traditional Russian Christmas delicacy that she could come up with. It was their last day of freedom before Pietr was scheduled to be at the arena the next morning for pre-game practice. Hence the interest in Pietr and Harper on the local TV station. Many hockey fans were amping up for the game. They'd already been photographed together locally at several of the attractions they'd visited. Both by fans, unknown photographers, and of course Pietr had posted a few photos to Instagram with his usual batch of ridiculous hashtags.

"Hey, baby." Pietr was stretched out on the sofa. Yuri was reading a newspaper in a recliner nearby. "Mama kicked you out of the kitchen?"

"There was some bullshit body language expert saying shit about us on her talk show," Harper explained.

"Like that we are madly in love?" He sat up, swinging his feet back to the floor to make space for her to sit beside him.

"Like that Isaac is standoffish and there's something going on between you and Misha."

"Well, Isaac was a little uncomfortable at the wedding," Pietr admitted. "And there is something between Misha and Me. You."

"That's not what they meant."

"I know." He put an arm around her shoulder before stealing one of the cookies. "Ignore them, *lyubov moya*. We know the truth." He nuzzled her cheek before taking a bite. "Speaking of, did you call Misha?"

"Not yet. He's doing stuff with Cecil and his parents."

"Don't put it off," he chided. "Even if it's short. He wants to hear from you."

"I know." Harper squeezed Pietr's knee. "Don't eat too many of these."

"If I can't cheat at Christmas, what is the point of living?" He teased.

Harper snuggled into his side, and they shared the plate. Pietr relaxed, content with the cookies and the light touch. He brushed crumbs out of his beard and Harper teased him to keep the crumbs for later, trying to tuck a chocolate chip into the wiry hairs.

"Rude!" He turned his head nipping her fingers. He snapped up the chocolate chip. "I don't think that would taste very good with all the product you put in this." He stroked his chin. "Is very soft though."

"I told you to stick with it."

"It is only because you take such good care of it. Like your own special pet."

"Your beard is my pet?"

He hummed, kissing her again. "It could use a little trim."

"I like it the way it is," she retorted, reached up and scritching her fingers into his cheeks. Pietr groaned.

"You two are indecent. Can't an old man read the news in peace?" Yuri grumbled from his chair.

"I thought old people liked seeing young people in love?" Pietr retorted.

"*Da, Da,*" Yuri waved a hand, "out in the world. Not in my own living room."

"Sorry, Papa." Pietr's arm tightened around Harper's shoulders. "We'll reel it in. Should we turn on the TV here? There are probably some good Christmas movies on."

"Or some really shitty ones," Harper rebuked.

"Hallmark has a marathon. You can turn that on," Yuri suggested.

"Oh no! Have you and Mama gotten into the Hallmark movies?" Pietr reached over for the remote. Sure enough, it opened up to the Hallmark Movie channel, currently showing something about a big city doctor moving to a rural Vermont town and falling for a chiseled, too-clean carpenter. Or something like that.

"It's kind of early in the day to start a drinking game," Harper said, "but we might need to if this is what we're doing all day."

Pietr covered a grin, rubbing her shoulder. "I'm sure they have some good stuff hidden away somewhere."

Harper split the last cookie on the plate with him and settled deeper into the couch. Smells from Anya's cooking began to permeate the apartment. Pietr's hand slipped down Harper's side, flirting with the hem of her t-shirt. Harper reached, squeezing his fingers. They'd been almost non-stop since landing in Florida. Taking advantage of the brief time they had with Anya and Yuri. Getting back to their hotel each evening had been spent winding down, brushing teeth, a kiss goodnight, and crashing. No energy left for love making.

"Maybe after lunch," Pietr leaned down to whisper to her, "we go back to hotel? Spend some time, the two of us?"

"That's not rude?"

"I'm sure Mama and Papa want us out of their space. Plus, we'll see them tomorrow before the game. You're all sitting together." Pietr murmured. "Is not rude. Just a break."

Harper nodded. "That would be nice."

Pietr growled something low in his native tongue in her ear. Harper didn't need a translation, coupled with the tight squeeze to her hip and a nip from his teeth.

"Behave." There was a loud swat as Yuri hit him upside the head with his newspaper. "You're a married man now. She's not going anywhere."

Pietr laughed, rubbing the back of his head. "Damn it, Papa, that hurt."

"Good. Knock some sense into you." Yuri broke off into his own string of Russian. He ruffled his paper back open, settling back into the recliner. "Ridiculous boy."

"I'm in love. I can't help it."

"Don't you find him smothering, Harper dearest?" Yuri asked. "If you ever need break, you come spend some time here with Mama and Papa."

"Thanks Yuri." Harper rubbed Pietr's knee. "I don't mind though. I've gotten used to it. I'd be more concerned if he wasn't like this."

Yuri grunted, shaking his paper some more. "Just keep it down over there then."

Pietr smiled, relaxing again. He traced light circles through her t-shirt into her side. Harper zoned out for a bit, content to be next to him. She was nearly asleep when Anya announced that lunch was ready.

"Oh good." Yuri closed up his newspaper. "Perhaps our son will control himself better once he has food in him."

"Or perhaps this is a refueling for more shenanigans," Pietr countered. "You never know."

"I am so happy you have found someone, *someones*, who will put up with you in your own old age, *syn moy*." Anya patted his cheek. "I am also so happy you live in your own, far away."

"Love you too, Mama." Pietr caught her hand, kissing her palm. "What did you make for lunch?"

"Nothing special," Anya retorted. She waved them over to the table just big enough for four as she rattled off the menu. It was more of an evening dinner than light lunch to be sure. Though, with most of the Russian food that Harper had sampled, she wasn't sure that there was much distinction. A lot of it seemed filling.

After lunch Pietr yawned. "Thank for a good meal, Mama. Harper and I are going to go back to the hotel for now."

"But we didn't make the *sbiten*," Anya argued. "And the—"

"Mama, don't throw everything at us in one visit. You and Papa can enjoy the *sbiten* and the other stuff. You'd make them whether we were here or not." Pietr kissed her forehead. "We're tired. It's been a busy couple of days. Aren't you exhausted? Following us around all the theme parks, and the garden, and the park..."

"I am not saying a nap is not in order," Anya said coolly. "Come back for dinner. Otherwise, we will not see you until the game tomorrow."

"Tell you what," Pietr began. "We will come back here at about six o'clock. We'll go out for dinner. Somewhere nice. My treat. Then we'll come back here for your *sbiten* if it is that important to you. Okay?"

"Fine." Anya nodded. "It would be nice to not have to cook, I guess."

"I love you, Mama." Pietr kissed her again. "Love you too, Papa. We'll see you later?"

"Yes, please, get out. You're suffocating us," Yuri teased, waving them off. "Shall I call and see if I can get reservations at your someplace nice?"

"If you want to pick the place, sure." Pietr nodded. "Surprise me when we get back." He turned to Harper. "Come on, *lyubov moya*. Let's go."

"See you later." Harper let Pietr pull her out of the tiny apartment.

Chapter Two

The hotel wasn't far. A short walk down the street. They were going to move to the team hotel the next day but opted to be closer to the parents for the holiday. It wasn't the grandest hotel, but it was comfortable, and they hadn't been bothered during their stay.

Pietr pushed Harper through the door into the room. He closed and put the security latch in place before beginning to shed clothes after they'd each kicked off their sneakers.

"What are you waiting for?" He prodded, realizing that Harper had not begun the same.

"I still need to call Misha," Harper realized. With the holiday hub-bub, they'd sent a few texts, but Misha had requested she call. He was spending time with Cecil and the Spitz family, but he promised to make time for her whenever she got the chance.

"Then call him," Pietr urged. "That's hot. Talk to your boyfriend while your husband eats your pussy." He stepped closer. His fingers moved into the waistband of her jeans. He waited until she kissed him before popping the button and unzipping them.

"He might be with Cecil. Or with Cecil's parents."

"Then you will have to be very well behaved so that he doesn't know what's going on. That's even more hot." Pietr coaxed. "I bet he's into it."

Harper smiled, pushing him away. "Let me call him. It will only be a few minutes. Then we can play all you want."

"At least *ask*." He stepped away, pulling off the last of his clothes before going to the bathroom.

Harper took out her phone, tapping up Misha's phone number.

"Hello *Kiska*. You have good timing," Misha's voice filled her ear. "Cecil just left."

"So you're home alone?" Harper asked.

"Yes. I'll go back to Edmonton in the morning."

"How was your holiday?"

"It was good to have some time with my husband," Misha admitted. "We did some talking, which was good. Had some of our own fun. How's Pietr? You're at his parent's place?"

"We just got back to the hotel. He's horny."

"Then why are you talking to me?" Misha laughed.

"I didn't want to forget to call you."

"I understand."

"Pietr thinks it would be hot to talk while he goes down on me."

Misha hummed. "Would you let me listen?"

Harper felt a flush rise to her cheeks. "Would you be into it?"

"I think listening to you try to keep it together, having a mundane conversation with me while Pietr is trying to make you cum sounds fun." There was a brief pause. "I'm sad you didn't call a few minutes earlier. I could have seen if Cecil would have played too. We could have done it at the same time."

"We'll have to keep that in mind for the future," Harper replied.

Pietr reappeared from the bathroom, a towel tucked under his arm. He frowned, motioning at her. "What is this? Take it off already."

"He sounds impatient," Misha said. "Let me talk to him while you do as he says."

Harper considered for a moment before she gave a slight nod. "Okay *Daddy*." She held the phone out to Pietr. "He'd like to talk to you."

"*Da*?" Pietr took the phone. "How are you, Meesh?"

Harper couldn't hear the response other than a soft rumble on the other end. She pulled off the LA Scorch hoodie she'd worn, long commandeered from Pietr's closet. A remnant of his time with his first NHL team. She had one of her plain black tanks on underneath it, no bra.

"We did some sightseeing. Very cute pictures at the Wizarding World. I will send you some. Harper's face –priceless. Is easy to forget she is giant fucking geek sometimes."

"You had fun too." Harper poked him in the side before shimmying out of her jeans. She tossed them aside before reaching down to peel off her socks.

"You drive me nuts." Pietr angled the phone away from his mouth. "Dawdling is what this is." He turned his attention back to the phone. "How was your holiday? Cecil sent a Merry Christmas text."

Harper wriggled out of her trunks, then finally shed the tank. She stepped close to Pietr, kissing his cheek. He let out a little groan, turning to meeting her lips. He reached down, giving her a smack to the butt before jerking his chin toward the bed and mouthing, "Bed. Now."

Harper got on the bed as directed. Pietr tucked the phone up with his shoulder, kneeling in front of her. He grabbed her by the back of the knees, pulling her flat to the mattress. Harper caught a laugh in her throat, not resisting. He unfolded the towel, making her lift her butt to tuck it under her.

"*Da*," he was speaking to Misha again. He said something in a string of Russian that Harper didn't even pretend to follow, not able to recognize any particular words after *da*. Then he smiled, handing her the phone back. "Here you go."

"Hi." Harper kept an eye on Pietr. He ran his hands up her thighs, pulling them apart to move between them. He leaned forward, pressing a kiss first to her chin, then trailed downward to suckle on a nipple. "It's not very nice when you two speak Russian, you know."

"I'm sorry," Misha's voice was a purr. "It's not so often that we get to speak our first language. Does it bother you?"

"No," Harper admitted, "but sometimes it seems like you do it just to have a conversation about me."

"Sometimes," he admitted. "It's not to complain or anything bad. Only ever good." There was a pause, followed by a slight creaking sound. "Has he started?"

"Yes," Harper admitted. "Ignore him though. I know you just said, but how was your holiday?"

"Good. Cecil's mom cooked for us on Christmas Eve. We spent all of yesterday just the two of us. He has a game tomorrow, or he would have stayed today too. I have a little longer break."

"Pietr has a game tomorrow too."

"I know. How has your trip been? You went to the amusement parks?"

"Yeah. We flew into Orlando. Anya and Yuri met us. We all stayed a night there, then came back to Tampa for Christmas Eve."

"What did your husband get you for your first Christmas as a married couple?"

Harper grinned. "The trip was the gift."

"You don't mind that?"

"I don't mind at *aaah*—" Harper reached down to touch the top of Pietr's head as he finally moved south. "Fuck. I don't mind at all. Gifts aren't everything. I'd rather we got to do things together than have a bunch of stuff."

"Very wise," Misha replied. "I'll keep that in mind for the future."

"What about—*Oh fuck, Pietr!*" Harper's fingers tightened in his hair. The phone slipped a little from her ear. "I know what you're trying to do, and don't you *dare*. We have to sleep in this bed."

"I put down a towel," he retorted casually.

"No."

He sighed, his breath hitting her wet center. Harper shivered audibly, making Misha laughed in her ear.

"Let him, *Kiska*," Misha chided. "It feels good, doesn't it?"

"I wouldn't say it's good. Or bad. It's just messy."

"You're embarrassed about it," he said. "However, I will point out that...it is hot as fuck. It is a rarity, to be sure. You're the first woman I've ever known to do it."

"It doesn't make it less...I don't know." Harper's mind was drifting between the feeling of Pietr's tongue on her clit and Misha's soft, reassuring voice in her ear. "If I do it, I prefer it be in my own bed. Not making a huge mess for some poor hotel housekeeping staffer to clean up."

"Try not to think about that. What's he doing to you right now?"

"I already told you. He's going down on me."

"No, I mean, where is his tongue. Where are his hands?"

"His hands are on my thighs," she answered. "His tongue is...licking."

"You are so bad at this," Misha chided. "You write such vivid scenes, but you can't tell me out loud that your husband is licking your clit?"

"I know. I'm absurd."

"Fast? Slow?"

"In the middle," Harper's voice caught as he began sucking instead. Two fingers slid back inside her, making slow shallow strokes.

"Does it feel good?" He asked.

"Yes. Pietr is an expert at making me feel good."

Below her, Pietr growled, pulling away long enough to nip at her thigh. Then came back to her clit, making her cuss under her breath.

"You going to cum big for him, Harper darling?" Misha coaxed. "How many fingers does he have inside you? Two? Three?"

"Just two."

"How wet are you?"

Harper laughed lightly. "Dripping."

"I bet you are, baby." There was another soft creak and rustling in the background. "Eating that pussy is a lot of fun but *fuck* I can't wait to bury my cock in you again."

"It's probably good we don't see each other too often," Harper teased. "I get to recuperate in between."

Misha laughed. "You're not the first to say such a thing to me. Is it really so big?" She could hear the telltale slicking noises as Misha stroked himself.

"It's a monster and you know it," she retorted.

"You take it so good," he responded. "You don't complain at all."

"You're good at taking it slow," Harper said. "You're very patient."

"Yes, I am. Are you close?"

"Not necessarily. Are you?"

"No but I'm plenty hard. I only need a little incentive," he prompted. "Tell me what he's doing to do you. Good details. Use your words."

Harper closed her eyes, letting her hand trail back up to tuck behind her head. She tried to focus between the sensation of Pietr's mouth on her pussy and the sound of Misha stroking his cock on the other end of the phone. She relayed Pietr's movement; the way his tongue flicked at her clit then sucked down hard. His fingers thrusting inside of her. Kissing his way across her thighs. The way his beard tingled against her skin. No holding back, but not flowery or overly detailed either. Matter of fact. Informative.

"Am I distracting you from your orgasm?" Misha asked.

"A little," she admitted.

"Put me on speaker instead. Let me listen. I'll be quiet."

"Hold on." Harper pressed the phone to her chest. "Pietr, Misha wants me to put him on speaker so he can listen. Is that okay?"

Pietr paused, looking up at her. "I have asked you to do that for me for *months* and you always say no! But for Meesh, you will try?"

"We're kind of in the middle of things right now," Harper said. "But if you don't want me to..."

"Do it," he growled, "but promise you do it for me at some point in the future too, okay?"

Harper nodded slowly. "Yeah, okay."

"Okay then. You all right?" He rubbed his hands down her thighs. "It all feels okay?"

"It feels great," she assured him. "Just, divided attention."

Pietr leaned forward, kissing her again. Harper let out a little noise of distress; his beard was a soggy mess.

"You deserve it," he admonished. "Now let him listen to me make you cum."

Harper tapped the speaker button on her phone and hesitated for a second before placing it on her stomach between the two of them. "Okay, it's done. Sound okay?"

"Sound is perfect," Misha replied. She could also hear him a little better; the way his hand was sliding smoothly across his cock. Slick, slightly sticky sounding meant he'd probably applied some lube during the lull. "I feel like I'm right there next to you."

"Blind folded," Pietr teased.

"Should we try that next? Sensory deprivation," Misha replied. "What do you think, Harper? Would you be willing to try it? Blind fold. Ear plugs. Cuffs to keep your hands out of the way. Let us do as we will to you."

"I was fine until the cuffs," Harper answered.

"It's okay, *lyubov moya*." Pietr kissed the inside of her thigh. "We could try me first. I trust you to take care of me."

Harper's breath hitched as he sucked down harder on her clit then, fingers moving faster. Misha's breath was a little louder too; a deep intake followed by a slow breath out. The slick sounds slowed slightly.

"Tell me when you're close," he requested.

"Almost," Harper promised.

"Cum big for us, baby," Misha purred.

Harper blew out a slow breath and closed her eyes. She tried to ignore the weight of the phone on her belly. She listened to the slick noises coming from both herself –as Pietr's fingers thrust into her and his tongue sucked harder at her clit, and from the phone where Misha was stroking himself and breathing hard.

Pietr moaned, sending a brief vibration through her. Harper released a short whine, a curse, and then the high-pitched sound that both men seemed to love so much. Pietr kept going, letting her ride out the wave of orgasm, switching from his tongue to rub his fingers over her clit instead. He leaned forward, forgetting about the phone and squishing it between them for a moment.

"Can I fuck you now?" He asked. He leaned forward, kissing her. Harper grinned, wrinkling her nose at the dampness that clung to his beard, but still put out her tongue to lick his lips, then suck away a little of the wetness. "I take that as a yes." He leaned back just enough to position himself before sliding inside of her. Harper moaned. She reached down, picking up the phone and setting it on the bed next to them instead.

"Sorry, Misha, you're in the way."

She heard him chuckle.

"It's okay, kitten. Do what you need to do," he replied.

Harper was more keenly aware of the sounds they both made. The slick wet noises as Pietr thrust into her, the rustle of the bedding, the creak of the mattress, and of course Pietr's heavy breathing –not much better than her own. The distraction likely kept her from a second orgasm, but Pietr didn't seem to take it personally, simply enjoying his own. She laughed as he was a little *extra* loud with his finishing groan.

"Was that necessary?" She teased as he collapsed on top of her.

"*Da*. Had to make sure Misha heard."

"Trust me," Misha sucked in a breath, "I heard everything just fine."

Harper picked the phone back up, tapping off the speaker. She picked her fingers through Pietr's hair as he pressed kisses to her shoulders as he settled heavily on top of her. Wallowing in the closeness.

"Did you finish?" She asked. "I was too distracted to listen."

Misha let out a soft laugh. "Yes, kitten. Right before your husband did. I was quiet, so as not to disturb."

"You're pretty quiet in general," she said. "Are you feeling okay? I've gotten used to you talking the whole time."

"I'm fine," he assured her. "Tired. Missing my husband. Missing you. Missing your husband a little too."

Harper laughed. "Are you counting down the days until I visit?"

"No, I'm not that pathetic," he chirped, teasing. "It's about nine weeks. Hopefully it will go by quick."

"I *am* that pathetic. It's sixty days," Harper informed him.

Misha chuckled. "I'm glad one of us knows."

The bed rustled as Pietr rocked against her again. Harper looked up at him, raising an eyebrow.

"Are you going again?"

Pietr gave a little laugh. "Maybe?"

"Shit. Really?"

"Just talk to Meesh," he encouraged. "Don't worry about what I'm doing to you."

"I *do* worry," she chided.

"All that noise and he's already going again?" Misha sounded surprised. "Has being around his parents put a kink in your love making, Harper darling?"

"A bit," she admitted. "With all the travel and sight-seeing, it's been a packed few days." She pet Pietr's hair, then tucked the phone more securely between her ear and shoulder. She dug her fingers into his beard, giving him the soft massaging scritches to his cheeks that he liked so much. He let out a low, contented growl and leaned into her hands.

"I should let you go. Focus on getting him satisfied." There was a brief pause before Misha laughed again. "This was fun though. We should do it again sometime. Maybe some video?"

"No, no video," Harper admonished.

"A guy can ask," he replied. "Talk to you later. Call me when you get back to New York."

"I will."

"Thank you. Bye, *Kiska*."

"Goodbye, Misha."

Harper let the phone drop away and she turned her focus back onto her husband. "Okay, Mr. Insatiable. I'm all yours."

Chapter Three

Back in New York for New Years, the next couple of weeks went by quickly. With Pietr and McKinley on the road, Harper tried to make more of an effort to reconnect with her best friend Tanner. It still didn't feel like long before Pietr was dropping her off at the airport with a "have fun" and Harper was on her way to Edmonton.

"I told you I could get to your place on my own." Harper said but was still relieved to clip the seatbelt into place after getting into Misha's sedan. Sensible, but not boring. It was definitely a luxury model with all the perks including cozy butt warmers.

"I know you could. You're a very capable person. It's one of the things I love most about you." Misha turned, learning over the center console. "Kiss me. Quickly, before the people behind me start honking."

Harper grinned. The kiss was too long. A loud honk from behind made her jump.

"Worth it," Misha declared. He tugged her back for another brief peck before straightening and shifting the car into drive. "How was the flight? The layover wasn't terrible?"

"It was good. Surprisingly smooth. I had enough time to use the rest room, grab a snack, and then was boarding again," Harper said. "I might almost say it would be worth the longer layover just for the breather."

"You got to me faster. I appreciate that. Plus, timing was good to come pick you up after my morning pre-game. Now we can enjoy a couple of hours together before I have to be at the arena. Take a nap?"

"Is that a euphemism? You already know Pietr's pre-game habit."

"It seems to work well for him." Misha reached over to squeeze her knee. "I'm excited you're here. Coming to my games."

"I can tell. I'm excited too. A little nervous," she admitted.

"Nervous? Why?"

"It's mostly going to be the two of us. Alone. No buffers. For a whole week."

"I know. Fucking finally. I don't have competition."

Harper laughed. "What if we find out over the course of this week that we don't get along, or click, outside the bedroom?"

"I already know that isn't true, *Kiska*. I adore spending whatever time together we get. Plus, we converse very well. I feel like I know you as well as if we were able to see each other more often," Misha said. "I'm not worried about anything like that. The worst thing that could come from this week is not wanting to send you back home to your husband. He would not be pleased with me. Nor would Cecil, so we'll have to keep ourselves in check a bit, eh?"

Harper took his hand between hers. "Is it a long drive to your place? I didn't realize how out of the way the airport was from everything."

"Only about a half-hour. My apartment is close to a lot of things. We can go out and explore a little tomorrow. Cecil is excited to see you, though he won't admit it." He glanced over at her. "Does that make you nervous too? Being alone with Cecil and me?"

"Not necessarily," Harper hesitated. "Not the way you might think."

Misha raised their hands to kiss her knuckles. "I *think* you have gotten used to Pietr being a bit of a white knight and always protecting you."

"I don't need protection from you. Or Cecil. I trust you both. What's more, Pietr trusts you, or he would have asked me not to come. At the very least would have said more than *have fun* when he dropped me off this morning."

"I'm glad to hear that. I know he thinks we play too hard when we're together."

"Oh! That reminds me," Harper interjected. "We better keep it tame this trip. The IUD is still adjusting."

"Is it not going well?"

"It's fine, but annoying. Spontaneous cramping. Spotting. When Pietr and I have been a little rougher, or broken out the big toys, it's not that it hurts exactly. I'm just aware of the difference and it's uncomfortable. If that makes sense."

"We can take it easy. Would you like if this was a sex free visit?"

"Do *you* want that?"

Misha grinned. "I don't want you to feel like that's the only reason I want to see you or spend time with you."

"I don't think that," Harper assured him. "We might have to switch things up a bit. With a little patience and experimenting, we'll be fine."

"Good deal. We can start immediately when we get to my apartment," Misha announced. "I suggest kissing and butt rubs? Then a nap. Maybe, eh, a sensual wake-up?"

Harper laughed again, squeezing his fingers. "That sounds nice."

Misha changed the subject and they discussed the itinerary for the rest of Harper's visit. Misha had a couple of games that week, but had planned for minimal work and maximum relaxation time.

"Are you sure that's a good idea? You're not putting anyone off on the team? Irritating the coaches? Causing problems?"

"I think asking for flexibility this week was well received," Misha said. "Some people need a break from me."

"Such as the defenseman you punched in December?"

"Breitbart? He's an asshole. He deserved it." Misha parked the car in the small lot outside an older looking apartment building. It was well kept, but not a lot to look at. Definitely not the sort of place that Harper had come to associate with hockey superstars.

"Speaking of," Misha unclipped his seatbelt and turned toward her, "while most of my teammates are solid, open-minded guys, Breitbart *is* an asshole. If, for whatever reason, you find yourself in a situation where he's around, please stick close to me or to one of the other guys. Blaze or Barnet are good options. Charlie Hennessey is our captain. Aiden Swan is an Alternate."

"Is he that bad?"

"His own ex-wife donated to a fund last month when Dylan DeLario cussed him out and got fined. Rio donated all the money that was sent to him to a charity, but still. Says a lot, in my opinion."

"Hopefully it isn't an issue," Harper said.

"Hopefully not." Misha gave her a reassuring smile. "Let's go in. It's cold."

"It's Canada. Isn't it always cold here?"

Misha laughed as they got out of the car. He waved her off, hauling her suitcase out of the trunk. The wheels clacked against the cement sidewalk toward the apartment. He held a hand out to her instead, which she took with a roll of her eyes. He let go long enough to open up the main door and usher her into an apartment near the middle of the first floor hallway.

"It's not big. What you see is what you get." He set her bag down to remove his jacket and kick off his sneakers. Harper did the same as he pointed out the important spaces. "Kitchen, living room, bedroom, bathroom."

"You warned me it was small, but I didn't expect *this* small," Harper admitted.

"It's comfortable," Misha said. "I'm here so little it didn't make sense to get anything bigger or nicer. The house has more personality. Mostly Cecil's personality."

"This is bigger and nicer than my place when I met Pietr. That was an efficiency. Cozy. I kind of miss it, but it was silly to hold on to it, even just as a writing space."

"I bet any space with you can be cozy." Misha took the handle of the suitcase again. "Let's test the theory in the bedroom."

While not meticulous, it was neat and clean. The bed was even made. Misha tucked Harper's suitcase near the closet door, then cupped her face in his palms to kiss her.

"Hi." He grinned.

Harper let out a breathy, nervous laugh. "Hi."

"Have I said I'm glad you're here?"

"You have," she confirmed.

"How about I show you how much?" He ushered her toward the bed and drew his henley over his head, tossing it aside. Lips met again as his fingers trailed under the hem of her t-shirt. Misha broke off long enough to draw it off. He slipped open the fly of her jeans, his lips moving to her neck.

Misha paused, hands on Harper's hips. "Do you need to text Pietr? Let him know you got here in one piece?"

"I did that while I was waiting for you."

"Good. I don't want him mad at me." Misha pushed her jeans over her hips. He shuffled her closer to the edge of the bed. "What did I suggest in the car? Kisses and butt rubs?"

Harper laughed against his mouth. "Yes, though you didn't mention if that was exclusive or mutual."

"I don't care, so long as we're skin-to-skin," he declared. He went for her neck, unhooking her bra and casting it aside.

Harper pressed closer as the rest of their clothes came off and were discarded. Misha's teeth sank into the sweet spot between her neck and shoulder. He hiked her up by the thighs, tipping her backwards onto the bed.

"Turn over, flat," he coaxed. He waited until she was comfortable on her stomach. Harper folded her arms under her head and Misha straddled her hips. He started at the base of her neck, kissing a line down her spine. His fingers dug into her flesh, skimming her back and sides. He spent a few minutes just enjoying touching her and sprinkling her with soft kisses and bites. He settled in after drinking his fill.

"Not too heavy?" He asked, bracing himself on his forearms as he covered her.

"No," Harper assured him. "You feel good."

He grunted, rocking slightly against her. "You feel good too. Soft. Smooth."

"Great, my back-ne is clearing up."

Misha snorted back a laugh. "Hey, I'm trying to be... what's the word I'm looking for? Sensual maybe? And you're making a joke."

"Couldn't help myself." She grinned, biting her bottom lip between her teeth.

Misha sat up, giving her a swat to the butt. "Okay, naughty girl. Maybe we should skip to the nap?"

"Spoons?"

"You remember when I was in New York and you weren't feeling well?"

"Yes?"

"Like that again. Lay on my chest?"

"You're sure you'll be comfortable?" Harper asked.

Misha moved, getting back off the bed for a moment to adjust the pillows and draw back the covers. Harper moved out of the way until he'd settled. Slightly reclined on a pillow, Misha beckoned her closer.

"Very comfortable," he promised. "Come."

Harper sank against him. Misha drew the covers over them both before resting his hands on Harper's back. She laid her head on his chest –then reached to pull off her glasses.

"Is there a safe place for these?"

Misha hummed, taking them to set on the side table. He leaned forward to kiss the top of her head, then relaxed again.

Harper felt a wash of exhaustion. She'd been awake since nearly four that morning to get to the airport on time. She hated flying, even though she had been on more flights in the last six months than in her whole life previously. Misha rubbed her back in small comforting circles. Whether it was like he was filling her, or he was absorbing energy, she couldn't be sure. She just knew it felt right. Necessary.

Chapter Four

Misha reached over, giving Harper a reassuring pat after she gasped awake. She had jerked upward at the sound of his far too loud alarm. The afternoon had bled into early evening. The windows were already showing a world starting to go dark.

"It's just my phone, baby," he said. "So much for a slow wake-up." He coaxed her to his side before getting up to grab his jeans. He pulled out his phone to finally silence the alarm and then slid back into bed with her.

"You have to get ready." She smiled sleepily at him.

"I have time. They won't start without me. As long as I'm there before warm-up, everything is fine."

"You really going to push that?"

"To spend every available minute with you? Yes, I am." Misha shifted over top of her, peppering her face, neck, and shoulders with kisses. Harper giggled, pressing her hands to his chest, but not pushing him away.

"We can leave together if I take my time. I prepped my sticks and all that before I left this afternoon. I literally just need to put on my equipment," he assured her. "If we go together, you don't have to get a rideshare. You can come in the player entrance with me. Avoid crowds."

"And by avoid crowds, you mean you'll protect me from paparazzi like that horrible Delly Forrester?"

He grunted. "Exactly."

"You can't protect me from everything," she chided. "Don't stress or burn yourself out trying, Misha."

"Rationally, I know that," he said. "Not so rationally, I'd rather put you inside a bubble for your entire stay, so I know you're returned unscathed to Pietr."

"Hey." Harper took his face in her hands. "I am a grown-ass adult. I'm not your responsibility. So, please, relax? Let's focus on having a good time together."

He took her hands in his, kissing both of her palms before nodding. "I will try my best."

"This is one of those times where I feel like you, and Pietr, have a tendency to shove me into a Woman Box."

"You *are* a woman," he said.

"My sex is female," Harper said. "But I'm not a *woman*, Misha. They're not mutually exclusive. And neither being female or a woman makes me incapable of taking care of myself."

Misha considered that for a moment. He squeezed her hands again before kissing her fingers. "I'm sorry. Non-binary is still a new concept for me. Though, I'll point out that you *do* refer to yourself as a woman at times. I'll do better to be supportive."

"You are," she assured him. "I know it's confusing, but try to keep that in your head the next time you're inclined to worry about me?"

"Harper, darling, I am going to worry about you," he laughed. "I love you."

Harper stilled. Part of her had sensed it was coming. She had been considering whether she was ready to say it herself yet. Even though she *knew*, somewhere deep, that it was true. She still wasn't prepared to hear it from Misha first.

He let a small, almost defeated looking smile pull at his mouth. "You don't have to say—"

"Misha, I love you too," she rushed to cut him off. "I love you so much."

He grinned, kissing her. One of the long, firm, soul-searching kisses that seemed to pour all of his want into her. Harper moaned. Misha released her hands, leaning over her. He nuzzled her chin up, moving to brush his lips to her neck.

Harper laughed again, pushing his shoulders lightly. "We –*you* don't have time for this."

"I have as much time as I need, *Kiska*," he chided. "It will be worth every minute it takes to hear you cum for me."

"What about you?"

"It won't take me long." He found her lips again. "Two minutes. Tops."

"I'd rather you enjoyed it a little more," Harper said.

"I enjoy all of it," he assured her. "I'll enjoy it more tonight, tomorrow, and every day until I drop you back at the airport next Sunday." He leaned back, taking in a deep breath. "Do you *want* me to skip ahead? I like getting you there first, but if you're really worried..."

Harper bit her bottom lip, rolling it between her teeth. Her cheeks flushed pink as she admitted, "I want you inside me. I don't care if I get an orgasm first. Or at all."

"Whatever you wish, kitten."

He kissed her one more time before he stretched for the side table. He grabbed a condom and quickly rolled it into place. Harper shifted, Misha's hands spreading her thighs wider as he angled the head of his cock to her center. He rubbed gently, coating the head with dampness before slowly pushing inside. Harper sucked in a breath as Misha settled in place.

"Okay?" He asked.

"Yes. Just tight."

"I know." He thrust gently, withdrawing just a few inches before pushing back in. "You always feel so good. Squeeze and hold –just like that, yes." He groaned, moving a little faster. "Tell me if it's too hard or too deep. I don't want to hurt you."

"A little faster, but not deeper. This time. Maybe we can ease back up full length."

He smiled, catching her lips again and rocking into her. The covers had fallen away from them. Pressed close, they were still wrapped in a bubble of comfortable warmth. Misha braced his arms against Harper's side. He let his hips roll, taking his sweet time.

Harper whined. Her hands came up to his cheeks. "You feel so good," she murmured. She followed the statement with platitudes against his mouth and cheeks, urging him on.

Misha growled, nudging her chin up to sink his teeth into her neck again. Short, quick rutting-like thrusts pushed him closer and closer to the edge. Part of his brain was going primal; wanting so badly to cum deep inside her. Hold her down, like breeding animals. Another part knew time was running short but *god*, it felt so fucking good to be together. And last, the smallest piece, wanted badly to hear Harper's orgasmic moan.

"Will you cum for me, baby?" He crooned. "I can hold back if you think you can."

Harper moaned, closing her eyes. "Maybe?"

"What do you need?"

Harper reached down between them, making him pause. "Do you think you can angle just a little higher? Then, just keep doing what you were doing."

Misha nodded, lips brushing hers again. His pelvis pressed into her, rubbing her clit with each grinding thrust Harper let out a soft *"oof—fuck!"* and grinned against his mouth. He turned focus on getting to hear her. Listening and watching for her little micro-reactions that would tell him she was close. Finally, just as the animal inside was about to get frustrated, he heard it. She tightened around him and dug her fingers into his sides. He hissed, drinking it in and letting her ride it out. He *finally* sat back, hooking his arms under her thighs to thrust harder into her.

"Ow—fuck!" Harper winced, pushing on his chest in surprise. But it was too late. He was already cumming. He caught her lips, slowing back to the soft, shallow thrusts.

"You okay? I'm sorry," he apologized. He let her thighs splay back open as he leaned forward to stroke her hair, and pepper her with more soft kisses. "You came and I just—"

"I'm fine," she assured him. "It was good. So good."

He rocked gently, savoring the warmth. "You asked me to be careful. I got carried away. Sorry, *Kiska*."

"I love you."

Misha grinned. "I like hearing that." He gave her one last kiss to her cheek. "I love you too. I really will be more careful, I promise." He leaned back again to let out a ragged breath as he pulled free from her. "Now I do have to get ready. Come take a shower with me. It's faster."

"Faster or more of a distraction?"

"Conserves water either way," he chirped. "Think of the planet. And my water bill."

Harper laughed, giving him a swat as he started to get off the bed. "Fine. For the sake of the planet –and your bank account."

Chapter Five

Misha kept a tight grip on Harper's hand as they made their way into the player's entrance. He gave her a final kiss before introducing her to one of the security team. She was issued a badge, similar to the one she had in New York. There was still time before the gates officially opened, but she got her ticket scanned and a personal escort to her seat. She was surprised to find it was just three rows back from the glass, behind the Roughneck's bench. Harper laughed when she realized and wondered what kind of strings Misha had needed to pull to make that happen. Even Pietr just took whatever seats were available from the pool, and neither thought much about where she was in the crowd.

With plenty of time to kill, she shot off a text to Pietr to check in.

[HARPER] How's it going?

[PIETR] I miss you. Come home?

[HARPER] By the time I got there, you'd be on your road trip.

[PIETR] Oh right. How's Meesh?

[HARPER] Good. He got me a great seat.

She included a photo of the arena with the text.

[PIETR] Damn. I will have to up my game. That is a great seat.

[HARPER] He told me he loved me.

[PIETR] Finally? Good.

[PIETR] And what did you say?

[HARPER] I told him that I loved him too.

[PIETR] Is something wrong?

[HARPER] No. Part of me knew it was coming. I've been thinking about how I feel about him for a while. I just didn't expect it today. The way it came out.

[PIETR] He didn't say it while fucking, did he?

[HARPER] LOL! No. The fucking was after I said it back.

[PIETR] Good. So you know he meant it. Was the sex good?

[HARPER] Duh. It's Misha.

[PIETR] I hope you have the same reaction when he or Isaac ask about our sex...

[HARPER] They don't. But if they did, I would. I love you most.

[PIETR] Not possible. I love *you* most.

[HARPER] It's not a contest.

[PIETR] Sort of is.

[HARPER] I married you. You can't win more.

[PIETR] I'm sure I could think of way.

[HARPER] You're being silly.

[PIETR] I am. It's boring being home w/o you.

[HARPER] Why don't you see if Isaac wants to play?

[PIETR] He's busy tonight.

[HARPER] ???

[PIETR] He has a date.

[PIETR] With Hollywood starlet Hannah Stone.

[HARPER] From Ameri Khan?

[PIETR] Yes.

[HARPER] How did he meet her?

[HARPER] And why didn't he tell me?

[PIETR] I don't know.

[PIETR] On both counts.

[PIETR] He probably only told me because I asked if he was available. And he perhaps didn't tell you because he knew you were with Misha this week and didn't want to bother you.

[HARPER] Maybe.

[PIETR] Are you jealous?

[HARPER] No. I want him to find someone who makes him as happy as you make me. I think he needs it.

[PIETR] Me too. I'm not sure an actress is the answer though.

[HARPER] I think he'd be happier with someone who would be around more. I'm not going to judge until it's more serious though.

[PIETR] If it gets serious.

[HARPER] Exactly.

[HARPER] If he tells you how it goes, keep me in the loop?

[PIETR] I'm sure he'll let us both know.

[PIETR] You're at the arena very early.

[HARPER] I came with Misha. They let me in early.

[PIETR] Well aren't you special. They must already like you to give you such treatment.

[HARPER] I think Misha is pulling some strings. I should tell him to stop.

[HARPER] He's worried something is going to happen to me "under his watch".

[PIETR] You're a grown up. You can take care of yourself.

[HARPER] I told him that myself. Also: Pot, Kettle, Black.

[PIETR] I don't understand.

[HARPER] You are also very overprotective of me.

[PIETR] Yes, because I love you and you are one of the most important people in the world to me. When you hurt, I hurt. Moreso when it is caused by something I could have prevented. Or could have been avoided.

[HARPER] Be honest with me. Do you see me as a woman?

[PIETR] I don't understand the question. You're non-binary. You're a woman. You are both.

[HARPER] You don't worry about Isaac the same way.

[PIETR] I suppose I don't. But I care for you in different ways. I love you both very much, but not the same.

[PIETR] If Isaac called tomorrow to say it's over because Hannah wants to be an exclusive monogamous couple, I would be hurt but we would still be friends.

[PIETR] If *you* called me to say you wanted a divorce and were staying with Misha I wouldn't just hurt. That would wreck me.

[PIETR] So it's not about your gender that I worry and want you safe. It's that I want to spend as much of the rest of my life with you as is possible.

[HARPER] Okay. Sorry.

[PIETR] You don't need to apologize. I am sorry if I ever make you feel like I don't respect your identity.

[PIETR] Sometimes it is easy to forget. To revert to old bias. I never do it on purpose.

[HARPER] I know.

[HARPER] I think I'm struggling with identity right now.

[HARPER] Again.

[HARPER] Constantly.

[PIETR] Because you switched back to She/Her?

[HARPER] Maybe? I don't know.

[HARPER] Do you ever feel like you're not queer enough?

[PIETR] Always. Even when I'm sucking cock, I wonder, hmm, does this make me more gay or just seem like I'm pretending?

Harper laughed but felt a little relieved at Pietr's honesty. She reached up, tucking a hair behind her ear. She had started feeling defensive in the conversation with Misha earlier. Admitting to Pietr that she was struggling was hard, but if she couldn't admit it to him, then who could she talk to?

[PIETR] Harper, you are enough and no one can tell you otherwise. Other people can think what they want, but if *you* say you're non-binary and queer, that is enough. That is all that you need. Just like people can look at us and say we're a straight couple. We know we are not. Our partners know we are not.

[PIETR] If you ever want to change your identity words, or your pronouns (again), I'll support you in whatever ways that I can.

[HARPER] I know that. Thank you.

[PIETR] Did Misha say or do something to make you feel like he doesn't understand or support that part of you?

[HARPER] Not exactly. I feel like sometimes all three of you, especially in regards to the protectiveness, default me to feminine.

[PIETR] Ah. I am 100% guilty of that. It' not on purpose. I will do better.

[PIETR] I know other people would use us being LGBTQ as a reason to hurt you or us. I am physically bigger. Stronger. I put myself between them and you. It's not about you being female. It's because I love you and I'd rather take the brunt of something painful than let you do it alone.

[HARPER] Being in a relationship, being married, means neither of us has to face that shit alone. Right?

[PIETR] You're right. I'll keep that in mind from now on.

[PIETR] The game will start soon. I should let you go. Get some snacks.

[HARPER] Yeah. People are starting to filter in.

[HARPER] I love you. Call you later?

[PIETR] I can't wait to hear your voice.

[PIETR] I love you too. Enjoy the game. Give Meesh a good reward for his hard work. Win or lose.

[HARPER] I will.

She sent him a kissy emoji before closing the screen.

Chapter Six

"Good game, Misha." Harper let him pull her into a hug as he arrived at the WAG Station after the game.

"Thank you, baby." He kissed her temple. "I'm happy you got to see me win for once."

"I've seen you win," she assured him. "Just not in person, as your girlfriend before." She grinned, giving him a quick peck to the lips. "Dinner?"

"Fuck yes. But lets order in a pizza or something." He drew his arm around her shoulders, leading her toward the exit. "I don't want to go out in this suit and I don't want to leave the apartment again after we go back."

"Do you have an app on your phone?"

Misha pulled the device out of his pocket and unlocked it before handing it over. "Here. You order, I'll drive."

Harper took the phone, swiping the screen as Misha steered her toward the car. There was a group of photogs and fans clustered near a gate. She could hear camera snaps and rushed questions but chose to ignore them until she heard a familiar voice.

"Harper Wyatt! Good to see you in Edmonton."

Harper's head didn't snap to attention, but she did look up. Misha visibly bristled as she was unable to keep herself from stopping.

"Delly," she replied. "I'd say it's a pleasure to see you, but that would be a lie. Should we be expecting you to harass us the whole time I'm in town?"

"Harass you?" Delly gasped. "Never. I simply love a good romance. Perhaps we could have a good sound byte for the blog?"

Misha swore under his breath, tightening his fingers on Harper's shoulder, trying to gently pull her away. "C'mon babe."

Harper ignored him, stepping closer to Delly and the other reporters. "I suppose that depends on what you'd like to hear. And how clever your sound editing is."

"I'm curious to know how you'll be spending your time in the city. Can we expect to be seeing you at more Roughneck games?"

"I'm in town for the week," she announced. "So I'll be at Tuesday and Friday's games as well. As for plans, Misha and I don't get to see each other often. We'll be making the most of it. Take that as you may."

"Harper," Misha grumbled, "don't poke the bear."

"How am I poking?" She retorted. "I'm being honest." Misha's flat expression spoke volumes. "Okay, fine." She turned back to Delly and the other curious reporters holding their phones and recording devices. "Thank you *so much* for your interest in us, but Misha and I aren't that interesting. We'd appreciate privacy as we figure out how to navigate the more unique structure of our relationship in the public eye. Have a great night."

Harper stepped away, now pulling Misha instead.

"Mx Wyatt, when you're ready, I'd love a full interview," Delly called after them. "You have my contact info! Call me!"

"You will call her over my dead fucking body," Misha swore. "Delly Forrester is a *cunt* –and I never use that word."

"Misha!" Harper gasped, surprised at the vitriol in his voice.

"Sorry." He softened. He pulled the keys out of his pocket. The car beeped twice as he unlocked the doors. "I cannot stand that woman."

"I know." Harper stopped as Misha opened the door for her. She turned back to him, pressing her hands to his cheeks. "But there is absolutely nothing that she can do to hurt us. You and me, we're being open and honest about our relationship now. I don't care what any of them say, or think they know. I love you."

Misha's lips pulled in a smile. "I really do like hearing that."

"I like saying it," she admitted with a grin followed by a feigned glance of concern. "Maybe don't tell Pietr how much I've said it? It took me a long time to be comfortable telling him."

"It's our secret," he confirmed. He let her pull him forward for a kiss. Slow, a little lazy, but sweet and refreshing. He pulled her hands from his face, kissing her knuckles. "Do I need to unlock my phone again so you can order dinner?"

"Shit," she swore, looking down at the phone. "Damn it. Yes."

He chuckled. "Zero-Six-Two-Four."

Harper felt a flutter in her chest as Misha trusted her with his security code. She tapped it into the screen and the order app popped back onto the screen. "Got it."

"Good." He kissed her again. "Get in."

Harper slid into the passenger seat and Misha waited until she was tucked inside before closing the door firmly and circling to the driver's seat. He was quiet as he started the car, driving the short distance back to the apartment. Harper asked him a few questions about the order, which he responded to. When she'd finished, she relayed the order back to him for approval.

"That sounds great, babe," he assured her. He reached up, loosening his tie. "ETA?"

"Twenty minutes?"

"Good. Long enough to change and fool around a little bit." He glanced over to give her a small grin.

"Pace yourself, Levin," she teased.

He laughed. A few minutes later, he'd pulled into his parking space. Harper didn't let him make his way around the car to let her out, meeting him at the sidewalk. The car beeped again as he locked the doors. Misha held her hand as they made the short journey up the walk and into the apartment.

"Make yourself comfortable," he said. "I'm going to change quick."

"I'm going to call Pietr to check in," Harper said.

Misha nodded, leaving her to her call.

Pietr picked up on the second ring.

"Hullo, *lyubov moya*." He sounded sleepy. "How was the game?"

"Roughnecks won, six to four."

"Good game then," he said. "You had fun?"

"Yes, it was a lot of fun," she said. "How was your night?"

"Boring. I played some video games. Double checked that I had everything packed to leave tomorrow. Checked in with Isaac about his date, but he didn't answer me." He yawned. "He is probably still on it. It's earlier there after all."

Harper smiled. "Did you find what I left you?"

"The hoodie? Yes. Thank you. I'm wearing it right now actually. It smells like you."

"You already miss me so much?"

"I missed you five minutes before dropping you off this morning," he said. "I'm glad you're getting some time with Misha though. I..." he faltered slightly, "I am trying not to be jealous."

"Why are you jealous?" Harper's voice softened. She took a seat on Misha's sofa. It wasn't anything special, but comfortable. A soft brown suede that matched a recliner, slightly off-set from the TV.

"Sharing you is hard sometimes," he said. "I want you to be happy. I like Misha. I like how you are with him. When it's the three of us is fun too. But, this, you going to see him and being alone with him. This is new. And now you're using the L word."

"Pietr, it doesn't mean I love you less."

"I know. I know full well that we are both capable of loving other people, having other relationships. That you and I are not less because of those relationships. But, it's still new."

"Sounds like we're both having to work through some shit today," Harper mused.

He let out a soft amused noise. "I guess so."

"Should I not have told you? About us using the L word?" Harper asked.

"I always want you to be honest with me," he said. "I like being included. That was a big step, for both of you. Especially with the distance and the time. I'm glad you told me."

"Okay." Harper rubbed a circle in the arm of the couch. "Is this something we should put a pin in and discuss when I get home?"

"I don't know," he admitted. "But let's try to sit down and figure it out, okay?"

"Yeah, okay," she agreed. "Anything else going on?"

"I don't think so," he said. "I should let you go. Enjoy your time with Misha. Don't worry about me, please. I love you so much."

"I love you too."

Pietr let out a soft hum and Harper smiled.

"Talk later?"

"*Da*. I'll call you when I get to the hotel tomorrow," he said. "But just for a few minutes. I don't want to get in the way. Seriously, please enjoy your time with Meesh. You both deserve it. Have fun. Don't play too hard."

"We won't," Harper assured him. "Bye, Pietr."

"Bye Harper, darling."

Harper paused for a moment, not really wanting to end the call. She was excited to be in Edmonton. Excited to be spending time one-on-one (mostly) with Misha. But, she had also grown very accustomed to being in New York, to Pietr's coming and going. Being the one away felt very different. Different than the month she'd spent with Isaac back in November. Being with *Misha* was different.

"Harper?" Pietr's voice brought her back to the present. "Hang up, baby."

"Sorry," she apologized automatically. "Love you. Talk to you tomorrow."

"Bye," she heard him say one last time before she ended the call.

Misha reappeared from the bedroom. He looked casual in a worn out t-shirt and a pair of loose sweats. He took a seat on the couch next to her.

"How is Pietr?"

"Sleepy," she answered. "Missing me. A little jealous."

"Jealous?" He repeated. "Why?"

"He says sharing me is hard sometimes," she offered.

"I get that," he said. He leaned his elbow on the back of the couch, looking at her curiously. "Do you like being polyamorous?"

Harper considered that for a moment. "I don't know. For as much as I love you and Isaac, I was content with Pietr before we went down this road. If something happened and our other relationships ended, and it was just the two of us again, I don't think I'd actively pursue it. You and Isaac just kind of happened. Well, okay, *you* happened. Isaac was Pietr's fault."

Misha smiled. "I have a terrible habit of shoving my way into people's lives."

"Is that what you did with Cecil?"

He chuckled. "Sort of. We lived down the street from each other when my parents moved us to Edmonton. I was walking down the street one day while my Mom was unpacking and my Dad was getting settled at the university. Cecil was shooting balls into a net in his driveway and I watched for a few minutes. He invited me to play, and...we've been friends ever since. We played together all the way until we were drafted."

Harper reached over, pressing a hand to his knee. "If you two have always been so close, then why keep the relationship a secret?

"After my parents passed, I fell into a sort of depression. Hockey and sex were the two things that kept me going. Cecil tried to get through to me, but I wasn't ready to hear it."

"How long did that take?"

"Awhile. He tried to talk to me about being self-destructive, which was valid. I accused him of wanting to control my life. Then I kissed him and didn't stop. The clothes came off, he sank to his knees..." Misha shrugged. "I have never once had Cecil comment on my size in bed."

Harper blushed and he laughed.

"It's okay," he shrugged, "it's big, but it didn't faze Cecil. He knows. He makes jokes in other places, sure. But, in bed –it doesn't matter how big either of us are. We just want to feel each other."

"Hard not to feel either one of you," Harper teased.

"Maybe it's good thing we found each other. I can feel his cock on my lips for hours after. I love that feeling. Like a secret memory."

"I'm familiar with that," Harper said. "I like it too. A little dirty reminder."

Misha reached over. His fingers traced her ear, tucking a lock of hair back into place. "Anyway, after that...whenever we would see each other, we'd hang out and it would be just like it always was until we'd hook up again." He frowned. "I was falling in love but he didn't seem to be feeling the same way. I felt like he was always holding me at arm's length. We were best friends, but when we started doing that, it was like he didn't know how to talk to me anymore as just my friend."

"But he was, falling in love, I mean."

"About a year before I was traded to Edmonton, I finally asked him what the fuck we were doing. He was in the news, having broken up with, ah...shit, what is her name? Grace Jin? She was in that sci-fi movie based on the show?"

"I know who you're talking about," Harper assured him.

"Good. They'd broken up after *dating*," his tone was sarcastic, as though he didn't believe the relationship had been real at all, "for over a year. I'd seen other people too. Mostly casual. Some regular Friend-With-Benefits situations, but...to me, Cecil was the only one who mattered. All he had to do was say stop and I would have dropped all of them for him."

"And you told him that?"

"More or less," he said. "We had another big fight. I felt jerked around. I was in love and didn't want to be his dirty secret that he used to cheat on his girlfriends with."

"What came out of that was you getting traded to Edmonton?"

"Turns out, he had been feeling the same way. He thought I was the one using him for quick, easy sex when we were in the same place. Like I had different people in all the cities that I was fucking around with, and he just happened to be another hockey player." Misha shrugged. "I did not, by the way."

"I didn't think so."

"After our fight, we started trying to communicate better. Figuring out how to make a real relationship work. I started talking to Edmonton, since I had the opportunity to be a Free Agent. They're a struggling team, but we came to an agreement and here I am. It was a homecoming. Cecil's parents are still here. We bought the house in Red Deer. We told our closest friends and his family that we were together."

"How did you decide to get married?"

"Ricky Beckham got hurt in a game," Misha explained. "The kid's girlfriend was distraught and the hospital staff wouldn't let her do anything or see him until his parents arrived. Ricky was a kid and it wasn't anything life threatening, but it was hard to watch Lindsey go through that. If that had happened to me, I would want Cecil to be the first to know and calling the shots. We decided we would take the risk of being outed in order to take care of each other. Maybe that is not best reason, but it's ours."

"Your HR departments know you're married?"

"Yes." Misha nodded. "Our HR and GMs."

"While you were doing the secret hook-up thing with Cecil, you were seeing other people. Were you serious with any of them?"

"Not really." He shook his head. "No one ever stuck the way that Cecil did. The way you do."

"Stuck?"

He reached over, sliding his fingers between hers. "When you're not around, you're still in my head. The both of you," he said. "I wonder if you're awake when I get up in the morning. I wonder what you're doing periodically throughout the day. Sometimes, when you text and I'm stressed out, I'll wait to read it as a reward for making it through the day."

"Is that why it sometimes takes you longer to reply? I always assumed you were busy."

"That too." He smiled. "But, whether it's you or Cecil texting –the guys always know it's someone special. Apparently, I have this *face* I make."

"Are they still teasing you about the Daddy thing?" Harper asked.

"Periodically," he admitted then continued. "But that's what I mean by *stuck*. With other people, and I've been with more than my fair share, there wasn't the same connection. Honestly, I thought that Cecil would be the only one I ever felt that with. It was confusing to meet you and have those kinds of thoughts for someone else." He squeezed her fingers. "I thought you were beautiful when Pietr introduced us. You seemed so at ease, but also a tiny bit nervous. I could already see how Pietr felt for you. He carries his feelings on the surface. It felt wrong at first, to keep thinking about you. Then, at the awards..." he laughed. "When you told me about Parker and how the two of you had opened your relationship. I felt like I had won the lottery. And I felt less gross about the occasional sex dreams I'd had."

"You had sex dreams about me?"

"Nothing crazy, but a couple. Have you ever had any about me?"

"No." Harper laughed. She brushed her hand through her hair, looking a little uncomfortable. Shy. "Not that I remember anyway. I'm sure if I had, I would remember it."

"True. Real life is better than dreams any day. Dream Harper didn't make nearly as much noise. Sounded more like Cecil."

Harper laughed as Misha's phone pinged. He looked at the screen before stretching and getting up from the couch.

"Pizza is here. I'll go down." He paused to kiss the top of her head. "Be right back. Grab us drinks? Water is fine for me. Help yourself to whatever you want."

Harper nodded. When Misha had stepped out of the apartment, she rose to go into the tiny kitchenette. It was basic, divided from the living room by a counter island. She checked the fridge first, grabbing a bottle of water for Misha and a soda for herself. She was considering glasses when Misha re-entered holding the pizza box. He dropped it on the island counter, an audible stomach growl following it.

"Did I order a big enough one?" She teased.

"I'm sure you did," he said. "Plates are in the cupboard by the fridge."

"Do you want a glass for your water?" She asked.

"No, no, that's fine. Less dishes the better," he replied. "I'm only suggesting plates because you're here."

She shrugged. "I don't care about plates. How messy is the pizza from this place?"

"The plates are probably a good idea."

Harper opened the cupboard, taking out two plates. "Is it the kind of place where I'm going to end up needing a fork?"

"That depends on how you feel about me licking any sauce or cheese off you," Misha retorted. "I don't mind, but if you want to stay *neat*, then maybe."

"I think I'll live."

Harper brought the plates over to the island. Misha opened the pizza box with another stomach growl as the smell of the melted cheese and assorted meats hit them both. He slid two slices onto a plate as Harper did the same.

"Should we turn on a movie or a show?" He asked.

"How do you usually wind down after a game?"

He considered for a minute. "Usually, I take my sweet ass time getting out of the locker room because I know I'm coming home alone. I place a pick-up order before the game, so I stop and get that. When I get here, I change out of the suit, sit in silence while I eat whatever it is. Maybe read. Check socials and texts. Sometimes I'll play a video game or watch some old reruns. I've usually ridden out the adrenaline from the game by midnight or so. Then I go to bed."

"Sounds a lot like Pietr's routine."

"We are creatures of habit."

"Let's watch something then. After we eat, we can go to bed and tire you out the old-fashioned way."

Misha let out a low growl. "I like that idea."

Harper chuckled, picking up her plate. "You better eat something then. Or you're not going to have the stamina I've come to expect."

"I have plenty of stamina."

The sound of his stomach once more betrayed him.

Chapter Seven

"Hey."

"Hey."

"Is that really how you two greet after not seeing each other for, what, two weeks?"

Harper raised an eyebrow as Cecil dropped his keys onto a hook and kicking off his sneakers at the door before entering the living room where Misha and Harper had gotten comfortable on the couch after arriving a few hours before. After Misha had finished his Sunday non-game day routine at the training center, he'd come back to the apartment. They had gone out for lunch, wandered around some of the sights of Edmonton, and then decided to go to Red Deer a little early. Both men had lucked out with a total rest day together the next day.

Cecil smirked, leaning over the back of the couch to press a kiss to Misha's cheek. Then he leaned over, doing the same to Harper.

"No," he said, "normally we don't say anything at all. He just throws me over his shoulder like a caveman and carries me into the bedroom. But you're here so I imagine he's fairly well satiated for once." He squeezed her shoulder gently. "One perk to trying this open relationship thing."

"You like it and you know it," Misha chided. "Do you want me to carry you into the bedroom? It's been awhile for you."

"I'm fine, thank you," Cecil assured him. "Have you two eaten dinner yet?"

"No," Harper answered, "we thought we'd wait for you."

"That was nice of you. What are we having then?"

"Chicken and roasted veggies," Misha replied. "If that's okay."

"Sounds great." There was a slight pause before he continued. "Is that in the oven now, or am I in for a wait? 'Cause, I admit, I am fucking starving."

Harper leaned forward, picking up her phone. "My timer says fifteen more minutes. Can you survive that long before your stomach eats itself?"

"It's going to be close, but I think I can manage." Cecil came around the couch. "How was your flight in yesterday? The layover wasn't too bad?"

"Good," Harper replied. "Layover was fine."

"...Are you wearing an LA Scorch hoodie?"

Harper looked down. "Yes?"

"Why?"

"It's cold and it's comfortable?"

He continued to look at her quizzically.

"It's Pietr's, from when he played," she explained.

"Right. We need to get you better merch," Cecil teased. "Hasn't he bought you an Osprey hoodie?"

"I have two. This one is cozier." She shoved her hands into the pouch at the front. It was hard to explain why exactly she liked the Scorch hoodie. It was a little oversized. Looking closely, observers could tell that Pietr had worn it often. The edges of the sleeves were fraying and the fabric had become extra soft with wear. He'd handed it to her on a whim when it was cold in the apartment one evening and she had never returned it. It was sort of like, he'd given her a piece of his past that she hadn't gotten to be a part of.

"Don't pick at her," Misha chided. "She can wear what she wants."

"I'm not picking. It's just an interesting choice. I wouldn't have thought it was Pietr's and Isaac has been retired long enough, I wouldn't think he'd have encouraged it."

"Neither of them encourage me to wear anything." Harper was the one who looked confused now. "I owned Osprey merch before I met Pietr and while I wear it often, it's mostly when we're together or at games. At games, I usually wear a jersey now."

"I see. I'm sorry."

Misha grunted. He slid to the edge of the couch before standing. "Harper, keep an eye on the timer. Cecil, come with me please?"

Harper bit her lip as Cecil, a pink flush creeping up his cheeks, followed Misha out of the living room. She heard a door close. Their bedroom probably. She sat quietly, half watching the TV and waiting for the timer to signal dinner. At the sound, she went to the check on the oven's contents. She'd acquainted herself with the general layout and location of things when she and Misha had worked together to prepare the food. She took down plates and started serving up portions of everything. She set them down at the small kitchen table and went to the fridge for drinks; beers for the two of them and a soda for herself. After adding silverware to the table, she hesitated about going to knock on the bedroom door. Before she could make up her mind, the two men re-appeared.

"Thanks baby." Misha touched her elbow as he moved around the counter. "You didn't have to do all this."

"You two were taking your sweet time and Cecil said he's *starving*," she replied.

"I am," Cecil piped up. He went straight for the table, taking a seat. "This smells so good. Was it a joint effort?"

"Yes," Misha replied. "Mostly it was Harper though. I just chopped things."

"Don't underestimate the importance of a good sous chef," Harper said. She and Misha took their own seats and picked up forks to dig in.

Conversation was polite. Harper still felt a panging wave of anxiety tighten in her chest. Why, she wasn't sure. Misha had given her the opportunity of an out to the visit including time with Cecil. She supposed, as she listened to the two men talk about what else they had going on, part of it had to do with unknown expectations. When the couple had visited her and Pietr in Wisconsin the previous summer, Cecil had been pretty clear that he wasn't sexually attracted to her. But, they'd still had plenty of fun between the four of them –including and not limited to Cecil becoming *very* familiar with Harper's squirting ability.

Misha reached over, tapping her thigh. "You're very quiet."

"Am I?"

"Yes and it's very unlike you," he chided.

"I'm fine." She gave him a short smile.

Misha raised an eyebrow at her but didn't push. He turned back to Cecil.

"What do you want to do after dinner, *lyubov moy*?" He cocked his head to the side. "You decide."

"What are my options?" Cecil asked carefully.

Misha sniffed. "Either something normal like a movie or a game, or something kinky like letting Harper and me double team your cock?" He shifted his gaze back to Harper. "If that is agreeable to her, of course."

Harper shrugged. "I'm game. Pietr said I should have whatever fun I wanted." She picked the tines of her fork over the potatoes on her plate. "Although," she glanced up at Cecil, "I know I'm not your cup of tea, so if you'd rather just have some alone time with Misha, I can occupy myself."

Cecil frowned. "What do you mean? Why would you think that?"

"Um, because you've said that. Several times?"

"When?"

"When you visited in August. You were quite adamant actually that you didn't find me sexually appealing, and you couldn't wrap your head around why Misha does."

"Oh. Wow. I was kind of an asshole, wasn't I?"

"Yes," Misha replied dryly. "You do have the habit, lately."

"Fuck, I'm sorry." The pink flush was creeping up Cecil's neck again. "That visit wasn't exactly my shining moment. I was still figuring out how I felt. I had negative feelings to deal with. I didn't realize you'd taken that to heart." He rubbed the back of his neck like he was trying to tame back the flush. "By the end of that weekend, I was pretty stunned with how much I enjoyed the experience." He took a short pull from his beer before looking at her. "You're right in that I'm not, like, conventionally attracted to you. But the time before was fun and I've been looking forward to trying again to see you how Misha sees you. Maybe not *exactly* how Misha sees you. Cripes. Do you know what I mean? Or am I making a bigger ass of myself?"

"I think I get it," Harper answered. "And that's fine. I had fun back in August too, or I wouldn't have done any of it. But I know the two of you don't get much time together so again, it's fine if you want to take some time to yourselves tonight and we can all fool around tomorrow, or whatever. I'm flexible."

"Yeah, Meesh and I have been busy lately, but I'm good. Are you?" Cecil asked Misha.

Misha looked nonchalant. "I'm content with whatever you want, babe. As long as I get to fuck one of you, good. Both of you? Fantastic." He popped the last piece of his chicken into his mouth and chewed thoughtfully. "You have until you clear your plates to make a decision."

Cecil picked at chunk of potato before admitting. "I'd love to get you to squirt again, Harper."

She sighed. "Of course you would."

Misha chuckled. "We have big towels. It's okay. We can put down extra. And Cecil can clean up the mess." He frowned. "The new IUD hasn't been a problem with that?"

"No." She sounded almost disappointed. "Pietr was very quick to test that out after I was feeling up to it."

"I bet he was. You should have let me listen in again," he chided. Then he perked up. "Is Pietr playing tonight?"

"Yes. They have a game in Washington," she said.

"Ah. We should find a good time to let him listen while you're here this week. Since you were so nice to let me when you were in Florida at Christmas."

"Are you three having phone sex now?" Cecil asked.

"Not really," Misha retorted. "Pietr wanted to fuck and Harper had promised to call me. Two birds, one stone. I liked it. It was good." He squeezed his hand on Harper's thigh. "What do you think *Kiska*?"

"We can try and call him later. He usually texts when he gets back to the hotel."

Misha hummed.

"Aaaaand," Cecil pressed, "you're good if we try the squirting thing?"

"What do I get out of it?" Harper asked, curious.

Cecil grinned. "What do you want?"

Harper considered that for a moment. "Could we try DP? You're both so fucking huge though..."

Misha laughed. "You want to try anyway?"

"Maybe a Spit Roast?"

"That we can definitely do," Misha said. "Cecil isn't quite as girthy as I am. Good cock for sucking."

"Thank you?" Cecil said, quizzically.

"I mean it in only the best way," Misha assured him.

Harper popped the last morsel of food into her mouth. Misha reached over once she'd finished, stacking their plates. "I was mostly teasing. I'll enjoy whatever you two want to do. But, if you really want to try and get me to squirt, towels are a very good idea."

"While Cecil finishes, I'll go set up? Make sure everything we need is handy," Misha suggested. "You brought along some of your favorites?"

Harper nodded. "The upper pocket on the front of my bag has the wand in it."

"Good choice." He stood up, pausing long enough to kiss the top of her head before carrying their dishes to the sink. "Come in when you're ready. Maybe grab a couple waters? So we don't have to get up for it after."

"Will do," Cecil replied. He waited until Misha had made his way over to the bedroom before looking up at Harper again. "I'm sorry about earlier too. The hoodie. I wasn't picking. It's just not a logo you see often up here."

Harper shrugged. "It's fine. Like I said, it's comfortable. It's something of Pietr's that I borrowed and didn't return. It...makes me feel closer to him when we have to spend time apart."

Something in that statement seemed to click for Cecil. He nodded thoughtfully. "I get that. I borrow one of Misha's North Face jackets all the time. He takes a pair of my U of A sweats. They're safe to wear in front of other people without suspicion."

"Can I ask you something and you won't get mad?"

"When you put it like that, I can't make any promises," Cecil countered.

"You know more players have come out, publicly and quietly. Have you thought more about telling people about you and Misha?"

"If I thought my teammates would be supportive, I'd do it in a heartbeat. But some, not all, of them would make my life a living hell. It's about timing. We manage and neither of us can play forever. It's tough now, but there's still a lot of life after hockey."

"True," Harper reasoned, "but you don't have to be miserable just because you're still playing."

"You think we're miserable?"

Harper frowned at him. "I know Misha isn't happy. I also know he loves you and will stay with you for as long as he can. I won't pretend to know how you feel, Cecil."

Cecil made a soft acknowledgement noise. He'd finally cleared his plate. The chair scraped against the floor as he pushed back to carry his dishes to the kitchen. He stopped, opening the dishwasher to begin loading it while he continued contemplating a response. When he'd finished, he turned back to Harper.

"I asked Misha to marry me because I needed the reassurance that I was a priority for him. That he was serious about making a life with me. At the time, I wanted to know that I was the only person for him. We've been a unit most of our lives. It's not perfect, and it's hard. But I'm not miserable. I wish I saw him more. I wish it didn't have to be so stressful and complicated. But our safety and security is worth more to me than our marriage being public. Maybe I'm paranoid, but I'd still rather not find out I'm right, as much as I want to be wrong."

"I get all that. But are you happy?"

"I don't think it's a matter of being happy," Cecil replied. "I love every minute I get to spend with Misha. I'm happy that he's able to fill some of the void he's been feeling with you. It helps him, having someone else to focus on."

Harper hummed, pushing back her chair from the table with a soft scrape. She circled the table to toss her empty coke can into the recycle bin. Hands emptied, she pressed them to Cecil's waist and had to rise onto her toes to press a soft kiss to his lips.

"Let's go fuck your husband."

Chapter Eight

As Misha awoke, it took him a few extra seconds to realize that his left side was colder than his right. His husband was pressed into his side, fast asleep. However, his girlfriend was no longer in bed with them. He held back a groan, gently shifting Cecil from his arm to slide out of the empty side of the bed.

He padded, still naked, out of the bedroom to the kitchen first. No Harper. He noticed a soft light from the living room and went in. There she was. She had gotten dressed and was lying on the couch. Approaching, he could tell she had drifted off with her laptop resting on her chest.

Misha paused, watching her sleep for a minute. He gently lifted the laptop and closed the lid before setting it on the coffee table. She stirred as he crouched beside her, pressing a soft kiss to her shoulder.

"What's wrong?" Harper murmured

"Nothing. Why are you out here?" He rested his chin on her shoulder, stretching an arm across her chest. "I woke up. You weren't there."

"Couldn't sleep. Came out here to do a little work."

"Come back to bed."

"Yeah, okay." She lolled her head to blink at him in the darkness. "You have to move first."

He smirked, leaning forward to kiss her. He slipped away, rising and stepping out of the way to give her the space to maneuver from the couch. He held out a hand to help pull her to her feet. Harper swayed, falling against him. Or, perhaps he pulled her. His lips found hers in a soft, wanting kiss. Fuck, he wanted her...

She pushed back and Misha groaned. He calculated whether it was worth waking up Cecil to continue in the bedroom, or just fuck her there on the couch. He hoisted her up, bracing her butt under his forearms. She squeaked, her arms wrapping around her neck.

"Sleep or sex?" He asked.

"You *really* want sex again already?"

"Yes."

Harper kissed him again before giving him a gentle pat on the chest. "Put me down and get comfortable."

Misha let her slide down his front, onto her feet. He did as she asked, taking a seat on the couch. She pushed back the coffee table to more easily pull open a drawer for a bottle of lube, then dropped to her knees in front of him.

Harper pushed his hands out of the way. He watched, curious and horny, as she tipped his still-hardening cock toward her mouth. He savored the wetness of her tongue. The sensation of the head of his cock passing her lips. She carefully moved her hand along his length in short strokes. His foreskin stretched open, revealing the head of his cock before retracting again. Misha realized she was playing with him, pressing a line of kisses up the shaft after letting it slap back against his belly. Harper turned her attention to his balls and he released a breath he hadn't realized he'd been holding.

"Fuck, *Kiska*. That feels so good," he whispered. He reached down, brushing her hair out of the way. "Such a good girl."

Harper gave a little amused noise but didn't deviate from what she was doing. Her tongue swiped up from the base to the tip, sucking lightly at his skin.

"It's a shame you got dressed," he hinted.

"Shh," she chided. "Be quiet, Daddy. Cum for me."

He growled. A deep rumble from his chest. He stretched his arms across the back of the couch, inviting her to continue. He was finally getting to his full erection. Too heavy to stand tall. Harper's fist wrapped around him, fingers stretched. She give him another lazy wash of her tongue before beginning to stroke him in earnest.

Misha bit his tongue, resisting the urge to coax her on. He knew that she, Cecil, and even Pietr had teased about how much he talked during sex. He couldn't help it. He liked coaxing and directing. Sometimes some light cajoling. He enjoyed every second and the words just slipped out. How good they made him feel. How good he wanted to make *them* feel. Asking questions. Harder, faster, more or less? But if Harper wanted quiet, she was going to get quiet. Or, he'd do his best at any rate.

Misha's bottom lip rolled between his teeth. The cap of the lube bottle cracked open, a little too loud in the quiet house at 3 AM. He inhaled as her now slick hands, both of them, wrapped around him in a tandem pumping motion. She leaned forward, licking a bead of precum from the tip.

Misha let out a soft string of Russian. He had to drop his arms from the back of the couch to dig his nails into the sofa cushions. The urge to haul her into his lap and let her grind against him was beginning to bubble.

The lube was starting to feel tacky. Harper contemplated for a moment before releasing him to draw off her bottoms and dip her fingers between her thighs. Misha groaned again as she wiped her own juices along his shaft. Another soft *fuck*.

"You okay?" She asked, amused.

"No. Come here." He gave in, moving her into his lap. She let out another light laugh, balancing over his lap, hovering.

"What are—"

Misha put a hand over the head of his cock, then pressed gently on her hips with the other.

"Sit back and slide. It should be good for you too."

"Like this?" Harper braced her hands on her thighs, rubbing her damp center along his length. Misha let out another contented groan.

"Just like that, baby." He moved his hand, guiding her hips, though she didn't need the extra aid. His cock twitched and he felt the tightness rising from his balls.

Harper draped her arms over his shoulders, letting him keep her steady. She moaned against his lips, intense want hidden in the kiss, to drive him a little crazier.

It wasn't intentional on either of their parts. Misha was breathing heavily, loving the feeling of Harper's folds rubbing his cock. One second, he'd coaxed her back, nearly to his balls and the next, he'd drawn her higher against him, his dick tipping at just the right angle. Coupled with a thrust of her hips. He swore softly as he slid inside. Harper let out a low moan. Misha would have said he had no idea what *sensory overload* felt like, but he had a good idea as she squeezed around him.

Harper gasped, her eyes flying open as she jerked backward. Misha, a second behind her reaction, caught her and held on tightly as he kept cumming.

"Misha!" An admonishment.

"Fuck!" He swore, his thoughts pulled different directions. No condom –bad! Soft, wet pussy on bare cock –good! So fucking good. The rules! Safety! Permission! But fucking christ, she squeezed and kept squeezing like she didn't want to let him go any more than he wanted to pull out.

He wrapped his arms around her waist, pulling her closer. It was already too late. It was done. He'd come inside her; the first time he'd been bare inside anyone in *years*.

Harper panted into his neck but had tensed up. Like she wasn't even going to let herself try to enjoy it. Misha kissed her shoulders, rubbing her back.

"I'm so sorry, kitten," he sighed. "I don't –that was not what I meant to do. At all. Shit." He couldn't help letting out a soft laugh. "It felt fucking amazing though." He kissed her again softly. "Are you mad?"

"I..." Harper seemed a bit speechless. She pushed away from him. Misha grunted as cool air hit his warm, damp skin. Harper stood, bending down to pick up her trunks.

"Harper?" He tried again. "You know it's okay. It *was* safe. I..." he paused, trying to read her expression. "I know it broke a rule, but it was an accident."

"Yeah."

"Baby," he scooted forward, taking her hand, "say something. Please?"

She seemed to really look at him for the first time, getting out of her own head. She tried to give him a reassuring smile that didn't even try to reach her eyes. "I'm not mad. We got too into it. And it *was* safe. I've got the IUD. You've had a vasectomy. We all have clear health."

"Then why do you look like a deer in headlights?"

"Because we were *not* supposed to do that. Not yet. Not without asking or telling. I...You said you wanted to keep using condoms. I never even considered talking to Pietr about it again after our last conversation. I didn't tell him about your vasectomy either. It wasn't my information to share—"

"Harper," he said her name as he got to his feet. He brushed hair back from her face before cupping her cheeks in his palms. "Did you not like it? Was it bad?" He cocked his head to the side. "Initial feelings. Not the other stuff. Just how it felt while it happened."

"I did like it." Her eyes cast downward.

"Good. I liked it too," he said. He leaned in close, his voice lowering to a husky whisper. "Filling you up with cum." He nuzzled her nose with his. "Felt better than I remember it ever being. It's been a long time since I did that, with anyone." He kissed her then. A soft, chaste kiss. "I love you." Another kiss. "I am so sorry. It will never happen again without expressed, verbal, permission." One last kiss, but this one was firm with his promise. "I take all the blame. I don't know what's wrong with me. I keep making mistakes. Losing control with you."

"I didn't stop you," she countered.

"No, you didn't," he confirmed, "but that doesn't make it right. We should tell Pietr. And Cecil."

Harper nodded. She patted his chest before pulling away from him. "Go back to bed. I need to go clean up a bit."

"Then you'll come back to bed too?"

"Yes. We can call Pietr and talk to Cecil in the morning."

Misha nodded. He tugged her forward for a brief hug. He murmured softly into her ear. "Even if Pietr is *really* mad, it was worth it, baby. Know that I definitely want to do it again sometime."

Harper let out a soft laugh. Not forced, but a note of anxiety to it.

"Hey." He tipped her chin up again. "You trusted me and I fucked up. It's reasonable to be upset with me."

"I'm not." She gave his arm a squeeze. "If I were, I wouldn't have stayed where I was, you know?"

Misha let her go, watching her disappear toward the bathroom. He paused in the kitchen, giving himself a quick wipe down as well. He stared down at his cock, on the large side even when not erect. Now at its smallest, the retreat into his foreskin was almost comical. As if it knew it had been bad.

Think with the bigger brain, asshole, he told himself. He tossed the damp paper towel into the trash. He returned to the bedroom, sliding back into bed with Cecil.

While they'd been gone, Cecil had curled toward the edge of the bed. With the movement, he let out a soft moan, turning back toward Misha.

"You okay?" He asked softly.

"Yeah." Misha got comfortable, resting back against his side. He leaned his arm across Cecil's side, rubbing his bare hip softly.

"Where's Harp?"

"Bathroom. Go back to sleep, *lyubov moy.*"

Cecil hummed. Harper appeared in the doorway, shuffling back toward the bed. She got in beside him. For a moment, his chest tightened as she seemed to be getting comfortable beside him rather than *with* him. Then, she turned onto her side and wrapped an arm across his waist. Her head rested on the pillow next to his, chin on his shoulder. He resisted letting out the sigh of relief. He reached up, his other hand stroking her arm. Content, for now, he let his eyes close, and he fell asleep between his two loves.

Chapter Nine

Pietr had stretched out on the hotel bed to enjoy a few minutes alone when his phone rang. He was rooming with Tim Jamieson this trip. While they had become good friends, a little alone time on the road was precious. He picked up his device and smiled seeing the photo of Harper he'd set as her icon and "Lyubov Moya Calling..."

"Hello my love," he answered. "Good timing. I just got back to the hotel."

"I'd hoped I'd timed it right," Harper said. "You have a few minutes then? I need to talk to you about something."

She sounded anxious, which didn't bode well. But, he reasoned, a lot of things that made Harper anxious rolled off him.

"I have plenty of time for you." He turned on his assurance voice. "What do you need to talk to me about?"

There was silence on the other end, then she swore. "I don't know how to say it except to just say it."

"Then why don't you do so and if I need you to elaborate, I will ask."

"Misha and I accidentally didn't use a condom this morning and he, ah, finished inside."

Pietr felt a wash of arousal rise over him. He could picture it –and it was hot. But that had also been one of their core rules over the last year: condoms with other partners. Always. Even when Harper had told Misha and Isaac about the IUD, there had been no extra discussion about stopping.

"Please explain accidental?" He finally asked.

"It was like three AM. I'd fallen asleep on the couch and he came to see why I wasn't in bed. We started kissing. I was just going to give him a hand job. It wasn't enough. He had me sit in his lap and, well, rub against him instead?"

"Pussy job. I get it. Okay. And then?"

"I don't know. We weren't thinking, just feeling. He pulled me close and everything lined up. Suddenly, he was inside me and cumming. He was halfway gone when it hit me."

"And...how was it?" He didn't even try to hide the excitement from his voice.

She laughed. "Messy."

"Did you like it?"

It took her a moment before she let out a soft, "Yes."

"Did Misha like it?"

"Yes."

"Okay. Did you feel safe doing that with him?"

"Maybe there are two things that I need to tell you..."

"There is more?"

"Misha had a vasectomy like ten years ago. He told me back in December. When I told him about the IUD. But we had agreed, he *said*, he preferred to keep using condoms."

"So it was safe. Well, our level of safe."

"Yes, I'd say so."

"Okay."

"Okay? That's it?"

"Harper, I love you. You love me. You love Misha. He loves you. I think we should have talked about that possibility beforehand because it does happen. It's happened to us. It shouldn't, but we're human. It's easy to get carried away with someone you love and want to feel *more* with. I'm not mad. I'm not even disappointed, except that I wasn't there to see it. I'm concerned for how you feel. I hope you haven't been worrying about this."

"A little," she admitted. "I'm so sorry."

"Sorry? What for my love? For having sex with your boyfriend? Please never apologize for that."

"I'm sorry for losing my head. I never—"

"Harper," he cut her off, "do not beat yourself up about this. It was one time. I'm not even going to ask you to not do it again. I trust you. If that's a change you want to make with Misha, that's between the two of you. We know he is safe, and Cecil is his only other partner. It's fine with me. You have my full support to do what makes you happy."

"Really?"

"*Da*. Really. In fact, it would be really hot to let him give you a big creampie before you come home. Bring it back to me?"

"Yuck." She sounded disgusted but laughed.

"No, no, I want it now. Get you home and clean it up with my tongue. Then fill you up again. Like dogs, marking territory."

"What is it with you and dog analogies?"

"I don't know. Do I make them often?" Pietr laughed.

"Enough," she said. There was a beat of silence before she sighed. "It's okay though? Truly?"

"Baby, yes. Don't fret about it." He relaxed into the pillows. "How has the rest of your trip been? Are you with Cecil today too?"

"Yes. We got to their house in Red Deer yesterday afternoon. Cecil got in later."

"Has that been fun?"

"Cecil seems more at ease this time," Harper noted. "We told him this morning what happened and he was surprisingly chill."

"Good."

"His first reaction was reminding me that Misha had a vasectomy and that he really doesn't have time to sleep with anyone between the two, or three, of us anyway." Harper let out another laugh. "So, he's got his priorities straight."

"I'm glad to hear it. What have you all been up to?"

"We had dinner last night. Fooled around. They fell asleep; I couldn't so I got up to do some editing. Fell asleep on the couch. The accidental creampie happened. Back to bed. This morning, we slept in. Made breakfast. Told Cecil. Fooled around some more. Just finished up lunch and now I'm calling you."

"What does *fooling around* include?"

Harper hummed.

"*Please*?" He begged. "I'm rooming with Jammer. He's here all the time. This is the first chance I have had to be alone since we got in last night."

"Last night, we did a spit roast. Lots of oral. This morning, we took turns. It's been fun."

"I bet it has." Pietr let out a little growl. "I miss you."

"I've only been gone two nights, Pietr."

"I know. Do you miss me?"

"I haven't been alone for any length of time to miss you."

"Cruel. You could at least lie to me."

"Of course I miss you, Pietr," she said softly. "I'm easily distracted."

"Too late," he replied, "I'm not buying it."

Harper laughed. "I love you. ...Does that help?"

"*Da*." He paused for a moment, just listening to her breathe on the other end. "You are enjoying yourself?"

"I am," she answered. "How's your trip so far?"

"So far is good. Game tonight is going to be a rough one, I think. I will be glad to be home for a few days after this trip. Seeing you." He yawned. "Misha and Cecil both have games tomorrow?"

"Cecil leaves for his own road trip tomorrow morning. He has to head back to Calgary tonight after dinner. Misha and I are going to stay another night. He thinks it's more comfortable here at the house. I think he's a little self-conscious about his apartment."

"Why?"

"It's small. Utilitarian. I don't mind either way. I came to see him, not where he lives. It's plenty comfortable." She paused then continued, "It's been interesting seeing how he lives alone versus how he lives with Cecil."

"Before I lived with you, my apartment was very plain too," he said. "I didn't even like my apartment. It was just available and reasonable. I really should have found something closer to the practice arena. Being close to the Garden is nice, but only because it's a faster trip home on game nights."

"I like our apartment," Harper told him. "It's close to the good stuff."

He hummed. "I don't mind the commute."

"You sound tired."

"A bit. I think I'll take my nap early. Maybe see if Tim will come be a warm body," he teased.

"Whatever you need to do to bring home the W, babe."

His chest rumbled with a laugh.

"I'll let you go," Harper said. "Good luck tonight."

"Thanks. We'll need it. Now, don't let missing me get in the way of having fun with Meesh. I'll talk to you later. Stay out of trouble."

"I will."

"Bye, Harper. I love you." He bid before ending the call so they weren't tempted to keep talking. He leaned over, picking up the end of the cord to plug it in to charge. Then leaned back into the pillows, closing his eyes. He let his mind drift back to what Harper had told him and he released a low groan.

He could just picture the scenario in his head. Misha's huge cock rising with her body and sliding inside. He knew what it felt like –having experienced it many times himself, as she tightened around his bare cock. He could only imagine what it was like for Misha, who probably hadn't gone bare inside a partner in years. He could imagine her pulling free, the flow of cum leaking from her pussy... Fuck, he missed his wife and she'd only been away from him for two nights.

He wasn't normally like this, he surmised. He traveled quite a lot for games. He and Harper stayed in good communication while he was out of town. It had been different when she was in Wisconsin with Isaac before Thanksgiving, and now this week she was spending with

Misha. He was happy she was getting the time to spend with her other partners but he missed the little things while she was preoccupied. Talking on the phone, steady texting, tagging each other on social media posts, watching shows and talking on the phone while they streamed the same episode.

He yawned again and shifted downward into the pillows. He was going to sleep, he decided. When he woke up, he could send her a little nudge. They could still find a way to connect, even if they were both very busy.

Chapter Ten

"It's just the two of us again."

Misha took the seat next to Harper on the couch after he'd returned from seeing Cecil out to his car. Cecil had a much earlier morning, leaving for a game in New Jersey. Misha just needed to be back in Edmonton by nine AM. Harper looked up at him from her laptop screen with a soft smile.

"Sick of me yet?"

"Never," he declared. "I wish Cecil could have stayed longer." He draped an arm over her shoulders, leaning in close to press his face into her hair. "I'm glad he's come around to playing with us." A soft laugh. "That he's come around to any of this, actually."

Harper curled her arm, reaching up to stroke his cheek. He leaned a little more heavily into her.

"I'm glad too," she said. "You seem tired. Do you want to go to bed?"

"It's only seven o'clock," he grumbled.

"We could watch the Osprey game," she suggested.

"We can do that." Misha pressed a kiss to her ear. Then he leaned back, looking at her for a moment. "Do you watch my games with the same regularity you watch Pietr's?"

"Pietr *is* my husband," she countered.

"I know. Still a valid question."

She grinned. "If they don't overlap, yes, I watch your games too."

"Good." He leaned forward, reaching for the remote. He took his time with the TV but settled back against her as the opening commentary and warm-up were ending. "What are you doing?"

"I'm going over editing notes," Harper answered. "They want some irritating changes."

"Do you like being a writer?"

"I like writing," she answered. "I like that I can make a living doing something I'm good at. But no, I do not generally enjoy being a *writer*."

"How so?"

"If I had stuck to self-publishing, I could write the stories I want to write. Regardless of their sales potential, the *line*, expectations and formulas. Traditional publishing is...stressful. While I generally like the stories I write, they aren't always sent to the public the way I would like them to be."

"Example?"

"I had to write this non-binary character as an A-M-A-B," she said.

"Would you have preferred to write them A-F-A-B?"

"No, but I would have enjoyed the option. To write and see *myself* in a book."

Misha hummed.

"I can't just take my novels and leave, either," she said. "I'm locked into a very good, very lucrative contract. It's frustrating."

"How many books do you owe them?"

"Three more," she said.

"Give them the three, then run," he suggested. "Write for yourself again. You have the fan base now."

"I know, but part of the reason I have that is because of my contract."

He grumbled. "Seems complicated."

"Like the business side of hockey isn't?" Harper teased.

"True, but that's why I have an agent."

"I have an agent too. And she tells me to keep doing what I'm doing."

"Sounds terrible. Get a new one."

Harper laughed, jabbing her elbow into his side. "My agent is fine. The book is fine. The editing isn't even that bad. Nothing I didn't expect to hear, to be honest. Some of it valid. Some of it...not. I don't have the energy to fight about it."

"When do you have to have this done by?"

"A couple of weeks," she said. "It's something to do when I have down time. I didn't bring a project with me on this visit."

"Good. Put this away then," he suggested, tapping the edge of the screen. "Snuggle with me to watch your husband work."

Harper closed the laptop before setting it on the coffee table. Misha pulled a throw blanket from the back of the couch, draping it over them both. They settled in for the game in a companionable silence.

During the break before the 2nd period, Misha got up to grab snacks. Osprey were ahead 2-0. When he settled back onto the couch, Harper was texting with a small smile on her face.

"Pietr?" He guessed.

She nodded.

"Do you smile like that when you are texting me?"

"Sometimes," she answered. She looked up at him, the smile widening. "Are you feeling jealous?"

"Why would I be jealous?"

"Because this is supposed to be our time together and yet I'm texting Pietr instead of paying attention to you."

"Baby," he cooed, "the week is only starting. Besides, I know how the two of you are together. He misses you, doesn't he?"

"Yes."

"Pathetic, but also sweet. And you miss him too."

"I do but I am glad to be here with you." She leaned heavily into his side. "I wish we could do this more often."

"Me too, but we'll figure it out. The Roughneck's season will probably wrap up quickly. Play-offs aren't likely for us at this point, so our last game will be April Thirteenth."

"I'm terrible and haven't been paying attention to Calgary. How are they doing?"

"Fairly well. They might make it in as a Wild Card team," Misha replied. "Why? What are you thinking?"

"What if you and I went and spent some time in Wisconsin while Cecil and Pietr are in the play-offs? The Osprey are likely; they've been having an amazing season."

"I know they have been," he said. "That could be nice. You're sure you don't want to be in New York for Pietr though?"

"I learned last year that play off season is crazy. He practically spends all his time between the arenas and just comes home to crash for a few hours. We hardly even did our morning routine. I am positive that if we went to spend a week together at the manor, he would appreciate not having to worry about me, amongst all the other things he has going on."

"Okay," Misha nodded with a smile, "I'd like that. Plus, by that time, your IUD situation should be better, yes? More settled."

"I fucking hope so, but the doc said it can take up to six months to a year."

"Ugh. Why did you do this again?"

"One less pill to take, which is only effective at the exact same time every day. It wasn't so bad when I was a repressed loner. But somehow I ended up with three boyfriends, so…"

"Lucky you." Misha drew an arm over her shoulders. He offered up the bag of chips he'd brought to the couch. "I'll talk to Cecil about a post-season trip, but I don't think it will be a problem. It isn't as though I'll go and cheer him on at his games either. We mostly leave each other alone during play-offs."

"We don't have to go to Wisconsin either," Harper said. "You *could* come to New York. I could come here. Or we could go somewhere completely different together."

Misha hummed. He pulled his fingers through her hair as he thought. "That could be interesting. Where would you want to go?"

"I don't know," Harper admitted. "Pietr and I talk about travel a lot. We went to the UK last year. This summer we're doing Spain and Portugal. Next summer is Japan. But, it wouldn't have to be anywhere extravagant. We could go somewhere that doesn't have a hockey team. Somewhere you've never been before?"

"If there isn't a hockey team, it would be less likely that we stick out."

"Hockey fans are everywhere, but yes. No one would expect to see us there. But, we could do some short trips around this area. Uh, the guy who did this tattoo," she held up her arm to flash one of her lucky cats at him, "has his shop in Boston. You could get more ink from a reputable artist."

"A tattoo road trip could be very fun," Misha admitted. "I bet that Helen could give us some great names, all within day-trip distance." He raised an eyebrow at her. "Does this mean that you want to get more?"

"I've been talking to Helen about doing a sleeve. The cats were kind of the beginning... And Melby drew up a Fauna that the more I think about it, the more I love it as a shoulder piece. ...Do you think it's a mistake getting so many so quickly?"

"I think you should do whatever you like. If you feel the connection to getting something put on you for life, then do it." He nuzzled her ear before kissing her cheek softly. "Tattoos are hot. I like picturing you covered in ink." He hummed happily, his lips moving to her jaw. "And I like the idea of us going to get some together. It would be a fun memory. Doing a thing we both like, together. It could be fun to go with Pietr and Cecil too sometime. Maybe even Isaac?"

"Get the whole polycule in on it?"

"Nothing crazy, like matching polyamory symbols or anything. That's a little cultish. Plus, we're still pretty new to all this. That seems like a big step. But, going together to all get a little ink. Cecil doesn't have any."

"Well, then you two really need to find a reason to be in New York at the same time. Helen *loves* a newbie."

Misha's arm tightened around her shoulder. "Isn't that how you got started?"

"Maybe. Hush and watch the game."

Misha grunted. He leaned forward, setting down the bag of chips, then slipped to the floor to kneel in front of her. He slid his hands up her thighs, pushing her knees apart.

"How about you watch the game and I bury my face in your pussy?"

Harper's cheeks warmed. "Is that what you want? You haven't had enough of that already?"

"Never enough," he responded. His fingers dug under the waistband of her sweats, but he didn't start tugging. "Only if you want it too."

"It sounds distracting."

"Less distracting than asking you to suck my cock," he countered. "Plus, you have done such a good job for me the last few days."

She leaned forward, pressing her palms to his face. She kissed him softly with a smile. "You're very good at making sure I'm taken care of, Misha. It's one of the many things I love about being with you."

Misha's hands slipped, tightening on her hips as he returned the kiss. When he sank back, licking his lips, he raised an eyebrow at her. "So...yes to the oral?"

She laughed, leaning back and lifting her hips. Misha tugged her hips closer to the edge of the couch as he tugged her sweats and trunks down. After they'd been tossed aside, he started at her knee, pressing warm kisses up her thigh. Harper rolled her bottom lip between her teeth, her eyes flicking between watching him and the flashy movements on the TV. McKinley was doing a victory lap after another goal. She spotted Pietr patting the top of his helmet as he got back to the Osprey bench.

Misha's tongue found her center. Harper let out a soft *hm*. He didn't look up, instead v'ing his fingers to spread her wider. His tongue dipped further inside. Savoring her flavor as the dampness began to spread. Harper's eyes closed, filtering the noise of the game commentary with the feel of Misha's tongue. He pulled his hands away, kneading her hips and thighs to do as he'd initially suggested –bury his face in her pussy. She let out a soft moan, reaching up to pull her fingers through his hair. He lifted his head briefly to kiss the inside of her wrist, before focusing his attention to her clit and stroking two fingers inside.

"Fuck, *Kiska*." He finally had to lean back to take a few deep breaths. His fingers continued stroking as he panted. "You're so wet. Should I add a third?"

"I can take it," she responded. "Just don't push too hard."

"I won't hurt you," he promised. "Nice and slow."

Harper's eyes closed again as he added the new digit. Misha watched her expression, making short thrusts with his fingers. He moved his thumb to brush over her clit and felt her tighten around him, her eyes opening again.

"Don't you dare," she warned.

"Don't I dare what?" He asked, innocently.

"Not in the living room."

"The mess would get on me. I have a washing machine." He shrugged. "Besides, you made a mess in the bedroom last night. You didn't seem to mind at the end of it."

Harper swore as he leaned forward again, his mouth replacing his tongue and sucking softly. She moaned, tensing as his thrusts went harder, more determined at his task. His free hand kept her thigh open even as she half-heartedly tried to wriggle free.

"*Oh! Fuck*!" She clamped a hand on his shoulder, squeezing tightly as a wave of orgasm washed over her –no extra bodily fluids involved.

"Keep going," he urged, still stroking.

"No, no, no," she pulled away. "That's enough."

"Come on, kitten," he urged. "I can make you cum a whole lot more."

"You can," she agreed with a laugh. She put a firm hand on his wrist, pushing him back. "Later. That was a really good one."

He let out a small sigh, but acquiesced. "Okay." He bent his head to kiss the inside of her thigh again. "A break then. Cool off. Then let me do it again."

She couldn't help but grin, shaking her head. "Come here."

Misha got back to his feet as she straightened on the couch. He straddled her lap, bending down for more kisses. Harper licked her own flavor from his lips and cheeks in between. He groaned, gripping the back of the couch as she ran a hand up the front of his shorts. He was half-hard, already straining at the fabric.

"No, no," he shook his head, "this was supposed to be your time. I get mine later. Plus, we seem to get into a lot of trouble on this couch."

"I didn't tell you about what Pietr said, did I?"

"No, but I assumed if he had been upset you would have said."

She reached up, pulling him close so she could whisper in his ear. "He wants you to fill me up again before I leave and to take the creampie home to him."

Misha swore, soft and husky and he pushed into her hand, still stroking the front of his shorts. He seemed to savor the idea for a moment before he leaned back. "Okay. Let's have a real discussion about it. Before we go too much further." He cupped her face in her hands. "I love you, but I don't need to do that to you unless you want me to. It really was an accident this morning."

"I trust you." She put her hands over top of his.

Misha's eyes closed again for a moment and he took in a sharp breath. "You're giving me a lot of power, *Kiska*. Especially when I feel like I fuck up a lot."

"Not on purpose. Never with the intention of hurting me."

He kissed her. One of the long, warm kisses that seemed to pass a bit of energy, leaving them both feeling drained yet rejuvenated.

"I *do* want to do that again. Intentionally. But not tonight. Tonight, I want you to enjoy yourself. Tomorrow, I think, after a late post-game dinner, perhaps we try pegging?" He brushed his thumbs over her cheeks. "You brought it with you, right?"

"I did," she confirmed.

"Good. So, that's tomorrow night. Then we can consider later what we want to do the rest of the week." He gave her a light lick to the lips. "Are you ready for orgasm two?"

Harper drew in a breath before she nodded.

"Should I go get your wand toy for this one?"

"I think I set it to charge on the table in the bedroom."

"I'll find it. Don't move." He kissed her again before backing onto his feet. "Take off the rest of your clothes, please."

Harper let out a soft sigh as he padded away toward the bedroom. However, she did as he asked and waited patiently for him to come back.

Chapter Eleven

"Jammer, are you using that other pillow?"

Tim Jamieson looked up at Pietr mildly confused. "I guess not. You okay over there?"

"No," Pietr answered. He caught the pillow and tried to adjust it in front of him. He sighed. "Damn it. Too thin."

"What are you doing?" Tim finally asked. "You look ridiculous."

"Promise not to chirp on me?"

"I never make promises I can't keep."

Pietr frowned, then sighed again. "I miss Harper. She's in Edmonton with Levin. I'm having some feelings about it."

"So you're molesting pillows?"

"I want the bed to feel less empty."

Tim considered that for a moment before he answered. "Do you want to share?"

"Elaborate your offer," Pietr's tone was reserved and skeptical.

"I'd like to not be kept awake by your tossing and turning. If the problem is an empty bed, then why don't we share? I don't care either way."

"It's not just the emptiness. I miss *her*. Spooning. How soft she is. The way her hair smells." Pietr lifted the front of his hoodie to his nose. It still had just the faintest whiff of *Eau du Harper*.

"You're pathetic."

"I can't help it. I know she's far away, having fun with Meesh. I'm happy for her. For both of them. But, they're moving faster than I expected. I don't know what comes next."

"What do you mean?"

"Misha told her that he loved her. And vice versa." Pietr opted not to fill him in on the No Condom Debacle.

"So? You both love Parker too, right?"

"*Da*, but Misha is only her partner. It feels different."

"Are you afraid he's going to steal her or something?"

"It's not like that. I know at the end of the day, Harper is my wife and is happy to be. I also know that, if it came down to it, we could go back to being monogamous and be happy too. We don't *need* the extra partners. They just happened."

"You really think that Harper would just dump Levin if you said you were done being polyam?"

"She wouldn't be dumping him," Pietr countered. "She just wouldn't be having sex with him. They would still be friends. She's –we're both allowed to have friends."

Tim looked at him, further confused. "I know I'm not a relationship and feelings person, but I do know how people act. You would stop sleeping with Parker if Harper said so? And still remain friends with him?"

"Yes. Isaac was my friend first. Plus, we had a relationship before. Isaac has said several times he never wants to come between the two of us. We've talked about how his feelings have changed. Being more protective over Harper after the incident at the convention."

"Okay, that right there. What happens if Isaac says it's too much and just wants to be with one of you? What then?"

"Then...that's Isaac's prerogative," Pietr said. "There isn't a formula to how our relationships work, Jammer. They just do. It's not a competition. It's a collaboration."

"Sounds complicated. I'll stay single," Tim announced. "Back to Levin. What are you worried about if it isn't Harper coming back and asking for a divorce?"

"When the two of them are together, it's...he's not me."

"No shit."

"I mean, you know how I am with her. He's similar, in public. Doting. Sweet. Can't keep his hands off her. But in private, their connection is more..." Pietr hesitated. He didn't want to overshare, but it was hard to explain. "They aren't into anything crazy, but they're more physical."

"You think he's going to hurt her?"

"There was an incident last summer. I know he'd never do anything on purpose. We've had an explicit consent talk since. All of us. But there's still this voice in the back of my head."

"Do I dare ask what happened?"

Pietr considered for a moment. "It depends on how much you really feel comfortable knowing about our sex life."

"...Tesla, you announced to both Vikky and me that you and Isaac watched Misha fuck your wife a couple months ago. You were a little drunk, but after that nothing surprises me when it comes to hearing about your sex life."

"You won't tell either of them –or anyone else, that I told you?"

"No. I don't spread shit around."

Pietr reached up, absently stroking the lilac tattoo on his pec. He told his friend the story of Misha announcing that Harper had used the safe word after he'd slapped her.

"If it had been the other way around, maybe not a big deal. Meesh is a big guy. He gets hit all the time. But Harper? Like, why would that even enter his mind? It's one thing to spank or scratch or bite. That I understand. But getting slapped across the face? I don't know. Not okay. And now it's just this *thing* I always worry and wonder about."

"I don't get it either, but it's actually a pretty normal kink," Tim offered. "Especially if they're into rough stuff. Soft BDSM." He cleared his throat, a little pink rising in his cheeks. "Anyway, Misha is a decent guy. Maybe a bit intense. Intimidating."

"Oh, right, you came from Edmonton before Calgary."

"Yup. It could be argued that I traded up. Misha is the best player on that team, and they all know it."

"Meesh likes to win," Pietr said. "He hasn't been doing much of that with the Roughnecks. But, going there was a compromise he had to make."

"What do you mean?"

"Not my place to talk about it," Pietr said. "Trust me, while he's not exactly in his best place for the W's, he's where he needs to be in other respects."

Tim grunted. There was another moment of silence. Then he spoke up again. "You still haven't answered my original question. Do you want to share a bed or not? I'll even let you be the big spoon if it'll help you sleep."

Pietr considered the offer before shrugging. "Sure. Worst case scenario, it doesn't work and we go back to sleeping separately."

"All right. Get over here then."

"You come here. I already have all the pillows."

Chapter Twelve

The rest of the week passed in a blur for Harper and Misha, while dragging on for Pietr. Harper texted him a few times, but knew he was resisting interrupting their time together. Which was sweet, but unnecessary.

"I will see you in April," Misha declared. He had escorted her to the airport and was struggling to let her go. "I miss you already."

"I'll text you on my layover in Toronto and again when I get home. If Pietr doesn't accost me before I get the chance. I love you."

"I love you too. Thank you for coming all this way for me."

"I came for both of us. We needed this."

"I don't disagree. Are you feeling better now? Feeling that we're compatible? It's not just about the great sex?" A grin parted his lips, showing off pearly white teeth.

Harper laughed, giving him a short nod. "A little bit. We survived without wanting to murder one another. Once we iron out our plans for post-season, we'll try it for a little longer."

Harper wrapped her arms around his neck, pulling him close for a kiss. She let him savor it, rocking her gently before stepping way.

"I gotta go."

"I know. Have a safe flight. I'll talk to you soon."

"Bye." She gave him another kiss and squeezed his arm before continuing on her journey home.

It was a relief to land at JFK and get in the cab home. As much as she had loved spending the time with Misha, his apartment didn't feel much like *home*. Especially when she was in it alone. However, Harper didn't even get to register saying a hello to her husband before Pietr picked her up, throwing her over his shoulder.

"Really?" She deadpanned.

"Really," Pietr repeated. "I came directly home to wait for you. I have never been so happy to see someone in my entire life."

"I missed you too." She laughed as he dumped her onto the end of the bed. He followed after her, covering her with his body. He peppered soft kisses across her face, then her neck. He tugged down the collar of the old Scorch hoodie to press one just below her throat.

Pietr slipped to her side, wrapping an arm around her middle and nuzzling her cheek. "How was your flight?"

"Long. The layover was longer. I'm glad to be home."

"Did you have a good time with Misha?"

"I did."

"Did you bring me home that creampie?" His tone was teasing.

"Gross. No."

"But, you brought home wet pussy, *da*?"

She laughed again. "Pietr, I *just* got home."

"I know. I'm teasing. Mostly." He pressed a soft kiss below her ear.

Harper turned into his arms, wrapping an arm around his waist. "You don't have team stuff to do today?"

"No, and I'm taking a rest day tomorrow. I need it. I need you."

Harper smiled. "I missed you too, Pietr."

He hummed happily before inhaling deeply. "I recognize that my obsession with you is probably not healthy. But fuck, I am so relieved you're home. With me. Safe."

Her smile dissipated. "Did you think I wouldn't be safe with Misha?"

"Is not that. I..." He tightened his grip around her. "I worry, is all."

"You know he'd never hurt me on purpose."

"I know this. I also know you are extra sensitive right now. And the way the two of you play... If there had been a problem, you'd have told me, right?"

"We only played hard once. He needed the outlet."

"How do you mean?"

"He was...agitated about an issue that happened after we got back from visiting with Cecil. Remember that teammate he punched in December? He lives down the hall from him and there were some words exchanged... Misha needed an outlet, so I cashed in the Level Nine."

"And how was that?"

"We both agreed that it wasn't something we wanted to do again immediately. It was intense. Misha didn't feel good about what I let him do to me. While I enjoyed part of it, I recognized that there were points where I should have stopped him."

"Why didn't you?"

"I'm not sure. Partly because I felt like if I didn't, he might take it out somewhere less healthy."

"Was it healthy to do it to you?"

"It was about channeling his frustration into something more productive."

"Potentially hurting you is productive?"

"No but making me cum six or seven times is." She reached up, pressing her palm to his cheek. "Pietr, he didn't hurt me in any way I didn't ask for. Explicit consent. And I got to give it back to him, so we're even."

"You are smaller than him. You don't have the ability to—"

"Pietr," she cut him off, "there are more ways to hurt someone than physically. Even in the bedroom." She frowned. "Do you...do you want us to stop? Misha and me, I mean."

"No." He reached up, pressing his hand over hers. "I want you to do whatever makes you happy. I want you to enjoy exploring. Figuring out what you want and like. I also want you to be careful."

"I am."

He let out a soft sigh before leaning in to kiss her again. He caught her lips this time, pushing her onto her back once more to half cover her.

She groaned out his name again. "You have to let me up. I need to pee, and then I need to take care of my bags..."

"I can't help with the first item, but I can go take care of your bag," he offered. "Then we come back here?"

"How about a late lunch?" She offered.

Pietr grumbled.

"I'm starving. Have you eaten?"

"No," he admitted. "I came straight home from the airport this morning to wait for you."

"You didn't have team stuff you should have been doing?"

"I think they were all glad to let me go. Including Tim. I may have groped him a bit over the last day or two. Purely on accident, but it was a line I didn't mean to cross."

"I'll have to send him something nice as an apology." Harper slid her hands up his arms, over his shoulders, then laced her fingers behind his neck. "I missed you too."

"No you didn't," he chided. "You had Meesh."

"And I enjoyed my time with him," Harper retorted. "But being with him isn't the same as being here with you. Just like I know he missed Cecil the whole time we were together."

"But the three of you got to have some fun too, *da*?"

"We did," she confirmed. "Just like Misha has had fun with us when he visits."

"Did you two decide anything about play-offs?"

"He's going to come here. We're going to do a Tattoo Tour," she smiled. "I already got a couple of suggestions from Helen."

Pietr smiled. "I see. You two are going to go get inked together?"

"Just some small pieces. I have some ideas for behind my ears, the top of my feet maybe, and I'm starting to warm up to Helen's pressure about the sleeve."

"I'm sure it's going to look good." He leaned forward to press a soft kiss to her lips again. "Did you talk to Bex?"

"About the therapy thing? Yes. She e-mailed me over a couple of names."

"Are you nervous? You know couples do therapy all the time, even when nothing is wrong. –Which, there is nothing *wrong* with us, Harper."

"That isn't true," Harper countered. "You've been more jealous lately. Or maybe I'm noticing it more? And my anxiety is less about *us* and more about everyone else."

"Is it better or worse since the wedding?"

"Neither. Just, targeted somewhere different."

"How was it while you were with Meesh?"

"Fine. We didn't go out a lot. We had coffee once with Radley Breitbart," she said.

"Really? Misha hates him."

"They had a good talk. After Misha punched him for a second time."

"Is that what the level nine fuck was all about?"

"Radley has an issue with filtering. His mouth moves faster than his brain."

"I see. Misha hit him so you let him take his frustration out on you?"

Harper frowned.

"I know. I heard it. I'm sorry. I will stop picking about it." He kissed her again before finally rolling away from her. "I had groceries delivered yesterday while Maria was here. What are you hungry for?"

"Something quick," Harper suggested. "You pick. I'll pee and take care of my bag while you get lunch."

Pietr made a grunt of agreement. He leaned into her as she came behind him to wrap her arms around his shoulders one more time. Harper pressed a kiss below his ear.

"I *did* miss you, bae. I'll show you how much after we both eat something. Agreed?"

"Agreed."

Chapter Thirteen

Harper leaned back in her desk chair. Pietr had left earlier that morning for another away game. He was only going to be gone overnight, but the apartment felt lonely without him. After spending so much time one-on-one with Misha and then coming home to an overly clingy Pietr... She sighed. She should be relieved to have a little alone time, but she would have given anything for the sound of someone else in the apartment.

She looked down as her phone pinged.

[TANNER] Come over? I'm bored.

She laughed, picking the phone up to respond.

[HARPER] Why don't you come here?

[TANNER] Because that involves me leaving the house.

[HARPER] Compromise. How about we go out for a drink at the Bison?

[TANNER] Fiiiiiiine.

[TANNER] See you in twenty minutes?

[HARPER] See you soon.

She pushed back her chair to move into the bedroom. Since she hadn't planned on going anywhere, she hadn't exactly bothered with getting dressed that morning. She exchanged her tank and shorts for a fresh T-shirt and jeans. Matched with her warmest boots and jacket, she stepped out of the apartment after grabbing her wallet and keys.

Tanner was arriving from the opposite direction when Harper approached the door of the bar. She'd walked, even though it was chilly. It had helped to clear her head. Tanner, who lived several blocks closer, must have taken his sweet time to be arriving simultaneously.

"Hey." Tanner gave her a quick hug. "Let's go in. It's too fuckin' cold."

Harper laughed, pushing into the bar. The TV sets were already playing the night's hockey game, but Harper noted one of the back sets was playing a Knick's game. Quinten was behind the bar chatting with another customer, but it otherwise seemed like a quiet night.

"Hey," he looked up at them as the pair slid onto stools, "it's been a while. What brings you out into the cold?"

"Boredom," Tanner replied. "Our husbands are out of town and we needed to get out of our apartments."

"Seth said the same thing, so I made him go do inventory."

"I'm bored but I'm not *that* bored," Harper scoffed.

Quinten laughed. "You want your usuals?"

"Yes please," the pair answered in unison.

A moment later, the bartender placed an apple cider in front of Harper, a rum and Coke for Tanner. Harper pulled out her wallet to pay, waving off Tanner's attempt to do the same.

"I've been a shitty friend lately. Let me pay for your drinks."

"You want a tab open?" Quinten asked.

"Sure. We might have a couple more. Is the kitchen open?"

"For you? Always. What do you want?"

Harper looked at Tanner. "How about a medium 4-meat pizza? Extra cheese."

"That sounds amazing," Tanner agreed.

"Coming right up. Anything else?"

"Mozzarella sticks?"

"Got it. Let me go put that in with Hudson. Then I'll get your tab started." Quinten tapped the bar in front of them before disappearing to the kitchen.

Tanner spun around on his stool to face Haper. He took a sip of his beer before speaking.

"So, what's new? How was your trip to Edmonton?"

Harper filled him in on the happenings. Glossing over certain parts and probably sharing too much on others –but Tanner *was* her best friend and had heard worse. She had most certainly heard worse from him.

"What about you?"

"Kinley is starting to get really worried about his contract getting renewed," Tanner said. "Like, he's worried about his performance. He's played less games than he did last year so far. Which, I mean, is nice for *me* because he's around more. Theoretically. Not playing seems to make him think that he needs to be in the gym or doing extra conditioning."

"I get it. But he's playing well –and that's why he's playing fewer games. They don't want to wear him out on games that aren't worth him playing. It's the same for Pietr. He's gone on a couple of trips and ended up being a scratch, which he finds annoying."

"I don't know what that means."

"A scratch? It basically means, that even though he's healthy, he doesn't get to play even though he was on the roster."

"...Right."

"You've been listening to me talk hockey with your dad for eons. You're *married* to an NHL player. You still haven't picked up lingo?"

"I tune you guys out," Tanner admitted.

Harper sighed, making an exaggerated roll of her eyes before taking a drink of her cider. "So, that's what Kinley is up to. What about you?"

"Nothing. Busy with work. Tax season is approaching, so there's plenty of that."

"Have you played any new video games lately? Isaac and I are always looking for new ideas."

"Kinley and I have been playing some Fall Guy together at night when he's away."

"Have you two figured out a better living situation yet, or are you still floating between both apartments?"

"We decided to wait and see what happens with his contract at the end of the season." Tanner took a long plug off his beer. "Harper, can I be really honest with you?"

"Tanner. I'm your best friend, am I not? A really shitty best friend lately, I know, but c'mon. We've been besties our whole lives. You can tell me anything."

"I'm worried about what happens if Kinley gets traded. I can work from basically anywhere. That's not the problem. When I do have to be in the office, I can fly in on corporate dollars. Not a big deal. But I don't know how to live somewhere without you."

"Without me?"

"We grew up together. We went to Chicago together. We came here together..."

"We haven't gone everywhere together. You managed to survive while I was on my Study Abroad."

"That was only three months, and it was agonizing."

"But you lived. And even if he does get traded, think of it as being a way for Kinley to improve his game. Pietr says he's a better player because of getting to play with different teams."

"I'm not really worried about Kinley. He's not nervous about getting traded at all. It's more like he thinks that it's an inevitable."

"You're worried about you and not having a support system where you're going."

"Yes."

"You know that I'm always going to be here for you." Harper squeezed his arm. "And, maybe they're not going to be quite the same as the group here, but you'd have the WAGs of the new team too. You might be their first husband to the group."

"Ugh. That's the only thing that has made this bearable. I'm not a novelty for the Osprey."

"Does Kinley have his agent working for a renewal with the Osprey or are they entertaining offers?"

"I'm not sure."

"Are you two not talking about the possibilities?"

"Not really."

"Tanner!" Harper threw her head back with an exaggerated sigh. "I thought your communication skills had improved, considering the swiftness of the wedding."

"We improved on the sex bit, but the rest of it is still coming along," he admitted.

Harper sighed, turning on her stool. She reached over, grabbing his knee to spin him toward her. "Okay, full blown honesty: you need to talk to McKinley about this. If his priority is getting resigned to the Osprey, then focus on that. If he *wants* to play for another team and his agent is exploring those options for him, then you need to get your shit together for a possible move. Please, please do not use me an excuse to be afraid of spreading your wings. I am going to be your best friend whether we're living in the same apartment, across the street, or across the country. Okay?"

Tanner gave a curt nod. "I know. I love you."

"I love you, Tan."

"Oh boy, are you two already that drunk? You're not crying, so..." Quinten returned with their mozzarella sticks and marinara sauce.

Tanner laughed. "No. Just dealing with some nerves. We're good." His stool spun back to the bar. He reached for one of the sticks, humming with enthusiasm as he bit into it and stretched a ridiculously long string of cheese from his mouth.

"Ah, well, alcohol is probably not the thing for dealing with anxiety. You want a second round anyway?"

"Sure. Then we'll switch to cokes –ah, I'll take a cider this time too."

"Sounds good," Quinten nodded. He served up two more bottles before moving down the bar to check on another customer.

"Thanks for suggesting we come out tonight," Tanner said. "I miss hanging with you since...well, it's not just your fault. I've been busy adjusting to McKinley too. Sorry if I've made you feel like you're the one dropping the ball."

"I can agree that it's been a mutual problem. Let's both try and be better?" Harper suggested.

"Agreed."

"Maybe you want to come play games with Isaac and me? We usually have hockey folks on, but it could be fun to do something with a fellow hockey spouse? Plus, you're good at video games. You might actually break my streak."

"Oh, I don't know about that. I'm getting rusty."

"No better place to find out than on the stream in front of a rabid audience."

"I'll consider it."

Chapter Fourteen

"Hey Harp." Isaac's voice filled her ears as her headphones settled into place.

"Hey," she answered. "How's it going?"

"Good. Or, good enough. I miss you," he admitted. "How was your trip?"

"Fun. It was nice getting to spend some actual time with Misha. Like, we actually click and it's not just a sex thing."

He smiled. "Would it be so bad if it was just a sex thing?"

"I think I prefer having a little more," she said. "How's it going for you? Anymore hot dates lately?"

Isaac wrinkled his nose at her on the laptop screen. "No. It's okay. I'm pretty content with how things are right now."

"Are you?" Harper asked, tone going serious.

"Yes," he assured her. "I'm happy focusing on the stream and us –and Pietr."

"All right. Let's focus on work then. I have a couple of ideas for next month's non-profit and what do you think about inviting Tanner to play with us? We could turn it into a regular segment; playing with a WAG."

"Okay, but if we're starting with Tanner, we gotta figure out a different way to say WAG, which is super sexist."

"There isn't a nice concise way to say Hockey Partners."

"Partners and Significant Others? P-A-S-O. Like pesos?"

Harper wrinkled her nose.

"All right. We can keep brainstorming it. I like the idea though. It's been kind of tough to get the current players to find the time for us. They're all trying to squeak into the play-offs. I can reach out to some contacts. You can check with the Osprey WAGs."

"Sure thing. And a lot of the wives know other wives from other teams because of trades and whatever, so...it's a whole network."

"Great. I love it." Isaac's face stretched in a smile. "What else have you got for me?"

They ironed out some other details for the upcoming schedule. Since January, Harper had become an official co-host to Play It With Parker. That meant changing her streaming schedule a bit. While she had routinely joined Isaac on Thursdays, playing with two retired hockey stars, she was more sporadic about playing on Tuesdays. Now, they played together every Sunday, Tuesday, and Thursday, while Isaac did a shorter solo review stream on Saturdays. They'd also begun making sizable donations from the revenue their streams garnered to non-profits, which had also caused a slight spike in their viewership.

"I know Pietr has a string of games to clinch play-off placement," Isaac said, once they'd put business aside. "Is it a good time to visit?"

"You know you can visit any time you want," Harper said. "I suppose it depends on whether you want to see me or if you'd like to try and squeeze in time with both of us. Which, if you're good just seeing me, I could come to you."

"It is warmer here," Isaac mused, "but I don't mind coming to New York. An in-between visit before CritCon."

"Oh! That reminds me, if the Roughnecks don't make play offs, Misha is coming to New York for a bit."

"Staying with you and Pietr?"

"Yes. Is that okay?"

"It's your apartment," Isaac answered. "I didn't mean it the way it probably sounded. I'm glad you and Misha are getting to spend some more time together."

"I sense a but?"

"No but." Isaac shook his head. "I don't get the appeal. I'm not sure I like the power dynamic you two play with. It's not for me. For the record, I like Misha. He's a good guy and I can tell he cares about you. That's the important part. What you two do in the bedroom has nothing to do with me. And I'd prefer it stay that way."

"You didn't like watching?" Harper asked.

"It isn't that I didn't like it," he offered. "But, no, I don't want to do it again."

"Okay." Harper shrugged. "Should we talk about CritCon? I got the list of panels from them, but I'm not sure I feel qualified to chime in on anything that isn't directly related to us."

"That's okay. Friday, we're on a late livestream with a couple of others. Plan for now is Fall Guys. We've got the LBGTQ-Plus Streamers, Streaming for Charity, and a Q-and-A with us on Saturday. Saturday night, I'm collabing with Monster Meeks to do a review of the new Aesop's Fables game. We were also invited to a live play tabletop game, if you're interested with Cassandra Poe and Bradley Jorgensen."

"Holy shit, really?" Harper's eyes widened. "She's on that show about the sisters...ParaNorma?"

"Yeah, that's the one. But she's a giant fucking geek who is in love with you, so maybe you should brush up on her work before you meet her? If she had used any more heart emojis around your name in the e-mail I would have thought she was drunk."

"No way."

"Way. It should be a good time. It's a party game, if I remember. Kind of a Cards Against Humanity."

"Fun," Harper said. "What about Sunday?"

"Sunday we've got our regular livestream, I'm doing a panel on branding, and we're both on a panel about working with guests. Don't forget that we also have our signings on Saturday and Sunday too. Yes, before you ask, I got the photos printed. They look great."

Harper had nearly forgotten about their little mini photo shoot they'd done while Isaac had been in New York for the wedding. Luckily, McKinley's sister Darlene had a flexible schedule and had been willing to meet up to take some nice shots of them being adequately geeky in front of a large "Play it with Parker" sign they'd gotten printed quickly at a local print shop, with a cardboard "& Harper" in Sharpie haphazardly tapped underneath it. Darlene had called it "hilariously charming" and "very them".

"Good. I'm glad that's taken care of," Harper said. "So, when are you coming to see us?"

Isaac blew out a breath. "I was looking over the shared calendar. Pietr has two home games next week."

"He does."

"I can get a flight in Sunday morning, so I'm there before the stream in the afternoon. Leave it open to leave when you two are sick of me?"

"More like, when you get sick of us." Harper grinned. "You're welcome to stay however long you like. You know that."

Isaac let out a soft laugh. "Yeah, I know. I miss you both."

"As soon as the season is over, we'll have the whole summer in front of us again," Harper assured him. "We'll have less of a time crunch –and we're doing the convention in Minneapolis in June."

"I know."

"Is everything okay?"

"Yeah," he nodded. "It's the same as always. You and Pietr being far away and..." he shrugged. "Sometimes the virtual thing doesn't feel like it's cutting it."

"I can't knock you for not wanting to try harder on the dating thing. I mean, Pietr found me in a bar bathroom. Neither of us were exactly planning on all of this happening." She waved a hand vaguely. "I love you, but I can only do so much for you with three thousand miles between us most of the time."

"I know," he replied. "It's a me problem, not an us problem."

"Isaac, it is an us problem," Harper replied. "Pietr and I are your partners. If you're not happy and there's something we can do..."

"All I want from you, right now, is the OK to visit. While I'm there, we can talk out some of the other stuff. But not right now. Not today."

Harper inhaled a bit too sharply but nodded. "Fine."

"I'm sorry. I know talking things out is important, but isn't it better if we're all together?"

"Yeah, it is."

"So we'll talk then." He gave her a soft smile. "I'll text you the info after I get the ticket?"

"Okay."

"I love you."

"I love you too."

"I'll let you go on with your day. See you tomorrow."

"See you. Bye."

"Bye, Love." Isaac waved before the screen went blank.

Harper pulled off her headphones. She rubbed absently at her ears for a moment before pushing up from the couch. If Isaac was coming in a few days, she'd better make sure they had a grocery order in, she decided.

Chapter Fifteen

"Hey baby." Pietr's arms wrapped around Harper's waist. He'd dropped his bag at the end of the kitchen island upon entering the apartment.

"You smell vaguely minty," Harper noted. "Are you chewing gum?"

"No," Pietr's tone turned to a grumble. "I forgot to refill my toiletries before I left and I ran out of shampoo. I borrowed Jammer's."

"I don't hate it." She turned, wrapping her arms over his shoulders. He grinned as she leaned up to kiss him.

He hummed happily, pushing her softly into the edge of the island. "Are you busy? We can go have Welcome Home sex?"

She laughed, letting one hand move from his shoulder to pat his chest. "We can, but first there's a surprise."

"Surprise? What kind of surprise? Is it food? Something full of sugar or salt? Lots of flavor."

"No, not food."

He hummed, pulling her hands to his wiry cheeks. She obliged him with a soft scritch while he pondered.

"Ooh, did you order a new toy? One of those vibrating anal plugs?"

"No."

"Well then, no offence baby, but I don't care."

She laughed, raising her voice slightly. "Did you hear that?"

"Yes, and I'm a little offended."

"Isaac?" Pietr's eyes brightened. He gave Harper another kiss before pulling away to move toward the living room. "What are you doing here?"

Isaac sat up from where he'd stretched out on the couch with a book.

"I missed you," he answered.

Pietr circled the couch, not at all shy about kneeling over top of his boyfriend to press some kisses to his cheeks before taking a longer savoring one from his mouth. "I missed you too. When did you get here?"

"Yesterday. I wasn't going to fly in until tomorrow, but I finished up some stuff at home and decided to try flying Stand By. I lucked out and surprised Harper last night."

"How long are you here for?"

"At least the week."

"Good. I'll see if I can get some tickets for the games? Harper wasn't going to come, but..."

"Don't worry about it. I already got them. For me and Harper."

"Let us reimburse you?"

"I can afford to buy Harp and me some game tickets occasionally."

Pietr kissed him again.

Isaac's hand slid up over Pietr's shoulder to the back of his neck, pulling him closer. Pietr moaned, shifting closer.

"You're going to break the couch," Harper quipped. "Take it into the bedroom, why don't you? Far more comfortable."

"Come with us?" Pietr asked.

"Why don't the two of you enjoy some time together?" Harper offered. "I'll get a start on dinner."

"What do you think?" Isaac asked.

Pietr rolled his bottom lip between his teeth. On one hand, it had been awhile since he and Isaac had gotten any one-on-one time. He was never one to turn it down, but he'd also spent the last nine days missing his wife. Finally he nodded. Harper wasn't going anywhere, and the three of them would have fun later.

"Come on." He got back onto his feet, holding out a hand to Isaac. "It's been entirely too long since I sucked that cock."

"If you want Harper, I can start dinner," Isaac offered. He held out his hand and let Pietr help him from the couch.

"I do want Harper," Pietr admitted. "More because I didn't expect you to be here, so my head has been on seeing her. You are still a very welcome surprise." He tugged him closer, kissing him again. "I fuck Harper silly all the time. You'll be a nice change of pace."

Isaac laughed, pushing him away. "Let's go then, Mr. Romantic. Way to make a guy feel special."

"You are my only boyfriend," Pietr reminded him. "Whom I do not see nearly enough." He laced his fingers with Isaac's, tugging him toward the bedroom.

Leaving the bedroom door open, they moved toward the bed. Pietr pulled his t-shirt over his head before reaching to coax Isaac's off as well.

"Why are you wearing a sweater? I know it's still cold, but you're inside," Pietr murmured, tugging at Isaac's sleeves.

"Hold your horses," Isaac retorted. He stepped back, pulling the sweater over his head on his own. "Better?"

"No. You still have jeans on."

"Pace yourself, Ivanov." Isaac stepped away, pushing Pietr toward the bed. "Go on. Let me take care of you for a bit. You played some good hockey over the last couple of games."

"*Da*. Was good team effort," Pietr acknowledged. He bit his lip again as Isaac sank down in front of him. "You really want to start there?"

"*Da*." Isaac mimicked. He tugged the front of Pietr's sweats down. Pietr sucked in a breath as Isaac's fingers wrapped around him. "Are my hands cold?"

"A little, but they'll warm up," Pietr replied.

He watched as Isaac took him into his mouth. Unlike Harper, whose oral skills sometimes had to be requested or were more of a nice surprise, his boyfriend had never been shy. In their early friendship, trading blow jobs had been an easy form of stress relief. Or that's what they told themselves (and each other). Even though they had been apart for several years, Isaac seemed to remember all the little extras that he liked. Wet kisses up his shaft. The way to squeeze his balls between massaging rolls. Tracing his tongue under the hood of his cock and playing a bit with the extra skin. It wasn't *better* than Harpers. Just different. And letting them share...that was definitely a treat.

"Oh fuck—can't cum yet." Pietr squeezed Isaac's shoulder. He nudged him gently away, bending to coax him back to his feet. He caught Isaac's mouth, turning the man toward the bed, letting him drop to the foot of it. Pietr's fingers began to work open Isaac's jeans.

Isaac lifted his hips, letting Pietr tug the fabric away. He let out a soft expletive as Pietr's mouth mimicked what his own had been doing just moments before. Pietr didn't have a lot of work to do. His lover already hard. Precum beaded at the head, and Pietr licked it up.

"How do you want to finish?" Pietr asked. "In my mouth? On me, somewhere? Fuck me?"

"Together, if we can," Isaac suggested. "Come here."

They shifted higher onto the bed. Pietr opened the side table, taking out a bottle of lube. With that in hand, he straddled Isaac's hips.

"Like this?" He asked. A little extra lube and their cocks slid together in a tight pocket between their pelvises.

Isaac hummed. He threaded his arms over Pietr's shoulders, pulling him in for a kiss. A leg came up over his hips, urging him to rock harder. Tighter.

Pietr groaned into Isaac's neck, taking his time. Savoring the feeling of warm skin-on-skin. He closed his eyes for focus, knowing Isaac was doing the same.

"Oh baby," Isaac grunted. "So good—harder?"

Pietr obliged, shifting his weight back to his hips and sitting up slightly. He brought his hand to the top of Isaac's throat and caught his lover's mouth in another kiss as he squeezed lightly.

"Yesss," Pietr let out a husky whisper. "Cum for me, Izzy. Let me hear it."

Isaac moaned into his mouth, as his nails dug into Pietr's sides.

"That's it," Pietr continued. "So close, yeah?"

Isaac hummed in agreement. "Yeah—*ahh!*"

"Yes, yes, yes," Pietr murmured, rocking harder. Another hard kiss. "Give me all that cum, baby." He swore, his own orgasm not far behind.

His thrust slowed until he went still for a moment. He shifted his weight again, leaning back on his knees. He cupped Isaac's face in his palms.

"That was too fast," he teased. "Did Harper not take care of you last night?"

Isaac laughed. "Actually, we took great care of each other last night, this morning, and after lunch."

Pietr chuckled, scooting off the bed to walk over to the bathroom. "So, you are saying I am lucky to have gotten that out of you?"

"Nah." Isaac waited until Pietr returned with a damp cloth. "I made sure to keep some in the tank for you."

"Appreciated." Pietr tossed the cloth to him. "Not that I am unhappy that you are here, but what's the occasion? You and Harper are meeting in Chicago in a few weeks. Then Minneapolis after that."

"Can't I miss you?"

"Of course you can." Pietr caught the cloth again after Isaac had finished with it. He threw it back toward the bathroom to take care of later. He got back onto the bed, setting next to his boyfriend once more. "You can come here whenever you want. You just didn't tell me you wanted to."

"You're so busy," Isaac reminded him. "I figured I would be more in Harper's way than yours. I was willing to settle for whatever time you could give me."

"Well, you are in luck. This is going to be an off week for me. I still have team stuff, but no games. Coach wants me to rest up until we play Boston again next week."

"Ooh, I am lucky."

Pietr kissed him again. Isaac shifted, letting the man wrap him up in his arms. The room grew quiet. They could hear the sounds of Harper playing some punk rock while she cooked along with the clatter of pots and utensils interrupted by the brief whirr of the food processor.

"What is she making?" Pietr asked. His lips trailed to Isaac's clavicle. Fingers reached up to pull the man's hair, tipping his head back.

"Chicken and pasta with pesto," Isaac said. "Or, that was her plan."

Pietr groaned. "Sounds good." He leaned back, loosening his hold. "How are things?"

"I needed to get out of LA. See the other coast for a bit. See you. Harper. Leave my house for something other than groceries."

"I get it. No luck on the dating scene?"

"I've had a few, but it hasn't been what I'm looking for."

Pietr brushed a hand over Isaac's hair, pushing a lock out of his face. "You always have us. Harper and me. For whatever we can do for you."

"I know." Isaac kissed him with a brief smile. "Love you."

"Love you too. ...Is it too soon to try and make you cum again?"

Isaac laughed. "Me? Definitely. I'm willing to give you another go though."

Pietr growled, shaking his head. "No. Better hold off. Don't want to be too tired for the wife later. She might get suspicious."

Isaac snorted, giving Pietr's chest a sharp tap. "Terrible. Should we get dressed and go see if she needs help with dinner?"

"*Da*. That would be nice of us. And when she kicks us out of the kitchen, we can go play a game together."

"Sounds like a plan."

Chapter Sixteen

"You two already done?" Harper leaned back into Pietr as he wrapped his arms around her waist. He kissed her neck before resting his chin on her shoulder.

"*Da*. We are very speedy when we don't have to get you to the end," he teased. "That smells good. How much longer?"

"The chicken has about fifteen minutes," Harper said.

"Do you need help with anything?"

"If you want to do something, you can set the table."

Pietr hummed, kissing her again. He gave her a squeeze before releasing her.

Isaac appeared at the corner of the island, looking down at Pietr's discarded bag.

"Why don't you go take care of your gear," he suggested. "I'll set the table. What do you want to drink?"

"Water is fine. I drank too much with the team while we were traveling. Ugh. No beer for awhile."

Pietr stooped to pick up the bag and swung it over his shoulder. As it thumped against his back, his eyes widened. "Oh shit!"

"What?" Harper turned away from the stove, a quizzical eyebrow raised at him.

"I totally forgot! Tim, Gregor, and Guy were coming over to chill. Play some video games. Nothing crazy."

"Do I have to feed them? Because this will keep until tomorrow, but I didn't make enough for three more."

"No, no." Pietr reached into the bag for his phone. "I should be able to tell them to fuck off. I can't believe I got distracted."

"You don't have to cancel on them," Isaac said.

"I spent nine whole days with them," Pietr replied. "I'd rather they were a little disappointed then have to give up time with you and Harper."

"You wouldn't be. Unless you want us to get lost?"

"You are okay seeing Gregor? After what happened? Have you even talked to him since...you know."

"Since he came in my face before I even so much as breathed on his dick? No, I haven't," Isaac retorted. "We're both adults. I think we can hold it together for the sake of being with friends."

"Okay, so," Harper cut in, "the guys are coming over. Do I have to feed them?"

"No, they're bringing snacks and drinks," Pietr said. "Guy and Tim just texted that they're on their way to pick up Gregor."

"Well, shit." Harper sighed. "I feel bad eating dinner if they're just bringing snacks."

"We can order a pizza or something later if they're hungry. Don't worry about it. It was my fault." Pietr circled into the kitchen to kiss her temple. "Let me go empty my bag. We'll eat and be mostly done by the time they get here."

Harper nodded and Pietr disappeared from the kitchen. Isaac scooted in to grab plates and silverware.

"What do you want to drink, Harp?"

"Could you just refill my water bottle for me? I think I left it by the couch."

"Sure thing."

"Hey." She caught his arm as he moved past her again. "Are you fine with Gregor coming over? We can go out instead. We could go out to the Bison or something."

"I'll be fine," he assured her. "Like I said, we're grown ass adults. Besides, that was months ago."

"I may not have the same amount of, let's say, *life experience* but I'm pretty sure a guy isn't going to forget about prematurely going off another dude's face, Isaac. Made worse by the fact that said dude *left without a word*."

"Okay, okay! In retrospect, I know that was a real shithead thing to do. However, I'll point out that it isn't like he's reached out at all in the last couple months either to call me on it. Guys just don't operate like that."

"Uh huh."

"You want me to apologize, don't you?"

"I don't *want* you to do anything." Harper reached over to turn off the timer on the stove as it began to sound. She grabbed a couple of potholders before opening the oven to withdraw the sheet pan.

"You're going to be disappointed if I don't."

"Do *you* feel like apologizing is the right thing to do?" She countered. The pan clattered as she set it on the stove. She looked up at him, her face a careful blank slate.

Isaac sighed. "I love you, but I hate you."

"I'm not your mother, Isaac Parker. I'm your girlfriend. I'm not going to tell you what you have to do. I *will* remind that, for as embarrassing as that whole thing must have been for both of you, Gregor is a sweet guy and he deserved better than to get ditched in his own apartment by a guy he had an obvious massive crush on."

Isaac frowned. "Fine. If I can find an appropriate moment without everyone staring at us, I will apologize."

"Uh huh."

"I will!"

"Give me the plates so I can serve."

"Hey, come on in." Pietr opened the door for his teammates a bit later. "We're just finishing dinner. I'm sorry –I kind of forgot about you all. I was surprised with Isaac visiting."

"Well, shit." Guy unloaded a six pack of beers into Pietr's hands. "Do you want us to get lost?"

"No, come on in," Harper called.

"We should have called to remind him," Tim apologized. "Honestly, I half expected him to answer the door naked."

"No," Pietr rolled his eyes, "Harper doesn't believe in eating naked."

"It's weird and gross," she countered. "There's nothing wrong with putting on pants. Especially if I'm putting in the work to cook something."

Pietr laughed. "I'm teasing you, baby." He leaned over her shoulder to press a kiss to her cheek. "What do you guys want to play? Isaac, maybe you have a suggestion?"

"Same device? Either Smash or Mario Party maybe?" He suggested. "If you guys brought devices or your phones, Among Us is easy enough."

"I can't play that on my phone." Tim shook his head. "I hate the fucking controls. I'm much better at it on my PS5."

"We've got two Switches," Harper countered, "and the Xbox."

"Yeah, but the Xbox isn't secret when you're the assassin," Guy said.

"I can set it up on the TV in the guest room," she offered. "Oh, or I can set my laptop up with one of the Xbox controllers and someone can sit out here at the table. Then you've got a little bit of privacy, but you're still close to the living room."

"I feel like it's less work to just play something off one of the systems," Pietr countered. "I'm fine with Mario Party. We haven't played that together in a while."

"Whatever you want. Just throwing out solutions." Harper started stacking their empty plates. "I made an apple crumble if anyone is interested."

"Is it as good as your blueberry?" Tim asked.

"It's on par."

"Then yes, please." He slid a chair out from the table and sat down. Then he looked up at her a little sheepish. "I mean...I can get it myself. You don't have to, like, serve me."

"It's fine. You can all sit. I'll go get more plates and the crumble." Harper patted his shoulder as she circled toward the kitchen.

"I can help," Gregor offered. His voice was a bit of a squeak, like he wasn't sure he was going to really make the offer.

As the two moved toward the kitchen, Pietr resumed his seat next to Isaac.

"Okay, so, Mario Party. I think it's a max of 4 players, but we can rotate. Harper, are the controllers charged?" He called out.

"They should be," she answered. "Do you guys want ice cream or is that overkill to your diets?"

"Pigeon, I will not argue if you choose to not serve me ice cream, but I will be sorely disappointed," Guy replied.

"Don't call me Pigeon."

Pietr held back a snort. "Sorry, baby. Is a hard habit to break."

"You can call me whatever you want when I'm not in earshot, or in an arena," she said, "but I don't have to answer to it in my own house."

"Sorry Harper," Guy chimed. "I don't deserve ice cream."

"Shut up. It's already on the plate."

Guy grinned. A moment later, Harper and Gregor returned with three plates a piece. Gregor dolled his out to his teammates, while Harper's went to her partners.

"If you want more, there's still half a pan," she said as she took one of the empty seats at the table. "I do have containers if you want to take it home with you."

"Are you already trying to get rid of us?" Guy asked, spooning up some of the ice cream and crumble. "We've only been here five minutes."

"You spent nine days together. Why do you want to spend more?"

"Because that was all *work*," Tim explained. "And none of us packed a system this time around. We ended up going out to bars and drinking too much."

"That's what Pietr said," Harper said. "It can't have been too bad. You only lost against Carolina."

"Yes, we are on a clear road to the play-offs," Gregor chimed in.

"You don't sound very happy about it," Harper chided.

"I am thrilled," Gregor replied. "I am also very tired. The second wind will hopefully hit after we have actually made it official."

"I am looking forward to my name on the cup again," Pietr grinned.

"Yeah, yeah," Tim retorted, "it's not a given. We still have to put the work in."

"Says the guy who wears his Grandfather's Stanley Cup ring like a trophy," Guy teased.

"It's a precious family heirloom," Tim quipped.

"All the more reason for it to be tucked up in a safety deposit box or something."

"It was meant to be worn. Back in the day, they weren't as garish."

"I like my rings," Pietr said. "I don't wear them because it seems like it could jinx a new team."

"Isaac, what about yours? You have two, don't you?" Guy asked

"Yup." Isaac nodded. "I wear them occasionally when I'm still representing the team. I'm still involved with the Scorch Foundation a bit. But otherwise, yeah, they sit in my wall safe most of the time."

"Neither of you were married. Did you gift your WAG rings to anyone?"

"*Da*. They let me give mine to my mother," Pietr said. "She took the first one, but declined the other two. I think they got donated to the foundation to be auctioned for charity."

"Would you wear a Cup Championship ring, Harper?" Tim asked.

"I already wear far more jewelry than I'm comfortable with some days," Harper replied. "I've seen some of those rings. I'd be afraid of getting mugged."

"It would be a very stupid thing to try and steal," Pietr assured her. "They are engraved to start. Not to mention that I would make a giant fucking deal out of getting it back."

"I know you would." Harper gave his shin a tap under the table. "Eat your dessert."

There was a brief stint of amiable silence as they all dug deeper into their food. When they'd finished, Harper waved the men over to the living room.

"I'll clean up," she announced. "You go have fun."

"You cooked," Pietr reminded her. "I can clean up. You go play."

"They're your friends," she replied.

"I would like to think that they are *our* friends, at this point."

"It's going to take me ten minutes, fifteen tops, to stack the dishwasher and put the leftovers away. By the time you're done with the first couple rounds and someone is ready to swap out, I'll be done." She gave him a quick peck to the lips. "Go on."

Pietr slunk to the living room, settling onto the couch next to Guy. Isaac switched on the television and Switch.

Then he handed out the controllers to the other four before taking a seat in Harper's chair at her desk, a little out of the way.

"You don't want to play?"

"I play video games for a living now," Isaac reminded him.

"And you are still terrible at them."

"People find me charming."

"Are you in town for something special?" Tim asked.

"No," Isaac replied easily. "I wanted to see Pietr and Harper. Get out of LA for a few days. Nice part about the job is flexibility. Plus, getting to stream in the same room as my co-host always throws my viewers for a bit of a loop."

"That's because your viewers are a lot of perverts," Pietr chided. "They know you're here to bang."

"You're not drinking so put your filter back in place," Isaac warned.

"I don't think he can overshare anymore than he did the night he'd announced the two of you watching Levin fuck Harper, so..." Tim shrugged.

There was a clatter from the kitchen followed by an audible gasp form Harper.

"He did *not!*"

"Uh, yeah," Isaac confirmed. "He was a little tipsy."

"I was asked a question and I answered it," Pietr replied.

"I don't remember the specifics," Tim leveled, "but I am one hundred percent positive I did not ask for that information."

"I admit, I maybe asked for a small elaboration," Gregor admitted. "And was told something about...infinity scarves?"

Harper mumbled something vague under her breath. "All right. I officially can't look of at any of you right now due to extreme embarrassment. Enjoy your games."

"It was months ago!" Pietr called toward the kitchen. "If they were going to tease you about it, or make comments, they had plenty of time before now."

"I wasn't part of that conversation," Guy chimed in., "but I'm willing to be now. What were the scarves for?"

"Misha tied Pietr up," Gregor explained. "I believe the explanation was, *he was too handsy*."

"I can see that being a problem of Pietr's. He can't keep his hands off his wife in public, how is he gonna do it in the bedroom?" Guy asked

"Oh my god!" Harper exclaimed, appearing at the edge of the living room. "Do the other wives deal with this or am I cursed?"

"You are special, baby," Pietr cooed. "Nobody cares what the other wives are doing."

Harper's eyes widened and Pietr sucked in a breath.

"That was not the answer you wanted to hear. I sense that now. It isn't like *all* the guys know. Just these three. Now. Like he said, Guy wasn't there. Sorry."

"Do I even dare ask what *else* you told them?"

Pietr blinked. "I think that was it?"

"You also informed us that you've slept with seven people, that Harper has slept with five, and you share three –four, if you include yourself," Tim reminded him.

"Why do you remember that?!" Pietr asked.

Tim shrugged. "I stand by my statement at the time that numbers are weird, but five still seems *really low* for the amount of spice in Harper's books."

"It wasn't just TMI about you either," Isaac assured her. "Gregor informed us of his use of SnapChat for virtual spicy time."

"I was offering a suggestion!" Gregor countered. "Pietr said he wouldn't mind some nudes and Snap is good for that."

"I'm out." Harper shook her head. "I'm going to go drown myself in the shower or something."

"No, don't do that..." Pietr got up from his seat on the couch. He paused as he began following her toward the bedroom. "You guys, go ahead and play. We'll be back."

Chapter Seventeen

"Alrighty then." Isaac picked up Pietr's controller. "Mario Party then?"

"Is Harper really upset?" Tim asked. "I thought she *knew* he'd told us that. You knew! Don't you all tell each other everything?"

"That was an odd night," Isaac offered. "That whole conversation slipped my mind until just now." He couldn't help sliding a glance at Gregor who flushed red.

Tim followed his look. "Oh yeah! You two hooked up that night."

"*Do prdele*!" Gregor swore. "Shut up. Please."

"Oh. Was it not...good?" Guy asked. There was a music as the game began loading.

Gregor grumbled.

"I take that as a confirmation," Tim retorted. "It couldn't have been that bad. You're sitting in the same room together."

"I didn't know he was going to be here," Gregor said. "Or I may have not come."

Isaac snorted. "I want to make a joke, but that would be inappropriate."

"Ugh! I am understanding Harper better and better." Gregor sank further down on the couch. "Please can we forget about it? Play the silly mini games?"

"Oh boy. Were you drinking? Were there *issues*?" Guy asked.

"My issue was not caused by drinking," Gregor retorted. "And it's none of your business. It was the most fucking mortifying night of my entire life and I'd rather not relive it right now. Or ever."

"It...wasn't that bad," Isaac offered.

"You left! Just walked out of my apartment. You haven't said anything to me in almost four months!" Gregor straightened, whipping around to look at him. "I can assume that Harper and Pietr both know? Considering, as Tim said, you all tell each other everything."

Isaac gave a small shrug. "Yeah, they know."

"Does Levin know too?"

"I didn't tell him," Isaac said. "I trust that Harper and Pietr wouldn't have had a reason to unless he asked."

"Okay, now I *gotta* know," Guy said. "Was it a Too Soon or a Didn't Happen situation?"

"Uh...an *over before it started* situation?" Isaac offered.

Guy and Tim both grimaced.

"Can we please just play the game?" Gregor begged.

"Yeah, of course." Tim gave him a small pat on the shoulder. "Relax."

They started the game in earnest. An hour later, after the first game ended, with Tim victorious overall, they realized that Pietr and Harper hadn't returned from the bedroom.

"If someone is going to go see if they're coming back, it should probably be you, Parker," Guy suggested.

"No, I think we should show ourselves out," Tim replied deftly. "Let the lovebirds enjoy their time. Thanks for playing impromptu host, Isaac." He set his controller down on the coffee table. "We should do this again while you're in town. With better warning this time."

"Sure," Isaac nodded, "that would be fun. We could stream, if you're interested?"

"That could be fun," Guy agreed. "I'll check my schedule and text Pietr."

"Sounds good."

"C'mon. Gregor, you want a ride back to your place?" Tim asked.

"No, I think I will walk," Gregor replied. "Thank you for the game, Isaac."

"No problem."

"Do you mind if I use the bathroom before I leave?"

"Go for it. You know where it is."

Guy and Tim shuffled toward the door while Gregor disappeared into the bathroom. They gathered their coats and caps. They gave Isaac another farewell and then disappeared out of the apartment. Isaac got up, setting the controllers back on chargers and powered down the system and TV. He was just starting to clear up the empties they'd collected when Gregor reappeared.

"Did Guy and Tim leave already?"

"Yes, just a few minutes ago."

"Oh." Gregor's cheeks pinked. "I'll show myself out then. Have a—"

"Can we talk for a minute?" Isaac asked. "Before you run away?"

"I was not *running*," Gregor countered, "but okay."

"I was an asshole for leaving that night without saying anything," Isaac acknowledged. "I wasn't mad or upset or anything. It just...I wasn't sure what else *to* do. I felt dumb and unsure. So, I left."

"It's probably better that you did."

"No, it's not." Isaac sighed. "I don't blame you at all if it put you off me, but," he winced. "I haven't stopped thinking about it. Not *that*, but how I left and I didn't wait to see what else could have happened. And I wasn't sure how receptive you'd be to a text... I didn't want to make things awkward. Instead, I let it go. Now, it's weird. That wasn't my intention."

"I'm not sure I understand," Gregor admitted. "Are you saying you want to try again?"

Isaac gave a small nod, his mouth quirked in a smile. "I'm curious, if you can stand letting me get close enough to do more than breathe on your dick, what it could be like."

"Now?"

"Harper and Pietr won't mind if we go to the guest room."

"You're not just fucking around with me? I know you think I'm young and probably stupid—"

"Gregor, you're not stupid." Isaac cut him off. "You're young, yes. But it's not that big of an age gap, all things considered. I feel old because I'm *retired*. You're full of potential and I'm a has-been. I don't want you to waste your time."

"What do you mean *has been*? You had a wonderful hockey career. You won two Stanley Cups. Now you have a second career as a successful internet streamer. People still know who you are, even if it's not for hockey. More people probably know who you are now than when you played."

Isaac rolled his eyes, feeling a flush creep up his neck. "Okay, okay." He heaved a sigh. "Do you want to go fuck around and find out, or should I just say goodnight?"

Gregor looked bit like a fish out of water for a moment, opening and closing his mouth. "I...if they really don't mind if we do it here, okay? Or we could go to my place."

"Here is fine, but let me check on them. They don't usually get *that* caught up in each other." Isaac said. "Can you take these into the kitchen? Recycle bin is the drawer closest to the sink." He handed Gregor the empties.

Gregor nodded, stepping back toward the kitchen with them. Isaac strode to the short hallway. He wasn't surprised to see the bedroom door closed. He knocked twice and waited for a moment. There was a murmur followed by Pietr's voice.

"It's open."

Isaac opened the door, popping his head inside. "Is everything okay?"

He wasn't sure what he expected, but it wasn't Pietr staring at his phone with Harper curled against his side, under the covers. He had a hand on her hip, while she'd drawn an arm around his waist.

"Everything is fine. Did the guys leave?" Pietr asked. "Sorry we didn't come back out. We had an argument and then....not an argument." He grinned. "Harper fell asleep. I didn't want to leave her."

"Guy and Tim just left. Gregor is still here." Isaac slipped inside, closing the door gently behind him. "I told him you didn't mind if we used the guest room."

Pietr's expression morphed to curiosity, then amusement. "If you need supplies, they are in the side table."

"Thanks." Isaac's neck warmed.

"He can stay if he wants," Pietr continued. "But if he goes home after, you come to bed?"

Isaac chuckled. "Yeah, okay. We'll see."

"And if he stays, maybe Harper and I make breakfast in the morning. Not waffles. So sick of waffles at the hotels..."

Isaac nodded. "Sure, Pietr."

"Go have fun." Pietr waved him off.

"Thanks."

Isaac stepped out of the bedroom. Gregor peeked into the hallway.

"Are they alright?"

"Yeah. Harper fell asleep," Isaac explained. "Come on." He cocked his head down the hall. "This way."

Even though he wasn't usually sleeping in it, the guest room still held Isaac's suitcase and looked a little *lived in*. He often still used the room to change and, admittedly, to get a little alone time. He closed the door behind Gregor before pulling off his shirt.

"I was thinking." Gregor turned toward him. "To ensure there isn't a repeat of last time, maybe we start with you?"

Isaac nodded. "I can see why that would be a good idea. Where would you like me?"

"Get comfortable?" Gregor suggested.

"Naked? Or are you the type who likes to do the undressing?"

"We can get naked," Gregor said quickly.

Isaac chuckled, beginning to unbutton his jeans. "Slow down, Ciklovich. Take the time to enjoy it this time, huh?"

"Right." Gregor cleared his throat. He pulled his sweater over his head, followed by the plain white t-shirt underneath it. He fumbled for a moment with the belt at his khakis, but eventually they fell away. Past his hips to pool on the floor.

After shedding the last of his own clothes, Isaac resisted watching and moved toward the bed. He didn't want to be presumptuous about how far they'd go, or what Gregor was into but he opened the side table anyway. He pulled out the bottle of lube and a couple of condoms, tossing them down on the side table. Just in case. Then he sat down on the edge of the bed, finally unable to *not* look at Gregor anymore as the man pushed his cotton boxer-briefs over his hips.

"Shit, Gregor, that's a huge fucking bruise."

"What?" Gregor twisted around to get a look at the mark above his hip. "Oh. That. It's nothing. You know how it is. Getting jabbed with sticks, stopping eighty-mile-an-hour pucks, elbows, falling on the ice..."

"You stop feeling the pain after a while."

"Something like that. I'll hit the cryo-tank tomorrow. That will help with the ache. Plus, it's just bruises. No tears, or breaks, or sprains." Gregor closed the space between them. He paused in front of Isaac. "Are you comfortable there?"

"Comfortable enough," Isaac nodded.

Gregor gave a small hum. "Full disclosure. As I alluded before, it's been awhile since I was with a male person. So, ah, you might have to give me a few minutes to warm up a bit."

Isaac didn't hold back the grin. "Take all the time you need.

Gregor sank to his knees in front of him. Isaac watched him take his first good look at the cock in front of him. A sense of determination passed over the man and Isaac took a deep breath as Gregor's hand wrapped around him, followed by his mouth.

Chapter Eighteen

Harper stirred as the door closed again behind Isaac.

"Are the guys still here?" She murmured.

"Guy and Tim left." Pietr moved his hand to stroke her hair. "Gregor stayed. He and Isaac are in the guest room."

She hummed. "They're trying again? Good for them."

"Are you waking up?" He asked. "It's still early. We could go out and watch something in the living room?"

"I didn't mean to fall asleep," she admitted. "I'm sorry for yelling at you."

"You didn't yell at me," he countered. "You spoke loudly in my direction."

She let out a sigh of a laugh.

"I'm the one who should apologize. I let my filter go because I was with friends I trust. There should be a limit on that trust," he acknowledged. "I will do my best to not overshare in the future."

"It's not that you told them about our sex life," Harper explained. "It's that you didn't warn *me* that you'd told them. When I say we're an open book, we still need to mutually agree who gets to be close enough to read it, you know?"

"I believe I understand your analogy," he confirmed. "In that case, you should know that I have also talked a little bit more about things with Tim. When we were on the road trip. While you were with Misha."

"Oh. Like what?"

"Like, he knows that Misha slapped you. It was a brief conversation, but we were talking about why I was worried about you being in Edmonton."

Harper didn't say anything for a minute. Her arm moved, reaching up to pat his belly.

"Pietr, you know Misha isn't going to do that to me again. He hasn't ever hurt me. Even then. It was more the surprise than actual pain." She shifted slightly to look up at him. "And it was months ago."

"I know." He pressed a hand over hers, holding in place. "I do. I need to let it go. It would be healthier to move on. Everything has been good, ever since then."

"Pietr, I don't know what to do to make it easier, other than to...stop."

"I don't want to do that," he assured her. "For one thing, I enjoy the relationship we have with Isaac. For another, you love Misha and it would be cruel of me to tell you to end that because of my own issues."

"I called around to some of those therapists that Bex suggested. I have an appointment for us on Wednesday. If you're up for it."

Pietr let out a soft laugh. "When were you going to tell me?"

"Well, you did head straight into the bedroom with Isaac. Then you sprung the guys visiting on me..." She reminded him. She sighed a little heavily, finally pulling herself up. "It's a tentative appointment, based on your schedule. There are a few other options, but I'll have to confirm it by tomorrow afternoon."

"Wednesday is fine. I have some stuff in the morning, but you already know that. Besides, I'm taking a rest week. I'm only doing what I absolutely have to do, work wise."

"It's in the afternoon," she confirmed. "I'll put the info in the shared calendar so you get the details and reminder."

"Thank you, baby." He scooped a hand behind her head to pull her in for a kiss to the forehead. "Do you want to get up? Maybe see Gregor do a walk of shame?"

"That *might* be amusing," she admitted. Harper glanced over to the shared wall, almost as though she hoped she could see through it. "How do you think it's going?"

"I have no idea," Pietr said. "It simply *cannot* be worse than last time though, yeah?"

"The only things that could make it worse are...eek!"

Pietr let out a rumbling laugh as he hauled her into his lap. "Let's forget about them and have a good time ourselves, yah?"

Isaac wasn't sure what he had expected out of Gregor's oral skills. It wasn't the best blowjob he'd ever had of his life, but something about Gregor's pure determination made it...strangely good. He was patient, took a little direction, and picked up on Isaac's micromovements.

"Okay, you gotta stop." Isaac pressed a hand onto Gregor's shoulder, squeezing gently. "I'm gonna cum and I don't want to do that yet."

Gregor leaned back, touching his fingers to his lips. Wiping away whatever was there, he looked up at Isaac. "What do you want to do then?"

"Come here." Isaac tugged him back to his feet. Gregor slid between his knees as Isaac's hands found his hips. Hands pressed to the top of Isaac's shoulders, he leaned down to kiss him. He hadn't forgotten since their last attempt that Gregor was a really good kisser. Soft lips, not too moist. His cheeks were, adding to his youthfulness, very smooth. Gregor grunted as Isaac's fingers dug into his hip

"Oh, shit." Isaac released him. "Forgot about the bruise."

"It's okay. I had almost forgotten about it too," Gregor admitted.

"Any other sensitive spots I should be aware of."

Gregor smiled. "The shoulders are always achy. I keep getting slammed into the boards. The pads only do so much."

"I remember."

"I'm pretty sure I have a couple of smaller bruises where I can't see them," Gregor admitted. "But it's fine. Don't treat me like I am, eh, fine china or something. I'm tougher than I look."

"You have to be to be at the level of hockey you've achieved," Isaac said. He wrapped his arms around Gregor's waist. "Do you want to fuck me?" His tone was a mix of teasing and challenge.

Gregor chuckled. "*Ano*, I would like that, but perhaps you should fuck me first. You're already very hard and we know from past experience that I might not last very long. Although, if we go that route, at least I wouldn't go off in your face again."

Isaac laughed. "It went up my nose. It was not pleasant."

Gregor let out another curse in Czech. "I can't believe you want to do this again."

Isaac grinned, nudging Gregor backwards just enough to stand back up. He caught his mouth again, turning him toward the bed. "If there's one thing I learned over years of being an athlete, it's to take every shot you get." He nudged Gregor's chin upward, his lips pressing to his throat, then into his shoulder before he pushed the man onto the mattress. "Let's start face down, ass up. Okay?"

Gregor agreed, grabbing a pillow. Isaac prodded him a bit, before picking up the bottle of lube and one of the condoms. He grimaced, settling behind the younger man. As Gregor had expected, his back was speckled with more small bruises and marks where his pads dug into his skin with every impact. He stroked a hand down the man's skin, feeling Gregor shift when he got too close to a sensitive spot.

"Sorry," Isaac apologized. "You do have a few more here. And you might need to refit your gear." He traced his fingers along one of the marks under his shoulder blades.

"I know," he admitted.

Isaac's fingers drifted further down to Gregor's rear. "Do you like rimming?"

"What is that?"

Isaac caught a laugh in his throat. "Uh, licking. The anus."

"Oh! Um...I've never had it done before."

"Do you want to try it or would you rather I just went right into fucking you?"

"I don't know," Gregor admitted. "Is that fun for you?"

Isaac leaned forward, pressing his mouth to the small of Gregor's back. "It isn't *not* fun. People that like it tend to *really* like it. Those who don't are more *meh* about it."

"Sure, okay. I'm willing to try."

Isaac's hands spread Gregor's cheeks apart. He didn't hesitate before setting to work. It didn't take long before Gregor let out another soft curse, followed by a moan. Nice and vocal. Isaac couldn't hold back the grin. A sense of relief washed over him that this time was going so much better than the last attempt.

Gregor let out string of Czech, a few words of what sounded like German, and even a little Russian before he shifted his hips away. "Shit, okay, you have to stop. I'm so fucking hard..."

"From that?" Isaac asked, a little surprised.

"Yah," Gregor admitted with a little laugh. He swore again. "Seriously, you gotta fuck me already. I don't mind so much if that's what finishes me, but I might be too embarrassed to look at you ever again if I cum from, what did you call it? Rimming?"

"Yeah." Isaac rubbed his hands over Gregor's buttocks again before shifting onto his knees. "Relax for a minute." The bottle of lube had been warming between his thighs so it wasn't exactly cold as he applied it. Gregor inhaled as Isaac's first finger dipped inside. He stretched him out to two, taking his time.

"Ready?" He asked.

"*Yes*!" Gregor's voice was a bit strained.

Isaac shifted again. The condom packet ripped open, getting tossed aside a moment later. Rolling the sheath over his cock with one hand, he pressed gently at Gregor's hip, lowering him just a bit. Then he took the plunge, not thinking too hard about it as the head of his cock pressed into Gregor's opening.

Gregor tensed. Isaac reached up, stroking is back.

"Relax," he chided. "I don't want to hurt you."

"You're big."

Isaac hummed. "I'm average at best, Gregor. Is it too much?"

"No! It's..." He shook his head. "Keep going."

"You're sure?"

"Slow and steady, right?"

"Right."

Isaac kept an even pressure, withdrawing slightly to apply a little more lube. His general rule of thumb was always: too much was better than not enough. Gregor moaned again, his shoulders sinking as he rolled his hips backward until he had taken Isaac's full length.

"Good?" Isaac asked.

Gregor nodded. "Yah."

Isaac withdrew, just an inch or two before sliding back in. Gregor sighed, his forehead resting against his arms. Isaac felt him tighten around him, but he kept stroking, building up speed and depth until—

"Oh *fuck*!" He didn't think twice about grabbing Gregor's hips, pulling him back against his pelvis as he came. Gregor let out a soft pained moan, a hand coming back to press on top of Isaac's and moving it lower. "Shit—sorry." His cock twitched as he continued to take shorter thrusts. Then paused for just a moment before slipping free. He stepped off the bed, feeling hot and over stimulated. He reached down, pulling off the condom and tossing it into the trashcan beside the nightstand.

"It's okay." Gregor stretched before sitting up. He reached down, rubbing a hand across his cock.

Isaac slipped back onto the bed, nudging Gregor back into the pillows. "You managed not to cum."

Gregor laughed, reclining against the headboard. His hand still stroked his hard on. "I promise I do have *some* self-control."

"Think I can manage to suck you off this time?"

"You're welcome to try," Gregor said. "I think I can hold it together this time. I've done well so far."

"You have," Isaac agreed. He leaned forward, catching Gregor's lips again. He sank lower, his hand replacing Gregor's on the man's cock. "Good job." He didn't waste time getting his lips around the head this time. If the guy was going to cum, he was at least going to do it in his mouth. Gregor reached up, his fingers raking through Isaac's hair.

Isaac resisted looking up at him, concentrating on the task. He listened to Gregor's hitched breathing. The way his thighs tensed. How his cock twitched against his tongue.

A string of mixed language gibberish, including a clear English, "that feels so fucking good –ah, I'm gonna—" and that uniquely sweet flavor washed over his tongue. Isaac sucked in a hard breath through his nose, swallowing what he could while stroking the base of Gregor's cock to empty the rest of it. He moved his hands to the man's thighs, rubbing softly as his tongue lapped up the last of it.

Isaac finally pulled away, letting out a little laugh.

"That was *way* better than last time."

Chapter Nineteen

"Oh, hullo."

Pietr and Harper couldn't help but notice the flush that burned up Gregor's neck as he stepped through the living room. Isaac was not far behind him.

"I thought you were sleeping," Isaac said.

"It was more of a cat nap," Harper said. "Did you two have fun?"

"Ah..." Gregor glanced between the pair and Isaac. The pink in his cheeks turned red. "I have to go home. And yes, *now* I am running away." He hesitated for a moment before pressing a quick kiss to Isaac's lips. "Please don't gossip about me."

Isaac grinned. "I can't promise that. Text me when you get home."

"Okay. Good night." He turned back to the other two. "Good night to you as well. Thank you for inviting me over, Pietr. Even if you did ditch us."

Pietr shrugged. "I think we're all ending the evening on a high note, are we not?"

Gregor didn't answer, moving toward the door quickly. He paused long enough to grab his coat and hat before the door closed again.

"I don't need details," Harper announced, "but I am curious. Was it at least better than last time?"

"Way better," Isaac admitted. He took a seat on the open end of the couch next to Pietr. "What are you two watching?"

"Ameri Khan. You went on date with Hannah Stone, didn't you?"

"Ugh."

"No good?"

"Hannah is a nice person. She is also very sexually curious. She wasn't interested in me as a person. She was interested in *us*, as a throuple. And she wanted me to be the way in."

"Oh!" Harper's eyes widened. "I'm not saying I'm *not* interested, but also...wow."

"Should I feel flattered?" Pietr asked. "She is a pretty girl but not my type." He put an arm around Harper's shoulders.

"Yeah. I didn't exactly agree to the date because she was *pretty*. I thought we legitimately had some, you know, shared interests. She's also a gamer." Isaac shifted in his seat. He'd left distance between himself and his partners and now he regretted it.

"She dropped her foursome interest on you on the first date?" Harper asked. "I didn't even tell Pietr about my DP fantasies until we were an official couple."

"That only took like two weeks, baby." Pietr grinned, nuzzling her ear. "You could have told me anything, any time. I would have only wanted you more."

"You say that *now*." Harper curled an arm upward to scritch her nails into his bearded cheeks. "If I'd dropped that on you during the walk back to my apartment after our first meeting, you would never have texted me."

"You forget," he chided, "I like all of that too."

Harper leaned forward, looking at Isaac. "Is that the problem? You don't want to share us?"

"It's not that, but also...yes," Isaac acknowledged. "I love the three of us together. But I want someone who's into *me*. At least, at first. I'm not saying it's out of the question for later."

"What about Gregor?"

"What about Gregor?" He repeated.

"How did it go? Are you going to see him again while you're here?"

"I think it's just sex," he said.

"You *think*?" Pietr said.

"It's not like we fucked around and then had a long *define the relationship* talk," Isaac chirped. "We had some fun, blew off some steam together, and...maybe we'll do it again while I'm in town. At his place next time, if you two are going to be creepy about it."

"Creepy?" Harper gasped. "We're sitting in our own living room, watching TV. How are we being creepy?"

"Harp, you can't just ask a guy I've slept with how it went."

"I asked if you two had fun! You assumed I meant the sex, but I could just as easily been asking about the video games."

"Uh huh."

"Come here." Pietr beckoned him over. "We will stop teasing you now. I'm glad it worked better this time. I don't think Gregor could have recovered from another disaster with you."

Isaac shifted across the couch, pressing into Pietr's side. The Russian wrapped his arm around his shoulder before leaning his head against Isaac's.

"You deserve someone who will make you happy. If that person might be Gregor Ciklovich, you should be open to exploring the connection. That is all I will say on the matter –fully recognizing that I was not exactly on board with his infatuation at first." He pressed his lips to Isaac's cheek. "Chill out with us for a bit while we have the chance."

Isaac let out a soft laugh before he nodded. "Yeah. Okay. Can we watch something else though? I'm not sure that I can watch Hannah Stone without thinking about what I know now."

Harper picked up the remote from the side table. "Your choice. Whatever you want."

Pietr rolled his shoulders as he closed his bag after his work out the next morning. He was looking forward to a couple of easy days, off the roster, to relax. Spend time with Harper and Isaac. Recuperate a bit from all of the travel and the stress.

"Hey." There was a light punch to his side. "What are you up to today?"

"Hey." Pietr looked up at McKinley. "Isaac is in town. I'm joining the livestream this afternoon. We're playing...I don't remember what."

"Fun. Never mind then."

"What?" Pietr pressed.

"I was going to see if you and Harper wanted to have dinner with Tanner and me, is all."

"Why don't you two come over to our place. Around six?"

"Only if we're not disturbing," McKinley said.

"We always have time for friends," he assured him. "Is something wrong?"

"No," Kinley shook his head. "We just need to get out of the apartment."

"Understandable," Pietr admitted. "I'll see you at six. I'll tell Harper."

"Don't let her cook anything. We'll pick something up," McKinley said.

"Got it. No cooking for Harper."

"See ya." McKinley gave him another pat to the shoulder before continuing on his way to wherever he had been headed.

Pietr hefted his bag over his shoulder and was just about to hit the door when a voice called him back.

"Pietr! I'm glad I caught you!"

"What is it, Felicity? I am trying to go home to my Harper." He turned back slowly, his shoulders sinking. "And my Isaac."

"Sorry," she apologized. Not sounding very sorry at all. "I was wondering if you could put a bug in Harper's ear about the Osprey Podcast."

"Podcast?"

"Yeah. We're trying to do some highlights on the families, and...well, you know how popular you and Harper are," she said.

"Popular?"

"People like you."

"More like they are morbidly curious and don't know how to stop themselves," Pietr retorted. "I will mention it to her. You can send her an e-mail? Or call her yourself with the details? I will just give her the heads up."

"I will send her an e-mail tomorrow. If she doesn't want to do it, all she has to say is no and I'll move on."

Pietr nodded. "Is that all? Can I go home now?"

"Yes! Of course. Sorry to keep you."

He turned, continuing on. His shoulders tensing as he got closer and closer to the door –until he broke free into the sunlight and managed to walk to his car without further interruption.

He didn't normally drive to the practice arena; it was about thirty minutes from his apartment, and it was more economic (and environmentally friendly) to carpool. But as he was getting a week "off" (not including tape day, a children's hospital visit, a charity luncheon, and a couple of appointments), he had decided to come in that morning on his own. The drive was quiet and felt long. He tried singing along with the radio, but he didn't listen to enough popular music to know more of the words. He was feeling antsy by the time he finally turned onto the block for the apartment and into the underground parking.

"Harper, baby." He wrapped his arms around her waist after entering the apartment. "Come to bed with me."

"I can't." She turned in his arms. "I have a chapter to finish before lunch. Then we're streaming with Isaac this afternoon." She gave him a quick peck to the lips. "I'm only in the kitchen to refill my water bottle."

When he frowned, her face softened. She reached up, digging her nails into his beard for a little scratch. He hummed, leaning into her right hand. It felt good, the little bit of attention. She grinned, leaning up on her toes to give him a more thorough kiss. His arms tightened around her waist, lifting her onto her toes.

"Why don't you come into the living room. You can read or something while I work. When I'm done, we can make lunch together."

"What is Isaac doing?" He asked.

"He's dealing with some scheduling stuff for one of the conventions," she said. "He's in the guest room if you'd rather go see if you can pull him away."

"No." He nuzzled her cheek. "I miss him plenty, but right now I want you."

"I'm flattered, seeing as how you *always* have me," she retorted. He let out a little growl as the scritches moved further back on his jaw. "How was your practice this morning?"

"It was fine. Felicity is going to send you an e-mail about something for the Osprey Podcast, by the way." He finally pulled her hands from his face to let her arms drape over his shoulders. "I don't know specifics. I was impatient to get home."

"Impatient? You? I hardly believe it."

Pietr grunted. He bent down, bracing his arms under Harper's butt to pick her up off the floor and drop her on top of the kitchen island. "We were mad when we fucked last night. I don't like it." He gave her another coaxing kiss.

"It's not my fault you and Isaac got so into Steedman's Rock that you didn't come to bed with me at a reasonable hour."

"It is good show."

"After lunch, I'll give you an hour. That will still give us some time before the stream."

He inhaled sharply before giving her another brusque kiss. "Fine. I accept this compromise."

"You have to let me down."

He grunted again. "I don't want to."

Harper grinned. She wrapped her legs around his waist, scooted a little closer to the edge of the counter. "I'll give you five minutes for kisses, but then I really do have to get back to my book. I've been making good progress today."

"I can do a lot more than kissing in five minutes." Pietr's hand slid under Harper's shirt, up her bare back.

"Just kiss me," Harper demanded.

The two broke apart as Isaac appeared a few minutes later.

"What are you two like when you *don't* have a guest?" He teased.

"I don't know what you mean." Pietr pulled him between Harper's knees as well. He put an arm over his shoulders. "You are not guest."

Isaac laughed, accepting a brief kiss. "Right, right. You're very horny."

"*Da*. Harper has work to do."

"That she does," Harper confirmed. "Let me down."

"One more?" Pietr requested.

Isaac rolled his eyes as Harper acquiesced with one more exchange.

"Okay you two. Am I going to end up doing the stream alone while you get this out of your system?"

"No." Pietr assured him with a smile. "I am very happy you are here too. Give Harper a little bit of a break from me."

"Is that right?"

"*Da*."

"Well, hate to break it to you, but I'm going out for lunch."

"What?"

"I'm having lunch with Gregor. I'll be back a little before two for the stream."

"With—He's, what?" Pietr huffed a sigh. "I lied. I don't like this at all. Gregor is a bad match. I forbid it."

"You what?" Isaac looked a bit flabbergasted.

"I..." Pietr caught himself, mouth gaping for a moment. "I am teasing, obviously."

"Right," Isaac patted him on the chest. He leaned up to press a brief kiss of his own to Pietr's lips. Harper squeezed past them to pick up her water bottle and circle back toward the living room and her desk.

"Where are you going for lunch?"

"Not sure. Any recommendations?"

"Close by? Hmm. Greasy Spoon is a few blocks over from Gregor's place. It's a nice day for a walk. Or over by Bryant Park, there is a pot pie place. Very good."

"Rock Salt is always good," Harper called the suggestion as she sat down. "And they don't usually have too much of a wait at lunch. No reservation required."

"We did like Rock Salt the last time I was in town," Isaac admitted. "I'll suggest it."

"Are you just getting lunch?" Pietr asked. He ran his fingers along the collar of Isaac's henley shirt, smoothing the fabric. "Or is this a hook up date with bonus food?"

"We'll see," Isaac shrugged. "You want me to tell you all about it when I get home?"

Pietr hummed. "I don't have any inclination to see you fuck Gregor. Or vice versa. I appreciate knowing you are taken care of, but I don't think that I need the details." He gave him one last brief kiss before finally pulling away. "Are you leaving now?"

"I have a bit of time. He texted me that he got back to his apartment. You must have left around the same time?"

"I don't know," he admitted. "I was very focused."

"Can you put out a feeler to see if any of the guys would be interested in doing a special stream with us on Friday night?"

"I'll send a text. What are you playing?"

"Mario Kart? We could play tournament style."

"Sounds fun."

Pietr went to one of the cupboards, pulling out a box of protein bars. He ripped the package open before turning back to Isaac.

"Is there something else?"

"No," Isaac shook his head, "I'm amused with how some things about you have changed. While other things definitely haven't."

"How do you mean?"

"You get home from practice and head straight to the kitchen. At least you went for the healthy option."

"Lunch isn't for at least an hour. If I'm lucky, Harper will agree to fool around first. I have to have my energy up for that."

Isaac laughed as he crossed the kitchen to press a quick kiss to Pietr's lips. He tasted a faint chocolate flavor. "I love you."

Pietr hummed. "Love you too, Izzy."

"I'll be back. Don't drive Harper too crazy." He squeezed his arm before stepping back. "Harp?"

"Yeah?" She called back.

"Don't make him wait too long. You know how he gets."

"You say that like I'm not making myself wait!"

"I'll be back later," Isaac assured them.

"Have fun," Pietr replied.

He watched Isaac move toward the door, picking up his coat and pulling on his sneakers. The door to the apartment closed gently behind him, leaving just Pietr and Harper again.

"Harper?" He called, a little note of hope in his voice.

"Seriously, I have to finish this chapter at the very least, babe."

He sighed, shoving the last of his protein bar into his mouth. Even though he had extra free time this week, it didn't seem as though he was going to get to enjoy it the way he'd hoped.

Chapter Twenty

"Hey baby. Sorry I'm late." Pietr pressed a fast kiss to Harper's temple. "Everything went to shit at practice this morning. Frank took a hit and they think he maybe broke a finger."

"How did he do that?" Harper asked. "Aren't the gloves supposed to protect your hands?"

"Sure, but he had taken them off to grab some water when Mattie slid into him at the boards."

"You guys seem very accident prone lately."

"No more than usual," he assured her. "Everyone is a little off because they lost last night."

"It was only one game."

"I know that. You know that. And we'll turn it around against Boston at the very least." He took a seat next to her. "I know I play better when I know you're there."

"Are you asking me to come to your game?"

"I always love to have you at my games."

"It shouldn't be an issue," she said. Harper returned the earlier kiss. "You aren't late. Dr. Balakin is running a little behind."

"Are you nervous?"

"Why would I be nervous?"

"You didn't really want to do this with me."

Pietr looked around the small waiting area outside the therapist's office. Dr. Deidra Balakin had been highly recommended by Bex and the doc had been kind enough to squeeze them in for an assessment appointment, from the sounds of it. He felt a bit bad that Harper had done the leg work on it, seeing as how it had been his idea.

"You're right. I don't. But, you want me to be here, so I'm here." She didn't sound defensive, but he did hear a note of exasperation.

There was a soft click as the office door opened and the little red "In Session" light beside it dimmed. A young woman stepped out of the office, Dr. Balakin right behind her.

"I'll see you next week, Kelly." The doctor's voice was quiet and even. "Have a good rest of your day."

The woman nodded, not acknowledging the waiting pair before scurrying from the office. Dr. Balakin turned to him.

"Harper and Pietr Ivanov? Am I saying that correctly?"

"*Da*." Pietr replied. "But Harper is still Wyatt. She did not take my name when we got married."

"Oh –how inconsiderate of me. My apologies." Dr. Balakin held the door open. "Why don't you come on in. Let me just swap some files around. Go ahead and get comfortable. Wherever you wish."

The pair followed her into the office. As she went for the desk, tucking a file away on a stack, they got comfortable on the couch across from a set of chairs. Pietr glanced around the office. It was rather boring, he decided. Mostly beige and brown. A bit dim, with the shades partly closed. The coffee table between them and the chairs had a wooden bowl with several decorative balls in it of various sizes, colors, and textures.

"So," Dr. Balakin sat across from them, "I find the best place to start is to ask why you're here. Or, what made you decide to make an appointment."

There was a brief pause as neither of them jumped to answer.

"There must have been something," she prodded. "Which of you brought it up first?"

"I did," Pietr admitted. "I have been feeling jealous lately. Of Harper's other partners. How much time she is spending with them."

"As opposed to how much she spends with you? You're married, nesting partners, correct?"

"Yes," Harper said. "Although, I don't think we've ever said it like that. Polyamory is still new to us."

"Is that the only thing that brought you here today?"

"I am worried about Harper's anxiety. How much stress she's under, being with me."

"Do you think you're anxious or stressed out, Harper?"

"Yes and no," she answered. "It's been a big change. I've had to learn a whole new language and culture to keep up with Pietr's job. And I'm not talking about Russian. There are a lot of unspoken expectations, which can be confusing and uncomfortable."

"Can you give me an example?"

"Like participating in team events. Talking to the other player's partners. There's apparently a dress code I haven't followed."

"There is not a dress code," Pietr chided. "Your clothes are fine, babe."

"I get away with wearing Osprey merch and nice jeans," Harper retorted. "But you can't look at how the other WAGs dress and me and not see the difference."

"The difference is, I don't give a shit if the other WAGs are comfortable. I want *you* to be and so you can and should wear whatever you want. If someone, including anyone from the organization doesn't like it, they can fuck off."

Harper sighed.

"Okay." Dr. Balakin adjusted in her chair. "This is obviously something we can unpack, but let's not dwell on it now. Tell me more about your relationship. When did you meet? How long have you been together?"

"We met in September of last year," Harper offered. "We got married December eighth."

"Does that seem fast to you?"

"I knew I wanted to marry Harper the first time I met her. Well, maybe not *marry*. That's a bit crazy. I knew I wanted to know everything about her," Pietr said.

"It's probably fast for some, but we clicked in a way I never have with anyone else. Pietr is all love-at-first-sight, but I admit it took me longer. He wears his feelings on the surface. I never have to guess with him. He just tells me. I'm not like that."

Pietr reached over, sliding their fingers together and leaned gently into her.

"How would you gauge your communication?" Dr. Balakin asked.

"I think we do a good job. Not great, but good. We're always honest with each other. Even when it's hard. Like this. Coming here," Pietr explained.

"We quickly found ways to stay connected, even when we have to be apart," Harper continued. "The only thing we ever really ask of each other is honest communication."

"Good. If you have that, then I find a lot of the other issues resolve over time and experience," Dr. Balakin said. "Why don't we start with the jealousy. Pietr, when was the first time you felt this way?"

"Probably when we were in LA. We spent a week in July with our partner, Isaac. Or, well, that was the week we confirmed that we were going to try being a triad."

"That was a mutual decision between the three of you?"

"Isaac had visited us a few months before," Harper said. "We had become friendly. I was a guest on his streaming channel. When he came, Pietr was recovering from his vasectomy. I...don't quite remember all of the specifics. One thing led to another and we ended up trying a threesome. I wasn't on board at first, at all, but it was...fun."

"Group sex is incredibly common." Dr. Balakin seemed unphased. "Is that the usual dynamic when the three of you are together?"

"Isaac and I had been in a relationship when we played for the LA Scorch together. We already had unresolved feelings for one another. They just reignited after that," Pietr said. "So, when we visited, I tried to give the two of them the chance to connect more. One-on-one. Which, I liked watching them fall in love too. There is still this little part of my brain that wishes I hadn't shared. That they could both be mine, separate from each other. Which is selfish and I am not a selfish person. I enjoy our relationship, both as Harper and me, and Harper, Isaac and me."

"And Isaac and you?"

"When we get those chances, yes, of course."

"So, it's Harper and Isaac that gives you the pause. Even though you encourage it?"

"Yes. I have bigger concerns about Harper's other relationship."

"With..." Dr. Balakin checked a note, "Misha Levin?"

"*Da.*"

"You're also friends with Misha. How is he different from Isaac?"

"For one thing, Misha is not also my partner. What the two of them do alone together is up to them. While we have done things together, it's different. Misha likes being in control. Being a leader."

"Do you prefer being in that role?"

"I suppose I am what you would call a *switch*?" Pieter admitted. "Harper and me, we take turns. Sometimes. We know what we like and how to get it from each other. But we always like to try new things. Having other partners has let us do that. Enjoy things with them that we can't with one another."

"What is it about him that bothers you then?"

"I don't want Harper to get hurt. Physically or emotionally. The way they are together when I'm with them makes me wonder what they do when I'm not."

"Misha slapped me," Harper filled in. "It was a onetime thing –during sex. He'd asked before we started and I was vague with a response. It hasn't happened again."

"How did that make you feel, Harper?"

"I don't know. Shocked at first. It wasn't a turn on. It wasn't him slapping me that made me use the safe word." Harper's fingers tightened between Pietr's. "It was more the pressure for a response afterwards. Asking if it was too much. If it hurt. If I could take more. If I was lying. I...I felt frozen. I didn't have the answers he wanted. I was too surprised that he'd actually done it."

"The two of you refrain from that kind of impact play?"

"There is a huge difference between slapping someone across the face and some spanking. No, I have never hit Harper," Pietr retorted. "Not in a way she didn't explicitly ask for in advance."

"We *learned* from the incident," Harper pressed. "Explicit consent from all of us before we do anything. No noncommittal *okays* or *maybes*. Anything other than a yes is a no."

"That's good. That kind of communication is vital for a healthy relationship." Dr. Balakins made a few notes on her pad. "Pietr, have you considered that what you are calling jealousy may more likely be a form of anxiety?"

"Possible, but it's different from Harper's in that case."

"There are lots of ways anxiety manifests. Can you tell me about growing up? What was it like getting into hockey?"

"I don't remember a time before hockey. I was on skates by the time I was three. My dad played and loved the game. I had talent, evident from very early. I never felt forced to play, but as I moved up and got involved in international games, it was more stressful. I was away from home, my parents.

My grandparents passed and I came to stay in the US. Got drafted and...it was fine."

"How is your relationship with your parents?"

"Good. I love and appreciate them very much, I'm happy to have them in the States with me. They sacrificed a lot to give me opportunities. Now I can take care of them."

"Did you feel a lot of pressure growing up? You say they sacrificed."

"Hockey isn't a cheap sport and my family is not wealthy. I started doing odd jobs around the rink, for neighbors, trying to help out when I was old enough for it to dawn on me how much it all cost. They never asked me to, but I know that they both went without things so that I could get what I needed to play. It made me a very careful adult. I make good money, but I can't do this forever. I'm already slowing down and I'm only nine seasons in."

"What about friends?"

"My team is my family, friends. We spend a lot of time together."

"How many teams have you played for over the years, Pietr?"

"Fuck, I don't know! Fifteen? Twenty? Including match-ups for All-Stars and Olympics and the shuffling around for the two years I was in the AHL..."

"How many of those past teammates do you stay in touch with?"

"Well, Isaac and Misha are texted regularly, obviously. When I play old teammates now, we might grab drinks or catch up for a bit, but it's sporadic."

"Is it possible that your anxiety, or your jealousy, may be related to your lack of lasting connections?" Dr. Balakin asked. "You found this person, the person you married. She is, for lack of better words, *yours*. You are *hers*, but you are also seeking other partners. Are you sure that polyamory is what you want to explore?" The doctor tilted her head, gazing at the pair. "There are a lot of ways to be non-monogamous while respecting each other's needs and desires."

"I...maybe?" Pietr considered the thought. It made sense, to an extent. But there were still things he *liked* about their relationships, just as they were.

"It's just a thought," Dr. Balakin assured him. "The next time your jealousy flares up, try to concentrate on the *why*. Then, it's rationalizing. If your anxiety is telling you something like, Misha could be hurting Harper, you *know* that they have boundaries in place to prevent that from happening. The consent aspect. The safe word. Open communication with you."

"I think I understand what you mean."

"If you would like, we can continue meeting and we can work on it some more. I'm purely guessing from the completely bias assessment from Dr. Beckett, but I'm leaning toward saying you have what we call an *anxious attachment style*. That could be part of your jealousy too. Harper on the other hand, seems to have more of a situational anxiety. If you'd like to work on that, we can also make the time. But, if this session today was just a check-in, that's fine. No pressure."

"I'm not saying I don't have issues that could probably use professional help," Harper said. "I feel fine. I like our relationship, the way that it is. When we do have problems, we figure it out."

"I like our relationship too," Pietr admitted. "I don't think it's a bad thing to have a formal check-in once in awhile."

"Do you want to keep doing this together?" Harper asked him.

"Maybe?"

"I don't need an answer today," Dr. Balakin insisted. "If, after you leave today, I never hear from you again, it's perfectly fine. It happens a lot. If you *do* want to continue, please know that whatever you say here, stays here. I take patient confidentiality very seriously. I'm familiar with polyam dynamics and kink lifestyles. You can say literally anything to me and I am not going to be surprised. Like the slapping? Incredibly common, particularly in BDSM and degradation or humiliation kinks. But, there are different lines for everyone. If that's not what you like, try impact play without the talking. As an example."

"We are already aware," Pietr replaced dryly. "Harper likes it rough –which is part of why she enjoys being with Misha. He's a more consistent Dom personality for her."

"Do you feel like you should be able to fill that urge for her better?"

Pietr considered that. "I worry more about overwhelming her. It isn't that I don't enjoy that kind of play, but I always hold back. If I let go completely, what happens when I let out something I can't reel in? What happens if I lose control of myself?"

"How do you mean?"

"I mean, I'm a big guy, very strong, with a physically demanding profession. It would not take very much effort at all to seriously hurt her –without meaning to. It would be very easy to...I don't know, rip out her hair, break her arm, leave marks and bruises."

"Pietr, you're not going to do any of that to me." Harper reached over, to rub his arm with her free hand.

Dr. Balakin tilted her head to the side, considering them for a moment. "Have you ever let yourself go, so to speak?"

"Sort of."

"You still held yourself back to an extent."

"*Da*."

Dr. Balakin was quiet for a moment, considering the pair. "Harper, how important is it to you that you have this rough play with Pietr?"

"It's not important. I don't *need it* at all. From him or Misha."

"But you enjoy it."

"Yes."

"Can you tell me why you like it?"

Harper's fingers tightened around Pietr's again as she hesitated.

"If you don't want to tell me, you don't have to," Dr. Balakin assured her.

"I spent a lot of my life feeling like I wasn't desirable." Harper chose her words carefully. "I still, even now that we're married and I have two other partners besides, have a hard time wrapping my head around the idea that they find me physically attractive. Or sexually appealing."

Dr. Balakin didn't say anything, letting her continue.

"When Pietr, or Misha as the case may be, are rougher with me, when it's more of a dynamic of them taking what they want from me, it," she shrugged, "I don't know how to say it. It makes me feel useful?"

"What about with Isaac?"

"We're not overly adventurous with Isaac, other than group sex. But, I suppose, there's an allure in being between two men who are, again, taking what they want from me. But, all of them —all three of them, are very good about making sure that I enjoy it just as much as they do. Pietr isn't satisfied until I've orgasmed at least twice."

Pietr let out a little hum. It was true. He hated the idea of leaving her disappointed.

Dr. Balakin hummed. "Regardless of whether the two of you want another session or not, can I make a small recommendation?"

"Of course. That's your job, is it not?" Pietr asked.

"I view my job as being more of a guide," she replied. "But yes, I do sometimes issue homework." She set her pad down on her knees and clasped her hands on top of it. "I want the two of you to try being responsible for your *own* orgasms for a while. You can set your own limits. Maybe try it for a week or two. Depending on your schedule and how often you're getting to be together. ...I assume you have a very active sex life?"

"*Da*," Pietr admitted. "It's as regular as it can be, given how much I travel this time of year."

"Understood. I'm not saying to do anything differently, necessarily, but Pietr, don't push an orgasm onto your wife. If she's not getting one and she wants one, then let her take the lead. Harper, if you legitimately enjoy that useful feeling, roll with it. Let Pietr take as much as you're able and willing to give him. Experiment with it. And, if you decide you want to book another appointment, you can tell me how it went."

There was a short *ping* as a timer on the desk went off.

"That's the end of your hour. Do you have any other questions for me?" Dr. Balakin asked.

"No," Pietr shook his head. "We will talk about coming again and get back to you."

"No pressure. If you want an uncensored opinion –the two of you are doing fine. Like you said at the beginning of the session, a check-in is always a good idea. I'm happy to help in the future if you just want to do another check-in." She gave them a warm smile. "It was nice meeting you. Dr. Beckett –Bex," she corrected, "always speaks very highly of you when talking about her friends."

She held out a hand and the pair each took turns shaking it.

"Thanks for making the time for us," Harper said. "This was interesting."

"I'll take that as a compliment." Dr. Balakin showed them to the door. "Have a great rest of your day." She stepped out into the waiting area. "Ah, Monroe and Jules. I'll be with you in just a moment."

Harper and Pietr said parting goodbyes before slipping from the office and to the elevator bay.

"What do you want to do now, *lyubov moya*?" Pietr asked. He looked down, realizing he was still holding her hand.

"It's a bit late for lunch and too early for dinner," she said. "Isaac was meeting with Gregor again so it's just us."

"Again? That's twice now since they hooked up on Sunday."

Harper shrugged.

"I could still eat something," he said. "Are you hungry?"

She hummed. "I'm not starving, but I could go for something sweet."

"There is a gluten-free, vegan bakery next to the parking garage I'm in. I noticed it when I walked over," he said.

"I'm willing to try it," she said. "But we could drive home and then walk over to SugarCube."

"You are bad influence." He laughed. He pressed a kiss to her hair as the elevator opened for them to step in. "Let's take a look at the vaguely healthier option. If what we get is terrible, *then* we go to SugarCube."

"Deal."

Chapter Twenty-one

A few days later, Harper accompanied Pietr to the practice arena to record an episode of the Osprey's Nest Podcast. Thanks to Felicity's haranguing, Harper had agreed to record the first of a new "WHOOSH" series of episodes, featuring the "Wives, Husbands, and Other Significant Humans" of the team. The new acronym seemed to be catching on; Marie had even changed the name of the WAG Discord server to "WHOOSH" and started a channel for other family members, like the older teens and parents.

Pietr had joined her at the end of the episode for some Q&A between the two of them. Afterwards, he wrapped his arm around her shoulders as they made their way down the hall, away from the tiny office that the podcast was recorded in.

"I have tapes yet. It will be about an hour or so," Pietr said. "Do you want to go wait for me in the lounge? Or would you like to come crash tapes? We're watching the highlights from the game against Carolina last week and Boston's game against Seattle."

"I'd just distract you," Harper said. "Wherever I'll be most out of the way."

"Out of who's way?" He chided. "You are never in my way." He paused in the middle of the hall. He turned, pulling her to a stop beside him. He turned, tipping her chin up with a finger and kissed her softly. He smiled against her mouth. "I love you."

"I love you too, but seriously. I don't want to interrupt or be in anyone's space."

"Come on." He laced their fingers more tightly together. "Most of us will be in the theater, so you can sit in the lounge."

The lounge was a spacious, open room divided with various furniture to create smaller spaces within it. It was attached to an open dining area with room for 40 or 50 people. There was a spacious kitchenette, surprisingly clean. An area with nice leather furniture included a large couch and several chairs around a large, mounted TV with an Xbox system. Finally, there were a few taller café style tables and chairs in another pocket of the room. The lounge was, Harper thought, oddly empty.

Pietr released her hand to rinse out his coffee mug at the sink. He set it upside down on the drying rack next to it.

"If you are hungry, my cupboard is this one." He tapped his knuckle against a middle cupboard. "Middle shelf. Everything is labeled. Anything in the fridge that doesn't have a name on it is free game. Help yourself."

"I'm fine, Pietr."

"I know, but if you change your mind." He looked up at the TV, which was playing some sports highlights from the previous night. "You don't have to listen or watch that either. The remote is usually on the coffee table. But it's almost eleven and Felicity likes to come in and watch that foodie show...The Spoodle?"

"I think you mean The Spatula?"

"Sure. That one."

"So I should stay away from the TV. Got it. Can I sit over there?" She motioned at one of the café tables.

"Yes, but not the one on the left."

"Okay?"

"Just trust me." He kissed her again. "I'll be down the hall, that way," he pointed, "third door on the left. It's labeled. If you need me."

"Should I need you for something?"

"Probably not. You are very independent, Harper darling." He kissed her again.

"Go watch your tapes." She gave him a little pat on the chest.

"Fine!" He stole one more brief kiss before backing up. "An hour, I promise."

She watched him leave before going over to one of the café tables –the first to the right, just in case. She got settled in the chair and pulled out a notebook from her bag. She hadn't wanted to bring her laptop. Sometimes doing some writing longhand helped her stay focused for longer. No internet distractions. She flipped the pages to a clean sheet and clicked her pen.

"Harper!"

"McKinley."

"What are you doing here?" He asked. McKinley walked to the kitchen, opening up a different cupboard from the one Pietr had pointed out. Harper saw just for a moment that each shelf was labeled, stocked with more labeled boxes. McKinley reached up for some protein bars on the top shelf of his cupboard before closing it again.

"I was asked to be on the podcast. They're highlighting player partners."

"You mean WHOOSH," he corrected. "Better than WAGs, I guess. Always made me think about dogs. Like our partners follow us around like happy puppies all the time." He rolled his eyes. "We got an honest to god *memo* about the WHOOSH thing. A memo! Who does that?"

Harper laughed. "I like it better than WAG. Now that you said it, I'm never going to get that puppy remark out of my head. Pietr makes enough dog references without that getting added."

"Sorry." McKinley smiled. "How was your recording?"

"I think it went okay. What are you and Tanner doing tonight? You should come over to our place and join us for the stream. I'm sorry you weren't invited before. It was the other guys at the house and Isaac decided to invite them, or I would have made sure you were included."

"We can't tonight. We're having dinner with Darlene and her wife. Then we're going to a play."

"What kind if play?"

"I have no idea. Some feminist one-woman show thing that a friend of Darlene's is doing. It's this tiny, tiny little theater above a Chinese restaurant."

"Is that where you're having dinner?"

"Yes. The food is amazing, so I'm not mad about that," he said.

"Why are you going for Darlene's friend?"

"I sorta broke her heart two years ago. She invited me. I have a feeling that I'm going to get trashed in the show."

"With your husband in the audience. Nice. Good job, Kinley."

"Tanner is looking forward to it. He seems far too excited."

"Of course he is. He's Tanner. Gossip and drama are the one area of his interests that is stereotypically gay. He can't be a boring accountant all the time."

"I think I talked him into getting back into doing Pokemon tournaments. I told him he could at least be trying to keep his ranking."

"Good." Harper replied. "Someone besides me needs to be reminding him that there is life outside work. And you."

McKinley chuckled as he went to the fridge for a bottle of water.

"You want one? There's cokes and other stuff in here too if you prefer."

"I'm okay, thank you."

"Okay." The bottles in the door rattled as he closed it again. "I better get to tapes. But! Maybe after we get back from our next road trip. We'll know whether we've clinched play-offs or not so we can maybe go out for a celebratory drink. I'll make sure Tanner and I have a couple evenings cleared for it either way."

"Sounds good. Have fun watching your game tapes."

McKinley nodded his goodbye and Harper turned back to her notebook. She had scrawled through nearly three pages, zoned in on her work. The flow of the ink across it smooth and readable really to no one but herself.

"Harper!"

She jerked upward. By the tone, she knew it was not the first time Felicity had said her name.

"I'm so sorry," Felicity apologized. "I didn't mean to startle you."

"It's fine. What's up?"

"Do you mind if I watch my show? It isn't going to disturb you or anything?"

"No, go ahead." Harper waved her off. "As you can tell, once I'm in a zone I tune out the rest of the world."

"Right. Sorry!" Felicity backed away toward the couch and TV. "Brock said you did a nice job with the podcast by the way. I can't wait to hear it."

"I didn't say anything I haven't said before," Harper replied. She looked back at the page. It had been a nice change to get sucked into the troublesome book for a few frantic pages. "Pietr started to overshare. It makes me worry about what he says about us when I'm not around."

Felicity laughed. "I promise, Pietr is a perfect gentleman. The only time I've ever heard about the guys teasing to phish out extra info in the locker room, he shut them down pretty quickly."

"Yeah, the locker room hasn't been my concern. Apparently, he gets chatty after games in the bar."

"Ooh." Felicity circled back to come stand at the edge of the table. "I did not hear anything about this."

Harper blinked at her. "I didn't want him telling the guys, I'm certainly not going to tell you, Felicity."

She frowned. "Right. We're not, like, friends. So, why would you? My bad. ...Which of the guys did he tell?"

Harper raised an eyebrow at her.

"I'm just going to take a wild guess and say it was probably...Jammer. Maybe Vikki? They've been spending a lot of time together –oh no way! Is Pietr hooking up with Gregor?"

"What? No!"

"Thank god. Kappy is going to owe me twenty bucks."

"You made a bet on my husband hooking up with...Gregor?"

"No! I made a bet that he *wouldn't*, because that's weird."

"Yes. They are."

"Also, I know Gregor *really* likes Isaac Parker. Has he made any headway on making that happen?"

"Not my place to say."

"Right! No gossip."

"You're missing your show," Harper reminded her.

"Shit –and Eric Ketchum from the Dallas Longhorns is on."

"Cheating on the Osprey?"

"Eric played for my college before his draft. They pulled him last year and he's been doing amazing," Felicity explained. "I think he's trying really hard for a King Clancy award, since he missed out on the Calder last year. That's why he's on the show. He's a spokesperson for Misha Levin—oh, jeez, you probably already know about Levin and Spitz getting other players for sponsors for their foundation."

"Misha and I don't talk a lot about the foundation," Harper admitted. "We don't talk about work, except when it comes to trying to see one another."

Felicity got comfortable on the couch. A moment later, the sports reel gave way to the mid-morning talk show on one of the network channels.

"That's probably smart," Felicity continued. "Sometimes when these guys get to talking about their passion projects, it never ends."

Harper smiled, turning her attention back to the page. The talk show was harder to tune out with its live audience and spunky hosts. Harper continued to dabble but wasn't as sucked in as she had been before the interruption. She paused long enough to watch the segment with Eric Ketchum and put him on a mental list to ask Isaac about reaching out for the stream. While they'd raised money for Misha's foundation before, having someone who *wasn't* Misha do it might be a good idea.

Chapter Twenty-two

Felicity didn't get up when the show ended an hour later, switching to a local noon newscast. Catering staff came in, pushing two large carts loaded with stacked boxes. A woman that Harper instantly pegged as the horrible Georgina followed behind them with a clipboard. She knew she had watched her for a moment too long when the woman flicked a glance at Harper.

"Harper Wyatt." Her voice matched her whole image of *disapproving headmistress*. From the tightly pulled bun to her kitten heels. The pencil skirt hugged her hips and thighs, and Harper would *swear* the woman had a corset on underneath the pink blouse, only just exposed under the only casual item she wore. A black and gold Osprey's zip-up.

"That would be me," Harper confirmed.

The woman gave her an appraising look. "You're smaller than I expected."

"Georgina!" Felicity whipped around in her seat on the couch.

"Oh. Right. I'm not supposed to tell people they're fat."

Harper blinked at her. "I am quite aware I'm fat. Thank you, very much."

"Please excuse her," Felicity retorted. "She has zero filter."

"I find masking an exhausting waste of time." Georgina replied easily. She looked at Harper again. "You know that you should watch your calor—"

"Excuse me. Georgina, isn't it?" Harper cut her off.

"My name is Georgina Halloway. I'm a gra—"

"Stop." Harper did it again. "You're not my doctor and you're sure as fuck not paid as my dietician. My weight is exacerbated by a recorded medical issue. Regardless, my caloric intake is none of your business. If you have an *actual* concern for my health, let me assure you that I'm perfectly fine."

If Georgina was bothered by the bluntness, she didn't show it.

"I prefer people *don't* use profane language around me. It has a strange...ear feel."

"I'd apologize but we're both adults and I'm sure you can respect that I'll use whatever language I like, particularly if you're going to be offensive."

That got Georgina looking more uncomfortable. "It was not my intent to be offensive, Harper Wyatt."

"Well you were. I have a feeling most of the guys just avoid you rather than tell you that."

"Working for the team has been an adjustment. I am very aware that most of them don't like me very much."

"You've almost killed at least two players by ignoring their allergies."

"Matlock's allergy is not anaphylactic in nature. He was fine after throwing up. And as for Meinich's gluten intol—"

"As a dietician, you should be more careful. You, of all people, should understand the effect of food, of allergies, on a body. What if you'd gotten them sick before a game?"

"I have completely memorized all the player and staff dietary needs files, thank you. There has not been a problem in months."

"Uh huh." Harper laid her pen down on her notebook before flipping it closed. "But these guys are more than pages in a file, Georgina Halloway. They're human beings, not machines."

"Food is fuel—"

"Food is one of the smallest pleasures we have in life and if you don't understand that, it's incredibly sad."

Georgina looked unsettled again.

"Go on. Say what you want."

"Food is literally nutrient—"

"Stop."

"But you—"

"You're right in the idea that food is what keeps us going. Sure, humans can survive on water and vitamin supplements for quite some time. But it's boring as fuck. Flavor is important. Diversity in your food is important."

"Harper, baby." Pietr appeared at her elbow, sliding a hand across her shoulders. "I see you met Georgina."

"She called me fat."

"I did not," Georgina retorted.

"It was implied."

Georgina pressed her lips into a thin line. She pulled herself together, tucking her clipboard under her arm. "I have to go finish setting out lunch."

"What did she say to you?" Pietr asked after the woman had disappeared to the dining room.

"She said I was *smaller* than she expected. When Felicity called her on it, she admitted she's not supposed to tell people they're fat. So, it was implied that was her intent."

Pietr muttered a string of Russian under his breath before sighing. "Let me guess, she doubled down because she didn't mean it offensively?"

"I'm assuming she's autistic?"

Pietr looked down at her, surprised. "Why do say you that?"

"Have you met her?" Harper watched him consider it for a minute. "I'm just guessing, but she said something about masking."

"Masking?"

"We'll talk about it on the way home. Are you all done?"

"*Da.*"

"Is Harper done yelling at Georgina?" Mattie's head popped around the door. "We didn't want to interrupt."

"I wasn't yelling at her," Harper retorted. "And jeez, it's your lounge. Are you *all* standing out in that hallway?"

"Not all of us..." Mattie strolled inside, a few of the other guys not far behind him. "Just most of us. Only Tesla was brave enough to interrupt. You can be intimidating, Pigeon."

"Yeah, we heard an F-bomb and knew it was probably serious." Kirk went to the fridge to grab out a couple of waters for himself and the others. "Did she tell you how profanity has a weird *ear feel*?"

"She did. I didn't give a shit," Harper replied. "She called me fat."

"Of course she did. She has no fucking filter." Von took one of the bottles from Kirk. He looked for a moment between Harper and Pietr. "Not that I agree with her! You've lost quite a bit of weight since we met you at the end of last season. ...Not that I'm commenting. Fuck." He opened the bottle of water and began drinking to shut himself up.

Pietr looked down at her. "Have you? Must have been slow, over time. I have not noticed."

"Not really," she replied.

"Good." He pressed a kiss to her temple. "Let's go get lunch. Something with flavor."

"Aw, take us with you," Mattie begged. "I swear, if lunch is another piece of fish today..."

"Lunch is *not* fish, Greer." Georgina appeared in the doorway to the dining room again. "It's Chicken, rice, and a roasted vegetable medley."

"She says that like it's any better," Mattie grumbled.

"Ivanov, you and Harper Wyatt are welcome to join us. There is extra." Georgina ignored him.

"Why do you say her whole name like that?" Pietr asked. "Just Harper is fine. Or Wyatt. Both is weird."

"Most of you refer to Harper Wyatt as *Pigeon*," Georgina replied. "Harper is too casual, and referring to a feminine person with their last name is...odd. I'm not sure what honorifics they are using, so the whole name seemed more appropriate."

"I think I get it now," Pietr squeezed Harper's shoulder. "I don't know why it didn't occur to me before."

"What?" Georgina asked. Her head quirked to the side.

"Is it appropriate to ask?" Pietr deferred to Harper.

"No," Harper admitted, "but it's a fifty-fifty chance on whether she'll be offended or not."

"I see." Pietr drew in a breath. "Georgina, are you autistic?"

"Yes. What does that have to do with anything? I am considered *high functioning*, or *low support need* depending on who you're talking to, if that's a concern."

There was a brief pause before the rest of the guys began muttering amongst themselves.

"What?" Georgina looked confused.

"Georgie," Von put a hand on her shoulder as he started to pass into the dining room, "sorry we've been short with you. Things make a lot more sense now."

"Being neurodivergent has absolutely no bearing on how I do my job."

"No, not your job," Kirk replied. "How you deal with *us*. You can be incredibly insensitive. And that, like Dutch said, makes a lot more sense now. It's not your fault."

Georgina shifted her shoulders as some kind of mixed emotions passed over her face. "Lunch is set. Go eat." She strode past the men and back out of the lounge. The sound of her heels tapping quieted as she got further away.

"I shouldn't have asked." Pietr said.

"She probably didn't say because she didn't want you all to give her a pass. People treat you differently when they find out things about you. She probably *preferred* the antagonism. Now you feel like you have to talk to her differently, right?" Harper asked.

"It's not like she can help it," Pietr replied.

"Trust me. Treat her the same way you always have. She'll appreciate that effort more than babying her."

"How do you know this?"

"Because believe it or not, I do occasionally have to go outside and talk to people, Pietr."

"Is this the beginning of an argument?" Kirk whispered loudly to Carter. "I didn't think Tesla and Pigeon ever argued."

"We are not arguing!" Pietr interrupted. "Trust me, you will know when we are."

"It's totally true. Isaac told—" Gregor stopped. "I'm going to go eat lunch. See you guys later."

"Wait," Harper called him back. "What did Isaac tell you?"

"Nothing."

"Why is Parker telling you anything?" Guy spoke up from the still milling crowd. "Have you been talking again since we played Mario Party the other night?"

"Yes," Gregor admitted.

"So, he got over the *incident*?"

"We're adults," Gregor replied quickly.

"Uh huh."

"What incident?" Carter asked.

"Nothing!" Gregor said loudly. "Can we please eat lunch? I'm sure Harper would like to go home."

"I'm kind of loving watching you squirm a bit, actually," Harper replied. She picked up her notebook to tuck it back into her bag. "But I also already know the details, so..." She hopped down from the chair. "I'll let you handle them. Where do you want to go to lunch, Pietr?"

"Your choice, Harper darling. Wherever you want."

"You already know what I want..."

"Sushi?" He guessed.

"Yurihana or Tanuki?" She suggested.

"Let's do Tanuki," he decided. "I like their rice bowls better."

"That's because it's Basmati," she replied. "Yurihana uses Jasmine."

"The fact that you can tell the difference is baffling," he admitted. "Let's go."

There were a few parting words as Pietr led her out of the lounge and down the hall toward the main exit.

"Did you have fun?" He asked.

"I don't think fun is the right word," she said. "I feel a bit better having told off Georgina for making you all miserable."

"She is just trying to do her job. It isn't like the food is *bad*," he offered. "It just...doesn't always taste like much. And she yells at us when we add salt. Or literally anything else. Did I tell you she confiscated Noodles' hot sauce? He had a brand new bottle of Sriracha in the fridge –gone. She dumped it down the sink."

"Seriously? Why?"

"She said something about spicy foods messing with metabolism."

"I highly doubt adding some hot sauce is going to be detrimental."

"She went on a rant about it messing up her calculations?" Pietr held the door to the parking lot open for her. "Joke is on her. Now he has a smaller bottle he refills and hides in his bag. Is like he uses it out of spite."

"Valid." Harper waited for him to join her. It was beginning to warm up and snow was melting. Pietr pulled his keys out of his pocket before taking Harper's hand again.

"I'm still sorry I didn't hold back more on her. She is, like you said, doing her job."

"Yeah, but maybe hearing it from someone outside the club means she'll take it to heart." Pietr opened the car door for her. "Do you want to go home first and we walk over to Tanuki's or should I try to find parking?"

"We can walk over," she said. "It's not far and it's nice out today. Even if everything feels damp."

"Okay. Watch your fingers."

Harper watched him stride around the front of the car to get into the driver's side.

"Hey." He leaned on the center console before turning the key over. "Thanks for coming in with me today. I liked it."

"It was interesting to actually see some of the space," she admitted. "I've mostly only seen pictures online."

"You can come in with me any time you want, baby." He stretched his arm over to hook a finger into the front of her t-shirt, and tugged her closer. "Kiss me before we leave. It's a long drive."

Harper laughed. "You're insatiable lately."

"I am stocking up. It's going to be a long play-off season. I can feel it. And you'll be spending time with Misha...." He shrugged. "Getting what I can."

"You can have whatever you want, when you want it." She kissed him and felt him relax for a moment.

"Mm. Maybe you put in an order on the app and we do a pick-up instead?" Pietr suggested. "Then we can fool around and take a nap after lunch?"

"We can do that either way."

"Yes, but if we stop and pick up on the way home, we don't have to walk anywhere."

"Oh, so this is you being lazy?"

"This is me being efficient."

Harper smiled, shaking her head. Then, she pulled out her phone.

Chapter Twenty-three

"Come in, come in." Pietr held open the door for his teammates later that evening. "We've got snacks on the island. Drinks too. Help yourselves."

"We're not late are we?" Guy asked. "Gregor changed his shirt six times. We almost told him to walk over."

"Six times and that's the one you landed on?" Pietr asked.

Gregor looked down at his polo with a small Osprey logo on the left pec. "What's wrong with it?"

"It has a collar."

"So?"

"You come over to play video games and think you're going to be comfortable in a shirt with a collar?"

"It's…" Gregor cursed. "Lend me something better then."

Harper laughed from the kitchen. "Gregor, you look fine."

"No, now I'm self-conscious about it."

"Come on," Harper beckoned him over, "let's go take a peek in the closet."

As soon as the two disappeared toward the bedroom, Guy leaned in conspiratorially to Pietr.

"I think Harper made Georgina cry today."

"Why do you think that?"

"I walked past her office on the way over to clinical. The door was closed –which it never is. And she had music on. Which she also never does. It was like standard sad girl, Swifty music."

"You want me to have Harper apologize?"

"I don't think Harper said anything wrong. But maybe you should apologize for asking about the autism thing? If she'd wanted us to know, to give her adjustments for it, she could have told us any time in the last eight months. Maybe she thought we already knew, or guessed."

"She's working with athletes. She should know by now that unless it's game related, we rarely notice shit most days."

"Still," Guy continued, "it wouldn't hurt to have a chat with her."

"Is there something you're not telling me?"

"She hasn't tried to kill me since Christmas," Guy said. "She was *very* apologetic the couple times she did."

"I find your behavior suspicious, but I don't think we have time to pull it out of you," Pietr said. "Where is Tim?"

"Parking. He'll be up in a minute."

"Right. Grab your snack and a drink and head in. Isaac is almost done reconfiguring the set up."

"Reconfi—oh!" Guy looked over at the living room. To adjust for the number of players, the triad had needed to move some things around. Guy could see not just the usual one, but four webcams linked back to a central laptop on a shelf near the large TV. There were six headsets, all wireless, along with four controllers set inside of small steering wheels on the coffee table. The couch was adjusted and flanked with Harper's desk chair and the recliner so everyone could sit and be seen by at least one of the cameras. Finally, there was a large microphone in the center of the coffee table.

"Hey Guy," Isaac greeted him. "I'm just double checking the camera switches and then we should be good to roll.

–Should I be concerned about Harper taking Gregor into the bedroom?"

"He's borrowing a different shirt," Pietr explained.

"Was there something wrong with what he had on?"

"No, but he was going to stick out with the collar and the rest of us looking more casual."

Isaac frowned but didn't have a chance to say anything as Gregor and Harper returned from the bedroom. Gregor had swapped his polo for a t-shirt that was a bit too big for him. At the same time, the doorbell rang again.

"That's probably Tim," Guy said.

"I'll get it." Pietr went for the door, letting the last of his friends into the apartment. "Jammer, welcome."

"It didn't start yet, did it?" Tim paused at the kitchen island, picking up one of the bottles of water.

"Not yet," Isaac called. "Let me give you all a brief run down. I had to modify things a bit. I've never had this many people in one room for a stream before."

"We tested everything with some folks from the Discord earlier," Harper said. "We should be OK."

"I still wonder if we should have gotten that auto-moving camera and mic instead of the multi-cams," Isaac murmured.

"We probably would have given someone motion sickness," Harper said. "How often are we really going to do this?" She gave his arm a squeeze as she passed him on the way to her desk chair.

"Right. Okay, so Harper and I are going to stay on Host duties and we'll let the four of you play," Isaac said. "I have two moderators on the chat tonight. Harper will keep an eye on questions and I'll stick to making sure our tech issues stay minimal."

"You are worrying too much," Pietr said. He reached to squeeze Isaac's arm and then press a kiss to his temple. "It's your show. People watch to see you play."

"People watch to see me make an idiot of myself," Isaac clarified.

"They like your charming personality," Pietr replied. He sat down on the end of the couch, nearest to Harper's chair. "Stop ripping on yourself and finish your spiel."

"You all know this is an all-ages, family friendly stream. Watch the profanity. We'll take a break after every couple of rounds."

"Can I ask a question?" Tim asked, raising a hand.

"What's up?"

"Wasn't the point of playing Kart that we could do a tournament or something?"

"I didn't get the board done in time, and the camera set up for it..." Isaac started.

"Don't worry about it. Are you nervous?" Pietr asked. "You do this every day."

"It's a big format change for a one off. And tonight's streaming revenue will go to the Osprey Foundation."

"Good to know," Gregor said. "You can relax. We will all be on our best behavior. Promise.

Isaac softened slightly. "I know that. Are you ready?" He picked up a small keyboard from next to the laptop.

The three guests took the last spaces on the couch. Isaac sat in the recliner. He tapped a few buttons on the keyboard and Harper pulled up the feed on Pietr's tablet as Isaac did his usual introduction. The guests introduced themselves and she focused on keeping an eye on the chat. When she had first started streaming with Isaac, trying to follow it made her feel a bit ill. But with the extra moderator fielding the chat, it moved at a slightly slower pace.

Over the next couple of hours, Isaac loosened up. He even took one of the controllers so Tim could take a quick bathroom break. After two hours, and more than a few rounds of Mario Kart, Isaac wrapped up the stream.

"We'll back to our regular routine tomorrow afternoon. Thanks for joining us live and remember to drop in and say hi on the Discord server. Have a great night everyone." There was a brief pause before the laptop popped up with a STREAM ENDED warning. "We're clear. That was fun."

"I'm starving." Gregor set his controller on the coffee table. "What's left?"

"You guys demolished the charcuterie," Harper said. "I probably have some meat and cheese left though. Or, do you want something sweet? I bought some cookies at SugarCube that I'm willing to share."

"What kind of cookies?" Gregor stood, following her out to the kitchen.

"They're a lemon sugar cookie with royal icing."

"Maybe? How are they decorated?" He asked, curious.

"Cross-stitch flowers." Harper pulled the plastic clamshell down from on top of the fridge.

"They're fancy looking."

"They're cookies."

"I don't want to take your fancy cookies."

Harper sighed, taking one of them out of the plastic clamshell package. She grabbed a knife out of the block, cutting it in half. "There, I'll split it with you." She shoved half at him, before taking a bite out of the other.

"I could eat some real food," Tim said. He got up, stretching his arms behind his back. "Anyone want to go grab a late dinner?"

"I better pass." Guy had pulled out his phone. "I have a text from a, uh, a friend. I better go check on them."

"You want a ride back to your place?"

"I'll grab a rideshare." He waved him off. "Thanks for a fun time, all. Sorry I can't stay longer."

"No problem. Hope your friend is okay," Harper said.

"I'm sure it's fine. See ya." Guy snagged a remaining cracker off a tray before making his way out of the apartment.

"Anyone else? Gregor?"

"Eh, sure." Gregor nodded. "Isaac?"

"Do you two mind if I go out?" Isaac asked his partners.

"Go." Pietr waved him off. "Let us know if you're not going to be back." He squeezed the back of Isaac's neck as he circled the island. "We'll clean up here. Have fun."

"You don't want to come with?" Tim asked.

"I had a huge lunch," Harper said. "We went to Tanuki. And then all the snacks."

"I'm good too," Pietr assured him. "I appreciate the rest of the evening with my wife." He wrapped his arms around Harper's waist, pressing a kiss below her ear.

"I'll text when I'm on my way back," Isaac promised. He waited until Tim and Gregor were closer to the door before trading a kiss with each of them. "I won't stay out too late. Promise."

"Just go have some fun." Pietr prodded.

"I will," Isaac promised. "Love you."

"Love you too," Pietr returned. "Show you how much later."

"Yeah? Don't wear him out, Harp," Isaac teased. "I'll put that to the test."

"Do my best," Harper replied. "Have fun."

Pietr waited until the other three had made their way out of the apartment before tightening his hold around Harper's waist. "How about I put all of this stuff away and you go pull out a couple of extras for some fun?"

"If I agree to that, does that mean I'm going to end up re-organizing all of my cupboards tomorrow morning because you've just tossed everything in?"

He hummed. "Okay, you clean up and I'll choose."

"Don't let your eyes be bigger than wherever you want me to put something," she warned.

"Ooh," he cooed, "can I take out the gifts from Misha? The cuffs, maybe."

"Is that what you'd like?"

"*Da*. I like how we play it with Misha," he admitted. "I'm curious though, letting you take over. Be Dom Harper while being just you."

He watched Harper hesitate for a moment as he released her. He turned her to face him, his arms wrapping around her shoulders.

"Harper, my darling." He traced a finger along her hairline, tucking a lock behind her ear. "What is that thing you say to me all the time? The thing that I have tried telling you is so dangerous."

"That you can do anything to me," she said.

"Exactly. I'd like you to take that to heart for once."

"I'm not sure how putting you in handcuffs translates to that."

"Keeps me submissive. My hands to myself." He kissed her lightly. "Plus, look at it as way to explore Dr. Balakin's suggestion. Own your own orgasm. Own them both tonight."

"I don't think that last bit was part of Dr. Balakin's suggestion. Unless you got something else from her in a solo session I wasn't aware of?"

"No, but I still think she would approve." He kissed her again, deeper this time.

She hummed contentedly, enjoying it for just a few extra seconds. She pushed his hips away.

"Okay. We can try. But not to the chair this time."

"We'll figure it out." Pietr gave her a pat on the behind. "Hurry up. I'll be waiting."

He left her in the kitchen, heading straight for the bedroom. He went for the closet first. He stripped down to nothing, tossing his clothes into the hamper. Then he took the purple wand they enjoyed off its charging cord. In the bedroom, he opened the small chest at the end of the bed Where they stashed some of their other toys. They'd tucked away the rope and the cuffs that Misha had brought on his last visit inside. They hadn't used them. In fact, Harper had hidden them deeper into the box, making them a bit harder to find.

"Ready?" Harper appeared in the doorway. She closed the door behind herself, leaning back against it.

"*Da*." He straightened, holding the cuffs out to her. "Here."

He watched her hesitate for a moment before crossing to the end of the bed.

"You're sure?"

"*Da*."

"English please." A smile pulled at her lips.

"Yes, my love. Do what you will to me."

"Safe word?" She coaxed.

"Same as always –lilac." He reached up, taking hold of her wrist. "And it goes both ways."

She hummed, looking down to fiddle with the buckles. "All right. Let's do this then."

Chapter Twenty-four

Harper slipped back into bed later that night. Pietr set his phone down on the charging pad before coming to settle beside her. The room was dark and quiet, the ambient hum of the air vents and a whisper of the traffic outside the only noise.

"Did Isaac text?" she asked.

"He's on his way back," Pietr replied. "They went out to get some drinks after dinner."

"He isn't going to Gregor's? Or is Gregor coming back here?"

"He didn't say. Maybe he is trying not to move too quickly."

Harper hummed. She shifted, trying to get comfortable.

"Baby?"

"What?"

"Did you have fun?"

"What do you mean?"

He let out a nervous chuckle. "Harper, you know what I mean. Did you like it?"

"I orgasmed three times, so I guess so."

"You can orgasm and not like something."

"Do we have to talk about it *now*?"

"No, we don't. But I value your immediate reaction. Before you can overthink it."

"Did you like it?"

"Mostly," he admitted.

Harper felt her stomach lurch. "What didn't you like?"

"Honestly?"

"Always."

Pietr traced his fingers along the low neckline of her tank. "I like touching you," he said. "I missed that. Otherwise, it was very enjoyable. Letting you use me."

"I missed that too," she admitted.

"So, is not something for all the time," he said. "Once in a while, for something different."

Harper nodded. The waves in her stomach lessened. "I can agree to that."

"Would you let me try them on you sometime?"

"I don't have a problem with not touching things I've been told not to," she teased.

"I know. You have great self-control." Pietr pressed a kiss to her shoulder. "But I think you'd look very sexy, cuffed to the chair. Or, sucking my cock with your hands behind your back."

"You're getting hard again, aren't you?"

He growled low in his throat. "Like you aren't getting wet?"

Harper laughed, swatting his hands away. "Save it for Isaac. You two can go to the other bedroom or at least the other side of the bed."

"Ooh, like porn? *Don't wake my wife, while we fuck in the same bed*?"

"If that's a turn on for you, sure."

"I like it more when my wife joins in," he declared. "Are we wearing you out?"

"No," she assured him.

Pietr settled his head on her chest as she finally seemed to rest on her back. She curled an arm behind him to stroke her fingertips over his hair.

"It was nice of Isaac to come though. I worry we get so wrapped up with each other sometimes, we forget about him," he said.

"You get busy. It's understandable," Harper answered. Pietr's hand moved up to return her touch, cupping one of her breasts in his palm.

"I don't forget about you though."

"That's because I'm here and you come home to me." She let out a soft sigh. "Pietr?"

"Hm?"

"Is something wrong? You've been clingier than usual since I got back from Edmonton. You could have gone out with the guys after the stream."

"I didn't go with them to give Isaac a little space. He likes Gregor. He won't say." He moved his hand to rest against her stomach. "Unless he has said more to you?"

"Not really," Harper admitted. "I figured he would say if it was turning into something we needed to be better appraised of."

"True enough."

They settled back into quiet, Harper continuing to brush her fingers over Pietr's hair. His beard rubbed coarsely against her bare skin. She had just begun to drift off when she heard the front door chime open. Pietr jumped at the unexpected noise.

"Shit," he laughed, "they must have been close by. That was fast." He shifted, looking up at her. "Sorry."

"What are you apologizing for?"

"You were almost asleep," he noted. "I was listening to you breathe, and your heartbeat." He moved against her side to nuzzle her hair. "I do that sometimes. When I don't fall asleep first. They are reassuring sounds. That you're here, with me. Relaxed."

"What about the snoring?"

"I don't mind the snoring." He smiled. "It's mostly cute. I can tell when you don't feel well though. It's louder."

There was a soft knock before the door opened a crack.

"Are you two still awake?" Isaac asked.

"*Da*. How was dinner and drinks?" Pietr asked.

"It was fun," Isaac confirmed.

"You didn't go back to Gregor's?"

"Gregor and I...I don't know what we're doing, but no. I didn't invite myself and he didn't ask me to. So, I came home."

"I hope this isn't going to be another McKinley and Tanner situation," Harper murmured.

Pietr snorted. He kissed her again before sitting up to look at Isaac, barely visible in the light of the hallway. "Are you coming to bed?"

"Yeah. I gotta go change. I'll be in in a minute."

Pietr nodded. Isaac closed the door again. He turned back to his wife.

"You think they could be as bad as those two? Kinley and Tanner."

"I sure as hell hope not. They seemed to have worked out their first little hiccup. But I'm not going to push." Harper rolled over onto her side, away from him. "If you two are going to fuck around, keep the noise down."

Pietr reached over, rubbing her arm. "Go to bed, baby. We won't wake you, I promise."

Harper let out a noise of disbelief, but didn't say more. Pietr shifted a little to the other side of the bed and waited for Isaac to return.

"Did I interrupt?" Isaac asked, getting under the covers beside him a few minutes later. "I didn't mean to."

"No. Harper is tired. I pushed her out of her comfort zone," Pietr explained. "I did leave something in the tank for you, as promised."

Isaac chuckled. "I'm good. Let's just go to bed."

Pietr grunted, feigning displeasure.

"I'll make it up to you before I leave," he promised.

"I'm sure you will."

Harper wasn't sure how, but she awoke the next morning squeezed between two bodies. Pietr was behind her, one arm under her head, the other curled around her. Isaac was in front of her, Pietr's free hand resting on the top of his head. His face was buried into her neck, and his hand holding her thigh, pulled over his waist.

She tensed, not wanting to wake either. She couldn't see the clock on the bedside table without her glasses. The blurry light in the distance could have read 2:00 AM just as easily as it read 5:55 AM. The longer she laid there, feeling Pietr's breath on the back of her neck, the more restless she felt.

Finally, Isaac stirred, pulling away from her. He blinked sleepily at her. A smile tugged at his lips as he saw she was wake.

"You need to get up?" He whispered.

"Yes," she nodded, "I'm trapped."

He let out a small laugh. The grip on her thigh loosened, and he let her slip it back. He reached upward, rubbing Pietr's arm to get him to loosen his grip. The other man groaned, pulling his hand free. He didn't seem to do more than stir, rolling onto his back and freeing Harper.

"Go on," Isaac coaxed. He grunted as she climbed over him.

She picked up her glasses. 5:37 AM. Annoyingly early considering that Pietr's alarm wouldn't go off for another twenty-odd minutes. She padded her way to the bathroom while Isaac took her place in Pietr's arms. She re-emerged a few minutes later and could see that Pietr was kissing his way down Isaac's shoulder.

"Did he not notice we switched places?" Harper teased in his ear as she got back to bed.

Pietr feigned surprise, looking between his lovers. "Why on earth have you tricked me this way?"

Harper chuckled. "Go back to sleep. The alarm will go off soon." She set her glasses back down and shifted under the covers.

"Or..." Isaac was surprisingly swift in wrapping his arms around her and sweeping her back between the two of them. "We use the fact that we're all awake a little early and have a little fun."

"It looked like you two were already having plenty of fun without me," Harper retorted.

"Nonsense," Pietr chided. His lips made a trail up her arm to her neck. "Is always more fun with you, *lyubov moya*."

Harper sighed. "You two are always horny so early in the morning."

"*Da*." Pietr palmed her face, tipping her lips toward his. "I am wrapped up in your scent all night. All I want is to devour you, first thing in the morning. What a wonderful way to start the day..."

"Shit," Isaac swore, "he's gotta be so romantic about it."

Harper laughed. "You two seemed to be doing fine without me."

"We were," Isaac continued, "but we're running out of time, the three of us. Pietr has the Boston game. I head back to LA soon."

Pietr hummed. "You don't have to leave. You can stay as long as you want."

"I have to go back eventually," Isaac said. "We can talk about it later."

Pietr hummed. He pressed a quick, rough kiss to Harper's mouth before leaning up on his elbow to stretch over her, pulling Isaac into one as well.

"*Da*. Later. Now –we make her cum."

Isaac grinned against his lips. "Right. I'll take over the kissing. Why don't you go south? I know how much you like that."

"I love how you just assume I—" Harper groaned as Pietr deftly pulled her shorts off and pressed his mouth between her thighs. She dug her fingers into his hair. Isaac's palm pressed to her cheek and turned her face toward his.

"We assume nothing," Isaac assured her. "Tell us what you want."

"The problem with that is, I want nothing," Harper replied. Her arm curled to scratch at Isaac's stubble. It was sharp and a little uncomfortable, but...she liked kissing him anyway. "It's the two of you that seem to want to cum so ba—aah! Oh fuck!"

"She complains but cums so easy," Pietr murmured. His hands slid up her thighs, squeezing her hips.

"What do you want, Harp?" Isaac pressed. "You want DP?"

"Oh god, it's too early in the morning for that." She laughed.

"Shall we just take turns with you then?" Pietr asked. "I have to get up soon." He straightened slightly. "I can fill you up with cum and then let Isaac enjoy you while I go get ready for the day."

Isaac groaned. "What do think Harper?"

"If that's what you want," she said.

"No, no, no," Isaac pressed. "What do *you* want?"

Harper sighed. "I don't care who fucks me just that one of you does. Both of you? Even better."

"You are not just saying that?" Pietr confirmed.

"No," she assured him. "it's a good way to start the day."

He lifted one of her legs around his waist as he leaned forward kissing her, then Isaac before Pietr slid inside of her. Isaac moved away from them just long enough to grab one of the condoms off the side table. He tucked it into Harper's hand.

Pietr traded kisses with each of them before he finally focused on a steady thrust. He repositioned Harper's thighs, pushing more deeply into her. He watched the way Isaac's hand moved to cup and squeeze Harper's breasts as he kissed her. Listened for the sound of Harper's panting against the other man's mouth.

"Cum, baby," Isaac murmured. His hand moved lower, his fingers rubbing her center as Pietr propelled into her. Slick, wet noises flooded the room along with Harper's panting. He felt her tighten around him followed by a hitch of her breath and a moan. He tried to will himself to hold on. The warmth and the wet, the sound and smell of sex and arousal...

"Oh *fuck*, Harper—" He squeezed her hips, holding her firmly in place. He knew she could feel the way his cock twitched as it emptied. He groaned, low and deep. He released her, leaning forward to find her lips again.

"That feels so good," Harper admitted. She smiled, wiping her fingers across his still damp beard. "You're a mess."

He chuckled. "When Isaac finishes, you'll have to come help me clean up." He kissed her, not really wanting the coupling to come to an end...yet, he knew it had to. He sighed, pulling away to make room for Isaac between her thighs instead.

Isaac sat up, taking the condom out of Harper's palm. "Damn, Harp, he did make a mess." Harper squeaked as he settled between her knees, lowering his mouth to her center.

"Isaac, you—"

Pietr hummed. He stretched out beside her, resting for just a moment to enjoy the show.

"It's different, tasting both of you at the same time," Isaac admitted. "Sweet and salty."

"Fuck me, please," Harper requested. "Before I'm too tired again."

Isaac laughed, ripping open the condom, then sliding it on. Pietr nuzzled Harper's cheek, coaxing her for another kiss, which she rewarded him with.

"I like starting our mornings this way too," he whispered to her. "Can you cum again for us, baby?"

"You're certainly going to make me try."

Pietr chuckled –then cursed as his phone began to emit its alarm tone. He moved away from his partners to pick up the phone and silence it. While he was gone, Isaac covered Harper, coaxing her to adjust her position just a bit. He braced his arms against her shoulders, pinning her down. Harper panted as he thrust into her; the bed quaking beneath them. As Pietr rejoined them, phone tossed down on the bed behind them, he distracted Isaac with a sharp swat to his backs side. Isaac flinched, stilling for a second.

"Hurry up," Pietr urged. "I need Harper to come shower with me."

Harper reached for him and Pietr laced their fingers.

"You have to go do your work out," she chided.

"This is my work-out." He murmured. "I won't get anything done smelling like sex now."

"Stop talking," Isaac interrupted. "Or I'm never going to finish."

That made both Pietr and Harper laugh. Isaac groaned, then sighed, then straightened again.

"Goddamn it, you two. I lost it."

"Oh baby," Pietr crooned, "come here. We'll help you find it again."

"No." Isaac leaned back, palming off the condom. "It's fine. We can try again later."

Pietr frowned at him. "I have plenty of time, Izzy."

Isaac shook his head, moving away. "It's okay. You two go shower. I'll go to the guest room to clean up and change. Get started on breakfast."

Pietr started to call after him, but Isaac slipped from the bedroom, leaving the door open behind him as he went.

"Did I miss something?" Harper asked.

Pietr sighed, shaking his head. "If you did, then I missed it too." He leaned over kissing her one more time. "Come on. Let's clean up."

Chapter Twenty-five

"Isaac?"

Harper waited until after breakfast and Pietr's departure for the day before wrapping her arms around the man's shoulders. He'd gotten comfortable with his laptop on the couch in the living room.

"What's up, babe?" He reached up, touching her arm.

"You want to talk about this morning?" She leaned her head against his.

"What about this morning? We had fun. Didn't we?"

"You didn't finish. And then you left us."

"Pietr had to get ready and your shower is barely big enough for the two of you –that isn't a crack at your size. It is an average size shower and Pietr takes up just as much space as you."

"Isaac."

"Harper." He tipped his head back to look up at her. "I didn't cum. It's not the end of the world."

"I know that, but we had time."

"My head just wasn't there. With you. That wasn't fair."

"Where was it then?"

"Just...somewhere else."

"With some*one* else?"

"Never," he assured her. "Not when I have the two of you right in front of me."

Harper hummed. She pressed a kiss to his temple. "Is there a reason you came home last night then after dinner and drinks?"

"It would have been odd. Tim was with us. I didn't want to put him on the spot in front of someone else."

"I don't think Tim would have cared."

"I'm not pressuring him. We're talking again. And..."

"And?"

"I like him, okay?" He sighed. "I'm kicking myself for being an idiot about him and..."

"And?"

"And I have to go back to LA, so I'm trying not to get too dragged in."

"Why do you *have* to go back to LA?"

"I can't live here with you and Pietr forever. For one thing, while Pietr loves to share you now, I would hate to think about what happens when he reaches his limit."

"I'm not sure he'd be so wild about sharing *you* either," she reminded him. She ran her fingers through his hair. "Is that what was wrong this morning? You wanted him, not me?"

Isaac sighed, he loosened her arms, coaxing her around the sofa to come sit with him instead. He set his laptop aside to pull her into his lap.

"Harper, I wanted you, I promise. Unlike one of us, I don't have an issue asking for what I want, when I want it." He gave her a soft smile so she knew he was teasing. "If I'd wanted Pietr, I could have had him. This morning was about time. I let you two giggling together distract me and I didn't want to rush to finish. I never want to rush with you. Either of you."

"Do you want to go make up for it now?"

"Just the two of us?" He raised an eyebrow.

She saw a mixed expression cross his face. "You can say no."

"I'm in the middle of e-mailing a guest for next month. And then checking confirmations for the conventions in July and August."

"Okay." She felt herself push down a rush of disappointment. Of feeling rejected. "I'm going to go work in the bedroom then."

"You can't work out here with me?" He asked, letting her up from his lap.

"I could, but I'll get more done without the distraction."

He gave her a short nod, letting her go. Harper could feel his eyes on her as she made her way to the guest room and her own laptop. The guest room was a quiet haven. Even when the apartment was empty, Harper preferred to enclose herself up, rather than working in the open space of the living or dining room, or even at the kitchen island. She tried to press down the feelings that had started bubbling and churning in her chest. It had been a long time since that kind of anxiety had reared its ugly head. It was difficult pushing it back down. Never really rid of it, just subdued.

Harper tried to put it out of her head. Dwelling on it wasn't going to help. Working herself up over it wasn't going to help. Besides, she needed to focus on getting the book done so she could write something –literally anything she damned well pleased. She didn't even care if it was good anymore. Though, she didn't want to give any of her characters a misjustice of a book. They deserved their happily-ever-afters, in her best quality. Didn't they?

Her word count didn't move up more than a few hundred words. The tightness in her chest was heavy. The ticking of the analog clock above her was deafening.

"Are you going out?" Isaac turned from his place on the sofa. Harper had strode past him to the door. The whole apartment felt suffocating.

"Just getting some air. Might walk down to the bodega. You want something?"

"I'm good."

She forced a smile. "K. Back in a little while."

Outside, her feet took her down several blocks. She hadn't been going anywhere in particular, but she wasn't surprised to find herself at the door of the Mounting Bison.

"Hey Stranger." Quinten was wiping down the bar as she entered. "It's early in the day for you to be here. You want lunch?"

"Johnnie Walker, Black Label. One ice cube. A double."

"Scotch? Oh boy. What's wrong?" Quinten had been serving her and her friends for nearly six years so he knew she stuck to ciders. Asking for scotch spelled one thing. "Writer's block?"

"No. Maybe. I just can't get out of my own head today." She picked up the glass, watching the ice cube clink against the sides as it melted. She took a sip. It burned the whole way down to her stomach. The backs of her eyeballs steamed.

"You know drinking isn't the answer," he replied.

"I'm not drinking. I'm having *a* drink."

"Does Pietr know about this habit?"

"What habit?"

"You hit a snag and you come down here for the hard stuff. Or has he only ever seen you drink ciders?"

"He's probably seen me drink other things. I've shared a vodka with him a few times. I think."

Quinten hummed. "Is there something else besides the writing? You look more uneasy than usual."

"Just feeling some anxiety, which is stupid and useless and wrong. I know it's wrong. I'm just not reasoning it away very well."

"Do you want to talk about it?"

"No offense, but no. It's not really a thing I...I have a hard time talking to Pietr about it, so talking to someone else just isn't going to happen."

"What about Tanner?"

"I don't want to bother Tanner."

"Okay. Well, take it easy on that. Don't make me have to call your husband."

"It's one drink."

"Technically two in the same glass."

"Semantics."

Quinten sighed and shook his head, moving down the bar as one of the other patrons beckoned him over. Harper took a smaller sip of the scotch. The heat didn't release the tension in her chest. She wondered for a moment what a heart attack felt like. That started with numbness in the arm, right? She took another sip. No, not a heart attack. Just the fucking anxiety.

She picked up the glass after dropping some cash on the bar for it, and carried it to a booth in the back corner. She pulled out her phone and settled into the dark to look over her notifications.

The WHOOSH Discord was buzzing with plans for a watch party for the game against Boston. Harper ignored it. Tanner texted about dinner on Saturday while the guys were on the road. She shot off a [sure] in response. Misha had sent a photo of his bare shoulder and the pillow on the other side of the bed with a [Wish you were here] and a cat emoji. Harper felt the tension loosen, just a little. She sent him back a [Miss you too. Just a couple of weeks] and a fingers-crossed emoji.

By the time the scotch was gone, she had made necessary responses to the notifications. She didn't feel any better, even though she knew deep down the drink hadn't been going to be magical on that front. She set the phone back down, closing her eyes and just taking a couple of deep breaths.

Focus on the book. Where was it going wrong? What needed to happen?

"Baby?"

She jerked up, surprised to see Pietr.

"What are you doing here?"

"I got home just after you left and Isaac said you went out. He said you seemed weird." He slid into the booth across from her. "I used the Find My Friend app and saw you were here."

"I'm fine."

"You are day drinking." He picked up the glass, giving it a sniff before tipping back the last tiniest dreg of the scotch. "Hard liquor at that."

"I wasn't making very much headway on the book."

"I'm sorry. That must be frustrating," he put the glass back down. "Do you want another?"

"I shouldn't."

"That was not my question, *lyubov moya*."

"No." She shook her head.

"You are sure?"

"Positive. It didn't help, so I don't think another is going to do anything either."

"Does it usually?" He asked seriously.

"No," she admitted. "It's more the *idea* that it could help."

"Is it just your book? Isaac..." He paused, thinking how he wanted to speak. "Isaac thought that maybe he upset you somehow. But you didn't say anything."

Harper felt the tightening again.

"Harper?" He watched her face closely. "Is it about this morning?"

"Yes and no."

"It can't be both," he chided.

"I asked what had happened this morning," she admitted.

"And?"

"And he said it was time. He didn't want to feel rushed."

"Valid. We had time, but it's not worth arguing about," Pietr replied. "Was that it?"

"I asked if he wanted to make up for it, just the two of us. And he said no," Harper said. Then she continued, with the rational explanation. "He was busy –sending e-mails and stuff for scheduling guests and conventions."

"But he said *no*." Pietr caught on to the tone. He leaned forward propping his chin on the heel of his hand. "Tell me how that made you feel."

"It's stupid. He was working. I *know* he was working. I wouldn't expect you to just drop whatever you're doing to—"

"Harper, tell me how it made you feel."

"Rejected."

"Baby," he shook his head, "you know that would never be his intention."

"I know. Rationally, I know that. He literally told me not thirty seconds before that he wanted me. That doesn't mean this asshole part of my brain accepted it at face value."

Pietr straightened, stretching his arm across the table to put a hand on her arm. "I am so sorry that people treated you the way they did to make this...normal for you. You didn't deserve it –no one does. I hate that you question how we feel about you. Don't think I don't know you still wonder about me."

"Well, you married me, so..."

"You're right. I married you, because I fucking love you more than anything in the world. I couldn't risk someone else coming along and trying to steal you –including Isaac. And even if we weren't fucking him, he is one of our best friends. He loves you. So much it scares him because he doesn't want to come between us. Honestly, *that* explains more about what happened this morning than anything else. I was in the way."

"You were not."

"Because you like fucking us together," he said. "For Isaac? I think he came more to see you this time than to see me."

"That's not true."

"He loves me. I know he does, but he came for you. Because you're here. You have the time for him. I don't. I barely have time for you, my darling."

Harper sighed, wishing she had taken the offer of another drink.

"Say what's on your mind. Don't hold it in and hope that everything will just resolve itself. That's not how it works and you know it."

"I like our relationship," she said. "The three of us. But having him so far away is hard. When he's here, I don't want him to leave again. Doing the stream together, more officially is great, but it's not the same as being in the same room together. Maybe it would be easier if we were just friends and sex, the intimacy, wasn't part of it."

"Do you want to stop?" He asked seriously.

"No."

"Can I tell you what I think?"

"Of course."

"I think we need to be patient. I have a year left in my contract with the Osprey. Depending on how this season goes, that could mean a big renewal in the future. Seven years isn't uncommon now. If we can say that we're going to be in one place for a while, I think Isaac would feel more comfortable moving closer. Whether that's here, or even Wisconsin or Minnesota. He doesn't want to live *with* us, and I get it. He wants to be an independent person. We also have to be patient, because he is looking for another partner. A primary. Someone who is just his. Depending on who that person is, we might have to make adjustment to our expectations."

"I know that."

"I want him closer too." Pietr rubbed her arm. "Considering how this visit has gone, we should be prepared in case that person for him is Gregor. His contract is up soon too, and he does well, but who knows. He could be traded any time. That's how it goes sometimes."

"I know. We also have to consider what happens after your contract ends."

"I'm not worried about my contract," Pietr said. "Are you? If we need to move?"

"I don't know. I've lived here for so long. Starting over somewhere, a new team, new set of expectations... It's scary."

"I know. But I'll be right there with you. Starting together. And I should be in a position to make sure that wherever we end up, we are there for a while −or my contract will stipulate that I can only go to certain places. Minnesota. LA. Florida. Maybe Edmonton or Calgary?"

"Not Calgary. Not after what I've heard from Misha and Cecil."

A soft smile pulled at his lips. "I doubt they'd want to deal with my bullshit anyway. But you see what I mean."

"Yes."

"Does that help? Knowing we can be a little more secure that way? Have say in where I end up?"

"I want you to play for as long as it makes you happy. For as long as you can, physically. If that means we have to move once, or twice, or even six times, I'll deal with it. I can work from wherever we end up." She finally laced her fingers with his. "It doesn't make me less nervous to start over. But if you're with me, I'll manage."

"Good." He lifted her hand to his lips, kissing her knuckles. "Is there anything else you need to get off your chest?"

She considered it for a moment. Talking had helped. The tension wasn't *gone*, but it was less suffocating. "I think I'm OK."

"Are you ready to go home?"

Harper nodded.

"Good. I took a rideshare. Do you want to get a cab home, or should we walk?"

"I walked here, so I suppose it's only right I walk back."

"We can stop at SugarCube on the way home. Buy you more cookies." He offered.

"I think I'm good on cookies, but I wouldn't turn down a cupcake."

"Whatever you want, baby," he assured her. "Let's go."

Chapter Twenty-six

"Okay, let's talk."

"Talk about what?" Pietr looked up from where he and Harper had settled on the couch together. Isaac plopped down on the coffee table in front of them.

"About this. Us. And...Gregor."

"Oh, you are going to talk to us about Gregor now?" Pietr stroked Harper's hair. "What has changed?"

After the game against Boston, Pietr had left for a game in Buffalo. He'd only returned that morning and Isaac was still there. Longer than he'd intended to be sure, but he just couldn't make himself book the ticket back to LA.

"I like him. A lot."

"Good for you." Harper offered. "We're glad it's working out this time around."

"I think he'd like to make it more official."

"And what do you want?"

"I might like that too," he said. "But, logistics aren't ideal."

"True, but they are not ideal with us either," Pietr said. "You are going to let distance stop you?"

"No," Isaac admitted, "but I might be visiting more. And maybe not staying here with you two."

"Okay." Harper nodded. "You know you've never had to stay with us, right? You could have gotten a hotel. An AirBnB. Whatever."

"I know that," Isaac admitted. "I just, I'll let you know when I'm in town because I obviously want to see you, but I might, occasionally, spend the night at Gregor's instead. Or, you know, be spending more time with him than I am here with you two."

"Thank you for telling us," Pietr said. "We are very happy for you."

"This isn't going to make things weird for you and him, team wise, is it?"

"I think it's a little late for that," Pietr admitted. "It should be fine. I don't want to sleep with him. Not right now, anyway." He smirked. "If he's interested in Harper, that is something the three of you will have to work out. You have my blessing, should it come up."

"Fer fuck's sake, Pietr, we're not even talking about group sex yet."

"Yet."

"Okay, I'm done talking about this now." Isaac pushed up from the coffee table.

"Wait, wait!" Pietr reached out, grabbing his hand. He pulled Isaac back toward him. "I am only teasing you, Izzy. I stand by what I said, because you never know."

"I don't want to sleep with Gregor," Harper said. "So, no worries from me on that front."

"Part of me wants to say thank you?" Isaac admitted. "Cool it, okay? It's still new. It's fresh. I don't know that anything is actually going to be permanent. Maybe it ends up being some fun for the two of us and not serious."

"That is fine." Pietr grabbed the waistband of Isaac's jeans, tugging him closer still. "Are you going out?"

"Yes, in a bit. We're having dinner. I'll probably go back to his place."

"You're going to stay the night?"

"I might."

"If you do, let us know so we don't worry," Pietr requested. "Or, so that I don't worry."

"I probably wouldn't notice until morning," Harper admitted. "Have fun. Be safe."

"I'm always safe," Isaac retorted.

"We are knowing this." Pietr released him, patting his stomach. "Go on then. I will make do with my wife for the evening."

"You say that like it's such a hardship." Harper snorted.

Pietr grunted, a smile tugging at his lips. He murmured something quiet in Harper's ear that Isaac couldn't hear.

Isaac took a step back from the couch. This...this was the part he didn't like about being in the triad. The way that Pietr and Harper were together was just so...wholesome. Maybe an odd word, given he knew their proclivities. Comfortable was perhaps a better one. Seeing the two of them, enjoying the time they had together. Even when that was just some quiet time on the sofa, reading. He felt like an interloper. And, as had flared up back in February at KongKon, his feelings toward Harper in particular were just so...

"Why are you staring at us like that?" Pietr's voice cut into his thoughts.

"I'm not staring. Just spacing out."

"Thinking about that nice Czech cock you're getting tonight? I get it." Pietr reached out again, dipping his fingers into the front of Isaac's jeans this time. "If you like, you can have a nice Russian cock to kick off your evening."

"I'm good," he laughed. "That's *not* what I was thinking about."

Pietr hummed. His hand fell away, and his other tightened around Harper. "Then what?"

Isaac knew, he *knew*, that if he was going to really have the conversation with the two of them, it should be then. Going to dinner with Gregor would give them all the break to mull it over in case it went badly. Or, even if they just needed the space to think. And getting it off his chest would feel good. Right? He sat back down on the coffee table.

"I feel like something has been off the last couple of days. Since the other morning when..." Ugh, he didn't want to say it. "We were running short on time, so I didn't finish with you."

"That's your prerogative," Pietr said. Isaac noticed him squeeze Harper's shoulder, reassuringly. "You didn't have to, so you didn't."

"It wasn't because I didn't want to."

"We know that."

"I didn't want you to be late."

"Me being late is my own problem. I would rather be late because of something like that than something serious. The guys wouldn't need to know. And is not like I am regularly late because we're fucking around."

"Okay, that's all very rational, but I'm still getting a vibe that something is off."

"Harper?" Pietr prodded her. "Do you have something you want to say?"

"Not really," she answered.

"Harper..."

She sighed.

Isaac tensed. So he wasn't insane. Something *had* been off. The two of them had talked about it and not included him.

"It's not a big deal. I'm over it," Harper declared.

"Is it?" Pietr pushed. Isaac wanted to open his mouth and ask why he was trying to force her, but he also knew why. Harper needed coaxing sometimes. She was so willing to just let people push her around. She liked to feel needed. And...

"Fuck." It dawned on him. "Afterwards, when you asked me what had been up. You asked me to go back to bed with you and I said no." He hadn't considered that Harper was *asking* him for something she wanted, in her roundabout way of doing so.

"You were busy."

"You were horny and our time is limited," Isaac retorted. "Nothing I was doing that morning couldn't have waited to take fifteen minutes to fool around."

"You don't have to drop everything to fuck me, Isaac," she retorted. "It just felt..."

"Felt?"

"It's stupid."

"It's not stupid. I hurt you and I need to know how so I can be more considerate in the future."

"It felt like you were rejecting me, which is stupid because obviously you were not. You were prioritizing your livelihood. Like I've prioritized getting my work done a bajillion times in the past when you, or Pietr, or Misha, have asked. It's the same thing."

"It's not the same," Pietr murmured. "You take it more personally than we do."

"I don't want to. I can't help it."

"I know, baby." Isaac watched Pietr reach up, smoothing her hair away from her face as a beat of silence passed between them. "What do we do about it?"

"I don't want you, either of you, to start treating me any differently. That isn't going to help."

"We can be more thoughtful to how we respond to certain things," Isaac suggested. "You asked me very clearly if I wanted to do something and it wasn't that I didn't. I should have either taken the few minutes to give you the attention or suggested another time, when I was done with what I was doing." He stared at her. "I need *you* to be clearer about what you want. We've talked about that before, Harp."

"I know."

"It is more than that," Pietr said. "We both, *I*, need you to trust us."

"I do trust you."

"You trust me with a lot of things," he admitted. "You don't believe me when I tell you how important you are. How much I love you."

"I do too."

"Okay, so you believe me. Do you believe him?" He cocked his head toward Isaac.

"It's not that I don't," Harper started.

"It is simple question, *lyubov moya*."

"I *want* to."

"But you don't. There is this part of your head that won't let you." Pietr looked up at Isaac. "And you, you are just as bad."

"What do you mean?" Isaac recoiled slightly.

"The other day. Why did you really stop?"

"I told you. Time—"

"No. We had plenty of time. There was something else."

"I don't know what you mean."

"You didn't stop because I was there? I was distracting you from what you wanted?"

"What? Of course not."

"Are you sure? Because I know that you came to be with Harper. You're still here to be with her. Well, now Gregor too."

"Are...are we having a fight now?"

"No," Pietr shook his head, "not unless you want to be."

"Pietr, I came because I wanted to. It's easier for me to pick up and come. To get to see *both* of you. Gregor was a fluke. I obviously didn't expect it. But, it happened. And, you're busy with the team. I'm getting plenty of time one-on-one with Harper."

"You know it's okay for *you* to ask for what you want too," Pietr declared.

"Pietr." Isaac leaned forward. "You are not in the way or second best or whatever else. Is this what jealousy looks like?"

"Yes." Pietr agreed. "This is me jealous. I want you. I want her. I don't always want you together. Particularly without me."

Isaac straightened. "Okay. Then...let's stop."

"Stop what?"

"Stop this. Being...this."

"Why?"

"Because I don't want this. I don't want you worrying about Harper and me when we're together. I don't want Harper feeling like I don't want her –because I do. I *really* fucking do. I'd rather we took the sex off the table and were just friends again if being in a relationship is going to stress us all out."

"I like the sex," Harper admitted.

"I like the sex too," Isaac told her. "All of it –being with one of you, or both of you. It doesn't matter."

"Okay." Pietr cut in. "We all like the sex. That is good. Something we agree on. We all want to keep being friends. Great. What isn't working? What makes this hard?"

"It's hard seeing the two of you together," Isaac offered. "How you are with each other. Like right now. We're having this serious conversation and you're there, together. You're a unit. I don't feel like I'm part of the unit, except when we're in bed."

Pietr didn't seem to have a response for that. Isaac considered whether he had shared too much. Surely not. It was an honest statement.

"I don't know how to fix that." Pietr finally managed. "I don't know that it's something we *can* fix."

"I'm not asking for a fix," Isaac leveled. "I'm just making you aware how I feel. How I've always felt. This is why I need someone else who isn't the two of you. It's why I want to give Gregor a chance."

"I understand."

"Harper?"

"I get it," she said. "This dynamic isn't easy. You two have a history that I don't share. I don't want to end this, but...what if we pulled back?"

"Pulled back?" Pietr repeated.

"We've been focusing on making the most of our time with sex lately. Can we try to make more of an effort do more...relation-shippy things? Going out. Being in public. People know about us now, but we keep hiding in the apartment. We had fun when we went out and did stuff when we were in LA, right? We can go out and do things together. The three of us. Or the two of us, and we don't have to worry about rumors."

"I suppose doing the stream isn't the same," Isaac admitted.

"No, it really isn't. That's your job. It's a thing I like doing with you. Helping you with. But it's not the same as going out and holding hands in public."

"I get it. So...you want to be more public. How do we start?"

"There is a fundraising event, for the Osprey Foundation, coming up," Pietr said. "I bet I can convince one of the guys to give up their plus one if it means they don't have to find a date. Or, you know, pay for a third ticket."

"When?"

"It's before the Minneapolis convention, next month."

Isaac bit his lip. His eyes drifted to the clock sitting on Harper's desk. Shit –he was supposed to meet Gregor for dinner.

"I'm not saying no," he began. "I'm saying, let me think about it. I'm supposed to go meet Gregor for dinner. Can we put a pin in this conversation and talk about it tomorrow?"

"*Da*." Pietr nodded. "I didn't mean for this to keep you from your date. Have fun."

Isaac nodded as he stood up. He paused in front of them then dropped a kiss first to Pietr's lips –solely because he was closer. Then to Harper's.

"I'll text if I'm not going to be back. Don't wait up for me or anything."

"We'll see you in the morning," Pietr waved him off. "Tell Gregor we said hello."

Isaac hummed. He paused, looking down at Harper. "I love you." His eyes flicked back up at Pietr. "You too."

Pietr sniffed, adjusting his hold on Harper but didn't say anything.

"I love you too," Harper said. "Go on, or you're going to be late."

Isaac tried not to think about how forced the words sounded. It was just residual from having the hard conversation, right?

"See you later."

"Bye. Have fun." Harper waved him off.

Isaac pulled on his sneakers and grabbed his jacket before stepping out of the apartment. He shoved down whatever feels he was having over the conversation. They'd finish it later. Right now...he had a nice Czech cock waiting for him.

Chapter Twenty-seven

"I'm sorry."

"Why are you sorry?"

Harper tipped her head back to look up at Pietr. They were still on the couch. Isaac had left a few minutes before. She had settled back against his chest again and re-opened her book. It was sort of research. Another author's hockey novel. It was good to know what else was out there. Pietr had mentioned he'd liked this one...he'd taken to picking them up from his Kindle suggestions and this one had been good enough he'd sought out a paperback. The cover model was not exactly her cup of tea. Too clean. Too muscled. Too broad. Too perfect. Attractive, to be sure, but not at all what she had come to know actual hockey players looked like.

"I put Isaac, and you, on the spot. I pushed too hard. Both of you. To be honest. It's very frustrating to me to know how each of you feel, and yet won't talk to each other sometimes." He set his chin on the top of her head. "I have feelings too, you know."

"I know you do. You can share them any time you want."

"Can I? Sometimes is like I'm so busy wrangling the two of you that I become the one most easily placated."

"Neither of us mean to make you feel that way." Harper closed the book again. She let herself relax, settling heavily against him. His chin moved from her head to her shoulder with the movement and he tightened his arms around her. She hummed contentedly, enjoying the wiry feel of his beard on her cheek.

"I know. That is why I am sorry. We're usually very good with talking things out." He sighed in her ear. "I'm tired now."

"It was a bit intense." Harper curled her arm to gently scritch his cheeks. "You want to go lay down? I can move so you can get up."

"I want you right where you are," he assured her. He rubbed his cheek against hers. "Have you managed to avoid more day drinking?"

She let out a light laugh. "Yes. Although my book still isn't really coming along. It feels forced. I'm not sure what isn't clicking."

"Do you want to talk about it? I have read enough of your novels, and other novels like it. Plus, you know, am professional hockey player. Maybe I can help?"

"I think I just need to take a break from it for a day or two."

"What about your deadlines?"

"I have plenty of time. The last one came so easily...maybe that's the problem. I had a lot of fun with those two characters, and I'm not ready to leave them."

"I imagine that is hard." Pietr's lips grazed her cheek. "I know I am always a little sad to get to the end when reading. The story this time –what is it?"

"Black Hawk and Tyrone."

"*Oh*! So was...shit, I can't remember who. Someone said Tyrone was bi?"

"No," she shook her head, "I'm not labeling him, but he's probably demi? He's been slowly falling for Black Hawk throughout the rest of the series, if you paid enough attention."

"It is incentive to go back and read them again." He grinned. "So what is the problem? You've been planning this for a long time."

Harper sighed. She wasn't sure where to begin explaining. Something just wasn't connecting.

"I might be starting in the wrong spot," she said. "I picked up at the end of the last novel, and maybe instead I need to go back to more like...the beginning of the series? Show the build from a different perspective?"

"It could be good to remind readers of what has happened. Also, they get to see the other couples falling for each other," he said. "Maybe that is what makes whatever clicks *click*."

"Maybe."

"Are you liking the book?" He tapped the page she was reading.

"It's fine."

"What is wrong with it?"

"The hockey-bro speak is really annoying."

He chuckled. "It was a little much. Accurate, but over the top."

"Are you sure you don't want me to get up?"

"I am positive. I like you right here." He groaned, giving her ear a nip. "I might enjoy you putting the book down for a few minutes. I can wait though. When you're ready."

Harper grinned, closing the book. "It's not going anywhere." She tossed it over onto the coffee table.

"Good. Now just sit here with me," Pietr requested. "Relax." His lips pressed to her cheek. He slid a hand down to the hem of Harper's hoodie –his hoodie. The faded LA Scorch emblem had seen better days. There were small holes starting at the top corners of the pocket. Fingers under it, he then had to track down the second hem of her t-shirt before he could finally touch the expanse of skin beneath it.

"We could go to the bedroom," Harper said.

"I can do everything I want right here." He chided. "Let me touch you. Feel you. Maybe kiss a little." He rubbed his beard against her cheek again. "Snuggle? That is such a dumb cutesy word but is what I want. Crave, even."

"You want to sit and snuggle on the couch? In silence?"

"*Da*. Listening to the way you breathe is better than music or some ridiculous TV show. That quiet little moan you have. Or the deep intake of breath when I make you feel good. Find the right spot that turns you on."

"The silence gives me too much of an opportunity to get into my own head."

"Don't go there," he requested. "Stay right here with me." He finally pulled his hands away long enough to tug the hoodie and t-shirt looser before snaking his arm back under the fabric to squeeze a breast. He hummed happily. "Focus on how good it feels, yeah?"

"I'm not going to complain if that's what you want to do to me," Harper said.

"Not to you," he corrected. "With you. You can explore a bit too, if you like."

"Pietr, babe, you're behind me. All I can really reach is your beard."

Pietr let out a little groan. "That works for me. It feels good when you do that scratchy thing."

"This?" Harper resumed the soft scraping of her nails into the coarse hair. Pietr hummed happily, leaning into the touch. His own hold on her loosened slightly.

"It might feel good other places," she teased.

"Maybe. Where would you like to try?" His interest was piqued.

"If you let me move —not leave, just turn around, I could start at your pecs and move down from there."

"Fuck." He rubbed the other side of his face against her cheek again. He made a contemplative noise, considering the worthwhileness of the terms to the amount of pleasure. Finally, he grunted. He removed his hand from under her hoodie. The fabric smoothed back into place as he straightened it, then more docilely wrapped his arms around her chest.

"No," he said firmly. "Later, please. I want to hold you for a bit longer."

They sat in a comfortable silence. Harper opened her book again. Pietr closed his eyes, inhaling Harper's scent. Even though they shared the same shampoo, soap, and detergent, Harper still smelled *different*. A sort of tangy sweetness that clung to her skin and clothes that was uniquely her. It was the best part about coming home after a road trip. If she wasn't there to greet him directly, he'd head straight to the bedroom. The smell could always be found in the sheets.

"Are you falling asleep?" Harper asked. They'd been quiet for some time. She had made headway on the book.

Pietr's hold had loosened slightly and his breathing was slow and steady.

"Maybe." He straightened slightly. "I have held you here long enough. You can move now, if you wish. But don't think you have to."

Harper chuckled. "Let me finish this chapter. Then we should get up and find something for dinner."

Pietr's stomach growled at the mention of food.

"Or maybe I better finish the chapter later."

"No, no," Pietr kissed her cheek, "you finish. I'll get up and start dinner. Did you have something planned?"

"No. Maybe some pasta? I have those tiny meatballs you like."

"I can handle that." He gave her one last little squeeze before he sat up more fully to scoot out from behind her. "You enjoy your book."

"You want me to help?"

"Let me cook for you." He crouched down next to her to give her a proper kiss to the mouth. "I love you."

"I love you too. Go easy on the garlic."

He grinned. "No promises, *lyubov moya*."

Chapter Twenty-eight

"Harper!"

She turned at the sound of her name. She'd just landed at O'Hare International in Chicago. She'd collected her bag and was about to reach for her phone to find out where Isaac was, but he'd already found her.

"Hi," he grinned, wrapping her up in a quick hug, "how was the flight in?"

"Good. Fast." She gave him a hello kiss before tightening her grip on her suitcase. "Have you scoped out the shuttle situation?"

"Yup. And I contacted the organizers. They know we're here and they'll be waiting for us at the hotel to get us checked in and settled."

"Good."

"We should have the night mostly to ourselves. There's a little mixer thing for the other guests and some of the convention staff and volunteers. Take advantage of the hotel being empty before everyone starts to arrive tomorrow. Do you want to check it out?"

"First, I want to settle in. You know I hate flying."

"I know." He put an arm over her shoulders and pulled her in to kiss her temple. "I'm sorry you had to fly alone. At least I'm heading back with you, right?"

"Small favors, but also a new source of anxiety."

"What do you mean?"

"Pietr finagled getting another ticket into that fundraiser, sure. Now we're going to be under a whole new type of scrutiny. It's the first time the *three* of us have been out together in public, for something big. Something work related."

"Have people been saying shit to you?"

"If they have, I haven't seen it."

"Hopefully we're not dealing with anything too stressful this weekend," he assured her. "We're here to have fun, talk about what we like, and spend some one-on-one time."

Harper paused, pulling him short with her. She turned to face him. "Is that going to be okay? Being one-on-one? We got a little of that with your last visit. More than a little. It's not going to be weird because we're here, completely away from Pietr, is it?"

"No. I want to be here. I want to be with you." He dropped his bags beside them to cup her face in his hands. "Harper, I know things have been off. I love you so much. You had a great point when we had that talk last week. Pietr and I have a history. We know each other very well because we've been close. You and I...we're starting totally and completely fresh. We jumped into this thing and I'm not sure that we've been taking the time to get to know each other the same way. Can we focus on that this weekend? We're here for *work* and *fun*. Let's spend some time together."

Harper nodded. "I think we can handle that."

"Before we get to the hotel, we have a double queen room. We don't have to have sex this weekend. We don't have to sleep together."

"Isaac." Harper pressed her hands over his. "I *want* to have sex with you. That isn't what makes me nervous."

He let out a sigh of relief. "Good. –I mean, I'm glad you want to." He pressed his forehead to hers with a little grin. "I want to too. Don't ever doubt that."

"No promises." Harper squeezed his fingers, pulling them from her face. "C'mon. Let's get that shuttle. We can talk about sex later. When there's less people around."

"Oh fuck, right. We're in an airport." Isaac chuckled. He laced his fingers with hers, picking his bag back up.

They made their way through the airport to the shuttle pick-up. Twenty minutes later, they were greeted warmly by a staff member of the convention.

"Welcome to AtomiCon. We are so happy to have you! I'm Laurie. She/Her. I'll be your point person all weekend." Laurie shook both of their hands and exchanged a few more pleasantries before continuing. "We've already got you all checked in. Here are your room keys. You're on the 5th floor; high enough away from most of the noise, but close enough to run up to your room in between panels and it's not too stressful if you don't want to wait for the elevator."

"Thanks. We appreciate that."

"Here are your welcome packets." She withdrew two folders from under her arm. Each was labeled with their names. "Inside you'll find everything you need for your schedule, a map of the hotel, the full convention schedule, meal vouchers for the hotel restaurant, a couple of bonus drink vouches for the bar, and of course, we hope that you'll join us at the mixer upstairs in the Willis Studio."

"We're looking forward to it."

They began walking as Laurie kept talking.

"If you need anything, my phone number is in there, as well as quick contact to the Con-Ops, security, and the front desk. Your badges are also in the folders. Your first panel is at eleven AM. A lot of guests like to walk the venue the night before and get a feel for the space. Make notes about where their panels are."

"That's definitely a good idea," Isaac agreed.

Laurie stopped in front of the bay of elevators, tapping one of the buttons. "So, here's the elevators. I'll let you two go get settled. If you need anything, I'll be here in the lobby greeting the other guests as they come in –or, like I said, call or text me. I'll answer as quickly as I can."

"Thank you," Harper spoke up.

"You're very welcome. If I don't see you before, I'll see you tonight at the Mixer." Laurie ushered them into the opening door. "Go relax for a bit before it gets too crazy."

Upon entering the hotel room, they each dumped their luggage onto one of the beds. Isaac wrapped Harper up in another hug.

"We have some time to kill. Should we be good, responsible guests and look through the welcome packet now? Or, should we take advantage of the free hotel room and fuck around?" He nipped at her ear as he shuffled toward the closest bed, making it clear which option he liked best.

"I am amiable to some naked time, but first you have to let me go to the bathroom. And maybe take off my coat and boots."

Isaac leaned over, looking down at her knee-high boots. "I'd be okay with you leaving them on."

"I can't leave them on and take off my leggings." She laughed.

"I don't need the leggings off either. Just out of the way."

Harper rolled her eyes. "I forgot about your frottage kink."

Isaac grinned against her lips. "It feels good. Being cock-to-cock with Pietr is fun, but you've got some nice tight spaces." His hands slipped down to her butt, giving her a squeeze. "These are soft though. Leave them on. Let me get them a little dirty."

"You are *not* going to get cum on my leggings. I have to wear these later."

"Do you?" He intoned quizzically. "You packed other clothes." He spun her around, a little roughly. Harper felt a spike of excitement as Isaac pushed her face down onto the bed.

"Fuck, Isaac. I like this –*really* like it, actually. But, I seriously, seriously gotta pee, babe."

Isaac paused before Harper felt him move away from her. "Shit, of course. You said that. I'm sorry."

Harper got to her feet again. She shrugged out of her coat, tossing it onto their luggage.

"Don't apologize and get that look off your face. You didn't do anything *wrong*," she chided. "Get naked. I'll be back in a minute. We can pick that back up."

"I'll text Pietr and Misha that we got here," Isaac called as she walked toward the bathroom. "It looks like they both dropped messages in the group chat."

"Thank you!"

Harper took her time in the bathroom and was mildly disappointed to find that Isaac had gotten as far as stripping down to his boxers. He'd opened the thick set of curtains to allow in some natural light before getting comfortable on the bed. She had unzipped the boots and kicked them off, as well as removing the Scorch hoodie she'd been wearing under her jacket. She tossed it onto the luggage pile before getting onto the bed.

"You still have the most important part covered," she teased.

Isaac looked up from his phone with a smirk. "You're still dressed too."

"You implied you didn't mind that."

"How silly of me." Isaac tossed the phone down onto the table between the beds. He wrapped an arm around her waist, hauling her forward. "Make a mental note that I will always take a naked Harper over a clothed Harper." He kissed her finger tips before he trailed under the hem of her shirt, up her back.

Harper let out a little moan. She cupped his face in her hands. While Isaac didn't sport a beard that she could dig her nails into, like Pietr did, his cheeks were fresh and smooth from that morning's shave. Inhaling, she got an intense whiff of his aftershave. Spicy and hot. Masculine. Him. Different from Pietr or Misha. He kissed differently too. Pietr liked lots of short, sweet kisses, whenever he could steal one. Misha was always good for long, soul-reaching kisses that left them both a little breathless. Isaac seemed to reserve kissing for greetings, partings, and sex.

"You're thinking very loudly," Isaac interrupted her thoughts.

"Just pondering how different my guys are," Harper admitted. "This is nice, but it's not where we left off."

"I might have gone a little overboard."

Harper leaned back, looking down at him. "What do you mean?"

"I shouldn't treat you like that."

Harper raised an eyebrow. "...Go on."

"It's not very respectful." His tone made the statement sound like more of a question. Like he knew that he was interpreting the situation different from Harper.

"Isaac." She shifted her weight in his lap, sitting back on his thighs. "You've seen firsthand how Misha pushes me around. Pietr too, sometimes. You shoving me onto the bed is nothing compared to what they've given me. And I *like* it. If I didn't, I would tell you."

"I do know how you are with them," Isaac admitted. "I respect that you guys like to do that together. I don't feel comfortable pushing your limits."

"Okay," she nodded, "but, I need *you* to make the mental note that my threshold for that is *way* higher than spinning me around and holding me down." She laughed, pressing her forehead to his. "It was a little surprising, coming from you. You're usually so careful."

"I don't want to hurt you. Pietr would kill me."

"Pietr isn't here right now," she chided. "From my personal perspective, doing some things with the both of you is far more likely to push my comfort zone than anything you've ever done with me while we're alone." She nuzzled him with a nose kiss. "I *like* when you take what you want."

He grunted.

"You wanna try again?" She tried to tempt him. "I was teasing before. I brought plenty of clothes for this trip. You can get these leggings as dirty as you want."

The grunt turned into a low growl. Harper let out a squeak and another laugh as he shoved her off his lap and onto the mattress. He wasn't *rough* with her. Not the way that Pietr and Misha would have been. She tried to stay loose, letting him push her around.

"You mean that?" Isaac's voice was in her ear as he held her hands behind her back. She could feel him behind her. The fabrics between them did absolutely nothing to hide Isaac's growing erection.

"Yes."

There was a brief silence as Isaac adjusted again. He pushed her tunic halfway up her back before he noticed— "Harper, are you not wearing underwear?"

She laughed again. "I don't own anything besides trunks anymore, and they show through so..."

"*Fuck.*"

Harper felt his cock against her backside.

"You're not going to get it in my hair this time, are you?"

"Hush." He let go of her wrists to press his palms into the mattress on either side of her. "I'm gonna cum wherever I cum and you're going to like it." He raised onto one hand to use the other to brush her hair away from her face before kissing her cheek. "If we were kinky, I'd tell you to keep wearing them after I'm done with you." His tongue traced the curve of her ear. "Covered in my cum and I *know* your pussy is drenched. You'd smell like sex all night. How many people would notice?"

Harper cringed shaking her head. She made a little noise of discontent. "No way."

He chuckled. "Don't worry. Best behavior. But you can take them home to Pietr? Ask him to unpack your bag and find the mess."

"He might like that. He'd probably ask why I don't do the same with him."

Isaac grinned, nipping at her skin now. "Pietr craves two things –oral and penetration. He enjoys this, the frottage thing, but he'd much rather taste or fill. Or be filled."

"True," Harper agreed. She pulled her arms free to lean up on her elbows. She had to twist slightly for the brief kiss to the mouth. "This feels good though."

"These leggings are butter soft. Did you buy them with this in mind?"

"No," she admitted, "but I'll look into getting a few more pair if you like it."

"I like it a lot. Can you feel how hard I am?"

"Yes."

"You want this cock inside you, don't you?"

His breath was warm in her ear.

"My *pussy* wants it. I'm wet as fuck. *I* want you to enjoy yourself."

"When I'm done, I'll make sure you cum too," he promised. Then he let out a little "oh!". "Hold on. I have an idea."

Harper whined he moved away from her.

"Come here," he instructed. He got comfortable again in the pillows. He'd discarded his boxers and he patted his bare thighs. "Come ride my cock."

"With the leggings on?" She confirmed.

"Yeah," he grinned.

"Well, at least with these on, we don't have another accidental creampie incident..." Harper's eyes widened as she realized. "Oh fuck, I didn't tell you about that, did I?"

Isaac raised an eyebrow. "I want to hear about it, but...I also want to finish. Can you tell me later?"

"Yes," Harper promised. She squatted over his lap.

"Goddamn, Harper." He wrapped his arms around her. "You're *so* warm and wet. You're totally lubing my cock."

Harper leaned back, pulling the tunic shirt off. She didn't have an issue with Isaac getting her leggings dirty –but the shirt was a different story. And this position definitely lent itself to a different mess...

"Harder."

Isaac dug into her hips, rocking her along his cock. For as soft and "buttery" as they were, the leggings were thin enough; Harper knew she was coating Isaac's cock with a layer of her own juices. The head ridge of his cock teased her clit –just barely. She didn't want to stop and adjust; to make sure it was sliding against the right spot...

"Oh fuck!" Isaac pulled her more tightly into his lap. "So good!" He didn't ask, wrapping her up and tipping her onto her back. He peppered kisses across her cheeks and down her neck as he thrust harder into her from above. Faster until he let out a very satisfied moan into her throat. He stilled for a moment, then made a few slower, gentler thrusts. He backed away slowly, looking down at the load of warm cum spread across the front of her leggings.

"So sorry, babe," he apologized. "I got carried away."

"No need to apologize," she assured him. "It felt good."

"Let's get these off you." He kissed her softly before settling back. He tugged the messy leggings from her hips, rolling them down her thighs and then off each of her ankles before tossing them in the general direction of the other bed. He looked down at her, giving a small shake of his head. "Like you said, wet as fuck."

Harper drew in a sharp breath as his tongue found her clit and he sucked softly. He slipped two fingers inside, stroking. She relaxed into his touch until she felt the familiar wave wash over her. She squeezed her thighs, reaching down to gently push him away.

"Okay, okay. Enough." She laughed lightly.

"That didn't sound like a very big one. Pietr will complain if I don't take care of you properly." Isaac grumbled as he stretched out to join her. He kissed her, then grinned as she took his face between her hands to lick the dampness from his cheeks. "I get it." He wiped his cheeks with a palm, before settling.

"So," he began after a few moments of catching their breaths, "you said something about an accidental creampie? I assume you mean Misha did this."

"It wasn't Misha's *fault*. It was a mutual accident."

"Uh huh. Please enlighten me as to how you accidentally cum inside someone?"

"It was when I was visiting him. We met Cecil at their house." Harper filled him in on the whole story, including

Misha's vasectomy status. She also added in Pietr and Cecil's reactions to the incident. Then the ultimate decision they'd made to *not* do it again.

"Why didn't you tell me?" Isaac asked.

"I don't know. When I got home, Pietr and I had another little talk about it. You didn't seem surprised when Pietr and I said we still planned on using condoms after I got the IUD. Even with Pietr, it was a while before we stopped using them. With the vasectomy, there's minimal risk. Not that I'm pressuring you! But there *is* a risk with you."

"I understand," he assured her. "I don't mind using condoms. When we don't want to, we do...this." He reached around her, giving her ass a light smack. "I'm not mad. If Pietr knew and was fine with it, I'm not worried. I just want to be part of the conversation."

"I didn't mean to leave you out of it."

"I know you didn't. That was a special trip for you and you got some well-deserved, much needed private time with Misha. Just like we've gotten time together."

"I did tell you that he's going to come to New York after his regular season is done? They're not likely to make the play-offs this year."

"You did tell me that one," Isaac assured her. He gave her another short kiss before giving her another swat on the thigh. "Come on. Let's get cleaned up and then go through that welcome packet, huh?"

Chapter Twenty-nine

"Damn, I'd hoped you would put on another pair of leggings."

"We both know if I'd done that, you would have been walking around with a hard-on *all* night."

Isaac shrugged. He slid one of the room keys into his wallet before shoving it back into his pocket. He picked up his phone and shoved it into a different pocket. "You ready to scope out the venue before we go to dinner?"

"Yes."

They made their way out of the hotel and back down to the ground floor. They had spent a few minutes in the hotel looking over their welcome packet and had mapped out the panel rooms. Walking around the mostly empty hotel made for quick work in finding the rooms themselves and Harper made mental notes on learning the pathways around. They were stopped a few times by other guests, saying hellos, then by convention staff asking if they needed help with anything. Eventually, they made their way into the hotel restaurant, presenting their meal vouchers.

"Are you ready for tomorrow?" Isaac asked, picking up one of the laminated menus.

Harper nodded. "I am not expecting any kind of repeat of the debacle at KongKon, if that's what you're worried about. For one thing, we're halfway across the country and Chicago has its own hockey team –and they beat the Osprey the last time they played. So, I doubt there's any kind of animosity there."

"True enough. But you're comfortable? We each have a couple of panels where we aren't going to be together."

"It's not like I've never spoken in front of people before, Isaac. I'll be fine."

"I know you will be. I just wanted to make sure *you* know you will be."

Harper rolled her eyes then skimmed the menu herself. "What are you thinking? Maybe the cavatappi pasta?"

They discussed the options a bit before settling. A waitress appeared with their drinks and then took their orders back to the kitchen. Harper swirled her straw around in the cola and ice.

"Are you excited about any of the other guests?" Isaac asked. "Someone you want to make sure to meet?"

"I honestly don't know who most of the other guests are, other than *Oh, I've seen that anime* or that I listened to an episode of their podcast. The band that's invited sounds fun."

"So, you did some research on the other guests?"

"I didn't want to run into someone and not know who they were when I should. Otherwise, they might revoke my Geek Card."

"You love three things. Writing, hockey, and video games." Isaac smiled. "Well, you love more than that, but those are at the top."

"You *do* know me!" Harper chirped before taking a sip of her cola. "What about you? Who are you excited for?"

"Well, I already know a couple of the other streamers," he said. "Through collab planning and whatever. A couple of cosplay guests are great –and they have Yuna Hita! I was in love with *Sensei Go!*. I have the complete series for both manga and anime.

"Such a nerd," Harper teased.

"You knew that when you met me."

"You were introduced to me by Pietr streaming with you, so...yeah, it was pretty evident from the very beginning." Harper grinned. "It has its perks. You don't tease me when I complain about sticky controllers or joy-con drift."

"Babe," he shook his head, "I will never do anything but agree with you about how annoying joy-con drift is. Worst controllers on one of the best systems. Such a downer."

"I am looking forward to trying to go to a couple of the other panels. There's a Disney Lore panel between our Q&A and my writing panel, and then there's some gaming, board games, stuff happening that could be a lot of fun."

"I didn't even look beyond the panels yet," he admitted. "But yeah, some board games for something different could be fun. The next time we're all together in the same room?"

"Play it with Parker branches out?"

"Diversifying has been working very well for us."

"For you," she countered. "My portion still goes to charity."

"You know if you ever need that to change, we can restructure," he said. "People aren't going to be mad."

"Pietr makes more than enough to support us right now," Harper said. "Not to mention what I make on my writing. Is it big hockey money? No. But it's enough to keep us comfortable. I *like* being able to do something that generates help for other people. Not that Pietr and I don't already give to a lot of other things, and of course; supporting the Osprey

Foundation. I even went with him to one of the children's hospital visits a couple of weeks ago. It's one that the team rotates visiting on an almost weekly basis. One of the kids asked Pietr about you and me. He was waiting for an organ transplant."

"I used to hate those trips," Isaac admitted. "You have to talk to them like they're a perfectly normal kid while knowing that some of them aren't going to make it to the end of the week, or the month. The ones we only met once weren't so bad. But the ones we'd talk to every visit? Those were hard."

"Agree. But you can also see that even the ones who couldn't care less about hockey, like the momentary distraction. It was interesting. I'm glad I went, but I don't want to make a habit of it."

"Was it a good visit? The kid?"

"It was. He was sweet. Very excited. We played a couple of rounds of Smash. Before you ask, *no* I did not let him win. I slaughtered him. Von and Pietr were nicer."

"Nah," Isaac shook his head with a smile. "You can't give them an inch. Otherwise they think you're just jerking them around. Trust me. That kid *loved* that you beat him."

"I think he also enjoyed seeing Von get worked up about it. He was looking forward to a rematch, since I beat him at that cook-out last June. Jazz said he's been practicing, but I didn't notice a difference."

"You're so mean." Isaac laughed.

Harper shrugged. "You know how I can be."

"I do –and that's why I like co-op games with you. You bring us all up, rather than tearing us down."

Harper smiled. "Yeah, yeah."

They were interrupted briefly as the waitstaff appeared with their orders. They chatted more over their meal. When they'd finished, Isaac tossed some cash down on the table for a tip.

"We have about thirty minutes before the Mixer is supposed to start," he said, scooting out of his side of the booth. "You want to go back upstairs or should we walk around the venue a bit more?"

"I wouldn't mind doing some more walking around. Check out the gaming area, maybe? And the mixer is way up on the top floor, right?"

"Right," he nodded. "I think the gaming stuff is on the other side of the center courtyard?"

Harper pulled out her phone. "I downloaded the convention app. Hold on."

"Good idea." Isaac hooked a finger into the belt loop on the back of her jeans. He peered over her shoulder as the app loaded.

Harper clicked through a few things on her screen, then rotated her phone. "Okay, so this way..."

They were crossing the "garden court", a large raised platform in the middle of the hotel. There was an open space on one end with a couple of different backdrops; Harper guessed it was the cosplay photo area. There were also a lot of open tables and chairs.

"Oh my gosh, you're Harper Wyatt!"

Harper stilled, automatically tensing. Isaac stopped with her, moving his hand to her back in reassurance. He turned her toward the voice.

"Uh, yes?"

"I'm so sorry! Did I surprise you? I didn't consider that. I'm Maggie. Princess Magnolia. I'm one of the special guests too."

Harper took in the woman in front of her. She was tall. *Really* tall. She had to tip her head back slightly to take in all of her as the woman got closer. Her own companion was trailing behind her, tapping away at a tablet.

"Nice to meet you." Harper shook her hand.

"And Isaac Parker too!" Maggie was grinning so hard Harper couldn't help but think it must hurt. "I love your stream. I watch it a lot. It's great background noise for when Jess and I are working on costuming. Or just, literally doing anything."

"Wait, wait." Isaac stared at her for a moment. "You're Maggie *Gravesen*. You played for University of Wisconsin hockey and were on the last women's Olympic team."

"Guilty." A pink tinge brightened on Maggie's cheeks. "You actually inspired me to get into cosplay! I thought, if a guy like you, who could have such a great hockey career, could go into something as nerdy as video game streaming –then, why couldn't I try being a cosplayer? Right now, it's a part-time thing. I'm also playing for the Minneapolis Snow Caps in the AWHL –the American Women's Hockey League. Women's pro-hockey is still finding its footing and its fans."

"No way!" Isaac's eyes brightened. "It's been on my radar, but I haven't been able to find the time to really look at teams. Congratulations. That's so cool."

"Congrats," Harper said.

"No –shit, I came over to talk to *you*, not about myself." Maggie waved a hand. "Being a jock is boring as fuck. We're all here to geek it up over the weekend, right?"

Harper laughed. "Something like that."

"Uh –so, I have to do this right now because I don't want to miss the chance." Maggie ran a nervous hand through her hair. "Thank you *so much* for coming out as polyamorous. Like, for both of you –and Pietr, for just being who you are. It means so much to so many people and you have no idea."

"I mean, we read the feed," Isaac shrugged. "We get occasional e-mails."

"Sure, but I don't think you can really be told enough how much having representation, not just in this community," she waved a hand toward the ceiling of the hotel, "but also in the *athletic* community, in the hockey community, matters. I've been out since high school. Gay as hell. It was never an issue. But when Jess and I opened our relationship, mostly so she could explore her bi side, we got *so much shit*. People thinking she was cheating on me. That I was cheating on *her*. When it's not like that at all! And like, no, I'm not interested in dudes in general, but we've made friends with each other's other partners. It's, weirdly, made us more social."

"Really?" Harper asked. "Sometimes I think it put us into more of a bubble."

"I like our bubble." Isaac shrugged.

"It's different for everyone. There isn't a *wrong way* to do polyam. Jess dates a lot while I tend to do more one-time hook-ups. Harper, you've got two boyfriends *and* a husband. Isaac, you date a bit."

"I just started seeing someone recently. It's not an official thing. Yet. Maybe. I don't know. But yeah, I get what you mean." Isaac's fingers flexed against Harper's back.

"That's so awesome!"

"Mags." The woman that had been hovering behind her gave her a poke in the side. "I don't want to interrupt your fangirling, but if we're going to grab dinner before the mixer, we should probably get going?"

"Shit! Yes. Sorry, Jess." Maggie slid her hand into her girlfriend's hand. "Uh, Jess, you are familiar with Harper Wyatt and Isaac Parker."

"You only make me watch their stream *constantly*. And the YouTube channel. And follow them on Instagram. And Twitter. And Facebook." Jess looked up at Harper. "I read your books. They're very enjoyable. Have you ever considered writing a lesbian hockey novel? I'd read the shit out of that."

"Uhh..." Harper faltered, "I'm not sure I feel comfortable writing lesbian fiction. I don't, er, have much...any...experience in that area. Dicks are just so much easier."

"Girl, I hear you." Jess rolled her eyes. Then stopped. "Shit. Sorry. You're nonbinary. I *know* that. My bad."

"No worries. I colloquially refer to myself in feminine terms all the time," Harper assured her.

"It was nice to meet you," Maggie said. "We'll see you later at the mixer?"

"We'll be there. We're checking out some of the other areas beforehand. We just finished dinner. We can recommend the pasta, if you like mushrooms, and the house burger," Harper said.

"Great. See you later then." Maggie smiled again. Jess pushed her lightly away from the other couple, murmuring something under her breath that Harper didn't quite catch.

"I thought you said you looked up the other guests?" Isaac moved his arm over her shoulders, steering her across the courtyard again. "How did you miss that *Maggie Graveson* would be here?"

"I just looked at the con website! All it said was stuff about her cosplay!"

Chapter Thirty

Pietr swiped a hand through his sweat soaked hair. They were tied against Washington at the end of the 2nd period, 2-2. He had resisted checking his phone during the 1st period break, but he couldn't do it again.

[ISAAC] Harper and I are checked into the hotel.

He let out a little sigh of relief. He hadn't actually been worried that they *wouldn't* make it to Chicago unscathed. That didn't mean he couldn't appreciate the confirmation.

[ISAAC] We just met Maggie Gravesen!

[MISHA] Who is that?

[ISAAC] Olympic Champion. Led WI Badgers to a NCAA Championship two years ago. Now she plays for Minneapolis Snow Caps in the AWHL.

[MISHA] What the fuck is the AWHL?

[ISAAC] You are shitting me, right? The American Women's Hockey League.

[MISHA] I didn't know there was such a thing.

[MISHA] I'm not saying women cannot or should not play hockey. I just wasn't aware.

[MISHA] You're obviously very excited. I'm glad you could meet this lady.

[MISHA] Is she cute?

[ISAAC] Yeah?

The first picture he'd dropped was of a very tall, and yes, attractive young woman in a Wisconsin Badger's uniform. The second picture was of the same woman, but in a revealing Lora Croft cosplay. The hockey thighs lent something to the costume.

[ISAAC] That's why she's here! She's a cosplayer.

[HARPER] She was very nice. She thanked us for our representation.

[HARPER] You know, being out as queer and polyam.

[MISHA] I understood.

[HARPER] She's a lesbian and polyam with her bi girlfriend, by the way.

[HARPER] Not outing her. She's public about it.

[MISHA] Safe space, Kitten. I get it.

[HARPER] Pietr, congrats on your goal. I just got the alert.

The little heart-eyes emoji made him smile.

[PIETR] Thank you baby. Glad you made it okay and are having fun.

He tossed his phone onto the shelf before sitting. He eased off the skates long enough to take a bathroom break, then ripped into a protein bar that McKinley handed him.

"You okay?" Kinley asked.

"Yeah. Harper and Isaac got to Chicago," he filled him in. "Trying to find that second wind for this last period."

"I feel ya." McKinley pressed a hand to his side. "Hedburg elbowed me when he slammed me on the boards at the top of the second."

"We can feel secure in a play-off spot with this win," Adam piped up on the other side of him. "So get it together."

"It is together," Pietr assured him. "I get it. Bring home the W. Primary goal."

In the beginning of the third, Pietr got an assist for Gregor making another goal. Matched a minute later by Washington. With five minutes left in the period, he managed a from-behind-the-net scoop over their goalie's shoulder, which the competition again answered with forty-five seconds to go.

Coach Harrows swore loudly and Pietr grimaced. In overtime, he joined McKinley and Gregor for the first line. Another five minutes on the clock was a battle up and down across the ice. He twice tried to get through their goalie's defense, but no luck. And they didn't fare any better. Shoot Out it was.

"West, Hale, and Ivanov," Harrows barked. "In that order."

"Fuck." McKinley swore. "I hate shoot outs."

"You got this." Pietr clapped him on the shoulder.

Their opponent's first shot went completely wide. McKinley's bounced off the pipe. The second, Rychtik didn't get his glove up quite fast enough and the goal alarm sounded. Adam flicked a last second backhanded shot into the corner pocket as the Goalie dived, tying it up. The third Washington shot, Rychtik caught easily, flinging the puck back onto the ice. Pietr took a deep breath. He could win this game now. He wanted that notification to go off in Harper's pocket. To get another sweet text, knowing she was paying attention to the score.

"You got this, Tesla!" He heard Gregor shout from box.

He zeroed in on the goalie. He was familiar with Henry York. He'd played for Washington for the last fifteen seasons. He was good, but he was getting old. He was slowing down.

He wasn't delusional. That "the arena fell away and it was just him and the net" thing that happened in the movies wasn't real. But he tuned out the crowd hissing at him. He focused on the feel of the ice under his skates and the puck tapping against his rainbow tape. He zeroed in on the right side of the net as York seemed to flinch left. He flicked the puck, almost effortlessly over York's elbow. A soft *ting* as it hit the back post of the net before tumbling down to the ice.

There was a cheer from the Osprey fans in the crowd, as well as from his teammates. Pietr felt a wash of relief, skating across the ice to accept congratulations from his teammates, then to go congratulate Rychtik on his efforts. He got pulled aside to talk to the media. It felt like an eternity, even though it couldn't have been more than fifteen or twenty minutes before he could pick up his phone again.

[HARPER] Congrats on your shoot out goal. Way to bring home the W.

Pietr grinned at the kissy face emoji at the end of the text.

[PIETR] Thanks love. On my way to the airport soon. Are you having fun still?

[HARPER] Isaac and I are at a guest mixer. It's pretty chill.

[PIETR] Can I call when we get home in a couple hours?

[HARPER] Of course. I want to hear all about your game.

[HARPER] I'm sorry I didn't watch. I'll watch the highlights later.

[PIETR] You're busy networking. Don't worry about it.

[PIETR] I love you.
[HARPER] Love you too.

"Pietr had a good game?" Isaac asked.

"Won in a shoot-out," Harper answered. "He and Adam both made goals."

"Good for them. Are you gonna put your phone away now?"

"Yes! I'm sorry!" Harper tucked the device back into her back pocket. "Your husband makes a winning goal and you send him a text, okay? It's like Wifey 101."

"You're so sweet," Maggie laughed. She'd found them almost immediately upon entering the mixer and beelined for them. They'd been chatting ever since. "Jess doesn't even bother coming to my games anymore."

"Jess isn't a hockey fan?"

"No way." Maggie shook her head. "We met in an Art History class I took as an elective. That's Jess's background. She's doing a master's program online and works at one of the museums in Minneapolis." She gave a wistful sigh. "She thought I was a dumb jock, I thought she was an uptight egghead. It was basically love at first sight. Or...first party hook-up, maybe? It's a little blurry. We've been together for like six years."

"Dang," Harper said.

Maggie shrugged. "When you find the one, you stick with them. And look at you and Pietr. You only met, what? A year and a half ago? You moved right in. Totally

U-Hauling. Then got married? Anyone who doesn't see you two as an obviously queer couple is blind."

"I try to ignore people who don't get it. We know it and that's enough."

"You guys are so cute," Maggie gushed. "Can I ask a super out-of-left-field question?"

"Sure?"

"What's your polycule policy for hooking up?"

"Oh!" Harper didn't hide her surprise. "I prefer talk to Pietr. We generally feel like we should tell each other out of courtesy."

"That seems easy."

"We haven't put it to a lot of testing," Harper admitted.

"Would you like to?"

"Are you flirting with my girlfriend in front of me?" Isaac asked, feigning a surprised tone.

"No, I'm horrible at flirting! But I know she's polyam, AFAB, and we've been having a really nice conversation so...like," Maggie shrugged, "I guess if you're interested in having a little fun together tonight, or sometime this weekend, I'm into it?" She cleared her throat. "Jess and I already chatted about it. She's cool and willing to give us space in our room for a bit."

Harper opened her mouth to answer, but no sound came out.

"No pressure! You're just, you're very cute. I'd kick myself for months if I didn't at least ask. You can so totally say you're not interested and—"

"I've never done anything with a woman before," Harper blurted. "Not because I haven't wanted to, or don't have an interest, but...uh, yeah."

"You alluded to that earlier," Maggie reminded her. She smirked, raising one shoulder. "I'm a good teacher?"

"You can do what you want, as far as I'm concerned," Isaac assured her. He tipped back the beer glass he'd been holding, draining the final dregs. "I'm going to go get another drink and check out the snacks. You two can discuss this on your own."

Harper's teeth clenched, wanting to make him stay. She watched him mosey to the bar then looked at Maggie. "Pietr is about to get on a plane. I can text him, but I'm not sure when he'll see it."

"I'm less worried about Pietr's answer and more curious if you're interested?"

"Yes! I mean..." Harper cleared her throat. "If you're okay with me being a total anxious newb, then sure."

Maggie grinned. "How about I give you my number. You can text Pietr and when you get an answer from him, you can let me know. We'll go from there."

Harper nodded, pulling her phone back out. She tapped the screen, opening up a fresh text. "Send yourself a message from my phone?"

Maggie took the device, tapping in some numbers. There was a quiet *whoosh* before she handed it back. Maggie's fingers grazed Harpers as the exchange was made.

"There you go. I hope to hear from you soon."

"I'll text Pietr right now," she promised.

"Good. I better go check in with Jess. Make sure she isn't going on some tirade about the hotel art or something. Talk later."

"Later," Harper repeated.

She blew out a breath she hadn't realized she'd been holding. She had a vice grip on her phone that she released too. She looked down at the screen, seeing that Maggie had sent herself a Peach emoji.

She tapped back to her message list and selected the group text.

[HARPER] Hey, so Maggie Gravesen wants to sleep with me?

[HARPER] ...Is that okay?

Chapter Thirty-one

Pietr was pulling out his phone to put it into airplane mode when he saw the text.

[HARPER] Hey, so Maggie Gravesen wants to sleep with me?

[HARPER] ...Is that okay?

"What's wrong?" Tim elbowed him. "You look like someone died."

"What?" He looked up, confused. "No. I'm fine. Harper is..." He cleared his throat. "Harper is making friends at the convention."

Tim didn't ask, tipping Pietr's phone screen to read the text. Pietr didn't stop him.

"Whoa, shit! –Who's Maggie Gravesen?"

"She is a hockey player for Minnesota Snow Caps. Was Wisconsin Badger player. Olympian."

"So, she's you with a vagina?"

"She is American," Pietr retorted. Then paused. "...Shit, I am American now too."

"You going to answer her before we get on the plane? Misha already gave it an OK.

Pietr looked down, not having registered the response.

[MISHA] I would be mad if I found out you had that chance and didn't take it.

[MISHA] Have fun. Be safe.

[MISHA] Take pics?

[HARPER] No! No pics!

Pietr swallowed hard. Misha had the right idea, and yet...there was this knot in his stomach. He'd been expecting this ask for months. Now that it was here?

"How long until we board?"

"Ten minutes or so?" Tim answered.

"I need to make a call."

"Hurry it up," Tim replied.

Pietr stepped away from the team to try and find a little quiet. He tapped Harper's name and waited for her to answer. When she did, there was a lot of noise in the background.

"Hi Pietr. Let me step out of the party..."

"It's okay. No rush." There *was* a rush. Tim was already eyeing him for pushing it.

"Are you not on your plane home yet? I didn't think you'd see my text for a few hours. Or, is this not about the text?"

"It is about the text, baby," he said. "I didn't feel like that was something I could say *go for it* to in a text. I needed to talk to you."

"You can say no, Pietr."

"I don't want to say no. I want to hear that you want to do that. That you like this woman."

"It's not going to be like Misha. Maggie likes hook-ups. It's a one-time thing. She's a fan of the stream. She's also...did you see the pics? She's fucking gorgeous, Pietr."

He let out a light laugh. "She is attractive, yes, but too...not you, for me."

"If that's you saying she's skinny or athletic or whatever, very sweet, but it's not about that and you know it."

"I know."

"You want to say no, don't you?"

"I have expected you to ask this for a while. I won't say that I am surprised. I am...nervous."

"Nervous? Why?"

"Because, what if you really like doing this? What if you realize that being with a woman is what you want more than..."

"More than you? Pietr, listen to yourself. Do you feel that way when it comes to me versus Isaac?"

"No. You know I like certain things with Isaac, that I can't do with you. Or, aren't the same."

"Exactly. So why would you think I'd be any different about this?"

"I don't know!"

"Don't yell." Harper's voice went soft. "Pietr, I'll tell her no if you're not—"

"I won't tell you not to do something," he declared. "I am going to ask you to...not tell me about it."

"What?"

"I hope you enjoy yourself. Have fun. Please don't give me the details."

"Pietr..."

He ran his hands through his hair. "I don't know why this is different. I usually like hearing how it goes." He let out a sort of bitter laugh. "I can't this time."

Harper was quiet for a second. "I know you're getting on a plane in a few minutes. I don't want this eating at you until we talk next. I'm going to tell her it's a no-go."

"Harper, please. Have some fun with your fan."

"We are having fun. She's very nice. Funny. This is a whim for her. I've never done a random one-night-stand sort of thing."

"You don't need my permission."

"I *do*," she pressed. "Pietr, you're my husband. I love you. While I want to try something new, I'm not going to let you get upset about it."

"I'm not upset."

"You are. Deep down in your gut, you don't want me to do it. Is it because you don't know her? Because it's a *her*? You had no second thoughts about ever including Isaac, or even questioning when I brought up Misha."

"They're different."

"They're your friends."

Pietr sighed. Tim was signaling him to wrap it up as the other guys started walking to the boarding area.

"Baby," he spoke firmly, "I have to get on the plane. Please, *please*, do it and have fun. I don't want to be the reason you miss out on this. I am sure she is a wonderful person, and she is going to take care of you. I hope you enjoy it."

"Pietr, you're—"

"I'm sorry, Harper. I have to go. We're boarding. Promise me, right now. You will not let me hold you back?"

She was quiet.

"Harper? I need to hear it *now*." He started walking toward Tim who was looking exasperated.

"If we do, I won't tell you about it. Unless you ask. So, make sure if you do ask that you really want to know."

"Agreed. I love you."

"I love you too."

"Don't be mad."

"I'm not mad. I'm exasperated."

"Same thing. I'll still try and call when we land. If you don't answer, I'll assume you're busy."

Harper was quiet again.

"Harper?"

"I'll talk to you later. Bye."

"Bye *lyubov moya*. Talk soon."

He tapped off the phone and swiped to click on the airplane mode.

"Is everything okay?" Tim asked.

"*Da.*"

But it didn't feel like everything was fine and he couldn't pinpoint why.

Chapter Thirty-two

"You look upset," Isaac noted as Harper sat beside him. He'd found a cozy nook in the back corner with his plate of treats and another beer.

"I don't know what to do."

"About what?"

"Maggie."

"I saw Misha was for it. What did Pietr say?"

"Pietr *said* yes, but he doesn't want me to."

"Why do you think that?"

"He said he was nervous. That if I slept with a woman, maybe I wouldn't want him. Which is stupid."

"Agree. That's the same shit that people say to us all the time. He's better than that." Isaac frowned. "Harp, you know that was just anxiety talking. He doesn't actually think that. He knows you love him."

"Of course, I do, which is why I feel like I have to give Maggie a pass."

"What? Why? He said yes."

"He did, but spontaneous hook-ups are not our deal. He isn't texting me to bang anyone he meets while he's off traveling city to city for days at a time. We have you, and I have Misha."

"But you've never done anything with a woman before. I'm not saying this is a once-in-a-lifetime opportunity, but it is Maggie Gravesen."

"I know. She's very nice, but I can't..."

"Okay, you know he's going to be mad if he said go for it and you hold back because of him."

"Maggie isn't the only woman on the planet," Harper said. "I have really got to branch out from hockey players. This is a whole new level of having a type. I'm appalled with myself."

"You like what you like." Isaac held out his plate. "Mini quiche?"

Harper popped the *hors d'oeuvre* into her mouth, thankful to have something to do with her mouth other than speak.

"Can I say something?" He sat up, leaning in close to her.

"Yes."

"I wouldn't have thought Pietr would have any qualms about this. It's your whole thing. Giving each other the space to grow and try new things, while supporting and loving each other. But, for the last year, the two of you have been so wrapped up in you adapting to Pietr's life, he hasn't had to make adjustments to adapt to *your* life." Isaac reached over to squeeze her knee. "Pietr was the first person to love you, just for being you. What would pre-Pietr Harper say to Maggie?"

"Pre-Pietr Harper would have blushed like crazy, laughed like a moron, and run away."

"And Current Harper?"

"Current Harper is nervous as fuck but *really* wants to know what eating pussy is like."

Isaac laughed. "Surprisingly crude, babe. I'd say it's like sucking dick, except not at all."

"I'm not exactly confident in my skills in that department either."

"You can practice on me anytime. I'm pretty sure Pietr and Misha have no complaints. I won't tell you that you're great. You wouldn't believe me anyway. But you *are* enthusiastic and you take direction well. When you're confident, and you want it, it's sexy as hell." Isaac squeezed her knee again. "Is there something else that's making you hesitate?"

"Pietr said he doesn't want to know anything about it. After."

"What's wrong with that? I don't want regular updates on what you're doing either."

"It was the *way* he said it. I don't know how I feel about keeping something like that from him. He likes to know what Misha and I do together. Highlights. Not like major rehashing. So, not being able to say anything about it? What if she does something amazing?"

"You can tell me," he offered.

"That's not the same. Pietr and I talk about *everything*. Having him tell me point-blank that he doesn't want to hear about this specific thing feels off. Like he's telling me it's *bad* that I want to. It's an unexpected limitation, or a punishment for even considering it."

"Another form of rejection?" Isaac offered.

Harper thought about that for a second before slowly nodding. "That's a good way to describe it."

Isaac shifted in the chair, popping the last little snack into his mouth. When he'd swallowed it, he followed it up with another sip of his beer.

"All right, Harper. Here's my honest opinion, which I recognize that you have not asked for, but I'm giving you anyway. Because you're my girlfriend, and Pietr is my boyfriend, and I love you both very much." He folded his hands together. "He's being a fucking idiot. If you want to have a long conversation about it later tonight on the phone, okay. But, I think if you want to have this experience, you should go for it. We're only here a couple of days. Who knows if you'll ever even see Maggie again. If it goes terribly, it's a decent size convention. You can probably avoid her. But I think you might like it. I think having a fun, casual night, to try something different, is perfectly reasonable. Plus, I've heard that females tend to be way better at getting each other off."

"Isaac, I almost never have any issues getting off with you guys."

"Yeah, because we're all fantastic, respectful lovers who *really* enjoy making you cum. But not all women are as lucky as you," he retorted.

She sighed.

"You're still conflicted," he guessed. "What's it going to take to get you unconflicted? Should we go mingle some more? Do you want to get out of here? Take a break? I think we've been polite enough if you want to call it a night."

Harper shook her head. "I don't want to cut your night short if you're having fun."

"We're going to have fun all weekend," he reminded her. "Calling it early tonight isn't going to impede that."

Harper shook her head. "No, no. You stay. Keep mingling. Making friends. I think I'm just going to go and take a walk around the hotel."

"You sure you don't want me to come with you?"

"Positive. I need some quiet. Maybe I'll go sit in the lounge by the lobby for a little bit. Or, I don't know, see if the Con Staff need help setting anything up. Anything to not be sitting here and being in my head."

"Text me when you're ready for company again. I'll probably head up to the room in another half hour or so."

She nodded. She pushed up from the chair, pausing to give him a quick parting kiss.

"Will do. See you in a bit."

She escaped from the party again, taking the elevator down to the first floor of the hotel. She passed an occasional group of staff, placing décor and putting up signs directing people to various places. She stayed out of their way, taking a seat on a chair in the back of the lounge when she found it again. She let out a breath she hadn't realized she'd been holding and pulled out her phone.

She clicked to open her most recent messages from Pietr. They weren't anything special. A [Have a safe flight] he'd sent earlier that morning, some mundanities like [Should I pick up milk?] or [What's for dinner?]. Scrolling further, the rack up of [I love you]'s was evident. It didn't make her feel any better about the fast conversation that she and Pietr had gotten to have before he got on the plane. Before he was cut off from everything for two hours...more, if including the time it took to get from the airport back to the apartment.

She swallowed hard. Having sex with someone who *wasn't* Pietr wasn't as important to her as her husband was. Sex or no sex. If he wasn't going to give her enthusiastic consent, she wasn't going to do it. End of story. Maybe that was her letting him make a decision for her. Maybe that was her being a push-over. But as much fun as spending an hour or two with Maggie would probably have been, the lifetime ahead with Pietr wasn't worth fracturing.

She tapped the text to Maggie.

[HARPER] Hey. I'm going to turn down the hook-up. Thank you for the offer. It's very flattering, but not the right time.

Maggie's reply was almost instantaneous.

[MAGGIE] No worries.

[MAGGIE] Is everything okay? You looked serious w/ Parker before you dipped out.

[HARPER] Yeah. All good.

[HARPER] See you around the Con

She added a smiley emoji that definitely did not match her current mood.

Chapter Thirty-three

Pietr had never felt more uncomfortable to be on a plane in his life. He'd done a lot of air travel in his 30 years. His first flight had been at three, flying from Omsk to Moscow. By the time he was a teen, flying was second nature. He thought nothing of getting on a plane. He'd flown in all kinds of weather and turbulence. He'd been on a flight from LA to Tokyo as a Junior Worlds player and his plane was struck by geese, taking out an engine. None of that mattered as he sat next to Tim on the flight back to New York. He just wanted to be on the ground. Preferably in Chicago, but he was going to have to settle for home in Manhattan.

"You okay, Tesla?" Tim elbowed him. "Are you even breathing over there?"

Pietr looked over at him. "What?"

"You're upset. Why?"

"I'm not upset," Pietr lied. Mostly because he didn't know *why*. Part of his brain had known for months that Harper was eventually going to meet someone, a woman or feminine someone, who would be interested in her. He had expected it. So why on *earth* was this hitting him so hard? Why was he caught so off guard?

"Right. So, you're not trying to pry up the armrest?"

"What?" He looked down, realizing his knuckles had gone white, tightening on the arm rest. "Fuck." He quickly released his grip. "I'm fine."

"You are clearly not," Tim pressed. "What's up, man? Are you upset about Harper's text? I thought that was like...your whole dynamic. Giving each other the space to explore."

"I told her to go for it."

"But..."

"No but. I told her that she should do whatever she wants."

"Pietr, if you were like this," he waved a hand in Pietr's general direction, "while you were talking to her before we boarded, all she heard was *don't*. Absolutely nothing about your tone or expression says you support that."

"What's up with Pigeon?" Guy stood turning around to lean over the back of the seat. "Sounds serious."

"Nothing."

"She texted to ask if she could sleep with a woman."

"Hot! –I mean, uh..." Guy rolled his eyes upward. "Wait, I'm confused. Do you not want her to? You're doing the whole polyamory thing, so, isn't that part of it?"

"Not necessarily," Pietr said.

"How does it work then?"

Pietr let out a huffy sigh. "We have to inform the other. I told her to go for it. Is fine."

"Is not fine," Tim retorted. "You're upset."

"Why would I be upset? My wife is in Chicago fucking my best friend and now some hot hockey chick I've never met."

There was an extra beat of silence before Guy blinked.

"Wow. First of all, I think you should apologize to Tim for telling him *he's* not your best friend in such an abrupt way."

"Matlock!" Tim scoffed.

"Second of all," Guy ignored him, "hot *hockey chick*? Harper has a type, doesn't she?"

Pietr scrubbed his hands through his hair for what felt like the dozenth time since he'd seen the text. "Her name is Maggie Gravesen."

"Whoa, what?"

Pietr looked up at Gregor who had stood up to lean over the back of the seat, above him.

"Isaac and Harper met Maggie?"

"Yes."

"Oh, he is getting a very long text message when we land. She is amazing. I met her at a training camp...shit, I can't even remember when. She was playing for Badgers. Before the Olympics. I can see her as Harper's type."

"I don't know what you mean," Pietr retorted.

"Maggie ticks all the boxes. Sexy hockey player, giant fucking nerd," Gregor said. "What is she doing at the convention?"

"She's there as a cosplay guest."

"See? Giant fucking nerd," he repeated. "Also...I think I still have her number. I should call her."

"That is all well and good," Pietr said. "Could you two sit back down now?"

"No, no." Gregor waved a hand over him. "I have been listening. Not on purpose. We are all very close together you know. Anyone not wearing headphones totally knows your business, Tesla. We are all concerned about you and Pigeon now. What's the problem?"

"There isn't a problem."

"You seem awfully pissed off for there to be no problem."

"Exactly," Guy agreed. "Walk us through your headspace, buddy."

Pietr muttered under his breath, rolling his eyes.

"I don't know this person," he finally said. "It was different when it was Parker. It was different when it was Levin. I know them. I know I can trust them. This woman, I don't know."

"I know Maggie. She's great. Her girlfriend, Jess, is a real sweetheart too. They've had an open relationship status for years. Jess is bi, likes to date dudes occasionally. Maggie is more...one-and-done, was the vibe I got. Very, eh, have you ever watched L-Word? I think she is a Shane."

"The L Word?" Tim repeated. "Gregor, how queer are you?"

"Pretty fucking queer, thank you," Gregor replied casually.

"Sadly, I know what he's talking about," Pietr admitted. "Harper and I watched it last summer. Shane was the most tolerable character. Especially after Di—"

"Stop," Tim cut him off, "I am not going to hash out The L Word with you."

"Sorry." Pietr replied. He tipped his head up to look at Gregor. "This Maggie. She is a good person?"

"She's fantastic," Gregor assured him. "Great leader, amazing skills –hockey wise. She's a lesbian, so no interest in me in the bedroom. I can't comment on that. She's nice. Funny. Charismatic. *Gorgeous*. Harper would have a good time, if that's what you're worried about."

"I don't know what I am worried about, other than something that is very, very stupid," he admitted.

"What's that?" Guy asked.

Pietr sighed. He'd already told Harper. It was ludicrous. Her sleeping with another AFAB person was *not* going to magically make her feel any differently about him or what they did in bed together. They'd been together for almost a year and a half. Hell, she could probably *learn* some things from the experience. He knew his own experiences with both sexes had aided him over the years.

"If she does this, what if she doesn't want to...I don't know. It's not that I think she's going to divorce me, but what if it changes how we are together? If I'm not enough."

"Pietr, buddy," Guy grimaced, "I say this with love, but she's at least semi-regularly fucking two more dudes besides you. Are you enough for her now?"

"Our relationship with Isaac is not about sex. We could stop any time and be just fine. I can't speak to the dynamic with Misha, but it's not like Harper is, what is the word?"

Sex addict was tossed out, along with *nymphomaniac*, *slut*, *tramp*, among others from around the interior of the plane.

"For fucks sake, do you all think that about Harper?!"

"None of us said we thought Harper was any of those things," Gregor quickly recovered. "You asked for a word and we threw some out."

"There *is* a rumor that Harper is...you know. Really horny," Tim offered.

Pietr swore again. "She is not like that!"

"I know!" Tim rallied. "You have made me very aware of Harper's interests –thank you for that, by the way!"

"You asked!"

"I did not!"

"Hey!" There was a bark from further up in the cabin. "Would you all pipe down back there? Some of us are trying to get in a nap. Eat a fucking protein bar or something and shut up."

"Sorry Coach," they called back.

Tim lowered his voice. "Regardless, no, none of us think about Harper in any way in particular. Cripes, she's your wife."

"Well..." Guy contemplated, "after the whole *we're seeing Isaac Parker* thing came out, I guess I did kind of *wonder*, but also...eh. Harper is sweet and a lot of fun, but like Tim said, too weird to bang a teammate's wife."

"You are an automatic no," Pietr informed him. "Absolutely not."

"Why?" Guy frowned. "I think I'd show Harper a nice time."

Pietr's eyes widened slightly.

"Okay, okay!" He sank back. "The point Tim was trying to make was that Harper is your wife. We respect her as such. The two of you doing the polyam thing is different. It makes people talk and say stupid things. Maybe you've been hearing some of it and that's what's got you worried. But Tesla, man, we all know you and we all know Harper. She isn't going to bang this Maggie lady and not want to be with you. Have you *seen* the way she looks at you?"

"We tease you a lot for the way you latch onto her," Tim admitted. "But the fact is Harper fucking adores you too. Like I said earlier, even if you verbally said yes, if you gave her any indication that you were hesitating, you know she wouldn't do it."

"I don't have a valid reason to be feeling this way. This is...this is..."

"Jealousy?"

"Anxiety?"

"Bad vibes?"

"No. Yes. Something I'm not accustomed to," he said. "I don't know this person and that bothers me."

"What are your rules?" Guy asked. "You two have rules, guidelines, right?"

"We have to inform the other person and we always use protection. That's it."

"She did that. She informed you. Your rules don't stipulate that you have to *know* the person. Or vet them in some way."

"I know that."

"Maybe they should."

"I can't just change the rules on her."

"No, that's not fair to Harper," Tim agreed. "But you *can* sit down and talk about it when she gets back from the convention."

"It's still not fair to her, to either of us. We have completely separate interests. How would we even go about making it fair? She can only sleep with my friends and I can only sleep with hers?"

"That sounds strict," Gregor admitted. "But you each know other people who know people. Like, I know Maggie. I'm willing to vet for her. Maggie is a sweet girl who likes to have fun. She isn't going to be interested in starting up something permanent, so is not like Harper is saying she has new girlfriend."

Pietr took a few minutes to think it over. Gregor had a point. He did trust his assessment of Maggie as a decent person. He could feel some of the tension in his chest and shoulders beginning to release. But it still didn't mean that he was *excited* about Harper doing something without him.

"You're still pensive." Tim jabbed him in the side again.

"Look, I *want* her to do this thing. Have the experience. I think she would enjoy it. I just...part of me doesn't like her doing it alone."

"What do you mean?" Tim furrowed his eyebrow, then his eyes widened. "*Oh*! Is this residual vibes from what happened with Meesh that one time? Dude, you have got to let that go. It was months ago and Harper has been alone with him since then. With your blessing!"

"I know that she has," he admitted. "I know that the same thing would not happen this time. But still. I can't shake this feeling."

Tim clapped him on the shoulder, giving him a light squeeze. "You can't be her white knight all the time, Ivanov."

"I'm missing something. What happened?" Guy asked.

"Nope," Pietr shook his head. "I'm done with you."

"Aw, is this because I contemplated for like ten seconds, one time, what it *might* be like to sleep with your wife? You can't fault me for being a little curious! I'm single as fuck and gotta entertain myself somehow." He paused, then shook his head. "Wait, no, that definitely did not sound right. I swear to *god*, Pietr, I have never thought about Harper while actually *doing* anything."

"Gross." Gregor wrinkled his nose. He looked down at Pietr again. "I too have never had such inklings about your wife. Your boyfriend on the other hand...well, we know how that has been going." He gave him a small grin. "Speaking of, you should remember that Harper is not alone there. If something goes amiss, Isaac is right there for her."

"I know."

"Are you open to compromising?" Tim asked.

"How do you mean?"

"They're both at this convention. Maybe you can talk to Maggie on the phone? Get a vibe. Get some answers as to her intentions. Maybe it would make you feel more comfortable to hear her voice. Or, you could do a video call. Even better. People are generally pretty terrible at hiding things when you can see their faces."

"It might already be too late," Pietr pointed out. "You are giving Harper much credit, but she could be with this woman right now."

"I doubt it." Tim shifted in his seat, leaning back. He let out a yawn. "Try and put it out of your head, man. You can call her again as soon as we land."

"It will be late," he retorted.

"She's waiting for you to call her."

"You seem very sure."

"I feel like I've gotten to know you and Pigeon pretty well over the last couple of months," he said. "This is getting blown completely out of proportion."

Pietr let out a soft *hmph*. "Glad to hear you are so sure of things, Jammer."

"You'll see. Relax. Eat that protein bar Coach suggested."

Pietr muttered about what Tim could do with a protein bar. Guy laughed, slipping back into his own seat.

"He's got a point, Tesla. You're going to be telling us in the morning what an idiot you were being tonight."

Gregor reached over, patting him on the shoulder. "Have some trust in her being with Isaac. If something does go amiss, he's your proxy. He loves her nearly as much as you do." He sank back into his seat as well.

The rest of the flight was quiet, Pietr still pensive in his seat. He tried to read, but the book couldn't hold his attention. He wasn't sure what made him do it. Maybe it was because he knew it was something Harper did when she was upset and he wondered if it would work for him. He disturbed Tim long enough to pull his carry-on out of the overhead storage and grab his laptop. Tim settled back into his seat, frowning, as Pietr opened up his word processor, and started writing.

Chapter Thirty-four

For the first time in their 18 months of romance, Pietr hesitated while staring at his phone. The picture he had set as her icon was one of them together. Her niece, Olivia, had taken it with his phone when they'd visited her family during their first Christmas together. They had been outside, watching the kids try to tempt the beef cattle with handfuls of hay. She'd dipped her hands into his pockets and he'd leaned down to kiss her. He'd found the photo on his phone later, along with dozens of other random shots. It filled his chest with a familiar, comfortable warmth when he saw it; every time she called or texted him.

Finally, he tapped on his message icon instead, shooting off a text message.

[PIETR] Home. You up?

His phone began to ring almost immediately, the photo filling the screen again. Bigger this time. He tapped "answer" and brought it to his ear.

"Hullo *lyubov moya*."

"Hey. How was your flight?"

Her voice was quiet. Too quiet.

"It was..." he paused, "frustratingly long."

There was a brief pause before suddenly both of them burst out simultaneously "*I'm so sorry*".

"Why are you sorry, baby?" Pietr asked. "I am the asshole here."

"You're not. We've talked about sleeping with other people in *theory*, but not about random hook-ups. With the other two, it was…less spontaneous. Safer. We both *knew* Isaac and Misha. Here, I'm suddenly throwing this stranger wanting to sleep with me at you. We've never discussed that."

"I've always said I want you to feel comfortable having new experiences," he said. "I never considered what a hook-up was. Neither of us have a history with those."

"Technically, Misha was *supposed* to be. But apparently, I'm irresistible to Russian hockey players."

Pietr felt himself lighten, laughing. "*Da*. You are scxy as fuck." He heard her light noise of amusement and more of the tension faded.

"Which," he continued, "is why it makes sense this Maggie lady would like to have some fun with you." He let out a soft sigh. "I'm sorry I was weird about it earlier. If you want to do it, you should. I've had time to think about it more. Turns out, Gregor knows her. Big fan."

"Small world."

"*Da*. Full disclosure: I did talk to some of the guys. Specifically, Tim, Guy, and Gregor. But, eh, we were on the plane and I don't know who else was eavesdropping."

"I get it. I talked to Isaac a little after we talked earlier too."

"I think we should talk about this more when you get home."

"Agree."

"It isn't fair for me to ask to change the rules, or add to them without us getting to have a proper face-to-face about it. But, we can start the conversation if you want?"

"I turned Maggie down," she said. "I texted her and said it didn't feel right. It's not the end of the world. She's not the only woman on the planet who might be into me. We'll see each other around the convention this weekend and who knows? Maybe I make a new friend. I like having friends."

"I know you do."

"Isaac pointed something out to me tonight." Her voice had gone quiet again.

"What's that?"

"Just that I've done a lot of adapting to your life. And you haven't really had to adapt much to mine."

"That isn't true."

But then he thought about it. He'd asked her to move in, so it was easier to see her when he got home from traveling. She'd quit her day job to focus on writing because he'd promised he could take care of her. She'd had to learn how to navigate with the WHOOSH. She'd also been the first to budge on opening the relationship too –because he'd asked. She'd been willing to move out of her comfort zone to try something new with him, trying that first threesome with Isaac. Had those been positives? Sure. But what had he done for her? A couple of coffee dates and going to karaoke. Hosting their first Thanksgiving together.

"Pietr?"

He realized that as he'd been rattling off relationship highlights in his head, she must have said his name at least three times.

"I'm sorry," he replied, "what did you say?"

"I said that it is true, but I think you realize that?"

"It is," he admitted. "I'm very selfish."

"Pietr, that isn't what I—"

"Is true," he cut her off. "I don't even *ask* you. I automatically expect that you'll do things. I don't know why."

"Because I'm your *wife*. I'm supposed to do it."

"No," he volleyed, "you are my wife but you are your own person. You have your own wants and needs and desires and...fuck."

"Pietr, I want, need, and desire to be with you." She let out a light breath. "Tonight, after we got off the phone, I talked to Isaac –who told me to take your yes at face value and to go have fun. I couldn't do it. I couldn't let *that* be the thing that might put a crack in what we have."

"Nothing will ever put a crack in our relationship."

"You were so upset earlier."

"I was..." He knew it wasn't worth arguing with her. He *had* been upset. "I was, but not with you."

"Part of me knows that," she admitted.

"Let's put a pin in this," he said. "It's exhausting and I'm already so tired." He let out a soft self-deprecating laugh.

"You should get to bed," she said.

"Tell me about your day first. Your flight to Chicago was good?"

"The flight was fine. I met Isaac right away, we got to the hotel fine. Checked in, explored, had dinner, went to a mixer with the other guests."

"How was that?"

"It was fun," she said. "A little loud. Good food though. Free drinks. Not that I imbibed."

" Are you back in your room now?"

"No. I grabbed my laptop and came down to the lounge. Isaac turned in about an hour ago."

"Don't stay up too much later," he warned. "You don't want to be tired at your panels tomorrow."

"I won't."

There were another few beats of silence.

"I love you, Harper Wyatt."

"I love you too, Pietr Ivanov."

"I will talk to you tomorrow," he said. "Text me, when you have a few minutes. –And, please, *please*, if the opportunity arises and it feels right, give it a go with this Maggie person. She is not really my type, but I can see the attraction."

She laughed. "I'm okay not doing anything until we can talk about it more. But, I can't say I'm going to go out of my way to avoid her. She is a very nice and interesting person."

He hummed. "Good night, my darling."

"Good night."

Pietr hesitated again. He didn't really want to get off the phone with her, but he did. He ended the call, flashing the photo on his screen again. She was only gone for the weekend, but it was going to feel like an eternity.

Chapter Thirty-five

Isaac shifted closer as Harper slid into bed a few minutes later. He wrapped an arm around her, pressing his chest to her back. His nose nuzzled into her hair

"Better?" He asked. "You were gone awhile."

"I was waiting for Pietr to get home," Harper admitted. "Yes, I'm better."

"Good talk then?" He pressed a kiss to her shoulder.

Harper hummed, contemplating. Calling it good wasn't her first reaction. Comforting was perhaps a better descriptor.

"We decided to put a pin in it and we're going to re-access our rules when we're together again."

"Good idea."

"Did you know Gregor knows Maggie?"

"No shit?"

"I didn't get specifics. But he likes her. Pietr felt more comfortable with his yes."

"Are you going to try and spend some time with her then?"

"I don't think so," she admitted. "I was flattered, and my initial reaction was *fuck yes*, but having sat on it now, that isn't me. I don't want casual. I like making a connection first."

Isaac didn't respond except for a soft noise of agreement. His hand moved up, squeezing a breast. Harper felt her lips tug in an automatic smile.

"Aren't you tired?" she teased.

"Very," he confirmed. "Not initiating. Just like boobs."

Harper laughed. She pulled away from him for a moment to roll onto her back. He groaned, draping himself across her. His lips found her cheek in the dark, then her mouth. Harper's fingers tugged though his hair, savoring it a little longer.

"Go to sleep, Harp." He settled back against her side. His hand went to her chest again. Oddly reassuring. "We've got a lot going on tomorrow."

Harper let him get comfortable and relax. Her brain was still on overdrive. Mulling over the situation with Maggie. The conversations with Isaac and then Pietr. The anxiety of the day ahead, being in person with people. Officially this time. And in the back of her head, the worry that another KongKon incident was possible.

Harper and Isaac made it through their first day of panels and a signing without any troubles. Most people were kind. A few people were rude and entitled, but not abusive. They took a lot of photos. Signed more, along with a couple of LA Scorch items, convention merch, badge ribbons, and someone even had a t-shirt of the new "Play it with Parker & Harper" logo. Isaac didn't say anything to them but made a note in his phone to follow up with his lawyer about a possible cease and desist.

"You doing okay?" Isaac asked when they had a bit of a lull. "Dinner break is coming up."

"Yes, I could use some food," Harper agreed.

"Voucher dinner or you want to go out?"

"I feel bad not using them. They already paid."

"That's a risk they take," he countered.

"I'm fine eating here," she said. "I might try the burger this time."

"It was good," he confirmed.

"Hey! You two talking dinner plans?"

Harper looked up at Maggie, barely recognizable in her Teen Titans Raven cosplay. It was odd to see it on her. Dark and foreboding. Pale skin was achieved with a surprisingly light layer of makeup.

"Hey. Yeah, we're just finishing up here," Isaac spoke up for her.

"Jess is wrapped up in an MTG tournament, so I'm on my own. Do you mind if I join you?"

"Not at all. We'd love that," Isaac continued.

"...Harper?"

"Of course!" Harper snapped out of whatever mental block had occurred upon seeing Maggie's skin-tight, nylon clad...everything. "Sorry. Went off in my own little world. Hazard of being a writer."

"No worries." Maggie smiled. It killed the Raven vibe entirely. "I'm actually going to go change into my evening costume. Meet you two at the restaurant in like twenty minutes?"

"We'll be there," Harper agreed.

Maggie bounced on her heels. Also very un-Raven like. "Great. See you in a bit." She waved before disappearing back into the crowd toward the elevators.

"Should I not have done that?" Isaac asked.

"It's fine," she declared, "I'm cool."

"Uh, yeah, it's common knowledge that anyone who says they're cool most equivocally is not."

"I'm hungry. Nothing more or less. And we're all eating at the same place, so it makes sense."

Isaac didn't voice a response. He was saved from having to do so by another fan coming up for a chat and an autograph. They made small talk with a handful more fans before Laurie finally set out their "closed" sign and began to pack up their photo cards and Sharpies.

Maggie was already standing outside the restaurant with her phone. She had swapped Raven for a more breathable Princess Zelda from Breath of the Wild. Harper was internally appalled at the way her eyes drifted to Maggie's exposed midriff.

"I was about to text you." Maggie had her smile on again. "Good timing."

"Your cosplay is nice," Isaac complimented her. "The details are great."

"That's Jess. She takes pride in the details. I handle the base layers and props. It's good bonding time for us; having a unified goal that is for something we both enjoy."

"Sorta like Harper and I doing the charity streaming," Isaac said.

Maggie smiled. "Sorta. Do you have something you do with Pietr, Harper?"

"Oh, uh...no, not off the top of my head. We do most things together."

A frown tugged at Maggie's lips, but she didn't say anything. They moved into the restaurant, presenting their vouchers again. They were seated near the middle of the restaurant and presented menus.

"I already have this thing memorized," Maggie said, setting hers down on the table.

"Same," Isaac said.

"You seem quiet." Maggie prodded the back of Harper's menu. "Is everything okay?"

"Yes?" Harper looked up over the edge of the menu that she didn't really need to look at either. She just needed something to do with her hands.

"Right. So, things aren't super awkward between us after I propositioned you?" Maggie arched an eyebrow. "You seemed into it last night..."

"I didn't mean for it to be awkward," Harper responded. "And I was into it, but..."

"But?" Maggie pressed. When the silence stretched further on, she continued. "I'm not offended if you changed your mind or Pietr wasn't into it."

"Pietr was *not* into it," Harper admitted. "But he still said I should do what I want."

"Oh! Well..."

"I want to have a conversation with my husband about it, face-to-face," Harper finished. "So, it's not going to happen this weekend." She shrugged. "He still said I should do what I want. He felt better after talking to a teammate –apparently you've met Gregor Ciklovich?"

"I forgot that Gregor plays for the Osprey!" Maggie's eyes lit up. "I haven't seen him since college. We were both at training camp in Montreal. Before he got drafted. ...I should call him and catch up."

Harper set her menu back down. "Anyway, hook-ups aren't a thing we generally do. At all. So, this was different. We thought we were okay with the possibility, but the more I think about it myself, the more I don't think I would like him calling to ask to sleep with a random stranger either."

"I get that. No hard feelings." Maggie gave her another easy smile. "You two are going to Mill City Con in a couple of weeks, right? And CONerole in June?"

"We are, yes."

"I'll be there too! Just as a regular attendee, not a guest. But I've signed up to be on a couple of cosplay panels for each. Let's try and make the most of getting to know each other this weekend, you can have a heart-to-heart with you hubby, and maybe we can talk about it again the next time we see one another?" Maggie suggested. "No pressure! I don't want you to think I'm *only* interested in sleeping with you. I just think it would be fun, and you said you didn't have experience. First timers are kind of a kink for me."

"Oh!"

Maggie laughed. "That sounds terrible."

The waitress appeared with their drinks and to take their orders. Harper waited until she had disappeared again before looking at Maggie quizzically.

"Can I ask you a question?"

"You can ask me anything."

"Why do you like hook-ups?"

"Because I already have a girlfriend I don't spend nearly enough time with," Maggie replied easily. "I'm not *averse* to another relationship, but it's easy when it's only sex. No emotional attachment. Just good vibes and getting off. I love

Jess, and I'm glad she's been able to make other connections, but...she's enough for me. Sometimes though, I meet someone and I think *huh, I wonder what they're like*. Sometimes we even do it a couple of times, but it's never more than that." Maggie cocked her head to the side. "Why do *you* have two boyfriends and a husband?"

"Pietr picked me up in a bar and hasn't gotten sick of me yet?"

Isaac swatted her arm. "Hey, no self-deprecating speak."

"My bad." Harper rubbed her arm, even though it hadn't actually hurt at all. "Isaac joined us on purpose. It was a thing Pietr wanted to try and I finally agreed to it. We ended up enjoying it. Misha was supposed to be a one-time thing, but then it wasn't. I think I just do something for each of them."

"You do something for them, but they don't something for you?" Maggie asked.

Harper hummed, contemplating. "It's not that. Pietr is my life partner. We do everything together. We talk about the future. Growing old. Isaac is more..." She turned to look at him, "I'm not sure how to say it. It doesn't feel like a dependency thing. We're together because we *want* to be, not because we feel compelled to be. And Misha...well, if Misha Levin wants to fuck you, you don't turn him down."

Maggie snorted into her soda.

"I'm mostly joking," Harper assured her.

"I mean, I turned him down," Isaac pointed out.

"Whaaa?" Maggie's eyes widened.

"Fuck." Isaac covered his mouth with a hand. "You didn't hear that."

"I did too."

"It was a group thing," Harper explained. "Isaac was an observer –and not interested in being a participant. No more details required."

Maggie stared at the two of them for a few extra beats before making a *huh* noise. "I guess it's been alluded that when you three say you're in a relationship, you're *in a relationship*. I so seldom see the three of you together, I imagined there was still separation there."

"We do things separately," Isaac pointed out. "Like this weekend."

"But if Pietr had been available, he would definitely have come," Harper said.

"True," he agreed. "We get plenty of time though. Harp and I do the stream, we've started doing these conventions. Pietr stopped by the last time he was in LA for a game. We'll let Harper work and go out for dinner or just stay out of her way at the apartment when I visit them. It's been tough because of the distance, but we're working on it."

"Have you considered moving to Minneapolis? Or one of the 'burbs," Maggie asked. "Nice central location, rather than being on opposite coasts. Close to the house in Wisconsin too, right?"

"It's about two hours," Harper said. "So, in the grand scheme of things, yes."

Maggie launched into trying to sell Isaac on a couple of the various areas around the Twin Cities. She pointed out that Minneapolis had a wealth of conventions, that would be right in his backyard, negating some of the travel. It was cold, sure, but Minnesota *was* the State of Hockey. And travel to and from New York was half the distance of LA.

"I've been considering it," Isaac admitted.

"Then what are you waiting for?"

"I don't want to move just for Pietr and Harper," he explained. "They're my partners, and I would love to be closer to them, but I also have to consider any *other* future partners. I'm...starting to see someone else."

"Ah. Right. In LA?"

"No, he's in New York too."

"Then move to New York!"

"We've been seeing each other for like two weeks. Semi-officially," Isaac retorted. "I'm not packing up and moving after just two weeks. Plus..."

"Dating him has the same problems of dating Pietr," Harper replied. "He's a hockey player."

"Well, well, well...the Osprey have a wealth of queer on the roster, don't they?"

Isaac laughed. "You probably already knew Gregor wasn't straight."

"You're dating Gregor?!"

"We've been hanging out," Isaac said. "It's still pretty casual."

"I bet you two are absolutely adorable."

Harper made an *eh* sound as Isaac shrugged. Isaac swatted her arm again.

"Not every couple can be as fucking adorable as you and Pietr."

"Pietr and I don't try to be adorable. People just perceive us that way."

Their food arrived and they switched topic of conversation to their plans for the rest of the evening. There were still panels happening until nearly midnight, as well as a lot of gaming. Party rooms had been advertised, that might be worth checking out, and there was a rave style dance from 8 PM to 2 AM.

"I think I'd rather turn in early," Harper said, "and make the most out of tomorrow night instead. Sunday, we can crash at the end of the day before we get the flight home on Monday."

"Sounds like a plan to me," Isaac said.

"I have to make rounds. Make sure people see the costume." Maggie motioned at herself. "Tomorrow I have the masquerade and I'm a judge for the competition, so that's like...most of the day."

"We have a panel up against the cosplay competition," Isaac said. "I hope we still get a decent turn out?"

"You will. There are always people who don't give a shit about the cosplay comp. They just see everyone when they're walking around the convention. I should know –until we got more serious about it, Jess and I were totally those people. What's your panel tomorrow?"

"I think tomorrow is our Q&A," Harper said. "Then I have one on publishing, Isaac has one on building a brand, and we have our live stream tomorrow after the dinner break."

"Awesome. Are you planning on going to the dance tomorrow night?"

"We could pop into it." Isaac shrugged.

"I'm not really a dancer," Harper said.

"Harper, honey," Maggie reached across the table, putting her hand on top of Harper's. "We're in a hotel full of geeks. Most of them aren't dancers –but they certainly try anyway!"

Chapter Thirty-six

"Can I ask you something?"

Harper grunted, leaning her head against Isaac's shoulder. They'd just changed after popping into the console gaming room. They'd chatted with some fans for a while, but finally made their way back up to the hotel room for the night. They'd changed and crawled into bed to wind down with some TV before trying to sleep.

"You can say no," he continued.

"What do you want to ask?"

"Would you tell me about your ex?"

"My ex?"

"The first guy you...you know. Before your dry spell."

"That's a polite way of putting it," she said. A few beats passed before she shrugged. "Not much to say. He was a little younger than me, immature, and we just didn't end up clicking. He thought I was too smart for him –and I was. In retrospect."

"What made him the one?"

"He was there." Her laugh was self-deprecating. "I was already twenty and the only one of my friends who hadn't. I'd barely even been on dates before."

"Why?"

"You'll just get mad if I say *look at me*, so..."

"There isn't anything wrong with the way you look, Harper."

"I'm still getting around to accepting that," she reminded him. She looked up at him. "I can believe that *you*, and Pietr, and Misha –and apparently Maggie, see something I can't. When it comes to looking at myself, it's hard to turn off all the negatives that have been thrown at me since I was a kid. It's what made me want to get out of my hometown after high school. Leaving didn't suddenly give me confidence though."

"Okay. So, what about this guy gave you the confidence to date him? Have sex with him?"

"God, Isaac, it was years ago. I don't remember the specifics."

He smiled, pressing a kiss to her hair. "Right."

"Why are you asking?"

"Curiosity," he said. "I wondered if something had happened, when you broke up."

"Oh." He felt her shoulders shift, tensing for a second. "I found out afterwards—which, I thought had been amicable, that he'd been cheating on me."

"What?"

"With someone I'd thought was my friend. We worked together at the campus dining hall. We didn't date very long, but I was suspicious when he started dating her immediately after our break-up. It was a friend of *his* that confirmed it for me. He just kept lying, saying I was making something out of nothing. That we had been getting distant for a while and they'd just been talking before we broke up."

"What an asshole."

She made a noise of agreement. "We were both kind of assholes to each other. It was my first relationship. And, it wasn't an enjoyable experience. That's probably why I didn't bother."

"Until Pietr."

"I'm not sure I *bother* with Pietr either." She looked up at him. "In a positive way, not a negative one. He's easy to be with. Usually."

Isaac rested his cheek against her head and slid his fingers between hers, on top of the covers. "He is." There was a short stretch of silence. "You're wrong about one thing though."

"I'm wrong?"

"You *are* confident. When it matters." He stroked his thumb across hers. "Your ability to put your reservations into check is very appealing."

She made another little noise; more of acknowledgement than agreeing or disagreeing.

"That guy, your first, was a fucking moron," he continued. "I'm glad you broke up with him."

She laughed. "Me too."

"If you *hadn't*, maybe you'd still be stuck with him now, and be miserable."

"God, I hope not. He has *not* aged well." Harper snorted. "Not that I check up on him. I still have a few mutual friends with his now ex-wife."

"He *married* the girl he cheated on you with?"

"Yup. Cheated on her too."

"Definitely an asshole. You dodged a bullet."

"Agree."

Isaac brought his free hand to Harper's cheek, turning her head to catch her lips. She returned the kiss with a light smile.

"If you want to fuck around before we turn in, all you have to do is ask."

"I'm always up to fuck around," he murmured. Harper let out a soft groan as he deepened his kiss. He released her hand and face. He twisted slightly, his arm wrapping around her waist and hauling her into his lap.

Harper pressed kisses along his jaw and neck, rocking against his cock. Isaac cupped her face, directing her lips back to his.

"How do you feel about practicing those oral skills?" He asked.

"If you like," she agreed. She kissed him one last time before shifting back. Isaac made quick work of taking his boxers off, tossing them aside. She settled between his knees, hands on his thighs and ran her tongue up the length of his cock. He was already at full length as her tongue stroked the ridge of his head.

He whispered compliments, letting her have her fun. When she kept having to toss her head to the side, trying to keep her hair out of the way, he reached down, gathering it in his fingers and holding it for her.

"Thanks." She licked the length again before pressing kisses to his thighs. Then she refocused until he drew in a sharp breath.

"Harp, if you keep doing that I'm going to cum," he warned.

"That is the goal."

Isaac grunted. A moment later, Harper laughed as he threw her onto her back. He held her in place while he stretched for the side table where they'd left a few condoms out for easy access. He pressed the packet into her palm before slinking down her body. He tugged her shorts down her hips, tossing them aside. He leaned forward, pressing his tongue into her center.

"I love how wet you get, sucking my cock." Isaac's voice was muffled as he moved to bite her thigh. She groaned as he sucked, trying to leave a mark. He continued stroking her clit with his fingers before dipping two inside of her. His mouth moved back to circling her clit until...

"Oh fuck!" She squeezed his shoulder, jerking forward. "—You can stop."

"You sure?" He leaned back, still stroking slowly with his fingers.

"Yes," she laughed, reaching down to push his hand away.

"My turn then?" He held out his hand for the condom. She handed it over, then shifted higher against the pillows.

Isaac nudged between her thighs after ripping open the package. He rolled on the sheath with one hand, leaning over her to kiss again. She lapped her tongue against his cheeks, tasting herself, before returning the kiss. His cock slid along her opening until he sat back, thrusting inside.

"Hurry up," Harper teased. "I'm ready to go to sleep."

He gave an exaggerated sigh. "I'll take as long as I need, Harper Wyatt, and you're going to like every minute of it."

For all his bravado, Isaac focused, leaning into her for more kissing as he thrust. He didn't last long. He sank heavily on top of her before shifting to her side.

"You got that out of your system now?" She asked.

"That was good," he said. "I should be set until morning."

"So, I shouldn't expect a repeat at four AM?"

Isaac grunted, kissing her shoulder. "I don't think so, but maybe."

Harper laughed, rolling her eyes. "I gotta go brush my teeth."

Isaac shifted, letting her out from under him. He rolled on his back, reaching down to take care of the condom. Harper picked up her shorts as she made her way to the bathroom.

After they'd traded places at the sink, Harper flipped off the TV and pulled out the corners of the covers from the end of the bed. She felt better with them loosened, tugging them a little higher under her chin. Isaac joined her again, getting in on the opposite side of the bed. They settled in together.

"So...that guy," Isaac spoke up.

Harper let out a sigh. "What guy?"

"The...your ex-boyfriend guy."

"Cripes, Isaac. What about him?"

"Did you care about him?"

"At the time, I thought I did. In retrospect, I think it was more I *wanted* to care about him. And when it didn't work out, I didn't want to try caring about anyone but myself. Because I was a hyper-independent bitch."

"You're not a bitch." He laced his fingers with hers. "Independent? Yes. Anyone who tells you that's a bad thing can go to hell."

"Why are you really asking about him?" Harper asked.

"We said we were going to get to know each other better this weekend. I wanted to know about that part of your life."

"Does that mean you have exes you'd like to tell me about?"

Isaac grunted. "You know about Pietr."

"Yes."

"...But we only more recently, mutually, agreed to consider that a *relationship*," he continued. "Other than him, there was a girl in high school. We broke up when I realized that I was crushing on her brother more than her. In college, I went through kind of a whore phase. Hooking up at frat parties and that kind of thing, but I dated two or three people. Very briefly. A few weeks, maybe six months at most. When I was playing, I'd pick up mostly women in bars, aside from hooking up with Pietr. Until Adrienne."

"Adrienne?"

"She worked for the Scorch Foundation. Team relations, so she was the one who was basically the gopher between the Foundation and the players. We weren't serious, then we realized that we'd been having sex and hanging out for almost a year. Then we made it more official for another year, but...things didn't change between us. We weren't making the effort to be more. Then I got hurt and forced to retire."

"And she broke up with you?"

"I broke up with her," he said. "I didn't handle the injury well. I was angry. Rehab took fucking forever. I didn't know what the hell I was going to do with my life after hockey. Five years in the NHL hadn't been enough. I know that's average, but I'd always thought I'd be better than that. Last longer. It all went to shit. By the time I was less angry, I realized that I hadn't missed her and I don't think she missed me."

"I'm sorry."

"Nothing to be sorry for," he said. "It was a good two years. We just weren't meant to be. We're still friendly. I have to talk to her occasionally when I do stuff with the Foundation now as a former player. She got married last year. They're trying to adopt."

"Huh."

"Since then I've focused on building Play it with Parker. I've gone on dates, I've hooked up, but...no other relationships until Pietr and you."

"What about Gregor?"

"Gregor and I aren't in a relationship. Yet. Maybe."

"Do you want to be?"

"I'm trying to be realistic. He's busy. He's still got a lot of years of hockey left. He could be traded."

"He could," she agreed. "Any of them could be."

"Do you worry about Pietr getting traded?"

"Not really." She shook her head. "We've talked about it. He's hoping for another contract with the Osprey next year. Stipulations for trades being specific. If he can get that, we're thinking about buying a house or an apartment more central between the training center and MSG."

"I'm glad you're talking about it." He kissed her cheek again. "We don't have to though. We should try and sleep."

"Agree."

"Good night, Harp."

"Night, Isaac."

Chapter Thirty-seven

It was Saturday afternoon when Harper sat down in the chair next to Isaac at the front of the panel room where they were doing their Q&A. People were beginning to funnel in. More than Harper had expected, given that they were up against the cosplay competition.

"How was your last panel?" Isaac leaned over kissing her cheek.

"I think it went okay." She shrugged. "A bunch of people wanted to chat afterwards. Yours?"

"Good. Apparently people don't like me. I managed to escape quickly."

"It was a couple of people who came through the signing line yesterday," she said. "Which, when is our next block?"

"About an hour after we're done here," he said. "You want to grab food after this?"

"Sounds good to me."

"Hey guys! So excited to be your moderator today." A bulky guy in a bright yellow STAFF t-shirt with the convention logo on it squatted between them. "I'm Mitch."

"Nice to meet you." Isaac gave him a nod.

"The way we set this up is pretty typical. We handed out numbers at the door. We always keep to thirty. If, by some miracle, we make it through them –or someone dips before they get their question answered, whatever, we can take a few from the floor. Sound good?"

"Sounds good to me," Harper agreed.

"Great. I'll lay down your ground rules, folks will come up to the mic in the center there," he motioned, "ask their question, and then when you've answered they'll sit back down. One question per person, and I'm willing to be an asshole about it." He looked between them. "I will *not* let another KongKon incident happen to you. Promise."

"Thanks, but I think we're far enough away from home that Pietr's superfans aren't a threat," Harper said.

"You never know. Maybe it's not Pietr fans this time." Mitch scowled. It looked unnatural on his otherwise friendly face. "But we've got your backs." He stood back up from his crouch, taking the chair on the other side of Isaac.

"You ready?" Isaac asked. He reached over, squeezing her hand.

"Yeah." She nodded, rolling her eyes. "If I thought that whole incident was going to be repeated, I wouldn't have come. I'm super over it."

"I know." He bumped her shoulder with his.

"All right! Before we get started, just a couple of reminders." Mitch had adjusted his microphone as another staffer closed the doors to the room. "We have handed out all of our numbers for questions so keep in mind, you may not get your question answered. We are only here for an hour and there are thirty of you. Depending on the questions and how in depth our guests decide to get with their answers, and having a conversation, things vary. Secondly, while we welcome and appreciate questions about diversity, we will not tolerate baiting questions, rebuttals, or anything broaching on argumentative. Our guests are here as just that: guests, and they are not obligated to answer questions which make them uncomfortable. However, that will not be a problem, will it?"

There was a murmur of *no sir* and the like.

"Excellent." Mitch sat back for a moment, shuffling the cards in his hands. "Now, you have one opportunity. If you think your question is going to violate the guidelines, I'll ask that you return your number to Bridget."

The woman that closed the door raised a hand.

There was a murmur. A teenager in an Isabelle cosplay got up, quietly handing the card back to Bridget. An older guy with a Nintendo hat stood up, returning his as well.

"Not a problematic question –my daughter is having a cosplay emergency," he clarified. "Sorry!"

"No problem. Anyone else?" Mitch asked. When there was no other response, he went on. "Okay, Bridget has two numbers. Was there anyone who has a question but didn't get a card?" A couple of hands raised. Bridget gave them to the first two she saw.

"All right, I think we're good," Bridget declared.

"Great. Then, when I call your number, you will form an orderly line at the microphone. I'll call you up three or four at a time so we avoid crowding. If, at the end, we have some time, we'll take some questions from the floor." Mitch set the cards back down, flipping three of them over. "First up is sixteen, four, and twenty-seven."

The first few questions were normal. Mostly about gaming, some of the tech that they used, and their selection process for the non-profit donations. Then, Harper was surprise with a question about her jewelry. Pietr's rings had been joined with a circular pendant from Misha that he'd given her upon her departure from Edmonton. With it's locking clasp, she never removed it and mostly forgot about it except as something to fiddle with when she was bored, thinking, or anxious. After that, they were asked questions on game strategy, upcoming game releases they were excited about, and whether they had any other special streams scheduled.

"My question already got taken so," a teen boy in a Link cosplay blinked at them, "how are you enjoying the convention?"

Harper laughed. "So far it's been a lot of fun. I went to college in Chicago, so I'm familiar with the area. I actually attended a couple of times back then, when it was still being held at the university. It's grown a lot."

Isaac continued, "It's always fun to go to new places and get to talk about the stuff we like to do. Get out and see people. Put faces to usernames. We have some of the best fans and it's always great to go places where we can spend some time with them."

"Four, Sixteen, and Ten," Mitch called out.

"I feel really dumb for asking this." A middle-aged woman in a My Hero Academia t-shirt stepped up to the mic next. "I used to watch Play It with Parker religiously, and then I had a medical drama and am just getting back to catching up and was really surprised to see Harper had an official co-host status. What was the reasoning behind making that a thing? Not that it's not cool! I was just surprised by it."

"It was pointed out to me that Harper has brought a lot of viewers to the show," Isaac said. "I was making a sizable amount of money off her presence and that wasn't very fair of me. So, we talked about it and came up with the plan for the fundraising. Doing that kind of thing is important to both of us, it gives us the chance to spend time together doing something that we like, and we can bring other friends and partners into it too, which is fun."

The questions dwindled and they had just a few minutes left as the last waiting person left the mic.

"Okay, I guess we can take a question or two from the floor," Mitch said.

Some hands shot in the air.

"You –Applejack." He pointed.

"Can I ask a question about polyamory?"

"You could have, but you're only allowed one question and that was it," Isaac teased. "Next?"

The Pinkie Pie next to Applejack raised her hand instead.

"I'm kidding," Isaac chided. "What's your question?"

"How did you decide that was something you wanted to do?"

"I'm not sure," Isaac admitted.

"It made sense to us. We all got along. Pietr and Isaac had been in a relationship before and never got closure on it. They still had feelings for one another. Over time, Isaac and I have connected as well. The way Pietr and I feel for each other is different from how we feel about Isaac. It would take a lot for us to stop being friends, even if we do ultimately decide that being in a romantic relationship doesn't work for us. And trust me –we access that regularly. It can be hard having a partner on the opposite coast."

A few more hands shot in the air.

Mitch pointed. "Roxas."

"How many tattoos do you have?"

"I have zero," Isaac said.

"Just three right now," Harper said. "The lilac sprig," she touched her sternum, "and then lucky cats." She leaned her elbows on the table, showing them off. "Misha and I are going to do some road tripping when his season ends, visiting a couple of tattoo shops recommended by a friend. So, more to come."

"You in the Chicago U shirt," Mitch pointed.

"Isaac, are you seeing anyone besides Harper and Pietr?"

"Oh look, we're out of time," Isaac looked down at his watch.

Harper nudged him under the table again.

Isaac made an exaggerated sigh. "Nothing official, but I've been spending some time with someone when we get the chance. They're a bit busy, and we're not ready to make any kind of formal announcement. So…just having some fun together."

"Okay, I think we can take one more before we close up," Mitch said. "But I'll take a second to remind folks that Isaac and Harper have a signing session this afternoon and they may be able to take a few minutes to chat then as well if we didn't get to you." He scanned the hands. "Uh, how about you, with the Louise Belcher hat."

"Are you two doing any other upcoming conventions? Or where can people find your appearance schedule?"

"Those are posted on our website, and on the Discord server," Isaac said. "Coming up we have two conventions in Minneapolis. Mill City and CONerole. We'll also be at HoboKon in New Jersey. We're likely going to be doing something in October, but that isn't finalized yet. We're still figuring out conventions, but we hope to keep doing them. They've been fun."

"Okay, that's it!" Mitch shuffled his number cards again. "Thank you to Isaac Parker and Harper Wyatt for being here with us at AtomiCon. We are so, so happy to have had this opportunity and to have gotten both of you to give us your insight into what the two of you do together as well as separately. Thank you so much. A round of applause for our amazing special guests, huh?"

There was a smattering of clapping and Bridget moved to open the doors again. As people began to file out, Harper stood from her chair.

"Food?"

"Yeah. I got a recommendation for a place you'll like down the street. Something different." Isaac smiled, joining her. "It's not far."

"What kind of place?" She asked.

"Your favorite."

"Sushi?" Her eyes widened.

"Maybe." He put an arm around her waist, pulling her in for a quick kiss. "C'mon. We don't have a ton of time."

"You don't have to tell me twice if there is sushi involved," Harper murmured. "Let's go."

"Sorry, sorry!" Isaac waved off a couple of people who had hung around hoping for a word. "We need food. Stop by the signing table or find us later. Or drop into the Discord!"

"Stop plugging the Discord, you nerd." Harper sighed.

"Hey, you're the one who secretly lurks in it," Isaac retorted.

"Hush!"

They made their way out of the panel room and down to the lobby, heading off anyone who tried to interrupt them by looking determined to get somewhere. They stepped outside into the bright late-winter air. The Midwest in March was always a crapshoot, really, but spring was definitely in the air. There wasn't a snow pile to be seen –a miracle on it's own, Harper thought, but it was a warm sixty degrees with a light breeze. They walked across the parking lot and down the street. Harper gasped, seeing the outside of the building.

"Oh my god, is this conveyer belt sushi?"

Isaac laughed. "You like?"

"I love! I haven't been to a conveyer belt restaurant since I was in Japan!"

"There are a couple of them in Manhattan," he reminded her.

"I know, but Pietr and I always order out...and they can get pricey really fast."

"It's on me." He tugged her close, giving her a quick peck on the lips. "Eat whatever and however much you like."

"Isaac, you *know* how incredibly dangerous that is. I can really pack away the sushi and it's priced by the plate."

"I know how it works. Enjoy yourself." He gave her a little squeeze. "Consider it an early birthday gift? Don't think I don't know it's coming up."

Harper frowned. "How do you know that?"

"One, I love you. Two, because Pietr and I discussed what we wanted to do for you. Misha is aware too, but he's kept his plans to himself if he has any."

"The three of you have a secret group chat without me?"

"Maybe." He kissed her again. "Come on. I can hear your stomach rumbling over the traffic."

Birthdays had never been a huge deal for Harper. She hadn't even reminded Pietr about hers the year before. He'd found out when she'd received a card in the mail from her parents. He had been mildly perturbed that she hadn't told him it was coming up. He'd had an away game anyway, but he had still surprised her with flowers and a cupcake delivery. When he'd gotten home, he'd apologized for not asking before and taken her to dinner. Then to bed. That summer, for Pietr's birthday, they had gone to a local fair and spent the day together exploring the surrounding areas. While Harper was familiar with places, Pietr was not, and things had changed since she had been a kid. It had been fun.

"When is your birthday?" Harper asked as they sat next to each other at section of counter.

"June fifteenth," he said. "You two had just missed it when you visited last year."

"Should we do something fun this year?"

"I'm not sure if it's safe to plan something. Pietr might be in play-offs then and..." he shrugged, "my birthday isn't a big deal to me."

"Uh huh –neither is mine to me, and yet here we are."

He smiled. He grabbed a plate of sweet potato sushi as it rolled by. Harper grabbed a spicy tuna roll that wasn't far behind it.

"What about Pietr's birthday?" She asked. "That's in August. Should we do something?"

"I think we should. But what?"

"We'll probably be in Wisconsin. I could see if there are any concerts or shows going on. Make it a weekend to Minneapolis? Or we could go to Appleton. They have the PAX. Sometimes there's fun stuff in LaCrosse."

"That could be fun. We've spent some time in Minneapolis, but not much exploring. I've never been to Appleton. Or Green Bay. Could we go to Lambeau Field?"

Harper rolled her eyes. "We could. Green Bay also has a train museum. And a natural science museum if I remember correctly. They're right across the street from each other."

"Fun. –Oh my gosh, this is so good." Isaac sighed, picking up a second piece of the sweet potato morsel.

"Sweet potato is one of my favorite non-fish sushi," Harper admitted.

Over next half hour, they sampled a variety, splitting plates between the two of them.

"Oof, Harp...I'm afraid to know how much we stacked up here," Isaac looked at their stack of color-coded plates. Harper had stacked them in color order, lowest to highest. While they'd been conservative with their high-end sushi selection, their middle plates were sure to add up.

"I'm stuffed," she assured him. "We should get back for our signing."

He nodded. "You carry half?"

She laughed, picking up part of the stack. They carried them over to the cash register where the cashier counted and entered their total. Isaac whistled at the price but didn't complain when handing over his credit card.

"Thank you. I could have paid though," Harper reminded him as they made their way back to the hotel.

"I know." He squeezed her fingers. "Like I said, early birthday gift since I won't be here for it."

"Do you know what Pietr is planning? He'll be home this year, but there's a lot happening that week."

"I may be appraised of some plans," he acknowledged. "Don't worry about it."

"I do worry about it though."

"He loves you. Very much," Isaac reminded her. "Let him dote on you for a day."

"If that meant staying at home and having him cook me dinner or something, fine. But if it's something extravagant..."

"Relax. Pietr isn't one to go crazy over things. You'll enjoy it. I promise."

She hummed.

The cosplay competition was releasing as they passed the main stage room. The timing was right for them to run into Maggie and Jess. Maggie was wearing a very elaborate looking cosplay that Harper didn't recognize. She squeaked, wrapping her arms around Harper's shoulders.

"Kismet! Are you busy?" She asked, ignoring Jess's warning about glomming people.

"Isaac and I are on our way to our signing," Harper said. "What's up?"

Maggie's face creased in a frown. "I was going to see if you would cosplay with me."

"Excuse me?"

"Jess has a family emergency. Her sister is picking her up in like an hour to drive up to Madison," Maggie explained.

"It's true," Jess said. "My Dad had a fall. He's going to be OK, but my Mom has limited mobility herself so..." She shrugged.

"How does that equate to me cosplaying with you?"

"You and Jess are about the same size..." Maggie eyeballed the two of them.

"It's a very forgiving cosplay," Jess assured her. "I think you'd look amazing in it."

"What is it?" Harper asked. "And how long would I have to wear it?"

"It's Petra, from Horizon Zero Dawn." Maggie bounced on her heels.

"I have no idea what that is," Harper admitted.

Maggie's eyes widened. "What?!"

"If it's not on the Nintendo Switch, I probably haven't played. We have an Xbox One but Pietr and I like the portability of the Switch. We can play together, even when he's on the road sometimes."

"Here." Jess pulled up something on her phone. "It's not too revealing or anything. It has a wig, so you don't have to worry about your hair being wrong. I haven't even worn it yet. We were going to debut it tonight."

Harper looked over the cosplay. The character looked...delightful, actually. Plus-size positive, not too gawdy or bulky.

"You wouldn't have to wear it all night," Maggie promised. "We were just going to keep them on for a couple of hours and then change for the dance tonight." She gave a shy shrug, which looked weird coming from Maggie. "I can do Aloy by myself, but having a partner is always fun. I don't want to steal you from Isaac if the two of you have plans."

"No, no plans." Harper shook her head. "Our signing slot is about an hour and a half. Is this going to take a lot of time to get into?"

"Not at all! Twenty minutes tops and most of that is just checking the wig and a little bit of make-up," Maggie assured her. "I've totally got all of it down to make it super fast and easy for you. You've literally just got to wear it and hang out with me. People might ask for photos –but it's up to you if you want to do it or not. Most people are chill."

"Can I think about it?" Harper asked. "I'll get back to you after the signing?"

"Yes." Maggie smiled. "I'm going to go help Jess pack up and change into my Aloy. I might drift around by myself for a while. If you want to join me, great. If you decide not to, no worries."

"Harp, we better get going," Isaac nudged her. "We're supposed to be at the table soon."

"Right! I'll text you later."

"Bye. Have fun!" Maggie called.

"You've got it so bad...." Harper heard Jess sigh behind her. "You gotta reel it in, babe."

"Shut up!"

Isaac held back a laugh. "You're *sure* you don't want to take advantage of her offer this weekend?"

"Yes!" Harper sighed. "What do you know about this video game?"

"It's fucking amazing –and you'd like Petra. She's a blacksmith." Isaac started going down the basic premise of the game and the two characters, finishing with, "A ton of people ship them. And you'd look good in it." He gave her an appraising look as they took their seats at the signing table. "If you do put it on, will you let me take a couple pics of you taking it off? Very tasteful of course."

Harper gave him a light smack with the back of her hand to his arm. "Ugh!"

"Pietr and Misha would like them too."

"You're all sex crazed," Harper retorted. "Put it back in your pants before people start talking to us."

Isaac laughed. He picked up a sharpie, sliding another over to Harper. They had a stack of their printed photos next to him, which a lot of people took advantage of. They'd learned the day before though –plenty of people had other things they liked signed. Actual autograph books, LA Scorch merch, Harper's books, convention programs, blank badge ribbons, and the like.

"Hi!" The teenager that had returned their number to Bridget at the Q&A rushed the table as soon as the staffer opened the staging area. "I was wondering if you'd answer a question for me?"

"We might," Harper said. "Depends on the question."

"Do you date women?"

Harper raised an eyebrow.

"You have three boyfriends, but you're queer right?"

"I have two boyfriends and a husband, actually. Where would I find time to squeeze in another partner, regardless of their gender?"

"Right, right, but would you?"

Harper shrugged. "Yes, I'm open minded to all gender identities. I'm not actively looking for additional partners though."

"Oh." The teen looked a little disappointed.

"...Why?" Harper hesitated in asking.

"Well, my sister –she's like your age," he said. "She lives in the Bronx and works in theater. She moved out of Aurora, where we live, when she came out at eighteen."

"Uh huh."

"She thinks you're cute!" The teen continued.

"Are you trying to set me up with your sister?"

"Not necessarily. She comments occasionally on the stream. Her username is in leet-speak, Kinky Boots? Maybe you've noticed her?"

"I'm sorry," Harper shook her head, "there are a lot of people who comment. I don't always catch the usernames unless they post *a lot*."

"She's on the Discord too! Mad Mandie."

"That's vaguely familiar," Isaac interjected. "Didn't she recommend we try a restaurant in Uptown, last week when we were talking about dinner plans?"

"Uh, you were talking about dinner plans. I was lurking. Like usual," Harper replied.

"Yeah! She said you should check out the Greasy Spoon. It's one of our favorites when I visit!"

"Right."

"So, like, maybe if you wanted, you could send her a PM?" He leaned in conspiratorially. "I'm not trying to hook up my sister –that's weird, but she could definitely use some friends. All she does is work and it's *really sad*."

"I'll think about it," Harper said slowly. "But no promises."

"Okay." He grinned. "Uh...can I get a signed pic?"

Isaac scrawled a signature on one of the photos, then passed it to Harper who did the same.

"Here you go."

"Awesome." He grinned. "And seriously –my sister is super cool! I think you'd like her!" There was a brief pause as he turned, realizing that a line had formed behind him. "Oh, uh...thanks for your time. Bye!"

They signed a few more photos and other items. Made small talk and answered questions about other upcoming appearances, how they were enjoying the convention, and so forth. They were running low on photos, and the line was finally dwindling when the Applejack and Pinkie Pie that had been in the Q&A came to stand in front of them.

"We don't want autographs or anything." Applejack waved Isaac off as he started to slide another photo off the stack. "We just wanted to say hello and thank you."

"Thank you?" Harper repeated.

"Well, mostly just for existing," Pinkie Pie said. "The streaming community has been great about creating inclusive spaces but having the two of you being open about not just your gender and sexualities, but also with your relationship structure means a lot. There aren't nearly enough open polyamorous celebrities. So, yeah, thanks for putting yourselves out there and being willing to talk about what it's like."

"I'm not sure I qualify as a celebrity," Harper scoffed.

"You're famous by association," Isaac said. "You're also a pretty popular author, Harp."

"People don't generally recognize authors on the street," Harper informed him. Then she turned back to the cosplayers. "Uh, you're welcome. Even though I'm not sure we really did anything."

"You're yourselves. All the time. And that's awesome." Applejack grinned. "Are you two ever going to get Pietr to come to one of these with you?"

"Maybe a summer convention," Harper said. "Otherwise, he's so busy during the hockey season it's not possible. Maybe when he retires."

"And when will that be?"

"If he has anything to say about it? Another ten years or so," Isaac said.

"That's so long!"

"For hockey?" Isaac said. "Yeah, it is. But he's already beat the average odds. Most NHL players only last for five. He's already on season eleven."

"Do you just know that?" Applejack asked.

"He *is* my boyfriend and best friend," Isaac reminded her.

"He's my husband and I try not to think about it," Harper teased.

Isaac rolled his eyes. "Doesn't he have a big milestone coming up? Like 1000 games or something?"

"I have no idea. Maybe?"

"He won a game in a shootout on Thursday night, didn't he?" Applejack asked. "How does that overtime thing work anyway?"

While Isaac began educating the ponies on the intricacies of NHL overtime procedure Harper pulled out her phone to look at the time and saw a text from Pietr.

[PIETR] Miss you. Is the convention going okay?

[HARPER] Miss you too. Convention is great.

[HARPER] Maggie asked me to cosplay with her tonight. Her girlfriend has to leave for a family emergency.

[PIETR] What is the cosplay?

[HARPER] Petra from Horizon Zero Dawn?

Pietr didn't respond right away. Harper looked up, listening to Isaac continue for a bit until her phone pinged.

[PIETR] I like it.

[PIETR] I'll buy us a PS5 so we can play it?

[PIETR] Is Maggie dressing as Aloy?

[HARPER] We do not need another console. And yes, Maggie is Aloy.

[PIETR] Game looks fun...

[HARPER] We do not need another console.

[PIETR] What is $500?

[PIETR] Or save $$ by getting Digital Only?

[PIETR] That is dumb. Would rather spend the money on a full disc supporting console.

[HARPER] WE

[HARPER] DO

[HARPER] NOT

[HARPER] NEED

[HARPER] ANOTHER

[HARPER] CONSOLE

[PIETR] Oh no!

[PIETR] What has happened?

[PEITR] Credit card already charged.

[PEITR] Will arrive next week.

[HARPER] Goddamn it. Where are we going to put it?

[PIETR] Don't worry about it.

[PIETR] You are hanging out with this Maggie then?

[HARPER] A little. I still haven't taken her up on her offer.

[HARPER] I won't take her up on it.

[PIETR] You should though, if you want.

[HARPER] I don't want. Isaac is more than enough this weekend.

[PIETR] Okay.

[PIETR] I have to go start my workout with Jammer and Kinley. Call me tonight sometime?

[HARPER] When will you be home?

[PIETR] Probably around 7, my time.

[HARPER] I'll make sure to find time after that then.

[HARPER] Love you

[PEITR] Love you too

Harper tapped her phone screen back off. Isaac was wrapping up his spiel as the girls' eyes were beginning to glaze.

"Isaac," she poked him, "we have a couple of people waiting again." She looked past the two girls at the few people who were waiting.

"Right! Sorry. You're sure you don't want us to sign anything?" Isaac asked.

"No," Pinkie Pie assured him, "we're more about *experiences* than about like keepsakes or whatever."

"If you change your mind, we have our last signing tomorrow morning at eleven."

"We'll keep it in mind. Enjoy the rest of the convention!"

The girls wandered off, linking fingers as they did so. Harper didn't let herself think about the conversation with her husband for too long. She turned her attention to the next fan who launched into a complex question about their opinion on Pokemon move sets. She let herself get carried away into the conversation again, to put Maggie's proposition, Pietr's reaction, and the continued prodding, out of her head.

Chapter Thirty-eight

"I'm so glad you agreed to do this with me." Maggie ushered Harper into her hotel room. She was already dressed with her make-up mostly complete. She only needed to pull on the wig and the head piece, if Harper was remembering the character art correctly. Like the other cosplay that Harper had seen her in, this one was immaculately put together.

"The only problem we might have are the boots," she continued. "Jess has huge feet; she's an eleven."

"I'm like a nine-and-a-half, ten," Harper said. "So they'll be a little big. Not the end of the world."

"I think she's, pardon the verbiage, a little bustier than you too, but we can make some modifications."

Maggie pulled a garment bag out of the closet and laid it across the empty bed before unzipping it. She pulled out a white tank with a deep V-neck and ruddy red harem-inspired pants. "You can change into the base layer in the bathroom. Afterwards, I'll help you with the rest of it. Okay?"

"Sure. Uh, was Jess planning on wearing a bra with this? I think mine is going to show."

"Right! How do you feel about pasties?" Maggie picked up a small carry-on bag, handing over two pale flower-shaped stickers. "It's more for modesty than that the fabric is actually see through or anything."

"I've never worn them before," Harper admitted, taking them. "I'll give 'em a try."

She carried the base layer over to the bathroom, leaving the door partially open. She could still hear Maggie, who had gone back to finishing her make-up in the full-length mirror.

"What is Isaac up to tonight?"

"We're meeting for the dance later, but he had a couple of panels he wanted to go to. And there's an unofficial Streamer's Networking thing in one of the closed party rooms. We were going to check out an RPG game, but it got cancelled earlier this afternoon."

"That's cool. Not about the cancelled game! That sucks, but now you can do this with me!" There were a few beats of silence. "Have you talked to Pietr today?"

"He texted to see how it was going."

Harper folded her clothes into a neat pile, leaving them on the far edge of the bathroom sink. She looked at the pasties first before shaking her head and taking the plunge. *So odd.* The fabric of the shirt was breathable linen that had a nice weight to it, without being too heavy. The not-really-harem pants were similar, with an elastic waist that was a comfortable fit.

"Should I tuck the shirt into the pants?" She asked.

"Yes!"

Harper adjusted the pieces before stepping back out into the bedroom. "Okay. Now what?"

Maggie gave her a look-over. "First, let's tighten up the tank a little. I don't want you flashing anybody." She picked up a couple of safety pins to pull the tank more taught, securing the back. Harper let Maggie do as she pleased. She had no idea how to help, so leaving it to the expert seemed to be the best course of action.

"Great. So, we broke the over-body piece into two. The upper body corset and then the lower...apron? That's what we called it anyway. I'm going to have to get a little handsy with you to lace it. Is that okay?"

"Gotta do what you gotta do," Harper declared.

Maggie smiled. "We're going to drop this part over your head. We can adjust the straps a little before lacing, but...no, I think they're okay. Is that comfortable?"

"It's heavy. Is it supposed to be heavy?"

"It's fake leather, so...yeah. Is it too much?"

"I'll get used to it. Just not what I was expecting after the bottom layer being so light."

"That was by design," Maggie explained. "The linen fabric option was both breathable in case it got too hot, when we do summer conventions, as well as flexible. You're not getting pinched, are you?"

"Nope." Harper shifted her shoulders a little. "It feels a little loose, but when it's laced that should change?"

"Yup. And like I said, we can adjust the shoulders if we need to. Now, this is not a regular corset. It's not shaping you in a conventional way. Let me know if it's too tight."

"The laces will get hidden by the big belt thing, right?"

"Right. You did a little research on the costume then?"

"I figured I should at least sort of know what I'm representing here," Harper said. She let a few beats pass before she said. "I told Pietr about it when we texted. He apparently went and bought a PS5 so we can play the game."

Maggie laughed. "They're fun games! Not sure it's worth buying a console for a single game, but there are a bunch of great PlayStation games. I'll have to text you some of my favorites. I admit, I'm a PlayStation fan. Jess is an Xbox person. We both like the Switch." She leaned back up from her lacing. "Not too tight?"

"No, it feels okay."

"Good. Next, we'll do the apron. This buckles in the back...." Maggie swung the split hip-coverings around Harper's waist pulling the straps at the back tight and into place. Then she picked up the belt, a big yellow-gold disk that rested around Harper's middle. After it was fastened, Maggie walked around her to get a better look. "Excellent. Still comfy?"

"Yeah, it's fine," Harper assured her.

"Okay. We'll wait to put the gloves on until we're ready to go downstairs, but here are the boots," Maggie stuck her hand into the closet, coming up with a pair of what looked like had been sandals in the past and been altered into complete shoes. "Tuck the end of the pants into the top. After that, we'll do make up, then wig and kerchief."

Harper nodded. She managed to take a seat on the end of the bed to pull the boots on. They were on the big side, as expected, but not so bad that she thought she was going to trip. As instructed, she tucked in the pant legs, tugging the tops of the boots over the fabric. More elastic kept everything in place.

"You look fantastic," Maggie assured her. "Stay right there. And, uh, I'm gonna get close to you again."

"You know you don't have to warn me, right? I assumed, as you're the one doing the work in making this look good on me," Harper said.

"I do. I also don't want to make you nervous or uncomfortable. Especially after propositioning you Thursday night. I feel really dumb for doing that, you know?"

"Why?" Harper asked. She tried to keep her tone curious but wasn't sure she was successful.

"Because I watch enough Play It With Parker and have heard enough interviews and stuff to know that your dynamic isn't random hook-ups at conventions." Maggie let out a sigh. "So, I'm sorry I put that out there. I can be impulsive."

"I wasn't offended or anything," Harper assured her. "If Pieter were *here*, maybe I would have accepted the offer. But...it's a thing we're going to have to talk more about. For whatever reason, this bothered him. We've had some incidences in the past, and he gets worried when I'm with other people now."

"What do you mean?"

"You want me to tell you, with the full knowledge that the number of people who know this information is limited, so I will know if you tell anyone?"

"My lips are sealed. Swear."

"I like rough sex. Or, *rougher* sex. Pietr humors me, but it's Misha who really pushes the limits." Harper averted her eyes so she didn't have to look at Maggie. The other woman started in with foundation, paling Harper's skin a bit. She explained the now infamous Slapping Incident.

"He's worried that you'll let someone else go too far and he wants to protect you," Maggie guessed.

"I get that he's concerned, and his feelings are valid, but..." Harper sighed. "I'm an adult. I want to choose who I sleep with. It feels like he doesn't trust me to make that decision."

"So you *do* want to sleep with me?" Maggie paused, lifting the makeup sponge from Harper's cheek.

"I told you when you originally asked that I was interested. You're very attractive, Maggie Gravesen."

Maggie fanned herself. "I'll try not to let that high praise go to my head."

Harper unsuccessfully tried to suppress a smile. Maggie went back to her make-up application.

"Do you want to talk about it? I'm an unaffiliated third party and a decent listener."

"No. It's something Pietr and I have to deal with on our own," she said. "Possibly with the help of a licensed professional, but we'll figure it out."

Maggie focused more on her work. Eyeliner, lip color, a wig and head scarf. A few more minutes and Harper's transformation was deemed complete.

"Okay, here are the gloves. I've just got to get my finishing touches on." Maggie handed over a pair of brown studded open-finger gloves. Then she began tucking her own hair into a wig cap to pull on a long red wig. After settling on her head piece, she pulled her bracers into place.

"Ready?" Maggie asked.

"As I'll ever be."

"Are you okay with photos? We can run through a couple of poses if you'd like?"

"I'm going to look dumb in any photos," Harper replied.

"You won't, I promise. Uh, just look at me the way you look at Pietr and you'll have Petra down to a T."

"The way I look at Pietr?"

"You've seen pics of the two of you together. You both post them often enough." Maggie paused for a moment, tilting her head to the side. "Actually...you two haven't been posting a lot on Insta lately."

"We've been busy," Harper said. She stood back up, shifting on her feet to get a better feel for the boots.

"Well, we'll make sure we take a couple together, yeah? Maybe Pietr will like them."

Harper smiled shaking her head. "Or it will exacerbate his unease, but photographic evidence will probably be required of this whole thing.

"Come here." Maggie picked up her phone. She put her arm around Harper's shoulders, pulling her in. "Now, turn your head and think about your husband."

Harper rolled her eyes, but...did as she was told. She wondered what Pietr was doing. He didn't have a game that night. She hoped he was out, doing something with his teammates. Having fun. Not sitting at home, worrying.

"Perfect." There was a *click*. Maggie shifted away, tapping her screen. There was a *whoosh* noise and then a ping from Harper's phone. "You can send that one to your guys. Let's go walk."

Chapter Thirty-nine

Pietr was sitting in a booth at the Mounting Bison when his phone pinged. Glancing at the screen, he saw he had several Instagram notifications. People tagging him and Harper on Instagram. He furrowed his eyebrows, contemplating clicking the app.

"What's wrong?" Adam asked. "You look annoyed.

"I am getting tagged on Instagram," he explained. "I don't know why."

"Maybe it's spam? Also, why do you leave those notifications on, man? They'd drive me nuts."

"To make sure anything rude is deleted right away. I don't like Harper to see some of the comments."

"You can't protect her from every mean person on the internet."

"I know. I'm beginning to think that I have to hire someone to manage our accounts. Felicity helps with mine sometimes, but..." He finally clicked and saw a photo of Harper and Maggie, together, in their cosplay. Even though he wasn't familiar with the game, he'd looked at enough pics when she'd texted him earlier to recognize the skill in the ensembles. "It's nothing to worry about. Harper is having fun at the convention. She is cosplaying with a new friend."

"That Maggie person you were talking about on the plane?" Adam asked.

"You were listening?"

"You guys weren't exactly quiet," Adam pointed out. "You want to talk about it? I know I'm not exactly part of your little *crew*, but maybe you need an outside perspective?"

"No," Pietr shook his head. "We had a chat when I got home. Worked it out so it wasn't eating at us. We'll talk it out more face-to-face when she gets back."

"I know it isn't my business," Adam said, "but...how's this polyamory thing working out for you?"

Pietr scrolled through the pics and comments. Screening anyone being rude, but...but there wasn't much except positivity. It was a nice change of pace from what he knew people were capable of.

"Mostly, is really good," Pietr said. "Sometimes is harder. But...Harper wants to keep going, so we do."

"Are you nervous about her being off with Parker?"

"No. Trusting him is not the issue. Trusting Harper is not the issue either," Pietr said. "It's...everyone else."

"You say that Harper doesn't want to stop. What do you want?"

"I don't want more," Pietr said. "I also don't want to stand in her way. She..." He had overshared enough with the others, he didn't want to do the same with Adam. "There are reasons that I want to give her as much freedom as she wants to take. I love that she is becoming more comfortable with certain things. I don't want her to miss out on something now, that she wouldn't have let herself do before we met."

"She was a bit of a wallflower," Adam acknowledged. "Honestly, I never even noticed her until Seth pointed her out."

"You're also super gay, *el Capitan*." Pietr laughed. "Why would you notice her?"

"I probably noticed Tanner. He's cute. Don't tell Kinley I said so." Adam grimaced. "And honestly, when Seth did point her out to me, I think I thought she was a dude at first. She really has lessened on the androgyny vibe since you two started dating."

"I think she looks exactly the same."

"That's not true. Has she lost weight?"

Pietr's shoulders tensed and the hairs on the back of his neck prickled. "I don't know. Maybe?"

"I'm not commenting on her size, dude. She looks...heathier lately."

Pietr's face contorted. "English is my second language, so I hope I am hearing that differently than you mean it."

"Shit. Sorry. You're right. She doesn't deserve any judgement based on her looks. That's an asshole thing to do, even if it's not on purpose."

Pietr looked more closely at the photos people were posting. The tank top underneath the heavier leather layer dipped lower than he really cared for. It was *hot*, yes, but...some of the comments were a little *too* nice.

"Pietr?"

"What?" He looked back up from his phone.

"You're distracted. Is that the cosplay? Let me see." Adam reached over, taking the phone. He scrolled a bit. "Dang. Pigeon looks good. I don't recognize the characters though. Are they from a video game?

"*Da*. Horizon Zero Dawn."

"How'd Harper get talked into it?"

"Maggie's girlfriend had a family emergency."

Adam handed the phone back. "The comments are a little...spicy."

"I noticed."

"I'm not really a boob guy," Adam said, "but uh, Harper isn't leaving a whole lot to the imagination in that. You sure you're okay with it?"

"If she is comfortable in it, then..." He shrugged, clicking the screen off then switched it into silent mode. He tucked it away into the pocket of his hoodie to pick up his beer. There was only a mouthful left and had gone warm. He swallowed hard. "I think I'm going to head home. Thanks for the invite."

"No problem. I figured you didn't need to be sitting at home alone," Adam said. "Sorry the other guys couldn't join us."

"It is okay," Pietr assured him. "I think I will go home and play some chel or something."

Adam laughed. "You play chel now?"

"No, but you would tease me if I said I was going to go take care of my Animal Crossing island," Pietr retorted.

"You're right, I would," Adam admitted.

Pietr tossed a few bills down on the table for the waitstaff. "See you tomorrow. Don't stay up too late. Game day tomorrow."

"Back at you," Adam said. He saw him off with a raise of his glass.

Pietr walked home. It was a nice enough evening, and it wasn't that far. The cold air gave him some clarity. Almost as good as some alone time on the ice, minus the sound of the scraping of his skates.

At home, he sank down on the couch. He hadn't bothered turning on any lights as he'd come into the apartment. He'd followed the glow from the electronic indicator lights throughout the apartment. He pulled his phone out of his pocket, staring at the screen for a moment.

What Adam had asked had come back to him.

"What do you want?"

He didn't want to hold Harper back. But he also needed to stop feeling...whatever it was he was feeling. There was only one way that was going to happen. He tapped on the text message he had with Isaac and Misha. They didn't use it often. Just to check in with each other about plans. Recently, it had been about Harper's birthday. Misha had mentioned a little about their plans when he visited in April.

[PIETR] Can I ask a favor of you two?

Responses were almost immediate.

[ISAAC] What do you need?

[MISHA] What kind of favor?

[PIETR] Can we put a pause on the sex stuff? Harper and I need to talk and I think it would be easier if that is completely off the table.

[ISAAC] Have you told Harper you're asking for this?

[PIETR] No, not yet.

[MISHA] That isn't a problem for me. I won't see her for another month or so. Even then, we don't have to fuck to have fun.

[MISHA] Is something going on that we should know about?

[ISAAC] Is this about Maggie??

[MISHA] Did Harper sleep with her? She didn't say.

[ISAAC] No, because Pietr is being weird about it.

[PIETR] It's not about Maggie.

[PIETR] I am not being weird.

[PIETR] I want my wife to just be my wife for a while.

[ISAAC] I need you to re-read what you just wrote and think about how that sounds babe.

Pietr did as Isaac suggested, biting the inside of his cheek.

[PIETR] I wrote what I wrote. I can't explain what's going on in my own head right now, but that is how I feel. I understand that you're with her in Chicago right now and I'm not asking you to change anything for the rest of your weekend. I don't know if she will even agree. I texted because it wouldn't be fair to just throw it at you or expect Harper to be the one telling you that it has to end."

[MISHA] End?

[MISHA] Are you asking me to not fuck your wife or are you asking me to break up with her? I won't do that. I don't want to do that.

[PIETR] No, I'm not asking for that.

[ISAAC] What about you and me? It's not fair to ask me not to sleep with Harper if you're not stopping either.

[PIETR] When I said sex off the table, I meant us too.

[ISAAC] Okay. What about the charity event? Should I not come?

[PIETR] I don't know.

[PIETR] I want to be able to have a conversation with Harper that is just about her and me. Then about everyone else and how we fit together. That conversation might end in making adjustments to our rules.

[ISAAC] Right. Well, let us know when you figure out your shit.

[MISHA] Isaac, are you mad?

[ISAAC] My boyfriend is dictating whether I can sleep with my girlfriend while we're on a private trip. I'm a bit irked, yeah.

[MISHA] I don't think that's Pietr's intention.

[MISHA] I appreciate that he wants to take some time... I'm a patient guy. It will be fine. Enjoy your time with Harper. Then let them handle their shit when she gets home.

Pietr waited, watching the text indicator pop up, then disappear, then pop up again. He sighed, closing his eyes. When he finally opened them, Isaac had responded.

[ISAAC] I get it. I even understand it. It doesn't mean I have to be pleased about it.

[ISAAC] Just keep me in the loop, okay?

Pietr blew out a sigh.

[PIETR] Of course.

He tapped out of the group text. He had to scroll quite a ways down his screen to find just Isaac's name.

[PIETR] I'm sorry. I love you.

[ISAAC] I know you do.

[ISAAC] I love you too. I love Harper. That's why the back and forth hurts, Pietr. If we have to go back to being just friends, then I need to know that. I don't want to rush you. Maybe you should think about seeing that therapist by yourself to talk about your issues with this?

[PIETR] Maybe. Finding the time is hard.

[ISAAC] Hard but not impossible.

Pietr clicked the phone off, tossing it onto the coffee table. He sank back into the pillows. He felt like shit and that didn't bode well. He let himself wallow for another five minutes before picking up the phone again. It was late, all things considered, but he figured that leaving a message wouldn't hurt.

"Hello, this is Dr. Deidra Balakin." There was a long pause as Pietr waited for the rest of the voice mail message and the beep. Instead, it was followed by, "Hello?"

"Oh! I did not actually expect you to answer. I'm so sorry."

"I'm always available for a patient. Who am I speaking to?"

Pietr cleared his throat, sitting up straighter on the couch. "Pietr Ivanov. I was in with my wife—"

"I remember, Pietr," she spoke kindly. "What can I do for you? Is everything all right? I didn't hear from you or Harper so I assumed that you had decided not to continue."

"I don't think she wants to," he admitted, "but, I...I need to."

"Need to?"

"The jealousy, the anxiety thing," he said. "Harper is at a convention this weekend with our shared partner. She had an offer for a hook-up from someone at the convention. I was uncomfortable with her doing it."

Dr. Balakin didn't say anything for a moment. "I'm not sure this is something we should discuss over the phone. Do you have time tomorrow? I can adapt to your schedule."

"It is a game day," he said. "I'll be at the practice arena most of the day. I am usually back in the city by two."

"Is this going to distract you if we wait that long?"

"I don't know."

There was another pause. "I have a clear morning. Would it be possible to meet with you on your own turf? Say...nine o'clock at the arena? Is there a place we can have a private conversation?"

Pietr thought about his own schedule and prioritizing. Finally, he nodded even though she couldn't see him doing. "*Da*. I can make that work."

"Okay. Is there anything I need to know about getting into the facility?"

"Just come in the main entrance. I'll let Security know. I'll see if we can borrow an office." He swallowed. "Thanks for making the time."

"You're welcome. I'll see you tomorrow at nine. Goodbye, Pietr. Try to get some rest. You have a busy day tomorrow."

Chapter Forty

"You did so good! You should do this again with me at the Minnesota cons." Maggie was packing away the cosplay pieces after they'd wandered the convention, taken what felt like hundreds of photos, and...had a lot of fun. More fun than Harper had expected. Isaac had met up with them after his panel and they'd grabbed a quick dinner.

Now, they were changing into something lighter before going into the dance. Isaac had made himself comfortable in the chair in the corner while they'd changed. He'd looked mildly annoyed while texting.

"What's wrong?" Harper asked. She had swapped back into her leggings and tunic. Maggie had popped into the bathroom to change and wash off her make-up.

He looked up, a small smile on his face. "You know, that Petra top would look good with those leggings."

"You just like how much cleavage was shown off."

"True. I liked seeing you step out of your comfort zone." Isaac reached for her, pulling her into his lap. "Did you have fun?"

"I did," she nodded.

"Good." He rubbed her back. "You ready for the dance?"

"The dance will be fine. You avoided my question. What's wrong? You were glaring at your phone."

He frowned. "I'll show you later."

"...Is it the pics? Have people been posting them?"

"Yes, you've been tagged in a lot of pics, but the comments are mostly kind. A little *too kind* if you get my drift."

"I doubt that."

"I reported one of them for TOS violation. I did *not* need the visual of some random dude's self-described horse cock getting anywhere near you."

"You're exaggerating."

"I assure you, I am not."

Harper wrinkled her nose.

"You did look pretty hot though," Isaac retorted. "Maybe we talk to Maggie and Jess about some other costumes..."

"Oh? Like what?"

"Anything you want, baby. Bonus points if it involves the cleavage and maybe some really tall boots..."

"What is it with dudes and boots?"

Isaac chuckled, tugging her in for another kiss.

"Wow you two are affectionate tonight." Maggie was combing out her hair as she came out of the bathroom. She'd switched into yet another cosplay –a very casual Misty from Pokemon. She gathered up her hair into an off-set pony tail; a little longer than the actual character, but she still managed to make it work.

"We're an affectionate couple," Isaac said.

"I'd say you're a *comfortable* couple," Maggie said. "When you're on the stream anyway. You don't use pet names or anything. But you have fun. Even when you're together, you're very careful about how close you all sit together and things like that." She tightened the ponytail, looking at them. "Is that on purpose?"

"I don't know what you mean."

"Never mind. Not important." Maggie waved a hand. "You ready to go?"

"Yeah," Isaac agreed. He patted Harper's hip. "Let's go."

The dance had officially started over an hour before and a line wound around the lobby area in front of the main programming room.

"Well shit," Maggie crossed her arms, looking at the line. "Do we attempt to use our guest cred to skip the line, or go to the end?"

"We could go check out some party rooms," Isaac suggested. "Kill some time that way. A couple of them have music and dancing if that's what you want to do."

"Princess Magnolia, Isaac, Harper!" A voice called from across the room.

Harper looked up, seeing someone in a yellow staff shirt waving them over.

"Hey Tori," Maggie said. "What's up?"

"You waiting to get into the dance?"

"We were thinking about it. Seems too rude to try and pull guest rank."

"Nah, that's a perk of your service," Tori assured her. "Go on in."

Harper recoiled at the noise and the lights. She'd been in the space earlier that day when it had been broken into two smaller programing spaces. With the adjustable walls removed, it was a giant space with a large thrashing crowd in its center. The stage housed a DJ and several costumed dancers. The giant display screens were showing bouncing equalizer screens; different colors spiking with the beat of the music. Convention staff hung out near the edges of the room, keeping an eye on the dancers. Occasionally, they'd direct someone to the nearest water station to rehydrate, or check on someone who looked like they might be inebriated or generally uncomfortable.

"You okay?" Isaac had to lean in and shout over the music.

Harper nodded.

"Come on." She was sure he said the words aloud, but she didn't hear them. He took her hand, leading her into the sea of people, tagging behind Maggie.

Harper tried to shut off her brain. Enjoy the music. Let Isaac pull her into a comfortable sway. Not *really* dancing. Not the way everyone else was, which was hard and fast. Maggie stuck close but moved between partners. After a while, Isaac handed Harper over to Maggie, motioned over toward the side where there were water coolers, and mouthed *be right back!*

Maggie wrapped her arms around Harper's shoulders, leaning in close. Harper felt her breath on her ear. "Are you having fun?" Harper knew she was shouting it, but it sounded like a whisper.

"I think so," she shouted back.

Maggie smiled. She said something else. Not as close this time. Harper looked confused. Maggie repeated it, and Harper shrugged, still not catching it. Maggie's hands came up to her face. Harper felt her expression change, but her brain didn't quite compute what that expression was. Then

Maggie's lips found hers. For a split second, it was like one of those movies, where the whole world stopped for just a second. Everything went completely silent. It wasn't attraction though. Harper *knew* what attraction felt like.

The world started up again as Maggie backed off. Her smile faltered and she took a step back. *Sorry* she mouthed *I'll go.*

"Wait!" Harper was too late as Maggie turned, squeezing through pockets in the crowd. "*Fuck.*" She blew out a breath, looking for Isaac.

She spotted him in the corner, watching someone swinging around some stupid fiber optic whip thing. She rolled her eyes, pushing through the crowd –not really caring if she was being rude or not. She pulled out her phone, sending off a text to Isaac to let him know they'd left. Then, she followed Maggie.

Maggie was looking strangely uncomfortable as she stood waiting at the elevator.

"Maggie." Harper waited until she was close enough to put a hand on her arm before speaking. She jumped, tensing, then let out a sigh.

"Fucks sake, Harper. You scared the crap out of me"

"Why did you leave like that?"

"Because I did something exceedingly stupid," Maggie retorted. "I'm *so* sorry."

"Why are you sorry?"

"You looked at me like..."

"I was surprised," Harper admitted, "but I didn't hate it. Did I look like I hated it?"

"No, but that still wasn't okay. You made it really clear that you—"

Harper wasn't sure what came over her. Maybe it was the residual energy of the rave. Or the pressure of whatever was happening with Pietr. It could have been any number of things that made her grab Maggie Gravesen by the cheeks and pull her in for another kiss.

Unlike the one in the rave, this one was kept very much in the present. It took an extra beat before Maggie returned the kiss. Her hands going to Harper's waist. They broke apart as a couple of whistles and other rude noises interrupted.

"Fuck," Harper swore. "Sorry. At least when you did it, we were in the dark and no one was paying attention to us."

"Biggest pitfall of being a special guest. A lot of people are paying attention to us." Maggie bit her bottom lip. "Should we go upstairs?"

"Maggie, I can't sleep with you," Harper said.

"I didn't say anything about sleeping with me," Maggie replied. "We could just hang out. Talk. Kiss some more, if you wanted." Her lips pulled in a wry smile. "I like kissing."

Harper licked her lips. Maggie must have put on a berry lip balm. "I like kissing too."

"Something else we have in common. Besides being giant fucking geeks." Maggie laughed. "Come upstairs with me."

Harper shook her head. "I better not. This time."

"This time?"

"We're both going to be at Mill City and CONerole. That should be enough time to sort things out with Pietr." She paused for a moment. "Maggie, he's the most important person in the world to me. As much fun as I think, that I know, we'd have, I just can't."

Maggie took a step back, nodding. "I'm pushing."

"You're not," Harper shook her head. "You're...pulling and I'm planting my feet. I have to."

"I get it," Maggie said. She forced a smile. "Maybe it's best if we cool off then." She reached over, squeezing Harper's arm. "Breakfast in the morning? Around nine?"

Harper nodded. "I'd like that."

"Good." The smile relaxed into something less strained. "Good night, Harper."

"Good night."

Harper hung back from the elevator bay as Maggie disappeared. She pulled out her phone to see if Isaac had found her text.

[ISAAC] Everything okay?

[HARPER] Yeah. You still at the dance?

[ISAAC] Leaving now.

[ISAAC] You can see the sweat mist over the crowd. Ew.

Harper laughed. She moved away from the elevator, going to wait for Isaac closer to the programming room.

"You okay?" He asked, sliding an arm around her waist a minute later.

"Maggie kissed me," she told him. "Then I kissed her."

"Sorry I missed that."

She elbowed him in the side.

"Was it nice?" He asked.

"Yes."

He kissed her hair, nudging her toward the elevator. "Let's go to bed, Harp."

In the hotel room, they stripped naked in the bathroom before getting into the shower together. While Harper had washed her face after changing out of the Petra cosplay, she could feel the layer of sweat wash away after being in the rave.

Isaac wrapped a towel around his waist after scrubbing his hair dry. He stepped out into the bedroom to let Harper brush her teeth and get dressed before swapping places. He turned on the TV to some old sitcom reruns.

"You going to tell me what was bugging you earlier?" Harper wrapped her arms around his neck after jumping onto the bed behind him.

Isaac reached up, stroking her wrist. "Promise not to get mad?"

"I'll try not to, but you know I can't actually promise that."

Isaac tapped his phone screen, then scrolled up before handing her the device. Harper frowned, taking it to read the conversation between her partners. She sighed.

"I hate it when you guys don't talk to me," she said.

"I know. But I know why he asked that of Misha and I rather than in the big group text," Isaac said.

"Because for as much as I love him, he can be kind of an asshole?"

"I told him he should schedule an appointment with that therapist you two saw," Isaac said. "Was that too much?"

"No. He needs to talk to somebody." Harper sighed. "I don't understand what's going on in his head sometimes."

"It's not you, Harp," Isaac assured, turning to face her. "You want my completely uneducated opinion?"

Harper let out a hard laugh. "Sure."

"You and Pietr aren't very different. That's why you two click so well. He didn't have that much more experience than you when you started dating. Having a lot of sex isn't the same as having a relationship. What he and I did? That wasn't a relationship. That was two guys in denial of our feelings, fucking around to fill an itch. His girlfriends...they weren't anything special. That's only three people."

"Four," Harper said. "Pietr has been with four other people, before me."

"Four?" Isaac looked confused. "Who else?"

"I don't know that it's my place to tell you that," Harper said.

"Tell me."

"No, I can't."

Isaac took his phone back. His fingers made audible sounds, stabbing at the screen and putting it on speaker phone.

"Isaac? It is late." Pietr sounded sleepy. "Is something wrong?"

"Who did you sleep with before me?"

"Eh?"

"You slept with the billet sister of your buddy, me, and your girlfriend in Florida before Harper. Who else?"

Pietr was quiet before letting out a soft, "Fuck."

"Sorry, Pietr. I thought he'd know," Harper said.

"Isaac, you were not the first guy I had sex with. I'm sorry if I let you think that you were."

"Is there a reason you didn't tell me?"

"Does this have to be now? It's nearly one AM."

"I don't know. Does this guy have something to do with why you're so fucked up lately?"

"I'm fucked up?" Pietr asked. "That is news to me, Izzy."

"You know what I mean. You've been weird about Harper spending time with anyone but you. You were weird about Maggie. You keep saying that you want her to be happy and to try things, but then you freak out on her. That's not fair, Pietr."

"Harper and I are going to talk it through when she gets home. I *know* I'm not...." He sighed. "Isaac, it has nothing to do with the guy."

"Then tell me who it was. How long it lasted. Did you care about him?"

"I don't want you to think differently of me."

"That's stupid. Why would I?"

"Because I was young. And stupid. I did some things because I thought going along with it would get me ahead."

"What do you mean?"

Pietr was quiet for another minute. "He was an assistant coach. I was fifteen. He didn't seem that much older than me. The same age gap now wouldn't phase most people."

Isaac tapped off the speaker, taking the phone to his ear. "You were assaulted by a coach?"

Harper couldn't hear Pietr's side of the conversation. She could feel the way his shoulders tensed under her hands.

"Pietr, you were *assaulted*. Consent doesn't matter when you're fucking fifteen years old. You had no idea what—he took advantage of you!"

"Isaac," she squeezed the back of his neck, "relax."

"Where is this guy now? Is he still—" Isaac was cut off. "He's fucking dead?" He inhaled sharply. "Why didn't you tell me? –What do you mean it wasn't relevant?"

Harper sighed. She moved from behind Isaac to crawl under the covers. She listened to Isaac get more and more perturbed.

"I don't even know you, do I?" Isaac finally said. "I thought I was your best friend." The bed shifted as Isaac stood, going toward the bathroom.

Harper heard the door close and she refocused on the TV. She had absolutely no idea how long they were going to argue. If it was an argument? Whatever adrenaline she'd been feeling earlier had completely disappeared, and now she was just exhausted. She slid deeper under the covers. Her eyelids felt heavy. Her ears tuned out the TV, focusing on the murmur still coming from the bathroom. She'd been having a fun weekend but she was ready for it to be over now.

Chapter Forty-one

Pietr was pacing in front of the entrance desk when Dr. Balakin entered.

"Pietr." She greeted him. "You look uneasy."

"I had a really shit morning skate," he told her. "Follow me. There is an empty admin office we can use."

Dr. Balakin hiked her messenger bag a little higher on her shoulder, following along behind him. When they were enclosed in the empty office, she glanced around while Pietr took a seat on one of the chairs in front of the desk. She took a minute to slip out of her jacket, scoot one of the other chairs across from him, and then remove a clipboard and notepad from her bag.

"Alright." She settled into the chair. "How are you today, Pietr?"

"I told you –shit."

"Why don't you tell me what's going on," she suggested. "Start with Harper and...Maggie, was it?"

"*Da*. She and Isaac are in Chicago this weekend at a convention. Maggie is a cosplay guest. She is also an impressive hockey player." he said. "She is an impressive person, but it was brought to my attention that I don't know her. Maybe that is why I felt uneasy about giving Harper permission to..."

"To?" There was a long silence. "Pietr, did Harper want to have sex with this woman?"

"Yes."

"Did you tell her that she could?"

"Yes."

"Even though you didn't want her to?"

"I don't want to hold her back from things. She doesn't need my permission."

"Why do think you hold her back?"

Pietr leaned forward on his knees. "I was only the second person that Harper ever had sex with. The person before me was a decade ago. It was short lived. He cheated on her. It took her...weeks, months, before she trusted I legitimately liked her. Loved her. Even now, this, I'm sure she is questioning whether I love her or am trying to control her.

Dr. Balakin scribbled a note on her pad. "Pietr, I want you imagine that the roles here were reversed. You were out at a bar, or a club –whatever you get up to when you're out of town with the team. A woman, who is very attractive, is introduced to you. Through a teammate, by chance, however. You're chatting and she invites you back to her place. What do you do?"

"I say no."

"Why?"

"Because I don't want to fuck another woman."

"But you want to have sex with other men? You like the experience of being with other men, with your wife."

"I like being with Isaac. I like experiencing things with Harper. Watching her experience things with other men."

"Exclusively men. Not women."

"It hasn't come up."

"Would you feel different about Maggie if Harper had met her here, in New York. If you could be part of the experience?"

Pietr considered that for a minute. "Maybe. Probably."

"Why?"

"Because when I'm there, I know she is safe. I can make sure that she's enjoying the experience. That she's not pushing herself."

Dr. Balakin's eyebrows knit together. She folded her hands together on her notepad. "Have you ever felt like Harper wasn't enjoying sex –with you, or her other partners?"

"No."

"Have you felt like she's pushing herself somehow?"

"When she asks to be rough, harder."

"Is she pushing herself or you when she asks for that?"

Pietr tensed before he nodded. "Me."

"How does it make you feel when Harper pushes you to do that?"

"Nervous."

"Have you asked Harper why she wants you to be rougher with her?"

"She says it makes her feel wanted." He shook his head. "I don't understand that. Hurting her should not be how I show her that I care about her. That I love her."

"Have you ever had another partner who was into kinkier play? More physical altercation. Impact play. That sort of thing."

Pietr's jaw tensed. The conversation with Isaac the night before flooded back. He had only talked about Oleg Alekhin twice since he was sixteen years old. Even then, he'd only told Harper and Isaac what they needed to know.

"Sort of," he finally answered. "When I was fifteen, there was a man who took advantage of me. I didn't know better. I thought that it was a way to get ahead. That he cared about me."

"Will you tell me about him?"

"Do I have to? I try not to think about him. There's no point. No closure coming. He died in prison."

"He was incarcerated for what he did to you?"

"No," he shook his head, "he was put away because of what he attempted to do to someone else."

"You never told anyone what he did to you," she guessed.

"No. I told Harper, about a year ago. Isaac asked me about it last night; I don't know how it came up. Just that it was a thing. Not the details."

"Do you want to talk about it? What happened."

Pietr shrugged. "It was twenty fucking years ago. What does it matter now?"

"It matters because it's impacting the relationship you have with your wife. With your other partner. And your wife's relationship with her other partners; established and potential." Dr. Balakin's voice was oddly soothing. "You can't have it both ways, Pietr. The two of you can enjoy an open relationship, with the rules that you've set together. Or, you can close your relationship and you need to be more cognizant of filling needs for her –including being willing to...rough her up a bit, if that's what makes her feel wanted. Sometimes, the way our brains process emotions, feelings, desire. It doesn't make sense. When Harper says she feels *wanted* when you're rough with her, it's not because you're hurting her."

Pietr bit the inside of his cheek before he nodded. "Fine. I will talk about it. What do you want to know?"

"You can start wherever you wish. Tell me what happened."

"Oleg was an assistant coach for Junior International Russia," he said. "I was part of the team for six or eight weeks when he found me on the ice one day. Everyone else had gone home. I hadn't been happy with my performance, so I was running drills on my own. Trying to clear my head, practicing my slap shot.

"At first it was harmless. Touching me to straighten my stance, reposition my stick. Things like that. Then, we lost a game. I felt like it was my fault. I didn't pull my weight. I was in the showers. Long after everyone else had left. Feeling like shit and trying to feel anything other than disappointed. Burning my back with the hot water, like that would help. He came in and said he could help. Give me something else to think about." He sucked in a breath, shifting in the chair. He could feel the heat across the back of his shoulders. The steam that had flooded from the stall. Oleg's bare chest against his back. His cock against his backside. His fingers dug into the arm of the chair.

"That was the first time. He didn't ask what I wanted. He promised that if I cooperated that he would make sure that I got ice time, more attention during coaching, that he'd put in a good word for me with the coaches at the next level when I was ready to advance. So, I did what he wanted. Over the next...two years?"

"You spent two years being molested? You didn't tell anyone."

Pietr shook his head. "I didn't dare. When I got the call to join the Russian Olympic trial team. I didn't make it, but I got noticed and moved to the US to join another team. I decided to put it behind me and not think about it anymore."

"You alluded that he was rough with you?"

Pietr's jaw clenched. "When I didn't want to do something, or I did it poorly, he'd slap me. Hockey is a tough sport. When you're covered with cuts and bruises, getting slapped probably doesn't seem like such a big deal." He motioned to his face, which sported a small cut over his nose and another on his temple.

"Is that why you got upset with Misha when he slapped Harper?"

"I know what it feels like to get hit. In the face. By someone who you think, that you hope, cares about you. Because otherwise, why the fuck are you letting them..." He swallowed hard. "He'd do other things too. Shove me against the boards on the ice, into lockers, force me onto the floor in the showers. ...After I left that team, and I got away from him, I realized that it wasn't normal. I'd been scared because I knew I wasn't straight. The sex...the sex was usually okay. I even liked it sometimes. But the way he treated me when we were alone, versus when we were around other people. In practice. I was so fucking blind."

"What happened to you was not your fault."

"It was. I let it go on for two years because I thought that it would keep me playing hockey. It *did*. If he hadn't paid so much attention to me, helped me, who knows if I would have made it to the NHL."

"He was a good coach."

"Yeah," Pietr laughed, "he was a great coach. But he had a real hard time keeping his dick in his pants and away from teen boys."

"How did you feel about him? While it was happening."

Pietr shrugged. "I don't know. It wasn't an attachment. I felt like he legitimately wanted me to be better. That using me, rewarding me, punishing me, was his way of making me better."

"Was the sex a reward or a punishment?"

"Both? When I had a bad game, he'd use it to make me feel better. When I thought I played well, he'd rip my game apart while—" He forced himself to release the arm of the chair. "I don't want to talk about this anymore."

"That's okay. I heard enough," she assured him. "Pietr, you are not this Oleg person. You love Harper. Right?"

"*Da.*"

"The man who abused you did not care about you the way that you care about Harper. You cannot equate your relationship with her to what happened with him. You understand that."

"*Da.*"

"Pietr." She leaned forward. "You are a good, kind, loving partner. That is all you need to be. You don't have to be a protector, or a gatekeeper, or anything else. Tell me, what do you do for Harper? Specifically."

"What do you mean?"

"What do you do for Harper that you don't do for anyone else."

"Everything I do is for Harper now. Making sure that I can give her the life she deserves. So she can be comfortable. Make sure that she is taken care of, so that she can focus on what she loves to do."

"What does she do for you?"

"She makes my life easier. Takes care of the day-to-day that I used to have to either pay someone to take care of, or just ignore until I had a few free minutes. She streamlines my routine. I like routine. Knowing what each day holds."

"It sounds to me like you both make each other's lives a little easier. So you can each do what you love to do."

"I suppose so."

"You know that, regardless of whatever experiences Harper has or wants to have, she's committed to you."

"Rationally, yes."

Dr. Balakin sat back, looking across at him. She didn't prompt him with another question. Simply waited.

Pietr sighed. He leaned forward, elbows on his knees as he raked his fingers through his beard and hair, then locked his fingers behind his neck. He stared down at the pattern on the carpet. A confetti of blue and black in teal.

"How do I feel better about letting Harper be with other people? People I don't know. People I don't know if I can trust." He finally looked back up at her.

"What are your current guidelines for extra-marital relations?"

"We have to inform the other and we always use protection."

"So, maybe you add another layer. Some examples: any kind of impact play or BDSM has to be negotiated with both of you. You need to talk to a person on the phone or FaceTime before they sleep together. Maybe you have permission to see each other's phones. So that you feel involved with her process."

"I don't want her to feel like I'm trying to control her." He released his neck, looking up at her again.

"Do you feel like those things are controlling?"

"A little."

"There is never going to be a perfect answer," Dr. Balakin replied. "So, your assignment, before our next session, is to talk to your wife. You should be honest with her about what happened to you. You don't have to go into the details, but it might be helpful to her to know what you experienced."

"I don't want her to think differently about me."

"Why do you think knowing what you went through would change how she feels?"

"Because I was young and stupid back then. I should have told someone. I should have had some sense of self-preservation. All I thought about was getting to the next level. To keep playing. Hockey was my way out of Russia. The way I was going to take care of my parents. Thank them for everything they gave up for me."

Dr. Balakin hummed, leaning forward in her seat. "It's very easy to look back on the past and think of the things we should have done. But *shoulding* ourselves doesn't help the present. Focus on the here and now instead. What you can do now."

Pietr didn't know what to say to that and so instead gave her a hum of understanding and half a nod. The doc made a few more notes before sliding the clipboard into her bag.

"I took the liberty of looking at your upcoming schedule. I think it would be good to add talking to me to your routine. I know things get hectic for you, but I'd like to help you if you'll let me. You don't have to come into the office. We can do video calls, when you're out of town. I can come here again. I can be a certain amount of flexible."

Pietr nodded. "I'll make it work."

"Good. Why don't we start with trying to talk every other week," she suggested. "I'll send you an e-mail with a couple of appointment times and you tell me what works for you."

Pietr nodded.

Dr. Balakin stood, pulling her jacket back on. After she'd tossed the strap of her bag over her head. She came to crouch beside his chair, putting a hand on his arm. "You're a good man, Pietr Ivanov. Harper and Isaac are very lucky to have you as their partner. Don't forget to let them take care of *you* once in a while. Okay?"

He forced a short nod.

"Have a good game tonight." She patted his knee. "This was a good start. I promise. We'll talk soon."

He straightened. "Do you need to me walk you back out?"

"I can find my way," she said. "Thank you though. I'm sure you have other things you need to be doing this morning. Goodbye, Pietr."

"Bye. Thank you, for coming."

She gave him a soft smile. A moment later, the door clicked closed behind her. Pietr felt a tension he hadn't realized he was holding in his shoulders release. He closed his eyes, leaning his head against the back of the chair. He took a few deep cleansing breaths before reaching to pull out his phone.

He paused for a moment before opening the big polycule text.

[PIETR] I've been an asshole lately. Forget what I asked yesterday. It wasn't fair of me. I'm sorry.

[PIETR] I'll do better. Promise.

Did you love *Ripple the Mesh*? Then you should read *Dark Little Town: Complete Trilogy*[1] by Sam LaRose!

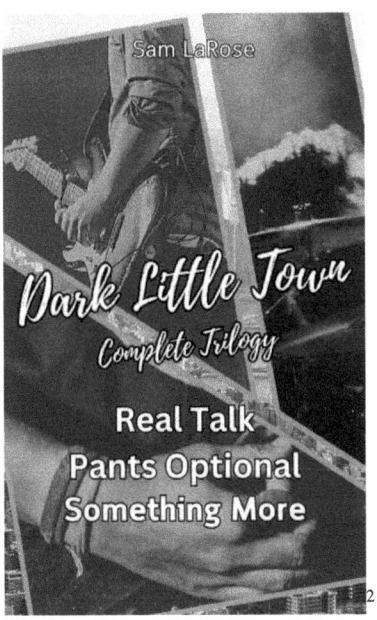

[2]

Collected in 1 volume for the first time, the Dark Little Town trilogy begins with Dylan Montomgery's banishment to Tynan, NJ. The connections made there kick off an intricriate web of connections between friends and lovers in Manhattan.

Real Tak: Dylan Montgomery's parents have reached their final straw. Banishment to Tynan, NJ seems like the pits, but is just what the troubled teen needs. It's there that he meets Tyler Norse; lead singer and guitarist for Dark

---

1. https://books2read.com/u/m0NMnW

2. https://books2read.com/u/m0NMnW

Little Town. As the summer begins to fade, the future looks dim on the relationship from Dylan's perspective, but as far as Tyler's concerned: it's just getting started.

Pants Optional:

Jack Piper is eighteen years old, living with his mother and twin sisters in Manhattan's Greenwich Village. He attends a selective private school, where he's honing his skills as a writer, aided greatly by his eidetic memory. It's been three years since his father passed away, inciting the move, and his first Christmas alone. When his friend Pixie invites him out for a Jewish Christmas, he doesn't expect the bend in the road his life is about to take.

Heath Gibson is a New Jersey transplant to the city. His band, Dark Little Town, is just inches away from real success. Since moving to the city, he's made plenty of friends and is open to making more. Especially if it means getting to forget how in love with his best friend he's been since he was thirteen.

When Jack and Heath recognize each other across a club on Christmas Eve, they don't expect to go home together. They certainly don't expect to catch feelings for one another. Jack isn't sure he wants to settle into a relationship with the older man. Heath is ready to hand over his heart, if Jack will just accept it.

And neither of them quite knows what to make of Jack's best friends; a gay polyamorous couple who want nothing more than to get one, or both, of them into bed with them.Something More:

Jordan Baxter has never considered himself to be anything other than a flirt. When his interest is piqued by not one, but two people, within days of one another, his world takes an unexpected turn.

Kyle is a talented artist who's smile makes his heart squeeze and his stomach tilt. ...But, he's openly polyamorous with his boyfriend Markus. Not to mention, he's also hooked up with Jordan's BFF Heath and Heath's boyfriend, Jack.Dani is a musician that lays most things on the table, like that they're non-binary and not entirely sure how the whole sex thing works for them. Unless they're drunk, in which case they stop thinking entirely.

Defining the relationships is put on hold while Jordan's band, Dark Little Town, tours for the summer. When the tour ends, he knows they'll all eventually have to make a decision about their romantic status, or just be friends.

Read more at www.samlarose.com.

About the Author

Sam is a nonbinary person in rural Wisconsin. They work as a libary director and live in an old farm house with a lot of cats, rabbit, and a flock of chickens.

Read more at www.samlarose.com.